HE KISSED

me

FIRST

SARA NEY

Copyright © 2017 Sara Ney
Cover Design by Okay Creations
Interior Formatting by Uplifting Designs

Second Edition: April 2017
Library of Congress Cataloging-in-Publication Data
He Kissed Me First
ISBN-13: 978-1544944418
ISBN-10: 1544944411

Thank you, Internet, for providing the inspiration for the dating quotes at the beginning of each chapter. They're all based on *real* conversations, pickup lines, come-ons, and texts between actual people.

For more information about Sara Ney and her books, visit:
https://www.facebook.com/saraneyauthor/

HE KISSED

me

FIRST

Prologue

Cecelia

"Do you ever wish you could just *un*-meet someone?" – me, wishfully thinking

Have you ever had a story to tell but just couldn't figure out a good way to start it? That seems to be my life these days: a veritable daily struggle-fest (as my little sister Veronica would say). Absolutely nothing has gone right for me today.

Nothing.

Allow me to tell you about the craptastic morning I first met Matthew Wakefield.

First, I didn't climb out of bed with grace. No. I stumbled. Of course, I still had my eye mask on (that's right haters, I wear an eye mask; it's not a crime, so get over it). Instead of peeling it off like a normal person, I blindly reached for the table next to my bed so I could balance myself before standing up, missed by a mile—naturally—smashed into that, and managed to knock over the lamp on my desk (the light bulb shattered; thanks for caring) which, incidentally, is halfway across the room.

Really quickly, can I note that at *no* point during all this loud crashing and banging around did anyone come to check on me (thanks Mom and Dad).

So yeah.

After that little introduction to my morning, let's fast forward a bit, to when I backed my car into my parents' recycling bins, had no change for a toll at the state line of Wisconsin and Illinois, and to top it all off, didn't pass a single McDonald's.

So it shouldn't surprise me that:

1. I am a hot mess. Hair falling out of my top knot, mascara smudges under both my eyes, and— bonus!—I just caught a faint whiff of myself, and all I have to say is…grody. I'm mostly sweaty and gross from lugging my damn bags, and it really would be tougher to get any grosser than this—*unless* you count the fact that there's almost a 100% certainty that my underwear are on inside out. #ratchet

2. I hashtagged myself. Deal with it.

3. I. Am. Starving, and my stomach will not let me forget it—it's all knotted up and growling, and my legs have also decided to start shaking from my plummeting blood sugar level. Wonderful. I'm pretty darn sure if you saw me on the street you'd think I was on *crack*.

4. My mom has been text bombing me since I left. Either she thinks I've been murdered, *or* she must have found the lamp…and the smashed light bulb. *Oops.* Oh well, the lamp was ugly anyway.

Lugging my tote down the long corridor in my apartment building, I fumble for the keys I've foolishly placed in my back pocket, and in the process drop my phone, sunglasses, purse, and several books I'd been holding on to by a thread.

Great.

Peachy.

Awesome.

The bag slung over my shoulder is so heavy it's weighing me down, thus creating no real way to bend down and pick up all my crap without also dropping the bag and/or injuring myself in the process.

This bag is *that* heavy.

It is actually dragging down the neckline of my plain white t-shirt, which I'm sure looks just *fabu*lous.

Cripes, why did I pack so much for the long weekend? It looks like I've packed enough to move back home, when really it's just a few pair of shoes, some jeans, shirts, underwear, a few bras, more books, makeup, curling iron, um… blow-dryer, robe, a few DVDs…oh, and a water bottle and workout clothes. I think I tossed my laptop in there too. Also, er, hairspray, a brush, and a comb, but those hardly take up any space.

Plus extra tote and slippers.

Eye mask…

All right, all right! You get the picture.

I try digging in my back pocket again and wonder what possessed me to wear such tight pants this morning (oh that's right…*they look awesome on me*) and end up palming the small wad of twenty dollar bills my mom surreptitiously stuffed into my pocket when I left this morning. Originally, she tried to get my *dad* to give me the extra cash, but as usual, he only pulled out one ten-dollar bill.

"Roger, that's not even enough for some snacks at a gas station!" my mom shouted at my dad from across the driveway.

To which my dad (aka Roger) replied, "She's almost twenty-three years old Margot; I would think at this point we wouldn't *need* to be supporting her."

My mom just shot him a dirty look, adding, "At least give her a hug good-bye."

I'll be honest: Roger always needs a reminder. He's not much for public displays of affection. I'm his daughter for crying out loud, and he blushes every time he is forced to hug me—not that I blame him. My grandparents weren't really affectionate either, and obviously the trait has been passed down to my dad.

Poor guy.

I'm the opposite, and my favorite thing to do is grab him, lock him in a bear hug, and squish him until he shoves me off.

It can get awkward sometimes, but a little awkward never hurt anybody.

You can quote me on that.

As I get closer to my apartment door, I breath a loud sigh of relief because hallelujah! I can hear the voice of my roommate inside. Although…it kind of sounds like she's arguing with someone. But hey, at least she's inside, because I'll probably need a hand with my stuff.

Instead of knocking, I bang the door with my hip, using all my might to heave the heavy tote like a wrecking ball so it slams into the door with a *thunk*.

I give a meek little "Help" and wait.

And wait.

Inside I hear a bang, like someone's smashed into an end table or desk, then I hear an "oomph" followed immediately by a groan.

Weird, and totally out of the ordinary.

Slightly panicked, I again bang on the door again with my hip, drop my bag, and fumble frantically for my keys.

Matthew

What the *shit* is that banging?

I look at my little sister Molly and she shrugs, trudging toward the door. I put my arm out to stop her. "Don't you *dare* get that—it's obviously some lunatic."

Molly rolls her eyes at me (the little brat) like she is always doing—and when I say always, I mean she's *constantly* rolling her eyes. I'm surprised they haven't gotten lodged permanently in the back of her head.

"It's either a lunatic or it's my roommate, so get out of my way you Neanderthal. This is *my* apartment."

Using all her strength (and trust me, she might appear scrawny, but she's way stronger than she looks), Molly manages to shove me out of her way, even as I attempt to block her path. In my attempts to stall her, my leg connects with the blue Rubbermaid bin she and her roomie have disguised as a coffee table, and the shit piled on top of it falls to the carpet.

Correction: the *dirty* carpet.

"Don't you dare open that door without finding out who it is first," I warn, sounding like our dad, while bending to scoop up a handful of Cosmo magazines from the floor. Kate Upton stares back at me from an August issue, and I stop reorganizing for a brief moment to admire her ample chest.

Damn she's good-lookin'.

Without hesitating, I start thumbing through the magazine, momentarily distracted by its contents. Shit, if the rest of these pictures are anything like Kate Upton's cover, I just might consider rolling this baby up and stuffing it into my back pocket.

"The door has no peephole, *moron*. Hey, stop touching my stuff! God you are so *annoy*ing," Molly huffs in outrage, boldly slapping the magazine out of my hand. "I still don't know why you're even here."

I shrug, not giving a shit about her bad manners. She truly sounds disgusted with me. "Why the hell are you in a building that has no peepholes? That's not safe. The least your landlord can do given these shoddy doors—which are basically made out of plywood—is put in some damn peepholes."

"Oh my gawd, you are such an idiot. Please say peepholes one more freaking time."

"Whoa, whoa, whoa, one insult at a time please. Can you stop being such a bitch for two seconds?" I ask, bending over a *second* time to rescue Kate Upton. Her boobs have gotten wrinkled from being dropped twice, and I pause to smooth out her pages.

It's the least I can do.

Then, before I can stop her, Molly uses a self-defense move *I* taught her and swiftly elbows me in the gut with a jab so quick I don't even see it coming.

Grunting, I teeter a bit and hold my stomach before I can stand upright. "That was a cheap shot," I croak out as the banging on the door gets louder. It sounds like someone's trying to break through the damn door with battering ram.

"What the *fuck?*" I march toward the door, palming Molly in the forehead to halt her and steeling myself against a possible assault. "Back *down* Molly. Christ. Do you really think Weston would want you charging the door when some mental person is on the other side banging it in? Step aside dammit."

She moves aside, biting her lip.

Well shit, that was easy.

At the simple mention of her pansy ass boyfriend's name, Molly's shoulders sag a little and she crosses her arms. I can tell she's debating about whether or not to give in as she continues chewing on her lower lip with a furrowed brow, deep in concentration.

I make a mental note to use Weston as my war strategy in the future.

Stalking to the door, I unlatch the deadbolt and throw it open, fist clenched at my side, ready to sucker punch someone in the face if necessary.

I open my mouth but don't have the chance to speak because I'm shoved aside by the girl standing in the hallway. With a giant mop of brown hair piled on the top of her head (that could honestly be a dead animal for all I know), smeared eye makeup giving her raccoon eyes, and a death glare, she pushes past me and demands shrilly, "Hey buddy, what the hell is going on in here? I could hear noises out in the hall."

Aw shit. She's kind of scary, actually.

The tall brunette rushes to my sisters' side, grabbing Molly by the shoulders and giving her a little shake. "Molly, are you okay? Is this guy bothering you?" the interloper demands, only turning for a quick second to shoot me another scowl and dump a pile of crap on to the couch—a pile, I can't help but noticing, that includes a bag of trail mix and a bag of Sun Chips.

Which reminds me, I'm *crazy* hungry.

"Yup. I was just trying to get him to leave, but he refuses." Molly, the little traitor, shoots me a triumphant look over her friend's head and winks.

Fucking *winks*.

Wait. *What?* "Hey! Now wait just one damn minute—"

The girl snorts indignantly out of her pert little nose and steps forward to jam her finger into my solid chest, so hard I can feel her nail. "No pal, *you* wait one damn minute. This is *my* apartment and Molly wants *you* gone, so it's time for you to go before I *pepper spray* your ass. Get out into the hallway and keep your hands where I can see them."

What. The. Fu...*ck*.

Out of the corner of my eye, I see my little sister continuing to smirk, her laughing eyes betraying her attempts to get me to leave. She's clearly incredibly entertained and therefore in no hurry to set this chick (who is *obviously* bat-shit crazy) straight.

I'm seriously going to murder Molly. Then when I'm

done, I'm going to dig up her dead, lifeless body and kill her all over again. Ah shit, do I sound bitter?

"Who the hell *are* you, anyway?" I ask.

"Who the hell am *I*? Hey, *I'll* be asking the questions, thank you very much. Hallway please. Seriously, I might be thin, but I have a black belt."

"Black belt?" Crossing my arms, I chuckle snidely. "Somehow, I seriously doubt that, so please don't make me laugh." I walk over to the couch and flop down on it. "What are you, a hundred and thirty pounds soaking wet?" I dismissively palm through the girl's discarded pile of stuff and snatch up the bag of trail mix from where it was sandwiched between a textbook and a curling iron. Without hesitating, I take custody of it and rip the plastic bag open savagely with my teeth—I mean, it was just *lying* there in the pile.

"Sweet, trail mix, my favorite."

"What are you doing, you *jack*ass!" Molly's irrational roommate-slash-bodyguard screeches (loudly I might add), trying to grab the bag out of my hands.

I hold it above my head out of her reach and flash her my pearly whites while looking her up and down. "You really ought to stop throwing yourself at me—it's embarrassing. Sorry, but you're not my type. Maybe if you cleaned yourself up a bit…"

I crunch down on a handful of nuts and pretzels, chewing noisily.

"Get the hell *out* of here!" the roommate fumes, white knuckles clenched at her sides. I can practically *see* the steam rising from her ears.

"Hey now, don't get defensive, I'm just the messenger," I soothe.

"Are you hearing me, asshole? I said get the hell out."

"You should listen to her, Matthew." Molly agrees with a shit-eating grin. She's leaning against the kitchen counter now, poking idly through a candy dish.

Ignoring them both and enjoying this scenario immensely, I spread my legs wide on the couch, tip my head back, and shake more trail mix into my mouth from the bag, which basically means it's mine now.

Fact: possession is nine-tenths of the law.

"Thanks for the snack," I say as I eat the last crumb and emit a satisfied groan. "I'll pay you back."

Or not.

I crumble the empty bag and toss it onto the coffee table, stretch my arms out behind my head, and groan again. "Mmm, that hit the spot. I was starving."

The roommate's mouth falls open, and for a brief moment she's actually silent. Thank god. I take advantage, adding, "Next time can you stock up on the Costco brand of trail mix? I like it much better than this gas station crap you bought."

"Oh my god, you are so rude! So *rude*! What the hell is your problem? *Get out*!" Again from the roommate in a high-pitched shriek.

All this squawking is giving me a headache. "Can you please chill the fuck out? Christ, you sound like a freaking shrew. In fact, you can make yourself useful by grabbing me an ibuprofen—wait, make it three," I say, rubbing my temples before snapping my fingers. "Oh, and a bottle of water. My trail mix made me thirsty. And maybe some different chips? These Sun Chips have no appeal for me right now."

I scratch my chin in thought while she stares, wide eyed.

"Actually, now that I mention it, never mind, I *will* just eat these. A bird in the hand and all that…" She stares at me, her feet rooted to the ground. To twist the proverbial knife deeper into her back, I add, "Be a good girl and run along now."

"*Security!*"

Cecelia

"I meant to behave myself, but...there were so many options that were more fun." – Matthew Wakefield

"Cece, I need you to do me a *huge* favor..." Molly's voice, thick with reluctance, trails off. I hear one of her IKEA dresser drawers open (the one that took two of us three hours to assemble even though the instructions said assembly time was only forty-five minutes), some light rustling, then the dresser being slammed shut. Papers shuffle on her desk, followed by a lot of muttering.

"*Terrific.* Isn't this just *terrific.*" Oh great. Now she's talking to herself.

Even though I can hear her just fine, I take the TV remote and point it at the forty-inch flat screen hanging on our small living room wall, turning the volume down a tad so I can hear her better—although actually, I would have heard Molly if she was whispering to me from inside her closet, buried under a blanket, with the door closed; *that's* how thin the walls in this apartment are.

I also put down the bag of Cheetos I'm stuffing my face with because, let's be honest, they're wicked crunchy, and who can have a decent conversation when they're snacking on these tiny nuggets of scrumptiousness?

Plus, I want to enjoy every delicious, fatty, orange morsel, and probably won't be able to once Molly starts making requests and I lose my appetite.

"Do I even want to know what this favor is?" I call out with a nervous laugh.

To be fair, usually the only favors she ever asks are mundane, like the time she wanted to borrow a pair of *my* shoes to kill a giant spider (by the way, I refused—I'm sorry, but that freaking spider was *humongo-giganto*), or when she needed to borrow my car because hers had no gas. There was also the time she borrowed my iPad for an entire week because she forgot hers at her parents' house.

See? Pretty harmless entreaties.

However, I have a sneaking suspicion—and can tell by the sound of her voice—that this 'favor' might be a doozy.

I hear more rustling from her bedroom. "Would you please just come out here," I request, exasperated, setting the remote down with a clank on the coffee table.

Molly sighs and appears in her doorway, leaning against the cheap plywood doorframe, and slaps her palms down against her jean clad legs in defeat. "I don't have my phone or my laptop."

I blink at her and groan. "*Ugh*, Molly, seriously? Not again."

"I know, I know. It doesn't really sound like that big a deal, but I have some people I really *really* need to get ahold of before this weekend."

It's Wednesday.

"Well…do you at least know where your phone and laptop *are*?" I'm feeling slightly less irritated and like it might be safe to resume eating Cheetos.

"See, here's the awkward part…they're in Westons' truck, and he's in, um… He's in Cleveland and won't be back until tomorrow night at the earliest?"

"Um, okay, are you *asking* me or telling me this?" I scratch my head. "I mean, don't you at least have a spare key to his truck?"

She rings her hands then throws them up in the air in exasperation. "Ugh, I wish! It wouldn't normally be a big deal, but this time the team flew to Ohio. He's got his truck at the airport because he missed the team bus this morning, and I'm not driving two hours to the airport just to fetch a laptop when he'll be home in less than thirty-six hours, but I need to ask Matthew now so he doesn't complain about me asking *last minute*." Molly throws her hands up again. "This wouldn't be a problem if he hadn't traded in his crotch rocket."

FYI: Her boyfriend Weston used to have a sporty green motorcycle, but he traded it in when they came to college. More practical, I guess.

AFYI (also for your information): Molly's boyfriend is a total, certifiable hottie.

Hey, I'm just saying!

I let out a huge puff of air and a tiny orange chunk of Cheeto shoots out. *Gross!* I freaking hate when food flies out of my mouth—it's so awkward. Wrinkling up my nose, I search for the speck and pick it off the arm of the couch before asking, "Soooo, who are these people you need to get ahold of?"

"Um…" Molly studies her nails, examining them this way and that before chewing on her coral-colored pinkie nail. "Mattmph…."

"Huh?" I squint, straining to hear her.

"My brothmph…" She looks at the ceiling and averts her eyes.

"Huh? What are you saying?" I'm so confused.

"*Ihavetogetaholdofmybrother.*" The words come out in rush and I actually have to cock my neck like a dog and play the words back in my head to try to make sense of them. *I have to grab hold of a gutter? I have to get fold of another? I have a bread load from a feather?*

Um yeah, deciphering her mumbling simply ain't gonna happen because none of it is making any sense. I majored in economics, not translating.

"Can you please repeat that, only slower and less… like a *spaz*?"

"You know I have this family dinner thing on Sundays and have to get ahold of my brother. I don't normally need a ride to my folks' place but this weekend I do. So…could you…um…" Molly's airily waving her hands to and fro.

I groan.

Not giving her a chance to finish her sentence, I loudly sputter and throw down the bag of Cheetos in a huff. A few Cheetos escape from the bag and land on the carpet. "*Ugh!* You know what Molly? You just *ruined* my entire afternoon. I can't even take one night to be lazy. How am I supposed to enjoy this junk food with an email to your evil brother looming on my horizon? Good god Molly!"

"Wait a second—are those *my* Cheetos?" Cheetos are Molly's absolute favorite treat and the one thing she *will not share.*

Growing up, she was never allowed to eat junk food because one time, her dipshit brother Matthew wiped his big, dumb, fat, Cheetos fingers all over the arms of her mom's favorite armchair, staining the fabric orange and ruining it *forever.* Molly officially refers to it as *The Incident of 2010 that Ruined it for Everybody.*

I mean, her mom must have been pretty pissed to banish *all* junk food from the house.

Molly narrows her eyes and I pick up the bag from the floor, only to shove it under an ugly throw pillow that's in the corner of the couch. "Cecelia Jane Carter, I'm going to ask you one more time: are those *my* Cheetos?"

Dammit. Busted. "Um….no?"

She rolls her eyes and steeples the points of her fingers together, not even a little pissed off. I can tell she's just had a eureka moment and I'm not sure I'm quite digging it. Slowly Molly smiles, the dimple in her right cheek appearing. "Tell you what, since I love you so dearly, and this is your first offense, I'll let this petty theft of yours slide, but you have to do me this one *small* favor."

"Two minutes ago you were calling it a *huge* favor. I'm sorry, but Cheeto theft or not, it's a no." Defiantly, I cross my arms and stare out the window with my chin pointed up. "The crime and the favor are not evenly matched, sorry."

Molly stomps her slippered foot like a petulant child. "Oh come *on* Cece! *Please!* Don't make me walk down the hall and ask Creepy Writer Guy if I can use his computer."

Dammit, she had to bring Creepy Writer Guy into this?

Crappity crap.

She knows me too well.

Creepy Writer Guy (CWG, or Pit Stains as Weston sometimes refers to him) is our name for the only other person in our apartment complex that we've actually ever met, and he's exactly what you're picturing: middle-aged, scowling, sometimes shirtless, always sporting receding hairline with a comb-over.

You know in *Friends* where Chandler, Monica, Phoebe, Joey, Ross, and Rachel talk about Ugly Naked Guy, the fat guy they watch from Monica and Rachel's apartment, and the guy they once poke with a large pole?

Well, Creepy Writer Guy is our poor girl's version of him. Maybe not so much the naked part, but he does live down the hall from us and every time we go into the hallway, he opens his door a crack to steal glimpses of us.

He's pretty weird, a total creeper, and we're pretty confident he has a collection of women's underwear inside a bathroom cabinet somewhere—but that's just speculation, so don't go quoting me on it.

I think once our neighbor kid next door said the guy was an author or a writer or something (is there a difference?), so Molly and I decided to give him a nickname because, well…calling him CWG makes him less threatening.

Less *rape*-y.

So even though we don't have to stare at him through a giant panoramic window like Monica and Rachel, we're not too keen on asking him for anything, or walking by his door.

Or talking to him.

Or *looking* at him.

Ever.

Although…I'm sure if we were given the opportunity to poke him with a long stick, we would totally do it. Yup, we'd totally poke him with a stick.

Hard.

Not because we're mean, but because he's creepy (hence the name) and probably deserves it—especially if he really does have stolen underwear in his place.

Ugh. Heebie jeebies.

I could go on and give you more details, but it would only incite nightmares, in you and me both. I know you're probably totally curious, but *trust* me on this.

When I finally remove my eyes from the window I've been gazing out and glance back at Molly, she is staring at me, bottom lip jutting out in the most unflattering way. Smirking, I ask, "What? Do you think you can influence me by pouting? I'm not your boyfriend."

Molly responds by widening her eyes and raising her hands up to her chin like girls do when they're pretending to be a kitten. I laugh because she's being utterly ridiculous. "Do you really think *that's* going to work—the pouty kitty act? What am I, a guy?" I reach under my lap blanket to retrieve the Cheetos hidden there, open the bag, and take a loud crunchy bite out of a big one.

The big fat ones are my favorite. Wait…did that come out sounding kind of pervy? Oh well.

The crunching is the only noise in the room besides Molly's fake meowing.

I lick my fingers and hold up the plastic Cheetos bag, peering inside to pick out another good one. I root around for a bit then hold one up, speaking to it. "Hey you, little orange guy. My, don't *you* look yummy." I pop it into my mouth, crunching down and chewing. "*Mmmm*, you taste so scrumptious. Thank you Molly for bringing these delightful little nuggets into our home."

"There's more where *that* came from. How about I make sure the cabinet is stocked at all times?" Molly sweetly attempts to entice me; she must be desperate.

I must say, her bribery is almost working.

But not quite.

I cock my eyebrow. "Are you trying to make me fat? What other offers do you have besides that?" I ask, popping another fat Cheeto into my open mouth.

Crunch.

Crunch. Crunch. Crunch.

"Please stop doing that," Molly says, wrinkling her nose in revulsion as I stick out my tongue at her. "Your tongue is *disgusting*."

"Well, please stop harassing me. I'm not going to cave just because you bring junk food home. You know I can't stand your brother—no offense," I add hastily.

"He can't stand you either. *Plus* he thinks you're a raging lunatic, so I guess you have something in common."

"What?!" I shriek. "What do you mean he thinks I'm a psycho? Why didn't you tell me this?"

"*Hello*, I didn't say psycho, I said *lun*atic—there's a big difference."

Oh really, I think sarcastically to myself, *that* is supposed to make me feel better? I'm not a psycho, I'm a lunatic? I don't have time to question it further because Molly continues. "I'm sorry Cece, but when he was here, all you did was yell and screech at him like a mental person, not to mention you threatened him with both mace *and* karate. So, yeah…"

Hmmm. She might have a point.

But still—whose side is she on?

I shift on the couch in a huff and point an orange, cheesy finger in her direction accusingly. "We both know it was a simple misunderstanding, and you were just *standing* there. You could have told me he was your brother, you jerk."

"I did tell you he was my brother…*even*tually." Molly awkwardly mumbles that last word.

Bored, I begin licking the cheese off my fingers, one by one, kind of like a cat cleaning itself.

Sensing herself losing control of the situation, Molly concedes. "Okay, okay Cece, water under the bridge, water under the bridge. No big deal." She presents her palms to me in surrender like she's trying to sooth a snarling dog.

"Yeah, maybe it wasn't a big deal to *you*. I'm the one who now has a reputation as a nut job. It's extremely embarrassing. Thanks."

"Well, I can definitely think of one way you can make it better and it would *really* be helping me out." Molly smiles and sits on the end of the couch, putting her arm around my shoulder and squeezing. "You know you love me."

That, my friends, is how I was manipulated into writing an email to Matthew Wakefield on behalf of his scheming little sister.

***

TO: Matthew Wakefield <imascoringmachine89@gmail.com>
DATE: September 13, 2014 at 5:07:04 PM CST
FROM: Cecelia Carter <carter.cecejane@gmail.com>
Subject: From Molly

To the World Biggest Asshole,
On behalf of your bratty, ungrateful sister, I wanted to let you know Molly needs you to pick her up this Sunday. Please don't come to our apartment because I can't stand the site of your ASS FACE. By the way, you owe me a bag of trail mix...

All right, calm down, I'm just kidding. I wouldn't actually send a note like that. Here's what I really wrote:

TO: Matthew Wakefield <imascoringmachine89@gmail.com>
DATE: September 13, 2014 at 5:07:04 PM CST
FROM: Cecelia Carter <carter.cecejane@gmail.com>
Subject: From Molly

Hi. Molly asked me to send this note because she left both her phone and laptop in Weston's truck, and therefore has no way to contact anyone. She wanted me to let you know to pick her up Sunday at 2 PM.
- C

There.

I did my part.

Short and to the point.

Boom, done.

I can't help thinking what a good friend and roommate I am, and I smile, pretty satisfied with myself, before hitting *send*.

I glance again at Matthew's email address, studying the jumble of letters more closely, and choke back a laugh when I realize what it says: *I am a scoring machine.*

Sheesh, *some*one is full of himself.

I know the guy is a great athlete and has a huge following, but man, that email address is super *lame*. On second thought, he's probably had that email since he was ten—only a kid would purposely call himself a scoring machine.

I hope.

I sit back in my chair and stare blankly at my computer screen, thinking how strange it is that after all this time living with Molly, I've only met her brother once. Sure, I've heard about him before in passing—not just from Molly herself, but from practically everyone else once they find out Molly Wakefield is my roommate—but I'd never interacted with him before the scene in our apartment.

Actually, he has been to our apartment a few times before, although we've never crossed paths (for whatever reason). Once was to help her move in, and occasionally he picks her up for their Sunday family dinners—that is, if he's even in the state.

His last year as a Badger for the University of Wisconsin, he was drafted by the Anaheim Ducks. I know he has an apartment in California where he lives during hockey season, and one halfway between Madison and River Glen, the Wakefields' home town.

So yeah, when people find out I live with Molly Wakefield, I get bombarded with questions about Matthew by default. *Have you met Matthew Wakefield before? What's he like? How tall is he? Does he have all of his teeth? Do you go to his games?* On and on and on it goes, simply because I live with his little sister.

Kind of explains why he's such a dick.

People love the guy.

TO: Cecelia Carter <carter.cecejane@gmail.com>
DATE: September 13, 2014 at 7:09:12 PM CST
FROM: Matthew Wakefield <imascoringma-chine89@gmail.com>
Subject: RE: From Molly
Dude, who is this?
MSW

Oh my god, really?

What an ass.

Matthew knows damn well who I am, but I guess I shouldn't expect a guy like him to make anything easy, or take me seriously. In his universe, I'm a nobody. Can't he just be nice because I'm doing his little sister a favor?

Having sent the message for Molly like she asked me to, there is no need for me to reply and get chatty with the guy.

Really, I should just ignore his quip and let it go.

On the *other* hand…

My fingers hover above the small keys on my smartphone and before I can stop them, they nimbly compose a new message.

Seriously. I couldn't stop myself even if I wanted to.

Which, if I'm honest, I do not.

TO: Matthew Wakefield <imascoringmachine89@gmail.com>
DATE: September 13, 2014 at 7:12:19 PM CST
FROM: Cecelia Carter <carter.cecejane@gmail.com>
Subject: RE: RE: From Molly
Your sister's roommate. - C

TO: Cecelia Carter <carter.cecejane@gmail.com>
DATE: September 13, 2014 at 7:23:16 PM CST
FROM: Matthew Wakefield <imascoringmachine89@gmail.com>
Subject: RE: RE: RE: From Molly
The angry one?
MSW

Oh my god, he really is infuriating.

Insufferable.

I reach up and palm my cheek, first feeling one and then the other, like I'm checking for a temperature. My face is hot, slightly feverish.

Once again, as if on their own accord, my fingers deftly hit *reply* and frantically start typing.

I am so irritated that *irritated* doesn't even begin to describe it.

Vexed. Furious. Peeved. Aggravated. *Take your pick.*

Not to mention, the fact that we're emailing is annoyingly inconvenient. I can't help but think this whole back and forth conversation we've embarked on would be *so* much easier if we were texting…

TO: Matthew Wakefield <imascoringmachine89@
gmail.com>
DATE: September 13, 2014 at 8:09:23 PM CST
FROM: Cecelia Carter <carter.cecejane@gmail.
com>
Subject: RE: RE: RE: RE: From Molly
The angry one? Try the ONLY one. I don't have
time to respond to your idiotic comments. - C

TO: Cecelia Carter <carter.cecejane@gmail.com>
DATE: September 13, 2014 at 8:12:18 PM CST
FROM: Matthew Wakefield <imascoringma-
chine89@gmail.com>
Subject: You are angry
I respectfully disagree, since you DO keep re-
sponding. I don't blame you—none of the ladies
can stay away.
MSW

Okay.

Now I'm freaking pissed. (That is a lie—I was pissed before).

I set my phone down on our scuffed up Formica kitchen counter and walk away, determined to stifle the urge to really give him a piece of my mind.

Counting from one to ten (twice), I walk into the hall and stand with my hands on my hips, thinking and surveying the apartment. I look around, trying to come up with something to do that will keep my mind and hands off that damn cell phone, and I am so desperate, I decide the large pile of laundry spilling out of our tiny hall closet could use some attention.

I tell myself I'll start a load of towels.

Yes, that's what I'll do; I'll start a load of towels.

I'm not going to think about it, I'm not going to think about it.

Seven minutes into going through the pretense of sorting light and dark colors, I cannot stand it anymore.

I walk back into the kitchen and snatch up my phone.

Yay me, seven whole minutes!

Aren't you impressed?

I know the things you're thinking—let me tick them off for you: You have no willpower. He's just a guy. He's a jerk. He doesn't deserve any more attention. You're better than this…the list could go on and on.

Believe me, I'm disappointed enough in myself for both of us. *What a fortress of willpower* I *turned out to be.* Roger would be so disappointed in me.

But guess what? Right now I couldn't care less.

Because Matthew Wakefield is so full of himself, I simply do not have it in me to resist the urge to knock him down a peg.

And so…

TO: Matthew Wakefield <imascoringmachine89@gmail.com>
DATE: September 13, 2014 at 8:19:31 PM CST
FROM: Cecelia Carter <carter.cecejane@gmail.com>
Subject: You are a jerk.
Oh, I'm SOOOO sure all the girls are beating down the door to your den of sin (I hope you're picking up on the sarcasm here). I will let Molly know I got ahold of you, and you can go fornicate the rest of

your evening away. No need to reply. - C

Okay.

I admit the email sounds catty and bitter, and *perhaps* I should have waited a little longer than seven minutes before I sent it.

Sigh. Too late now, I guess.

TO: Cecelia Carter <carter.cecejane@gmail.com>
DATE: September 13, 2014 at 8:22:07 PM CST
FROM: Matthew Wakefield <imascoringma-chine89@gmail.com>
Subject: Fornicate?
Den of sin? Wow. I LIKE THAT!!! But you're giving me WAY too much credit. And why would I go fornicate when this is so much more fun? Question: are you this big of a bitch to everyone, or is this just my lucky night? P.S. I bet a hundred dollars you reply to this message. And that you're wearing sweatpants.
MSW

I sit on the couch with my mouth hanging open and look down at my gray sweatpants. What a dick! Of all the nerve! Excuse me, but I happen to have a great ass *thank you very much*, and I do not need to flaunt it in low-rise jeans every hour of the damn day.

I huff loudly.

Then I huff again, stalking into my bedroom and flouncing onto my bed, bouncing up and down because the mattress is such a cheap piece of crap.

I'm so irritated my hands are actually shaking. Suddenly, I begin to feel like the lunatic he accused me of being. I need to get a grip here and fight the power, because the bastard knows I'm going to respond to his email.

Actually, *he* knows it *and* I know it.

I hit *reply* and change the subject line, giggling out loud at my own wittiness and wondering if he'll notice.

> TO: Matthew Wakefield <imascoringmachine89@ gmail.com>
> DATE: September 13, 2014 at 8:35:14 PM CST
> FROM: Cecelia Carter <carter.cecejane@gmail. com>
> Subject: YOU HAVE A STUPID EMAIL ADDRESS
> I am not a bitch. And for the record, I am NOT wearing sweatpants. - C

Am I going to hell for being such a liar?

I look down at my sweatpants again, and I at least have the decency to blush. Cringing, I delete the entire message and send this instead:

> I am NOT a bitch, but I guess since I'm replying to your damn message, this means I owe you a hundred bucks. Good luck collecting.
> - C

Matthew

"How did I get into her pants? Well that's an easy one. I whispered the three words every chick wants to hear: *I play hockey.* – Jay Mendelson, teammate

A few thoughts occur to me as my email notification goes off for the sixth time in an hour:

1. This is fun.

2. I have work to do tonight to prepare for tomorrow's game and shouldn't be wasting time playing around on my phone.

3. My sister's boyfriend Weston (who's sleeping in the hotel bed next to mine) sounds like a goddamn chainsaw that's having a seizure when he snores. In fact, I want to suffocate him with a freaking pillow. I wonder if Molly knows how loud he is, but then this thought immediately reminds me that he is probably *sleeping* with my little sister, which doesn't just make me want to smother him, it makes me want to beat the shit

out of him, too.

Speaking of Weston, I glance over to where he's sleeping and curl my lip. It's dark, and he's sleeping, but the sight of him irritates me nonetheless. How do I always get stuck rooming with this guy?

You might be wondering at this point how I even ended up in a room with him to begin with. Well that one is easy: I play professional hockey for the Anaheim Ducks, but in the offseason I come home to Wisconsin, where I keep a condo near my folks' place.

When my first season hiatus with the NHL began, it seemed like a natural progression to begin working as one of the development coaches for the hockey team at my alma mater, the University of Wisconsin Madison—you know, in my "free time." Whoa, that was a mouthful.

Basically, my job in the offseason is to coach certain collegiate players, train with them in the fitness room, make sure they're keeping their grades up, work with them on and off the ice. I occasionally travel with the team, and when I do, for some ungodly reason, the team's travel agent insists on sticking me in the same room as McGrath, probably as some sick joke to torture me.

The guy is a *pain* in my ass.

You think girls are high maintenance in the bathroom? This guy takes the cake: he brings his own shampoos and aftershave lotions, changes into special flip-flops for the shower, and travels with his own pillow.

Oh, and I forgot to mention that as soon as he walks into the hotel room, he yanks all the covers off the bed so he doesn't have to touch any semen-infested linens (his words, not mine).

What was that? You don't think that sounds so bad because you do all those things too? Well trust me. It's really annoying and against Mother Nature for a guy to act like that—girls yes, guys no.

Plus, he brings food but won't share it.

I glance over and eyeball a bag of his Sun Chips, letting out a loud sigh. If I take it, he'll hear the crinkle from the bag and wake up, and that's the last thing I want.

Adjusting myself on the bed to get comfortable, I click off the bedside table lamp and relax against the headboard before opening the new message, laughing when I read the subject line of Cecelia's email, and laughing again when I read the content.

I am NOT a bitch, but I guess since I am replying to your damn message, this means I owe you a hundred bucks. Good luck collecting. - C

Not a bitch? Bullshit.

That chick is *too* a bitch, and I've witnessed it firsthand. Not only have I experienced it myself, judging from the way she looked the first—and only—time I met her, she is probably totally sitting around right now in some kind of sweat or yoga pants. Trust me, I know girls, and that's totally what she's doing: pacing around that shitty apartment of theirs in a complete tizzy.

I click *reply*.

This is too easy. I think for a bit about what might piss her off the most, knowing already that it doesn't take much.

TO: Cecelia Carter <carter.cecejane@gmail.com>
DATE: September 13, 2014 at 8:47:24 PM CST
FROM: Matthew Wakefield <imascoringmachine89@gmail.com>
Subject: BUT I'M USUALLY ALWAYS RIGHT
If you don't have the cash, I can collect it in other ways...IF you know what I mean.
P.S. What was your name again?
MSW

I chuckle at my own wittiness and toss the phone onto the shitty hotel bedspread that's folded down at my feet, hoping that later when I hold the phone up to my ear it doesn't give me an STD or something because it landed in something gross—you know, like a bodily fluid, since it's been on this bed since approximately 1982.

Okay, so maybe Wes has a point about ripping off the bedspread… I make a mental note to rub my phone down with hand sanitizer.

Crossing my arms behind my head and flipping through the sparse cable channels this hotel has to offer, I finally settle on a rerun of *The Breakfast Club* and briefly close my eyes. Maybe if I try hard enough, I can conjure up a mental picture of my sister's roommate Cecelia (yes, I know her name), which isn't easy because we've only ever met once, and that was a few weeks back. However memorable the encounter was, I can honestly only remember a few things about what she looks like—mostly a pile of messy hair and smudged makeup.

Not a good look for her.

I do think I remember her being kind of tall, fit, and—most importantly—she had a shit ton of food in her freakishly heavy overnight bag.

You might not think this is important, but trust me, it is.

My phone chimes, and the little green email light flashes.

How weird—my pulse actually accelerated…or maybe I'm just imagining it. Why would I get excited over some unkempt chick I think is incredibly annoying and quite possibly a total bitch?

Maybe something is wrong with me. I put my hand to my forehead and feel for a temperature.

Hmm. Maybe I just need to get laid. It *has* been a while.

> TO: Matthew Wakefield <imascoringmachine89@gmail.com>
> DATE: September 13, 2014 at 9:06:23 PM CST
> FROM: Cecelia Carter <carter.cecejane@gmail.com>
> Subject: JACKASS
> Stop emailing me. I get dumber every time I read one of your messages. - C

This has me throwing my head back against the headboard and laughing out loud. Out of the dark comes an angry, muffled "What the fuck? I'm trying to sleep." Weston's head pops up and he's glaring at me from his side of the room, his hair sticking up in ten different directions. Dude needs a haircut. "Whatever it is you're doing, knock it off."

"Sorry," I answer…but I'm not.

Not at all.

Cecelia

"All I could hear when he was talking over the loud music was 'Blah, blah, blah, I'm a rude asshole.'" – my best friend Abigail Darlington

Leaning against the damp counter in the small bathroom of Lone Rangers, the one bar in Madison not entirely dominated by the under twenty-one crowd, I look up and study myself in the cracked mirror.

There are girls standing around waiting for a stall, some of them slumped against the tile wall—a few because they're drunk, others because they're bored from the long wait. Realizing I need to make it quick because of the growing line, I pull out a tube of gloss (Cover Girl Baby Lips in Pink Punch, my favorite in case you were wondering) and swipe it across my lips.

I give my boring, plain white tee a onceover (only some of it is wet from leaning against the counter), note that my face isn't *too* shiny (thank goodness), and observe that my hair hasn't lost much of its volume. Considering how freakishly hot it is in this damn bar, I take that as a good sign, because there's no telling when my friends will want to leave. In fact, people might have to look at me for a few more hours yet, and I'd rather they not to have to stare at my hair when it gets frizzy.

Although my eyeliner is a tad worse for wear, I leave it and grab my drink off the counter before yanking the door open.

Noise assaults me, and my eyes do a quick scan of the room, spotting my little group of girlfriends at the front of the bar (figures, since I'm all the way in back). A virtual sea of people separates us, and elbowing my way through the sea of people is not an easy task, let me tell you.

Someone even grabs my ass.

Drunk people are so *rude.*

And then there, in the middle of the crowded floor, is none other than Matthew Wakefield.

Wait, where did *he* come from?

I falter for a brief moment, tripping slightly on the short girl who suddenly appears in front of me, and I study him. Immediately the metaphoric wall goes up, and I paste a passive expression on my face…but pretending not to be affected by him is easier said than done.

I'm sorry, but have you seen him?

Matthew Wakefield is like a bad episode of some low-budget MTV show; think *Awkward*, for example—it's a terrible show with even worse acting, and it's gotta be a fact somewhere that you get stupider watching it. And yet, some sick part of you wants to see what is going to happen to that dipshit main character.

So much so that when your little sister walks into the

room and rudely changes the channel, you scream at her to change it back.

Er…not that it has happened to me (cough).

I won't insult your intelligence by gushing that Matthew is the hottest guy I've ever seen. Time is not standing still right now, nothing is moving in slow motion, the crowd is not parting like the Red Sea when our eyes meet across the room—too cliché. But you know…there is *definitely* something about him.

Maybe it's his arrogance that I'm warming up to.

Maybe it's his rich auburn hair, which is incredibly thick, unruly, and seems like a terrible waste on such a man.

Or maybe it's the sinewy biceps that have *actual* defined edges and can be seen beneath his shirt.

Or his dark green, expressive eyes that are hooded, sharp, and never miss anything.

And the freckles—can you say *swoon*!?

Not to mention the shallow dimple in his cheek. It's not a deep one, but I'd lick it anyway.

Holy shit—oh. No. I. Did. *Not*!

I'd lick it anyway? What the hell is wrong with me?!

Shocked with myself, I slap a hand over my mouth and stifle a groan. Shit. Guess I have a dirtier mind than I give myself credit for.

Then I think about his white, toothy grin—the one he gives so freely, even when he's being a prick.

All right, all right! Enough already!

So, even though we spent a good part of the week

sending each other what basically equaled, well, *hate* mail, I would still never have the nerve to venture to his side of the room, or publically acknowledge him.

Or say hello.

Or for that matter, look directly at him.

Not on purpose, anyway.

Some girls might have the lady balls to do it, but *I* am not one of them.

So I stand here, taking in every detail but pretending not to watch him, which—believe you me—is a skill few have mastered at my level, but is not impossible to learn.

Want to know what my secrets are? Simple:

1. I always make sure I'm looking *above* the person I'm watching—like, above the top of their head. Find something fascinating on the wall behind them; trust me—you can stare at someone without *ever* looking directly at them. And whoa! *Never* in the face. That could be the kiss of death. I mean, do you *really* want to be caught staring?

2. If you are caught? Do. Not. Panic. Do not find the nearest exit. Do not run away. Stiffen your spine, raise your chin a notch, and give a wave. No, no no! *NOT* TO HIM. Pick someone near the object of your affection...*anyone!* The bartender, the wingman—give them a wave. This will give the illusion that you were staring at someone *else* the entire time. Crisis averted. Congrats, you no longer look like the stalk-arazzi.

3. Or, if you're feeling brave, go right ahead and keep on staring. One of two things is sure to happen:

   a. The person you're staring at will freak out

and think you're a creepy stalker, and it's possible he will tell his friends to steer clear of you, which is *ter*rible—e*specially* if his friends are cute.

b. Or! The person you're staring at will think you're cute. Yay you! He will be intrigued and stare back, which could turn into either a staring contest, *or* (if you're lucky) he will have big enough balls to walk over and strike up a conversation.

Now, I wouldn't exactly call these *proven* methods, and if you try to pull this off and fail miserably, don't blame me. Plus, I wouldn't recommend trying them straight out of the gate—practicing on a friend first is probably your best bet.

Also, while we're on the subject of these mundane details, it's important to note that I'm sharing all this because girls have to stick together. I mean hey, it's entirely possible you don't have a friend who is sharing bits of dating wisdom with you. I consider it my civic duty to inform you some of the things I've picked up on over the years.

But I digress…

Back to Matthew.

I can hear the deep baritone of his vulgar voice booming over the crowd, and even though I can't understand what he's saying from here, it must be pretty freaking *hilarious* because the throng of groupies hanging on him is nothing short of obnoxious. Their giggling and laughter isn't charming. It isn't cute. It's downright aggravating.

It's not just girls either—guys are laughing at him too, like he's a damn comedian.

Well I have news for you: there's a difference between

being funny because, well, you're actually *funny* and having people laugh at you because they feel forced into it by some messed up obligation to kiss your famous ass. I have a feeling with Matt, it's the latter.

I don't know if I would *want* to be popular because I'm a conceited asshole; it isn't exactly an endearing quality, and eventually it does catch up to you. Professional athlete or not, karma can be a bitch.

Even with the ridiculously loud music being pumped through the speakers and people shouting to be heard, I can tell a lot of the laughter surrounding Matthew is fake, mostly because he's surrounding himself with groupies.

We all know *those types* (see: desperate) will force out a laugh over anything to get attention, even if it's not remotely funny.

Ugh, I bet the arrogant ass is telling stories about himself.

Figures.

It occurs to me that I am being judgmental, and for a nanosecond I am overcome with guilt, so what do I do? Shoot up a quick prayer toward the ceiling of the bar, of course.

Dear Lord, please forgive me for being a judgmental bitch and for anything else that comes out of my mouth and is directed at Matthew Wakefield tonight. I just can't seem to help myself. Amen.

My eyes drift back to the open neckline of Matthew's shirt. He's gesturing wildly, beer bottle in one hand and forearm flexing on the other, and as he talks, the dark plaid flannel shirt with its open top few buttons strains from the brawny pectoral muscles across the front—clearly an open invitation for my perusal.

Hey, I might think the guy is a complete douche, but I am human.

And female.

I sigh and continue on my way, although it's impossible to make any progress without throwing an elbow here or there just so I can get through to the bar. Embarrassed that I caught myself mentally undressing my nemesis, I purposefully lock eyes with my best friend Abby at the bar. Standing next to her are Molly and Molly's best friend Jenna, and they all wave to me from their position across the room.

They've actually managed to get seats. Nice.

Rising on her tippy toes, Jenna gestures wildly and mouths, *"Hurry up!"*

Bright disco ball earrings dangle from her dainty lobes, sparkling wildly under the dim lights and causing me to grin. Only Jenna could wear disco ball earrings out in public and pull it off without everyone thinking she's crazy; quite the contrary, in fact: everyone thinks she's cool.

Well, except for Weston, who is a tad weirded out by her because she used to have a huge crush on him…not to mention, she used to stalk him a little when they were in high school. It wasn't like *Fatal Attraction* and no rabbits were boiled, but still, guys hate stalking in any capacity, so do yourself a favor and never do it.

Molly is leaning across the counter, balancing herself on the bottom rim of a stool like a total champ with a twenty-dollar bill extended over the bar top. No, actually, she is tapping the bill impatiently like she's at the bar every day and has the system down pat.

Glancing around, she yells, "This place *sucks* when it's so crowded."

What she means is, it's packed because the Badger hockey team had a home game this week, and they're here celebrating their recent win against Cleveland…and where there are bad boys of Badger hockey, the crowds—and girls—will most definitely follow.

I roll my eyes and hand her my empty glass. "Can you get me a water? My head is killing me."

She nods and sticks her arm back out to signal the bartender. "This song sure isn't helping." One Direction has just come over the sound system, blasting out their hit from last year, "Best Song Ever".

"What, you don't like boy bands?" I tease.

"Not *this* one! What are we, twelve?"

Jenna, who has been Molly's best friend since grade school, makes a face of disbelief and her eyebrows shoot up to her forehead. "Don't you dare lie Molly Wakefield! I *know* you have this CD because I've *seen* it on your desk. You totally think this is the *best song everrrrrr!*" Jenna shouts this last part loudly, singing along and throwing her arms in the air like she's at a rock concert while I do a twirly little hip-hop dance move on my toes to the beat. This of course immediately sends me toppling over a little bit.

I have no rhythm.

Anyone watching us would think we were drunk.

Abby groans loudly, covering her face with the palm of her hand. "Oh my god you guys, please stop." (She's way more serious than the rest of us).

"You guys are idiots." Molly laughs as she smacks me

in the shoulder and sticks out her tongue.

Jenna shrugs in agreement. "Yeah, but you love us…"

"So, I don't see Wes…what's he up to?" Abby kindly asks.

"He busted his lip open during the game." The bartender sets down their drinks and my water. Grabbing her glass off the bar, Molly turns and takes a dainty sip out of the tiny red straw. "Actually, a left wing for the Buckeyes did it for him when they got into a brawl second quarter. Punched him right in the face with his glove after Weston checked him into the boards. The guy didn't even bother to take the damn glove off." She makes a face, wrinkling her brow. "He's going to have a huge scab on his lip. Ugh. No offense to Weston cause I love him and all, but it's *so so* gross."

Now *I'm* making a face. "Uh, *yeah.* Sucks to be you."

"Tell me about it." Molly turns to slowly scan the crowd. Her eyes lock on a group of guys across the bar and get real wide before she groans and turns back to us, embarrassed. "Oh geez, would you look at my brother? What the hell does he think he's doing?" She takes another sip of her Cosmo and squints in Matthew's direction. "*Oh my gawd*, what a tool."

My eyes dart over to the other side of the bar. Indeed, Matthew Wakefield is acting like a first class dipshit, banging his hands on his chest like a gorilla while one of the Badger players pours a beer into his big, fat open mouth. Of course, the beer isn't making it down his throat, or even in his mouth, instead running down the front of his flannel shirt in steady stream of wet, yellow foam.

Head tipped back, Matthew's Adam's apple bobs as

he swallows and his gloriously unkempt hair falls into his eyes. I can't help admiring the sexy unshaven five o'clock shadow straining over the cords of his thick neck as it disappears into the dark recesses of his flannel.

I avert my eyes and snort. "Maybe you should take a picture of the dumbass and post it on Instagram."

Molly looks at me like I've lost my mind. "No way! Hello! My mom is one of my followers and would be so pissed at us both."

Confused, I ask, "Why would she be pissed at *you*?"

Molly levels me with a stare. I rack my brain for a nanosecond, and luckily it only takes me that long to catch up. Realization dawns on me.

Ding, ding, ding—we have a winner.

Molly isn't 21 yet (unlike myself, who turned a magnificent twenty-two last May) and can't post drinking pictures on any social media. Her parents would K-I-L-L her.

Slowly. Surely.

For me, twenty-three is right around the corner—only a few months away, in fact (hallelujah)!

"Ahhhh…" I draw the words out in a really loud yell so she can hear me over the music. "Right. Gotcha!"

At that exact same moment, chanting interrupts what she's about to say, and to Molly's horror, her brute of a brother is loudly shouting—wait, no, shouting isn't the right word…it's more of a chant.

Yup.

The moron is definitely chanting his sister's name in a crowded bar.

"Seriously Matthew, what the F!?" Molly shrieks.

"Could you *not*?"

Matthew, now having gotten her attention, continues shouting, "Moll-y, Moll-y! Molly, come here! Molly!"

Unceremoniously, Molly yanks my arm and hauls me behind her through the crowd, pushing her way through like a prize fighter, toward her brother as he begins belting out the words to "Parking Lot Party" (a song by Lee Brice, in case you didn't know), which isn't even the song blasting out of the sound system.

Nope, not the song at all, but he's singing it anyway.

And he's not the only one; half the team is singing—maybe not to Lee Brice, but in one seemingly messed up redneck chorus. In the middle of all the chaos is, unsurprisingly, a group of skanky, half-dressed puck bunnies that are grinding on several happily drunk members of the team.

To a country song.

The one that's actually playing—a country song about saving horses and riding cowboys.

Seriously.

My lip curls in disgust as I'm forcibly dragged toward them—completely against my will, I might add.

It's not really the small crowd of skanks I object being pulled toward, it's...

Okay, I'm lying.

It's the skanks.

Matthew

I have a confession to make: I'm not really drunk.

Not *one* bit.

Another confession: I'm glad my sister is dragging that angry roommate behind her, and not her best friend Hockey Stalker Jenna, as I like to call her. I've heard horror stories about *her* from Weston, and believe me, I'd rather not voluntarily put myself in the path of a fan girl. Regardless, all night, Jenna has been watching me with beady, calculating eyes and she's wearing some freaky ass disco ball earrings. Even from here, I can tell she's just barely occupied with the other girl enough to not follow Molly.

Barely.

She wants to come over, but doesn't.

I stumble a few paces toward my sister, putting on a small show. It's easy to act drunk with a soaking wet shirt full of beer and loud music blasting all around you, and the drunk act is actually a good excuse to get a few words in with my sister without having to walk over to her.

She can't resist stomping over to discipline me.

Truth is, we don't get to see each other all that often, and…I miss the little shit, even if she is a pain in my ass most of the time.

But she's stubborn, and independent, and I know that unless I force her to come over, she would remain on her side of the bar all night, judging.

Molly and Cecelia get jostled a bit along the way, and I keep a close eye on the crowd as they make their way through it, shrewdly prepared to step up in case anyone touches either of them. I know how guys are, and both my sister and her roommate are looking pretty damn cute tonight.

Shit. Was I seriously just thinking that?

Thank god I didn't say it out loud.

Cecelia follows behind—not willingly, if the frown on her face is any indication. Man, does this chick ever smile?

Prude.

I take in her plain white V-neck shirt and faded denim jeans, looking her up and down. Even though Cecelia is *obviously* not here to hook up with or impress anyone of the male persuasion, I can't help but wonder why she didn't make more of an effort.

Isn't it, like...girl DNA to truss themselves up when they go out?

Though, to be honest, her stark white shirt is *just* tight enough, and *just* sheer enough that as she stalks over, I can make out the outline of a white bra and...an *ample* swell of breasts.

Which are kind of awesome.

She isn't wearing much makeup, and her long wavy hair is a loose, tangled, sexy mess.

Molly breaks my visual of her roomie by rudely marching up and getting right in my face like a drill sergeant. "What do you *want,* you imbecile?"

"I forgot." I resist the urge to laugh out loud when Cecelia rolls her eyes and sighs loudly, and of course my attention shifts immediately to her. "Hey Cecelia, isn't that the exact same outfit you were wearing when you accosted me in Molly's apartment?"

Beside me, I get a swift nudge in the ribs from my sister. Jeez, what is it with the elbowing? At this rate, I'm going to have three bruised ribs by the end of the night.

"That was *not* a gentlemanly thing to point out, Matt,"

Molly says with a sneer as Cecelia rolls her eyes (for the second time in less than sixty seconds, I might add) and crosses her arms resentfully—a move that pushes her breasts up even higher into the neckline of her tee.

I get a great shot of cleavage.

Nice. Very nice.

Instead of staring at Cecelia's boobs like I'm instantly drawn to do, I shrug at them both. "Merely making an observation. I calls it like I sees it." I take a casual sip of beer and smirk.

I get another jab in the opposite rib. This elbow belongs to Neve Vanderhalt, my good buddy and recent graduate who is also a fellow coaching staffer for the Badgers. His smile spreads wide and his dark blue eyes are pinned directly to my sister's roommate with unconcealed interest.

Cecelia returns his interest with a perusal of her own.

Damn him for being so good-looking—makes me want to knock a gap in his teeth.

"Hey Wakefield, wanna introduce me to your *friend*?"

"Nope, not really."

Cecelia plants her hands on her narrow hips before tossing her hair indignantly. "Hi. Just to be clear, Matthew and I are *not* friends. Consider us *anti*-friends." She sticks her hand out for a shake. "My name is Cece. I'm Molly's *older*, wiser roommate."

Cecelia sends a flirty wink—actually fucking *winks*—at Neve and smiles. As their hands make contact for the handshake, her long willowy arm dissects me across the middle of my stomach just as her palm connects with Neve's.

The contact from her elbow sets my nerves tingling, and something quivers in my nether region, even though I'm pretty sure she was trying to punch me in the gut, not turn me on.

Neve perks up at the news that Cecelia and I are not in any way involved, and he gives her a megawatt grin full of perfectly white teeth. He is all dark, brooding, and suave—everything I'm not.

Neve clears his throat and says, "At the risk of sounding corny, do you come here often?"

"That doesn't sound corny, it sounds *idiotic*," I complain and cross my arms, hoping it draws attention to my biceps. I glance down at them and flex a few times for good measure.

Cecelia doesn't notice.

"Well, *you* would certainly know idiotic," she says, briefly glancing at me with a raised eyebrow and pursed, glossy lips before turning away.

I *pfft* indignantly. "Oh, real classy."

Now she's got her eyes narrowed and is poking me in the chest with her fingernail. "Ex*cuse* me? I'm *wayyy* classier than those 'groupies'"—she puts her fingers up and does air quotes when she says this—"you have hanging all over you all the time, waiting for your sloppy seconds. It's dis*gust*ing. No. Thank. You."

"Those '*groupies*'"—great, now *I'm* using air quotes—"as you call them, are called puck bunnies, and following me around is a *respectable* hobby. They boost my morale. Maybe you could learn a thing or two if you acted more like them, like how to take a guy deep—"

Neve interrupts before I can finish my sentence. "That

is *enough* Wakefield. Christ, what is wrong with you, man? Could you shut up for five seconds so I can talk to the pretty lady?"

"Yeah she's *pretty*, but then she opens her fucking mouth."

"Matthew, don't be an ass," Molly finally chimes in, yelling over the noise.

"Yeah *asshole*, don't be an ass." This from Cecelia. The corners of my mouth unwillingly tip up into a smile at her sass.

Call me crazy, but I kind of like it.

Even though she's already holding a glass in her hand, Neve ignores everyone and pushes through the banter to ask her, "Cece, can I buy you a drink?"

Cecelia raises her chin a notch, cocks her eyebrow, and shoves her full drink into my one empty hand, the clear liquid (and a few ice cubes) spilling onto my hand from the force. "Neve, I would *love* that."

I have no choice but to take it.

Neve seizes the opportunity and takes her arm, leading her away and shoving a path through the crowded bar, an easy task given his impressive 6'1 height and imposing stature. No one is getting in *his* way, I begrudgingly admit, and I watch as he places his large calloused hand on the small of Cecelia's lower back to guide her through the crowd.

My lip curls in frustration.

I only tear my eyes away when Molly's voice cuts in. "You know what Matthew," she starts in on me with a huff. "If you weren't such a dickhead, you might have a shot at a relationship with a nice girl like Cece. But *noooo*, you—"

"Jeez, would you shut up for a damn minute," I demand, putting a finger up to silence her before shifting my gaze back to watching Cecelia from across the bar. Pulling the cell out of my back pocket, I unlock the screen.

Molly throws her hands up in frustration. "See, this is your whole freaking problem…" She continues ranting, but I tune her out. She's going on and on about me *always* being on my phone, how I'm *such* a jerk, and *blah, blah, blah*, who cares.

You didn't seriously expect me to listen, did you?

As if.

Ignoring my sister, I'm unable to resist the temptation across the bar. I click open my email (since I don't have her cell number), hit *compose*, and tap out a quick message before hitting *send*.

> TO: Cecelia Carter <carter.cecejane@gmail.com>
> DATE: September 15, 2014 at 11:27:18 PM CST
> FROM: Matthew Wakefield <imascoringmachine89@gmail.com>
> Subject: Try SMILING
> Just a suggestion.
> MSW

I look back up at my little sister, who is staring at me with a curled lip.

"Okay. Now you can go back to the part of your speech about Cecelia being nice. I need a good laugh," I say, tapping my forefinger impatiently on my cheap plastic cell phone case, holding my cell in one palm and a beer in the other.

I wait and watch.

Impatient, I feel like crushing the phone in my hand,

but I perk up considerably when I finally see Cecelia bend her head and pull out her *own* phone. I watch as she squints at the small screen in concentration, then frowns.

I turn away with a smirk and lift the beer to my mouth, hiding a laugh in the plastic cup, foam ticking my upper lip as I take a long drag.

Ahhh, victory tastes good. So cold and refreshing.

Covertly, I watch her again. Even from here I can see her nostrils flaring, and she sharply whips her head up to meet my gaze, coolly acknowledging me with narrowed eyes before lowering her head again.

Several seconds later, my phone chimes.

> TO: Matthew Wakefield <imascoringmachine89@gmail.com>
> DATE: September 15, 2014 at 11:30:23 PM CST
> FROM: Cecelia Carter <carter.cecejane@gmail.com>
> Subject: You're a dick
> Get a life. - C

> TO: Cecelia Carter <carter.cecejane@gmail.com>
> DATE: September 15, 2014 at 11:33:14 PM CST
> FROM: Matthew Wakefield <imascoringmachine89@gmail.com>
> Subject: I AM a dick.
> And I've got a big one. If you want to see it, all you have to do is smile pretty and ask nice.
> MSW

> TO: Matthew Wakefield <imascoringmachine89@gmail.com>
> DATE: September 15, 2014 at 11:37:26 PM CST
> FROM: Cecelia Carter <carter.cecejane@gmail.

com>
Subject: Seriously?
You're disgusting. Or maybe it's the alcohol. In any case, leave me alone. I'm in the middle of getting picked up by your hot friend. Total panty melter.
- C

TO: Cecelia Carter <carter.cecejane@gmail.com>
DATE: September 15, 2014 at 11:40:57 PM CST
FROM: Matthew Wakefield <imascoringma­chine89@gmail.com>
Subject: MEH.
Neve isn't man enough for you. Ask him about his dolphin figurine collection if you don't believe me. I dare you. Besides, I'm not drunk—what would give you that idea? My sopping wet shirt full of beer? Don't lie and say you weren't admiring my masculine physique when my shirt started sticking to my chest.
I saw you.
MSW

TO: Matthew Wakefield <imascoringmachine89@gmail.com>
DATE: September 15, 2014 at 11:45:19 PM CST
FROM: Cecelia Carter <carter.cecejane@gmail.com>
Subject: (Rolling my eyes)
This conversation is ridiculous. I'm not going to stand here EMAILING someone from across the room when I can't even stand talking to them in person. - C

TO: Cecelia Carter <carter.cecejane@gmail.com>
DATE: September 15, 2014 at 11:47:09 PM CST
FROM: Matthew Wakefield <imascoringma-

chine89@gmail.com>
Subject: Ouch.
That hurt my feelings a little.
MSW

Cecelia

"How annoying. He is seriously starting to interfere with her being single." – Jenna, my roommate Molly's best friend

Okay, I'll admit it—after that last email, I feel kind of bad. I sit up in bed and grab my phone to check the time: 8:27 on a Saturday morning.

Ugh.

Then, since my phone is already in my hand, I tap open the last message from Matthew Wakefield.

That hurt my feelings a little.

Trust me, I've dissected the reasons why I'm giving him the brush off a million times, and here are a few I came up with:

1. He is Molly's brother. There's, like, a girl code about liking a friend's brother somewhere…isn't there?

2. He is an ass.

3. Matthew is a hockey player for a professional hockey team. So out of my league, on so many levels.

4. Better to reject than be rejected....right? I mean, could he possibly be interested in someone like me for reasons other than to drive me insane?

5. Please see #2

Despite all of these things, I do the opposite of what any self-respecting girl would do: I pick up my phone and email Matthew back, even knowing that it's probably not necessary (him being a dickhead and all). Nonetheless, he is my roommate's brother, and I suddenly have a stab of guilty conscience.

TO: Matthew Wakefield <imascoringmachine89@gmail.com>
DATE: September 16, 2014 at 8:32:07 AM CST
FROM: Cecelia Carter <carter.cecejane@gmail.com>
Subject: This is awkward.
I'm sorry my last comment was so rude last night. I didn't mean to hurt your feelings. - C

TO: Cecelia Carter <carter.cecejane@gmail.com>
DATE: September 16, 2014 at 8:47:17 AM CST
FROM: Matthew Wakefield <imascoringmachine89@gmail.com>
Subject: Apology accepted.
Hurt my feelings? I'm a guy—our feelings don't get hurt. We get pissed.
MSW
P.S. Still, apology accepted.

I'll be honest: for a while, I sit in stony silence, cross-legged on my bed, completely fixated on the tiny screen of my cell, not quite knowing what to do or how to respond. I open and close my email app several times, reading and rereading his words, rolling them around in my head.

Should I respond? What do I say? Is there any way possible to play it cool?

My bedroom door is ajar, and I can hear Molly shuffling around the kitchen. I crane my head and try to get a visual on her through the small crack in my door, catching a brief glimpse of her bending to dig a pan out of the cabinet, still in her pajamas. I lean back against my headboard, frustrated, and blow out a puff of air, which sends the hair in my face flying in soft wisps.

How do I get myself into these messes?

TO: Matthew Wakefield <imascoringmachine89@gmail.com>
DATE: September 16, 2014 at 9:11:22 AM CST
FROM: Cecelia Carter <carter.cecejane@gmail.com>
Subject: RE: Apology accepted.
Okay. I guess I won't feel so bad then. I was wrong to assume you even *had* feelings in the first place. My bad.
- C

TO: Cecelia Carter <carter.cecejane@gmail.com>
DATE: September 16, 2014 at 9:15:48 AM CST
FROM: Matthew Wakefield <imascoringmachine89@gmail.com>
Subject: Hitting on all cylinders this morning?
I'm going to ignore that AND your sarcasm. Too early in the morning and I give zero fucks about

your crappy attitude.
MSW

Whoa.

Again, I sit stunned on the bed.

Several emotions wash over me all at once before I can stop or analyze them. Embarrassment. Shame. *Anger.*

Why are things always going from bad to worse with Matthew? One minute we're having fun and flirting in our sick, twisted way—and the next he's cursing and calling me sarcastic.

And not in a good way.

It's not really a situation I know how to deal with. Typically, I get along with everyone—well, except maybe my sister growing up, but she hardly counts since she's family). And okay, I'll admit there was this guy once at the public library I argued with over the only copy of Othello (I needed it for a class at the time), but in my defense, he wouldn't leave me alone, kept following me around, *pestering* me for the damn thing.

Which, as I already pointed out, *I. Needed.*

So yeah, there was that guy.

Confused, I stare up at my ceiling. Just when I think maybe Matthew and I *might* be getting along, I say something dumb and he takes it the wrong way.

Sheesh. Is it my fault he's so sensitive?

I was really hoping that at this point we could get along—you know, for Molly's sake, not because I think he's cute or something. One minute we're bantering, and the next we're bitching at each other.

TO: Matthew Wakefield <imascoringmachine89@
gmail.com>
DATE: September 16, 2014 at 9:45:03 AM CST
FROM: Cecelia Carter <carter.cecejane@gmail.
com>
Subject: So this is awkward...
Okay. That last email threw me for a loop. I feel
like I should apologize again for being such a...
ugh, I can't even say it. You get what I'm trying to
say right? Without me having to spell it out? I think
for Molly's sake it would be great if we could get
along. I'm really not as bad as you probably think
I am. If it's any consolation, you've seen me both
times at my worst. I mean, can you say smudged
eyeliner? - C

The inbox on my phone dings.

TO: Cecelia Carter <carter.cecejane@gmail.com>
DATE: September 16, 2014 at 9:46:12 AM CST
FROM: Matthew Wakefield <imascoringma-
chine89@gmail.com>
Subject: RE: So this is awkward...
Smudged eyeliner.
MSW

Then, *just* as I'm about to get pissy and send him a tart
reply, my inbox dings again.

TO: Cecelia Carter <carter.cecejane@gmail.com>
DATE: September 16, 2014 at 9:48:45 AM CST
FROM: Matthew Wakefield <imascoringma-
chine89@gmail.com>
Subject: RE: RE: So this is awkward...

I bet that last message pissed you off, didn't it? LOL. I think I have you all figured out by now—are you an only child by any chance? One hundred bucks says you are—oh wait, you already owe me one Benjamin, and you probably can't afford to pay me two.
MSW

TO: Matthew Wakefield <imascoringmachine89@gmail.com>
DATE: September 16, 2014 at 9:53:09 AM CST
FROM: Cecelia Carter <carter.cecejane@gmail.com>
Subject: RE: RE: RE: So this is awkward...
Wow, you think you're pretty clever, don't you? Never mind, don't answer that. Actually, smart-ass, I am NOT an only child. I have a younger sister who's going to be a freshman at Nebraska (go Cornhuskers!). So now the parents have one daughter working on her master's and one just entering another Big 10. My dad's pretty excited about that. P.S. You're never getting your money so you might as well give up. - C

TO: Cecelia Carter <carter.cecejane@gmail.com>
DATE: September 16, 2014 at 9:55:49 AM CST
FROM: Matthew Wakefield <imascoringmachine89@gmail.com>
Subject: WHOA
Holy shit, another actual paragraph. Don't stop, you're on a roll today, and I'm impressed—you've only been bitchy once today, which is a vast improvement from the other night at Rangers.
MSW

TO: Matthew Wakefield <imascoringmachine89@

gmail.com>
DATE: September 16, 2014 at 9:58:04 AM CST
FROM: Cecelia Carter <carter.cecejane@gmail.com>
Subject: Kudos to us both.
Yeah, and you've managed not to be a complete ass. Still an ass, of course, but maybe not so douchie...don't you go changing my mind either. I'm a tough nut to crack. - C

I am lying on my bed now, spread out on my back, phone propped in the air. I wouldn't admit it to anyone, but I have such a big grin on my face, I have to bite my bottom lip to suppress a giggle.

TO: Cecelia Carter <carter.cecejane@gmail.com>
DATE: September 16, 2014 at 10:01:12 AM CST
FROM: Matthew Wakefield <imascoringmachine89@gmail.com>
Subject: Tough nut?
Challenge accepted.
MSW

Oh shit.

Matthew

"How do you stop from choking on the bullshit coming out of your mouth?" – Weston McGrath

I watch the puck wiz by me through the glass, letting the whistle between my lips fall out of my mouth and hit the front of my sweatshirt with a soft bounce. Leaning against the short wooden wall of the rink, I prop my elbows and let my eyes roam the ice, impressed with what I see. From my vantage point on the bench, the young players skating laps in front of me are in top form today, each member transitioning from forward to backward skating with ease.

I keep my eye trained on Elliot Nelson, an eighth grader with a lot of talent for both defense and offense, but who might be a little too passive aggressive to pull off a starting position in the center of the rink when the puck drops.

Weston skates circles around them all, his skates slicing the ice in fluid movements, shouting out critiques and encouragement. I hate to admit it, but he's a damn good player and is turning into a damn good coach. He glances over at me and taps his wrist.

I nod and grab the whistle, raise it to my lips, and blow hard to emit a shrill shriek loud enough to garner everyone's attention, forcing them to look over.

I take my forefinger and circle it through the air, my sign for *let's wrap it up and bring it in.*

I'll be honest, when Molly offered Weston and me up for this volunteer position—coaching at-risk middle school boys enrolled in the afterschool program where she works—at first I balked. Actually, Weston and I *both* did because we just had to be difficult assholes; you know, not thinking of anyone but ourselves. No way did we want to spend any more time with each other than we already had to—we see each other enough. Plus, didn't I already mention that I'm stuck with him on any road trips I'm available to take?

Yeah. Exactly.

We're selfish bastards, but after countless lectures from my sister (she made some pretty valid points), we both caved—me because she had a point about giving back to the community that was so supportive of my hockey career, and Weston...

Well, he caved because he's a goddamn pussy, but mostly because Molly threated to cut him off—*if you know what I mean.*

Long story short, we've been coaching this group—the Madison Lightning—for a few weeks now, and not to brag, but they've gotten pretty damn good.

Weston ushers the small motley crew to the boards surrounding the ice and steps up next to me by the player's bench. He nods his head and holds out his clipboard. I glance at it briefly before clearing my throat. "Okay guys, nice work. Nelson, we wanna see you work on getting a little more aggressive." I point to a kid named Stewart Rosenthal. "Stu, next time someone passes you the puck, don't hog it. Keep your eyes watchful and when someone is open, get rid of it. If we see you do it again in a game, we're pulling you off the ice. Everyone else, get lots of rest and don't eat a bunch of crap." Weston looks pointedly at a chubby kid named Phil. "We have a game against the Racine Avengers next week and they're 8 and 3, so we have our work cut out for us."

Weston takes over. "Okay guys. We only have one more practice before our game, so make it count. Be here an hour early." He glances at me, raising his eyebrows at me with a questioning smirk on his face. "Anything else Coach Wakefield?"

Smartass.

"Nope. Go hit the showers. See you next week."

The kids skate off toward the locker room, some more skillfully than others. One kid actually smashes into the wall and almost biffs it. I make a mental note to work with him on the angle of his knees. *Shit.* I have a feeling I'm going to have to start all over with him on the fundamentals of hockey—as in, basic stances and walking on skates.

I sigh. I've seen enough of the two-foot glide for the day.

"I take it you just saw Dickey Winters almost take a digger?" Weston asks.

"Dickey Winters? I though his name was David."

"It is. Dickey is my special pet name for him because

he's slow."

"You're an asshole."

Weston shrugs. "Yeah, so?" He sits on the long bench where the substitute players sit during games and begins unlacing his skates before glancing up at me. "So what's the deal with you and Cece?"

"Nothing. There is no deal."

"That's not what Molly says."

"My sister needs to mind her own business."

"Don't get defensive man, I'm only repeating what she told me."

"What exactly *did* she tell you?"

He shrugs again and bends his head to loosen the laces on his other skate. "Apparently nothing, since there is no *deal*, right?"

"Don't be an ass."

"I can't help it. It's my special brand of humor," he says this with a laugh as he begins putting the blade guards on both his skates.

I clench my jaw, perturbed. "Just fucking tell me what Molly said."

Weston laughs again. "Just that the two of you go at it like two alley cats. Oh, and that you're totally a dick to her—but of course we all knew that."

"I can't help it. Cecelia is a total bitch."

"Oh, it's *Cecelia* now, eh?" Weston smirks at me while he bends to grab several loose hockey pucks on the ground and shoves them into an open practice duffle bag.

"Why are you saying it like that?"

"Don't get defensive man, I was just making a point. No one calls her Cecelia."

"Well I didn't *know* that. What do they call her then?"

"Her friends call her Cece. Obviously if she liked you she would have corrected you, but she doesn't, so…" He shrugs and pulls his sneakers out of the duffle before stuffing a goalie mask inside.

"You know, it's times like this I cannot fucking stand you."

Weston laughs. "The feeling is mutual, bro."

I stand there glaring at his back for a few moments—probably only a few seconds, in all actuality—not saying anything before shifting my weight and leaning my hip against the hard plank of the half wall. He looks up at me and twists his mouth into a grin.

Annoyed, I ask "What?"

"Look at you, dude. It's driving you crazy, isn't it?" He laughs again, zipping the duffle shut and hefting it onto his shoulder.

"I don't know what the fuck you're talking about."

"Yeah, *okay*." With that, he starts walking away (in his socks, by the way), leaving me staring after him. It's never easy with this kid; he just doesn't give a shit.

Nonetheless, I only hesitate briefly before calling him back.

"Wait." Weston stops and turns, brows raised, a questioning look on his face. I run a hand over my face and blow out a puff of air.

He smirks. "Well? Spit it out, I've got Molly waiting."

"Give me her phone number."

Silence fills the air, and he just stares at me. Finally he contorts his face and looks at me like I've lost my mind—and who knows, maybe I have. Nonetheless, his reply doesn't surprise me. "*Hell* no. Five seconds ago you were calling her a total bitch."

I snort. "What do you care?"

"I don't."

"Then just give it to me."

"*That's what she said.*"

I stare at him and shake my head in disbelief. "Seriously? Just give me her damn number. I already have her email address."

"Fuck off. I want nothing to do with this." He turns and starts walking the stadium stairs, taking them two at a time toward the lobby of the hockey arena.

Frustrated because I can't stand not getting my own way, I call up after him. "McGrath, what's it going to take?"

Slowly, Weston stops in his tracks.

And I know I've won.

Cecelia

"I caught myself smiling for no reason...then I realized I had been thinking of you." – Cece Carter

At some point in a person's life, you need a direction.

For me, on this particular day, that direction was toward the closest Starbucks.

I sit in a corner table up against the wall, my laptop, latte, water, and books all spread out in front of me...well, as spread out as one can get on these tiny squares they pass off as tables. Technically I'm *scrunched* in the corner table, but it works for me because at least here I can work without being interrupted.

Any time I work from home, there are bound to be distractions, usually in the form of Molly coming into my room to talk, or Molly making a smoothie in the kitchen, running the blender until there are no chunks in it, or Molly laughing during a phone call. Then, at least once or twice during the week, there's Molly dragging Weston to our apartment, only to disappear into her bedroom, and call me crazy, but I don't want to imagine what's going on behind *her* closed door.

Basically what I'm getting at is, my roommate is loud.

Not on purpose. It just...happens.

I glance up and gaze outside the window: it's drizzling and overcast, and I'm bundled up in an Irish cable-knit sweater, bright scarf tied around my neck to keep the chill out, leggings and boots. My hair is in a messy top knot, kept tidy by a thin headband.

Perched on top of my head are reading glasses.

Everything is laid out just so, and the dark weather outside makes it perfect to concentrate. People come in and out of Starbucks, and the hustle and bustle—combined with my iTunes library—is the perfect recipe for pounding out this thirty-page thesis, the subject of which I am far from an expert on.

I'll tell you the topic, but you have to promise not to get bored. Okay, are you ready? Here it is: *The United States was once a dominating force in all global economic industry; when did the shift of control to other countries occur, and why?*

Sounds simple enough, right!? The thing is, it really is. I could go on about this topic for days and days, but fact is, I cannot exceed the thirty-page maximum, and therein lies the problem.

Curbing my enthusiasm for the topic.

My phone chimes on the white Carrera marble café table.

291-555-2700: *Knock knock*

I stare at the number, wracking my brain for who it could possibly be. I hate responding to unidentified messages.

Me: *Who is this?*

291-555-2700: *The correct response is 'who's there?'*

How annoying. I roll my eyes and tap out: *FINE. Who's there?*

291-555-2700: *Didn't your mother teach you not to talk to strangers?*

Me: *Didn't your mother teach you not to talk to strangers who*

291-555-2700: *Wait, that wasn't part of the joke.*

Me: *Goodbye.*

291-555-2700: *You can't ignore me. You owe me.*

Me: *Owe you???? Are you nuts! I don't even know who you are.*

291-555-2700: *Yes you do. You've been waiting for me to text you all day.*

Just then, my phone chimes again, only this time it's Molly.

Molly: *Don't kill me.*

Me: *What are you talking about?*

Molly: *Weston just told me he gave my brother your number.*

I stare at the screen on my phone, the message illuminated in a tiny yellow bubble and blinking back at me. I can't even formulate an intelligent response.

Molly: *I'm soooo sooooo sorry!!!!!! He said Matthew was asking for it, and he had no choice.*

Molly: *Don't worry, I'll take care of this.*

Me, to Molly: *Too late.*

291-555-2700: *Hey.*

Me to 291-555-2700: *If I stop responding, will you eventually leave me alone?*

291-555-2700: *Didn't we cover this once during an email?*

Me: *(loud sigh) Yes, but then you pissed me off and I had no choice but to respond.*

291-555-2700: *See, it's like I said: the ladies can't resist me. Plus there's that issue of the 200 bucks you owe me.*

291-555-2700: *It's kind of a lot of money, and I'm hard up.*

Me: *(Snort)*

291-555-2700: *LOL. Hard up. Get it?*

Me: *You're an idiot.*

291-555-2700: *See, there you go insulting me.*

Me: *Because you're acting like a 15-year-old. WHAT DO YOU WANT FROM ME?*

291-555-2700: *Can you just ask Molly if she's going to our parents' house for dinner next weekend?*

Me: *Seriously?*

291-555-2700: *No.*

Me: *OMG. You're so annoying.*

291-555-2700: *I'm pretty sure that's what you love about me.*

This guy is proof that evolution *can* go in reverse.

I don't respond. Rather, I sit and look at the phone and thumb through all the previous text messages and emails Matthew and I have exchanged in the past few days. A few of them even make me chuckle. One of them makes me cringe.

Boy do I sound like a bitter bitch.

Here's something I don't get, and you might be wondering the same thing yourself: why is he sending me messages? I grab my pen and start tapping it on the table, a nervous habit I picked up when I first began my master's thesis (which is nothing compared to my friend Sylvia, who started smoking cigars when she started hers).

291-555-2700: *Knock knock.*

I roll my eyes before responding: *Who's there?*

291-555-2700: *See? Now you're catching on!*

Me: *OMG would you finish the joke?!*

291-555-2700: *I can't. There IS no joke.*

Me: *I don't have time for this.*

291-555-2700: *Yeah, I'm pretty sure you do…*

Me: *Um…….*

291-555-2700: *Gotta go. TTYL*

Wait. What?

Matthew

"If it makes you feel any better, I don't have a favorite child. You both annoy the crap out of me equally." – Clayton Wakefield

I'm not sure what possesses me to do so, but I cannot make myself stop sending messages to Cecelia. Sure, at first I was doing it simply to piss her off and get a rise out of her—which, honestly, is super easy. The real bonus here is that Molly had *her* email *me*—that itself was like a Christmas gift, all wrapped in a tidy bow, dropped into my lap for my very own personal amusement.

At first it was entertaining, then it became fun, something to look forward to. Now…it's kind of becoming *a thing*.

I absentmindedly fiddle with the tab on the top of my beer can and lean against the counter in my parents' kitchen, watching my mom put the last plate in the cabinet after unloading the dishwasher from the family dinner we all just shared—and yes, before you jump to conclusions and climb up my ass about just standing around doing nothing, I helped. Actually, I'm the one who loaded the damn thing.

It was my job growing up, and one I still do whenever I pop in.

The aluminum tab makes a hollow *ping*, one that's loud enough to cause my mom to glance over her shoulder.

"Everything okay sweetie?" she asks, shutting the cupboard door and turning to face me with a look on her face that only a mom makes.

I scrunch up my brow, instantly annoyed as Molly flounces into the kitchen carrying what's left of the taco dip tray. She narrows her eyes at us; so suspicious, that one.

"What are you two talking about?" she immediately wants to know, setting the tray on the counter and running the sink.

Jeez she's nosey.

Mom gives me a knowing look and gives Molly's shoulder a little squeeze. "Nothing. I was just asking your brother how he's been." She winks at me and I roll my eyes; she thinks she's so sly when we actually *were* talking about *nothing*.

"Oh *reallyyyy*." Molly smirks, dragging out the word before crossing her arms in a defensive pose and making a loud *pfft* sound (which is just short of snorting). "Did he happen to mention he's been harassing my roommate?"

My mom's head rears back a tad, surprised, and she cocks her head as she studies me anew with narrowed eyes. It's a move that runs in our family, and it's meant to be intimidating. "Do tell."

Before I can get any words out, my dad walks into the

kitchen, Weston nipping at his heels.

Great, an audience.

Just fucking great.

Weston looks at me, looks at Molly with her arms crossed, and at our mom who's still glaring at me suspiciously.

"What's going on in here?" he asks cautiously, like a dog that's been kicked a few times but still wants a treat.

"Nothing that's any of your business," I shoot back, sounding nastier than I probably should.

"Matthew!" Molly scolds, moving forward to peck her boyfriend on the lips. "Don't mind him, he's just pissed because I told Mom he's stalking Cece."

Weston's eyebrows shoot up, but for once he's smart enough not to open his big mouth. Instead he grabs a chip out of a nearby bowl and drags it through the taco dip tray, even though it's been in the sink with running water.

Disgusting.

And to think, my sister kisses that mouth.

Still, if I'm going down, he's coming down with me.

I point to Weston and casually add, "Yeah, but *he's* the one who gave me her phone number." I grab an apple out of the fruit bowl and take a big bite, chewing slowly but crunching loudly.

"You blackmailed me!" Weston shoots back cautiously.

"Dude, *please*. It hardly took any convincing." I snort and take a drag of beer.

"Matthew!" My mom scolds, looking around the room. "Can someone please tell me what's going on?"

Molly, the blabbermouth, steps forward. "Oh, I'll tell you all right. I had Cece send him *one* innocent email on my behalf, and suddenly he won't leave her alone. He is driving her *nuts*."

"She said that?" my mom whispers, looking absolutely horrified, the kind of look one might have if they found out their child was a serial killer. A bit over dramatic but... there you have it.

"*Hello*," Molly says sarcastically, holding up her fingers and ticking off my many offenses. "First he emails her back incessantly after she sends him one measly note. He even freaking emailed her at a bar *from across the freaking room.* Cece sooo doesn't have time for his BS mom!" Molly holds a second finger perched in the air, and now pokes at a third. "*Secondly,* Matthew gets her number from this one." She pokes Weston in the chest. "Thirdly, now in addition to emailing, he's also texting her. I can't take it anymore!"

"Man Wakefield, I knew you were hard up, but I didn't think you were *des*perate." Weston laughs, and my sister has enough loyalty to smack him in the arm.

My dad shoots him a stern look; he is clearly not as amused as the rest of us as he stands, arms folded in the corner, sipping from the long neck of his Pale Ale bottle.

Weston swallows guiltily and clears his throat. "Uh, sorry, sir."

Dad nods and points at me with the hand holding his beer bottle. "Son, maybe Weston has a point. Are you, in fact, stalking her?"

Defensively, I say, "No, goddamn it, I am *not* stalking her."

Molly starts fake coughing like a twelve-year-old boy. "Lies."

"Is anyone even going to let me defend myself?" I begrudgingly ask—and I'll admit, it kind of sounds like I'm pouting. There's a lot of silence that fills the room, and this is the moment my dad chooses to bite down on a carrot that was lying on the counter.

His loud crunching is the only noise until my mom gently says, "Sweetie, maybe you should just leave Cecelia be." She pats my arm. "Besides, I don't think you're her type."

Agitated, I shout, "Jesus Christ, I am not bothering her! And what the hell do you mean I'm not her type? *I'm everyone's type!*" I shoot Molly a dirty look and slice my flat palm across my neck the way I used to when we were younger, a move that clearly says *I am going to murder you.*

Molly, completely unthreatened, shrugs, raises one brow, and rolls her eyes at me—all at the same time. It's an understated move she's been perfecting for years, one that has always managed to *completely* piss me off. "Well, you haven't exactly *denied* the cyber stalking now, have you?"

"Would you please. Shut. Up." I glare at my sister, seriously wanting to duct tape her to a kitchen chair like I did one time when we were younger.

Okay, it was three times.

But all these accusations and crunching and eating are taking their toll.

Until…

"Well, I personally think you should send her an apology note," Mom says in an attempt to be helpful, having moved to the sink to scrape the cream cheese from the taco tray down the garbage disposal. She slaps Weston's hand away when he goes in with another chip.

"Mom, no!" Molly shouts, throwing her hands up in the air. "Are you in*sane*? Seriously mother, that's so counterproductive and not what I meant at all. He needs to stop. Period."

I scratch my chin, which is stubbly from lack of shaving, pretending to mull the idea over, and then I snap my fingers. "Hmmm, the idea *does* have merit. Good thinking Mom." The words come out slowly.

Weston, the big dope, just stands there silently shaking his head, even though his eyes are covertly meandering back and forth to the heap of cream cheese at the bottom of the sink.

"One last note and then you are done young man. Do you hear me? Then you leave that poor girl alone," my mom lectures from the sink. She pokes at me with a wooden spoon. "I'm not kidding. If I hear any more about this, I'm calling her myself to apologize on your behalf."

I grin. "Got it. One last note and I'm done. Thanks for the advice, Mom."

Winking at my sister, I saunter out of the room with spring in my step.

Cecelia

TO: Cecelia Carter <carter.cecejane@gmail.com>
DATE: September 19, 2014 at 11:32:12 PM CST
FROM: Matthew Wakefield <imascoringmachine89@gmail.com>
Subject: One last note.

Hey. My mom is making me send you this letter. She said I have to leave you alone and not send you any more messages. You have Molly to thank for this—she ratted me out. I told everyone you liked me and that when you received this letter you'd most likely slip into a deep depression. Don't blame me; blame my family.
MSW

"Um…Molly, can you come in here for a second?" I yell out my bedroom door. Granted, it's eleven thirty at night, but I can still hear her banging around in her room.

Her head appears in my door a few moments later. "What's up?"

I hold up my phone and shake it around. "Take a look."

She walks over, bends at the waist, and reads the small screen. Her face gets red and contorts her features into what I call her *ugly face*. It's similar to her *ugly cry*, but minus the tears. "What the fuu… That asshole!"

I shrug. "Hey, you said it, not me."

"This is *bull*shit! I'm telling my mom." I laugh when she storms out, and her door slams across the hallway. When she's gone, I reread message and lay flat on my back in the center of my bed. A bubble of laughter escapes my throat. Can you blame me? I mean really, this shit is kind of funny.

Matthew's note, and Molly's reaction to it: *priceless.*

I scan it again, committing every line to memory. I flip over onto my stomach and tap out a reply.

TO: Matthew Wakefield <imascoringmachine89@

gmail.com>
DATE: September 19, 2014 at 11:38:23 PM CST
FROM: Cecelia Carter <carter.cecejane@gmail.com>
Subject: LOL
I'm sorry, but this is hilarious: your sister is in her bedroom having a meltdown. You better brace yourself. Don't say you haven't been warned. - C

TO: Cecelia Carter <carter.cecejane@gmail.com>
DATE: September 19, 2014 at 11:45:45 PM CST
FROM: Matthew Wakefield <imascoringmachine89@gmail.com>
Subject: RE: LOL
You're warning me - does this mean you care?
MSW

TO: Matthew Wakefield <imascoringmachine89@gmail.com>
DATE: September 19, 2014 at 11:47:23 PM CST
FROM: Cecelia Carter <carter.cecejane@gmail.com>
Subject: RE: RE: LOL
NOOOOOOOOOOOOOOOooooooooooooo! - C

TO: Cecelia Carter <carter.cecejane@gmail.com>
DATE: September 19, 2014 at 11:52:36 PM CST
FROM: Matthew Wakefield <imascoringmachine89@gmail.com>
Subject: RE: RE: RE: LOL
How does that old saying go?
Me thinks thee protest-eth too much. (That's Shakespeare I think.)
MSW

TO: Matthew Wakefield <imascoringmachine89@

gmail.com>
DATE: September 19, 2014 at 11:55:13 PM CST
FROM: Cecelia Carter <carter.cecejane@gmail.com>
Subject: Well color me surprised.

Whoa, I'm impressed. That is Shakespeare, but the actual line is: "The lady doth **protest too much**, methinks." (Maybe you should have stayed in school a little longer than six years.) - C

TO: Cecelia Carter <carter.cecejane@gmail.com>
DATE: September 19, 2014 at 11:58:19 PM CST
FROM: Matthew Wakefield <imascoringmachine89@gmail.com>
Subject: Uh...

!!!!!!!!NERD ALERT!!!!!!!!!!! I don't even want to know how you know that. I'm going to have to assume you're a total bookworm. And just for your information, I was only in school FIVE years. I, um, changed my major a few times?
MSW

TO: Matthew Wakefield <imascoringmachine89@gmail.com>
DATE: September 20, 2014 at 12:01:25 AM CST
FROM: Cecelia Carter <carter.cecejane@gmail.com>
Subject: RUDE

Why am I not surprised you just called me a nerd? Oh! I know! Maybe it's because you are so RUDE. I cannot believe someone as sweet as Molly is related to such a huge jackhole. - C

TO: Cecelia Carter <carter.cecejane@gmail.com>

DATE: September 20, 2014 at 12:11:04 AM CST
FROM: Matthew Wakefield <imascoringma-
chine89@gmail.com>
Subject: Don't get your panties in a twist.
That is, if you're wearing any—scratch that, you
definitely ARE, and I bet they're great big white
granny ones of the Hanes variety. Speaking of
which, did you know Molly wore diapers until she
was like 4? And she wet the bed practically forever. Just saying.
MSW

TO: Matthew Wakefield <imascoringmachine89@
gmail.com>
DATE: September 20, 2014 at 12:18:03 AM CST
FROM: Cecelia Carter <carter.cecejane@gmail.
com>
Subject: OMG
I will admit, that made me laugh. Molly would have
a heart attack if, OMG...I can't even... What a terrible
brother you are. In fact, I bet I could go next door
and find out a few nasty things about you... Actually, since Weston gave you my cell phone number,
I should probably get some dirt on him too. Why
were you sniffing around for my phone number
anyway????? - C

TO: Cecelia Carter <carter.cecejane@gmail.com>
DATE: September 20, 2014 at 12:23:27 AM CST
FROM: Matthew Wakefield <imascoringma-
chine89@gmail.com>
Subject: I was drunk.
That's the only reasonable explanation.
MSW

TO: Matthew Wakefield <imascoringmachine89@

gmail.com>
DATE: September 20, 2014 at 12:26:17 AM CST
FROM: Cecelia Carter <carter.cecejane@gmail.com>
Subject: In that case...
This is where I sign off. - C

Matthew

"What are you talking about, dude? This isn't sweat. It's liquid-fucking-awesomeness oozing out of me." – Weston McGrath

"**H**ey dipshit, did you know you have a knack for pissing women off?" Weston asks as he skates past me, the puck gliding back and forth in front of him as he smoothly maneuvers it through a group of players. He glances over his shoulder and does a crossover so he's skating backward, shooting me a dark look from underneath his helmet that I can see even from where I'm standing in the penalty box.

Suddenly, Weston is charging the goalie and the whistle is being blown. For those of you who aren't familiar with hockey jargon, charging any player—even the goalie—is a penalty, even if the goalie is playing outside the goal crease.

Good. Maybe he'll use some of that aggression and score a few goals this weekend against Penn State.

Even while I'm thinking this, I raise my hand and flip the middle finger in his general direction as he angrily skates his way toward me, tearing his gloves off and throwing them into the box before stepping into it.

"You should really learn to control your temper. This is only a practice."

"Fuck you," he spits out, taking a chug from a water bottle and swishing it around in his mouth before spitting it on the ground.

"What the hell did I do to you?"

He stares at me, an incredulous look of disbelief spreading across his face.

"Thanks to you, Molly is still pissed at me for giving you Cece's number. That little stunt you pulled by writing that last letter—she showed that shit to Molly and now I'm cut off."

"I thought the letter was pleasant! My mom told me to write it. Besides, Cecelia likes the banter—"

He cuts me off before I can finish my sentence. "Dude. Are you fucking crazy? Knock that shit off. You're starting to sound like a pansy. And stop calling her Cecelia." He straps his helmet back on, slaps the side of it, and waits for the ref to signal his reentry into the practice game.

A few moments later, he skates off and leaves me standing there.

Cecelia

Matthew: *So I was told to stop calling you Cecelia…*

The text comes out of nowhere, several days after our last emails were exchanged, and from what I know from Molly, the guys are out of town and on the road until Monday.

The phone is balanced on the arm of the couch, along with my Kindle and the remote control for the TV—an clear indication that I've not only been here for a while, but that am in it for the long haul. To round out the evening I have planned, a big glass of iced Crystal Lite sits on the coffee table, a hand crocheted blanket is spread across my legs, and I'm donning my favorite chenille socks.

Me: *Actually, I don't mind it.*

And really, I don't.

I don't really know *when* everyone started calling me Cece, or why, but there's something lyrical about my given name that I actually quite enjoy.

And no, I'm *not* talking about the Simon & Garfunkel version they play in bars. You know the one that goes *Cecilia, you're breaking my heart (clap clap), you're shaking my con-fi-dence baby / Oh Cecilia (clap clap) I'm down on my knees, I'm begging you please to come home, o-o-ome…*

Um, yeah. Thanks Simon & Garfunkel for turning my name into a drunken frat boy serenade…kind of the same way everyone in a bar goes crazy when they play "Brown Eyed Girl" or "Piano Man". It's unavoidable—and unfortunate—that whenever "Cecelia" gets played and I'm at a bar (and it always inevitably *does* get played), drunk guys find me and go through a routine that basically goes something like this:

1. Clutch their chests like they're having a heart attack or stroke

2. Fall to their knees in front of me like they're praying to Jesus.

3. Scream (or screech) out the lyrics as if their sloppy lives depend on it.

And where am I during all this? Why, pretending to be somewhere else, of course.

And where are my *friends* during all this? Usually falling all over themselves in hysterical laughter. It actually wouldn't surprise me to discover they were the ones requesting the song...

Guys must think an inebriated serenade is romantic.

Which it...is...not. Not even remotely close. I mean, get up off the damn floor for crying out loud! It's freaking disgusting down there—people spill their beers, food, and lord knows what else. Oh! And let me remind you about the time I saw some guy *peeing* in a corner that was most certainly *not* the bathroom.

The point of all this is: except for those times it's being slurred by a tanked-up guy, I really do love my first name.

Anyway, back to Matthew.

Matthew: *That's good to know. Wes chewed my ass out.*

Me: *For calling me by my name???*

Matthew: *Yes. That and because Molly showed him the last email I sent you.*

Me: *LOL*

Matthew: *It wasn't a biggie was it? I mean, you and I both know it was a joke.*

Oh really? This is news to me, and it leaves me wondering: which part did he think was funny?

Me: *A joke...obviously.*

Matthew: *I mean, she's your roommate, & don't girls always show each other private shit?*

Me: *No. Not always.*

Me: *I only showed her because I thought it was a funny message. I honestly didn't think she'd flip out.*

Matthew: *Seriously?*

Me: *Yes. I'm being serious. I never would have shown it to her otherwise. I'm generally a very private person.*

Matthew: *That makes 2 of us.*

Matthew: *Why do you think I swear so much?*

Me: *Um...????*

Matthew: *So people leave me alone. Are YOU going to bother someone telling you to fuck off?*

Me: *Hmmm. Good point.*

Me: *My tactic is to just put my Beats on and pretend I'm listening to music...*

Matthew: *LOL. Good strategy.*

Matthew: *Unless it's me, of course. Then you just whip out your karate.*

Me: *Please don't bring that up. I'm still so embarrassed.*

Matthew: *Sorry, that lives in my memory. Forever.*

Me: *Great. Just great...*

Matthew: *I'll admit, that was not the greatest first impression, but at least it was a memorable one.*

Me: *Feel free to blame Molly for not mentioning you*

were her brother. I thought you were some pervert raper.

Matthew: *Well most people think Molly and I look pretty similar, so there is THAT...*

Me: *But still. It was a very heated moment and you so could have been a raper.*

Me: *Plus, then you started eating my food. Not cool.*

Matthew: *I don't know if you've noticed, but I'm a growing boy. I get hungry.*

Matthew: *And I wasn't eating your food until you threw it down on the couch. I considered that an open invitation, and I never turn down free food.*

Me: *I thought you weren't supposed to be sending me any more messages*

There is a long lapse between responses from Matthew, and then:

Matthew: *Is that what you want?*

Matthew

"I speak Italian. Just kidding, I speak Italian *menus*...
because I like the food." – Matthew Wakefield

I sit and wait for my phone to chime again, and after a tense fifteen minutes of no reply from Cecelia, I'm convinced I fucked the whole thing up. I mean, fifteen minutes is way longer than I would have liked—what could she possibly be doing?

Jumping jacks? Shampooing her hair?

The odd thing is, the entire time I'm waiting for my inbox to chime, my heart is racing—not like me at all. Anxiously waiting is amateur boy shit, not for grown men with lucrative careers.

In the bathroom next to our room, the hotel shower shut off, a good indication that I only have a few minutes before Weston busts out, probably wrapped in a towel, and gets all up in my business.

Fortunately, my phone finally lights up.

Cecelia: *I'm not sure.*

Me: *What aren't you sure about?*

Cecelia: *What all this means…?*

Cecelia: *Why the sudden interest from you? I don't understand.*

That makes two of us, I want to say—but don't.

Me: *It can't hurt to have more friends, right?*

Cecelia: *LOL. Yeah, I guess.*

Cecelia: *I guess maybe we can be pen pals.*

Cecelia: *I'll pretend you're a little boy from Italy.*

Me: *Mi piace la pasta*

Cecelia: *WHAT. THE. HELL. WAS. THAT.*

Me: *LOL. It means 'I like pasta.' It's Italian.*

Cecelia: OMG. *That did NOT just happen…*

Cecelia: *Did you Google that??? (still dying here)*

Me: *LOL. No. Yes. Maybe.*

Me: *Would you believe I did a semester abroad?*

Cecelia: *Um…no. Yes. MAYBE???*

Me: *I guess you'll have to wonder then.*

Me: *Cosa stai indossando?*

Cecelia: *You know I can look that up…*

A few seconds later, she figures out the translation: What are you wearing?

Cecelia: *You are the biggest moron!*

Me: *LOL. You're wearing sweatpants aren't you?*

Cecelia: *OMG. NO!!!!! K...maybe.*

Cecelia: *Why Italian?*

Me: *Mostly because German isn't as sexy*

Cecelia: *You are so vain.*

Me: *Hey, wasn't that a song in the 70s?*

Cecelia: *Yes! Here, let me sing it to you: (singing) "You're so vainnnnn, you probably think this song is about youuuu!!!!!*

Me: *Yup, that would be the song.*

Cecelia: *So, are you seriously holed up in a room with Weston?*

Me: *Yes. He's in the shower, and once he comes out of the bathroom, all my fun will be over.*

I grab my kindle off the bed and power it on. Once Weston is in the room, I'll have no privacy and will have to stop messaging Cecelia.

Cecelia: *LOL*

Me: *I won't be laughing in about five minutes so I'll just enjoy this while I can.*

Cecelia: *...this? As in...this?*

Me: *LOL. You're funny.*

Cecelia: *I am, actually...! Don't you think so?*

Cecelia

I stare at my phone, not happy that Matthew has suddenly stopped messaging me back. Granted, I know it's probably because Weston came out of the bathroom or something, but still. I'm annoyed.

Who just...stops? Talk about random—and rude.

I generally feel like a horse's ass for being the last one to send a message. It taunts me as it sits there unreciprocated.

Ugh, I feel like such a loser.

I palm my phone and click it again to check the time then set it back on coffee table upside down so I'm not tempted to check it...even though it chimes when I have a new message so there's actually no need to check it unless I hear that sound.

Have you ever done that—kept checking your phone to see if you have a message? Then checking it again...and again, even though you *know* you don't have it on silent.

Yes. Logically, I *know* I don't have a message, but that doesn't stop me from checking it a thousand times like a deranged teenager whose mere existence is validated by Snapchats and text messages, people *liking* their Facebook statuses, Instagram, and Twitter posts.

Speaking of teenagers, my cousin Sadie is the worst. She's almost sixteen, and no matter what family function we're at, she has her phone out at all times—even when she's being bitched at by my Aunt Shelley to put it away.

But, like an addict, she refuses. At our other cousin's baby shower,

Sadie stood in the corner taking selfies by the fireplace—and then there was me, watching her. It was so bizarre. I mean, not to completely get off topic here, but... have you ever sat and really watched someone taking selfies in public? Do you think they have any clue how idiotic they look?

Hilarious.

Anyway, my point is: here I am, eleven o'clock on a Thursday night, sitting on the couch, channel surfing and texting my roommate's brother, who, by all accounts, is only nice to me via social media.

And now he won't even message me back.

Go figure.

Cecelia

"Keep talking, I'm diagnosing you." – overheard between a girl and her date in the university café

TO: Cecelia Carter <carter.cecejane@gmail.com>
DATE: September 23, 2014 at 04:13:27 PM CST
FROM: Matthew Wakefield <imascoringmachine89@gmail.com>
Subject: Waz Sup.
How was the rest of your weekend?
MSW

TO: Matthew Wakefield <imascoringmachine89@gmail.com>
DATE: September 23, 2014 at 05:11:44 PM CST
FROM: Cecelia Carter <carter.cecejane@gmail.com>
Subject: This is what I think about you waiting days to message me.
[blank stare]

I wonder if he'll get that I'm pissed—and yes, I really do think guys are that clueless.

TO: Cecelia Carter <carter.cecejane@gmail.com>
DATE: September 23, 2014 at 05:24:32 PM CST
FROM: Matthew Wakefield <imascoringma-chine89@gmail.com>
Subject: Whoa.
Ok, maybe I deserved that, but in my defense, if I didn't have to shack up with McGrath so often, I would have more time to sit and enjoy myself. That moron is always interrupting my fun by being a nosy SOB. So this weekend after he came out of the bathroom, he ambushed me, took my phone, and shoved the battery down his boxers, and I had to literally tackle him before he started doing lunges. That dude is a freak.
MSW

TO: Matthew Wakefield <imascoringmachine89@gmail.com>
DATE: September 23, 2014 at 05:28:09 PM CST
FROM: Cecelia Carter <carter.cecejane@gmail.com>
Subject: LOL.
I think I just peed my pants laughing. I know that's not a ladylike thing to say, but you've already called me a psycho and a banshee, so I hardly think it matters at this point. I mean, we are pen pals after all. Are you guys back from your road trip? Wanna hear something hilarious? Your MOM sent me a note…but I'm not going to tell you what it was about. - C

TO: Cecelia Carter <carter.cecejane@gmail.com>
DATE: September 23, 2014 at 05:40:32 PM CST

FROM: Matthew Wakefield <imascoringma-chine89@gmail.com>
Subject: WHAT???????????????????????
Okay, FIRST OF ALL, you cannot drop a bomb like that and then not tell me what it said. You know that if you don't I'm only going to call her, right? Knowing her, it was to find out if I'm leaving you alone. My damn sister can't mind her own business. Does she boss you around too? To answer your question, yeah, we are home, for two weeks actually, and I'm not sure I'm going on the next road trip. Wes and I coach this youth hockey group and they have a small invitational they're playing in so one of us needs to be at that. Since I'm only staff, it'll have to be me. Plus, I'm the better coach—and you can mention that to Dipshit the next time you see him.
MSW

TO: Matthew Wakefield <imascoringmachine89@gmail.com>
DATE: September 23, 2014 at 06:15:03 PM CST
FROM: Cecelia Carter <carter.cecejane@gmail.com>
Subject: Where to begin.
Wait, did I already know you two coached a youth league? That's so great! For a while I majored in Early Childhood Development, but then I changed my mind—obviously. Yeah, that was random... As for your question about Molly bossing me around—I think we BOTH boss each other around. Honestly, she's so easy to live with. The only time we've fought was that day you came over and I almost laid you out ;) She didn't care for my high-handed tactics. Also, there was an argument over some missing Twinkies... How do you like coaching kids? - C
P.S. Your mother's note started like this: "Dear Ce-

celia, Please excuse my son..."

TO: Cecelia Carter <carter.cecejane@gmail.com>
DATE: September 23, 2014 at 06:42:12 PM CST
FROM: Matthew Wakefield <imascoringma-
chine89@gmail.com>
Subject: Would You Rather: Embarrassing Mom
Edition
Have your mom *randomly* email a girl (or in your
case, a guy) and apologize for your behavior, *OR*
have your mom show up at your university wear-
ing a t-shirt with your face screen-printed on it?
MSW

TO: Matthew Wakefield <imascoringmachine89@
gmail.com>
DATE: September 23, 2014 at 06:45:22 PM CST
FROM: Cecelia Carter <carter.cecejane@gmail.
com>
Subject: Um...
That's an easy one—I would rather have my mom
show up to my university wearing a t-shirt with my
face screen-printed on it. But wait, I have a feeling
YOUR mom has done that already, so does that
question actually count...? I played lacrosse growing up, and if you know anything about that, it's not
really a sport your parents show up to wearing the
same kind of paraphernalia that say, hockey parents show up in. My mom's getup was more the
polo shirt variety <snore> Do your parents ever go
to watch the team you coach? Next line of your
mom's email: "Even though I tried my best, sometimes his manners fail him." - C

TO: Cecelia Carter <carter.cecejane@gmail.com>
DATE: September 23, 2014 at 06:55:07 PM CST
FROM: Matthew Wakefield <imascoringma-

chine89@gmail.com>
Subject: No Words.
Do my parents ever come to watch me coach? Nah. It's way too far for them to drive all the way from River Glen to Madison just to watch a group of 12-year-olds massacre the game. Sometimes it's painful to watch, but there are a few kids that seriously crack me up—I still have to tie up this one kid Isaac's laces. He can't skate for shit, but his heart is in it. It's something you really gotta come see; you would think it sucks coaching an underdog team, but it's really rewarding. I get more satisfaction out of it than I would coaching a winning team, and Wes feels the same way—*NOT* that we sit around discussing that shit or anything...
MSW

TO: Matthew Wakefield <imascoringmachine89@gmail.com>
DATE: September 23, 2014 at 07:18:54 PM CST
FROM: Cecelia Carter <carter.cecejane@gmail.com>
Subject: Deep Thoughts.
I didn't take you for a guy who sits around discussing his feelings, but I guess I was wrong (wink wink). No use in denying it. Truth: I know for a fact Weston likes to have "life chats" with Molly, promptly followed by, well...*YOU KNOW*... - C

TO: Cecelia Carter <carter.cecejane@gmail.com>
DATE: September 23, 2014 at 07:20:14 PM CST
FROM: Matthew Wakefield <imascoringmachine89@gmail.com>
Subject: You bitch!
WHY WOULD YOU SAY THAT??????????????????
MSW

Matthew

"I'm jealous of me, too." – Neve Vanderhalt

*I*stare at the email on my phone, experiencing the horrible visual of my sister and her boyfriend screwing, thanks to her horrible roommate. Instead of emailing Cecelia back, I go with the quickest option and tap out a text.

Me: *Thanks for the visual. My retinas are burning.*

A few seconds later...

Cecelia: *Well at least you don't have to HEAR it.*

Oh my god, I'm going to kill this girl.

Me: *What the fuck.*

Sorry about the harsh language (but not really). No one ever accused me of being a gentleman, and I make no apologies for the frequent cursing.

Cecelia: *(Shrug) Truth sucks, don't it?*

Me: *Kind of.*

There is a long pause in the conversation, and she doesn't respond—not that my message gave her anything to respond *to.*

A word to the wise: if you're ever trying to have a conversation with someone, always—and I mean always—use open-ended statements that end with a question mark so the other person has something to respond to.

I type out another message and change the subject.

Me: *So what did you end up doing today?*

Cecelia: *Some of my thesis paper for grad school. I'm just about done.*

Me: *No shit—when do you graduate?*

Cecelia: *LOL. I graduated last year with a BS in econ. I'll have my MBA in a couple months.*

Me: *So…how did you end up roommates with Molly if she's a sophomore and you're in grad school?*

Cecelia: *Good question. Answer: Facebook.*

Me: *WTF. Do my parents know Molly found her roomie on the internet?????*

Cecelia: *Whoa buddy, don't get offensive. It's not like I'm a creeper. My friend Abby's friend is Jenna's cousin so it all worked out.*

Me: *Oh, like one of those "my sister's cousin's daughter's boyfriend" type of deals.*

Cecelia: *Exactly!*

Cecelia: *Match made in heaven (wink). Plus I get the added bonus of her giant boyfriend as a bodyguard, not to mention he has some really HOT friends.*

Me: *Um…*

She doesn't stop there.

Cecelia: *Speaking of which, guess who called me?*

Me: *Do I want to know?*

Cecelia: *Your friend Neve. He asked me out. Yay me!*

I stare at the phone for a few stony seconds before lobbing it on to the glass table in my dining room, irritated. It lands with a loud crack, skids across the surface, and falls to the rug below. I ignore it and stalk to the kitchen, throw on the water in the sink, pump some foaming hand soap onto my palms, and scrub my hands angrily.

What the fuck is Neve doing asking her out? Is she nuts saying yes? They only just met! Not only that, he never ran it past me. I mean, where did he even get her damn number from?

Never mind. I already know the answer to that one: my sister's idiot boyfriend, who is clearly becoming a wealth of information where Cecelia Carter is concerned.

The more I think about it, the more pissed off I become.

I shut the water off, yank a hand towel off the oven handle, and dry my hands before stalking angrily back into the dining room and swiping my phone from the floor in a testosterone-fueled fury.

I shove it in my back pocket and purposefully set my mind to taking my mind off the whole thing. If I stay busy, I won't have to think about it anymore.

So in the next few hours I manage to:

1. Run five miles on my condo complex's treadmill in under thirty minutes flat while watching almost two entire episodes of *Full House*. Thirty

minutes is military speed, thank you very much.

2. Organize and rename all the pictures on my iPhone into tidy little files.

3. Clean the toilet and sink in my master bathroom.

4. Clean them again.

5. Order a large Toppers pizza, a two-liter bottle of Cola, and dipping sauce. It's way over my allotted caloric intake for the day, but at this point, I couldn't care less.

Despite accomplishing all that, two hours later, Cecelia's excited *Yay me!* text is still grating on my nerves, and I curl my lip. I don't realize it now, but tonight when I look back at this moment, I'll recognize it for what it is: jealously.

Even though I'm not completely over myself yet, I text her back, albeit hours later.

Me: *Great. Have fun.*

Yeah, even I know that sounds sarcastic, and yes, I know I'm acting like an immature dick, but *I. Don't. Give. A. Shit.* I'm pissed. Oblivious to my mood, or just completely ignoring my sarcasm, she quickly responds: *I will—I am SOOOO excited!*

Honestly, could she have added any more Os to that sentence?

I take my phone's battery out and abandon it on the kitchen counter for the rest of the night.

Cecelia

"You seriously haven't ever heard of a water bra? It's, like, standard issue in a woman's revenge toolkit." – Jenna

"Hey Moll, do you mind if I come in for a minute?" I hesitate at Molly's bedroom door, biting my lower lip. She's at her desk with the light on, textbook open and Pandora softly playing a track from Ed Sheeran.

She looks up. "What a question—of course you can come in. Have a seat." She points to the bed and closes her book, turning to straddle her desk chair. "What's with the sad face?"

Flopping down on the bed, I let out a loud sigh and throw my face down into her pillow. "Ugh! I've gone and done it this time."

"Oooh, I like the sound of *that*," Molly says, chuckling softly.

"Oh god, now you're starting to sound just like Jenna—which isn't a compliment, considering she's a sexual deviant."

"Mmm, she'd like to consider herself more a continental woman of mystery..."

"Isn't it *international* man of mystery? Continental makes *no* sense whatsoever."

Molly shrugs. "Jenna makes no apologies. Plus, she's strictly mysterious in United States, sometimes Hawaii."

"You two are so weird."

"Jenna's weird. I'm simply relaying the message."

"Okay, okay, this conversation has gotten completely off track." I take a deep sigh. "So the reason I'm here—and you know this isn't easy for me to say...I'll probably choke on my words a few times..."

"Would you spit it out?"

"I can't! It's embarrassing."

"Cece, you're a grown ass woman. Spit it out."

I look down at my chest. "Grown woman? Please. My boobs aren't even fully developed."

Molly laughs. "You are so full of shit. I happen to think your boobs are way too big for your frame."

She's lying, but I love her for it anyway. My boobs are fine, nice even, but I won't be sending in any photographs to Playboy magazine. I'm a B cup on most days, sometimes a C when I have my period, and my bras totally suck because I'm way too cheap to shell out fifty bucks for a decent one at Victoria's Secret.

"So, I have this date with your brother's friend Neve." I say the words and for some reason, I have to wait for the excitement that should come along with such an announcement.

Molly blinks at me and puts a hand on her chest before saying, "Oh god. I thought for a second you were going to say you had a date with my *bro-ther*..."

Yeah, not really sure how to interpret that comment... Is she saying this in a *relieved* kind of way because her brother's a big dope, or is she disappointed I don't have a date with him...?

I push on. "Well, I mean, I told him and he seemed pissed. He didn't text me back."

"Wait...who was pissed?"

"Your brother."

"I thought you said your date was with Neve."

"It is."

"So wait...what?"

"I told him I had a date and he didn't text me back."

"Who didn't?"

"Oh my gawd! Are you even paying attention?" Frustrated, I shout this last part and flap my arms like a duck.

"Whoa Nelly. *Chill*. Start over. You have a date with Neve...but...who didn't text you back? Neve, or my brother? I'm sooo confused."

I take a deep breath and count to five. "Neve called me for a date. I accepted. I told Matthew. Now he's not talking to me."

Molly stares. In fact, she stops blinking.

"Did you hear me?"

I wave a hand in front of her face. "Yoo-hoo..."

She shakes her head and then says, "Whoa! For a second there I thought I heard you wrong. It *soun*ded like you said you and Matthew were texting each other!" She gives a little giggle. "I know *that's* not happening because you would have *told* me about it, right?"

Guiltily, I look away.

"Cecelia Jane Carter! What the fack! You little slut!" Molly grabs a decorative pillow (one of *many* on her white, eyelet-lace themed bed) and hits me in the face with it--not once, but twice. "How could you withhold this information?!"

If only she knew how easy it was...

Too easy to keep it a secret.

Too easy with *him*.

Easy, easy, easy.

I sigh and flop down on the bed.

Molly groans. "Ugh, spare me. I don't even freaking believe this." She flops down next to me and we lie there, staring up at the white popcorn ceiling. "How the hell did this all come about? All this time, Weston's been running interference, and you two are secretly *still* doing it anyway!"

"I didn't mean for it to be a secret. It just sort of *happened...*"

"Oh barf. Everyone says that. *I* say that."

"Well it's true! After your mom made him send the *I can't email you anymore* email, it just kept going. I mean, he *is* kind of funny—well, I mean, most times he's not, but it doesn't really matter because he's been so kind. Did you know he coaches a youth hockey league?"

The look on Molly's face is priceless, and she stares at me like…like I've just swiped the last pair of clearance Tory Burch flats out from under her at a Neiman Marcus sale.

In other words, horrified.

"Are you *trying* to make me nauseous? Ugh, you should see the sappy look on your damn face." She smacks me with the back of her arm. After taking a deep, calming breath, she finally says, "So, you've been emailing…and texting too? And now he's ignoring you because…?"

The word hangs there.

"Because the last text I sent him was about my date with Neve. He never responded. Here, see for yourself." I lift my hips and dig the phone out of my skinny jeans, setting it in her open palm.

Thumbing over the messages, Molly's lips curl. "I think I'm going to throw up. What's this shit about him speaking Italian?" She raises her eyebrow and looks over at me, laughing. "Seriously? I need to take a screen shot of this and use it to blackmail him. What a tool." What began as a giggle is now out-of-control laughter, complete with a hiccup at the end.

I'm laughing too. "I know Molly, but I can't help it. I totally didn't mean to keep emailing him. It's just…he's getting so damn adorable."

She lets my words marinate for a few minutes, and I let the silence linger in the air without feeling the need to fill it.

"Well, it seems pretty obvious to me that he's jealous. I know my brother, and he's going to ignore you now because you've pissed him off. Sorry, that's how he is." She tosses the phone on the bed. "But look on the bright side! You have a date with Neve, and he is so hot—wayyy hotter than Matthew…"

I hesitate, mostly because I don't agree that Neve is better looking, and give a noncommittal shrug. "Uh, yeah, I guess?"

"Yeah, I guess…*but*…?" She twists her wrist in a circular motion, encouraging me to go on.

"But, I don't *like* him like that."

"So what are you saying? That Neve doesn't make your lady parts the least bit wet?"

My palm slaps my forehead. "I can*not* believe you just said that."

"Sorry. I heard it from Jenna and she's kind of a freak. You *are* still going on that date with him, right?"

"Do you really think I should? I mean, isn't that leading him on?"

"Are you kidding me right now? No, it's not leading him on—it's a date, not a marriage proposal." Molly pats my leg. "If I know my brother—and I think I do—he is going to find out the details from Neve and show up. It's a move directly from the official Matthew Wakefield playbook." Molly blows on her nails and then brushes them across her sweater in an *I got this* move. "He's like a freaking little baby that doesn't like to share, and when he shows up to *ruin* his friends date—which he *will* try to do—boy is he going to regret not getting to you first."

Matthew

"I don't care where we eat, as long as it's not one of the 12 places you just named."

So, not gonna lie: this isn't my first dip in the espionage pool.

One time, my buddy Alan—a really nice guy from some small town in Iowa—was dating this wacky chick (Stephanie, I think her name was) back when we were sophomores at Madison. Stephanie had a penchant for un-returned phone calls and texts, and 'forgetting' to show up for dates.

Well, we finally convinced Alan she was probably cheating on him with some dude, and we were convinced it was someone on the rugby team. After all, she went to a lot of their house parties.

It actually took a lot of convincing, because, well… Alan *loved* Stephanie—or what he thought was love any-way. I mean, what were we, nineteen? Not to mention,

Alan wasn't just a geek, he was *the* geek (think plaid shirts tucked into khakis).

Basically, Steph was way out of Alan's league.

He knew it, and he worshiped her for it.

Alan's chickenshit, passive aggressive refusal to confront her was the opportunity we all needed to go spy on her. We set up special ops, gave ourselves code names, wore black shirts and black masks—the whole nine yards.

I can't say that we blended into our environment: in an unfortunate twist, half of us were well over six feet tall, and collectively we weighed over eight hundred pounds.

Plus, Manny Cushman wouldn't shut the fuck up.

From one shitty house party and bar to another, we loudly tailed Stephanie all over Madison , and I can tell you this: turned out Alan was right—she wasn't cheating on him with a dude from the rugby team.

Nope.

Stephanie was cheating on Alan with some girl from the drama department.

An *opera* major.

Talk about a dramatic end to an evening of surveillance. Jesus Christ. I don't remember who cried harder after she was caught red-handed: Alan or Stephanie.

So yeah, I don't mean to brag, but I'm pretty damn good at espionage.

Definitely am not going to classify this particular trip across town as stalking because in my defense, I have seen Cecelia Carter go all kinds of crazy with my own two eyes, and I figure it's my civic duty to protect Neve from any unforeseen outbursts.

As his friend, the least I can do is protect him from a crazy woman.

At least that's what I told myself as I climbed into my Tahoe, fastened my seat belt, and drove the twenty-something miles out of Madison city limits to the quaint restaurant where Neve's date is taking place.

I'm definitely not crashing this date because I'm jealous.

Pfft. That would be ridiculous.

In fact, I'm so not jealous that I even invited my friend Stacy along to act as a decoy. Wait. Did I just say decoy? I meant, as my date. After all, I can't just *waltz* into the same restaurant *alone* (one that's way across town and completely out of my way) and pretend to bump into Neve and Cecelia and have it look like a coincidence, now can I? Nope. I need a decoy-slash-date.

Otherwise it's just weird.

To be honest, I'm not sure my sidekick Stacy is clear on what being a decoy *actually* entails.

I glance over at her, concerned. "Stacy, a decoy wouldn't put their hand on my thigh while I'm trying to drive." Gingerly, I remove her manicured hand and return it to her side of the truck. I give her hand a pat as a goodwill gesture. "Safety first."

Oh god, now I sound like a daycare teacher.

"But Matty," she whines. "Can't we still have fun anyway? Why are you sitting so far away?" Her red bottom lip sticks out and she casts me a coy smile.

I'm pretty sure she has lipstick on her front teeth.

Gross.

Okay, if I'm being frank, Stacy is one *duh* short of a dozen. She's all foam and no beer. Although she *does* fill out her tops well with her artificially enhanced assets, I worry that her elevator doesn't go all the way to the top floor.

You could write everything she knows on to one sticky note.

What Stacy *is* is…convenient, amiable, useful…and most importantly, available on short notice.

A willing pawn on the saving Neve Vanderhalt crusade, albeit a very blonde and clueless one.

"Matty, I'm hungry. Why are we going so late?"

It's 6:00.

I sigh. "Stacy, I already told you: we are not going there to eat. We're going to help a friend. You remember Neve Vanderhalt, right?"

She giggles shrilly and twirls a lock of platinum hair. "Ooh, *yes*," she says breathily. "The really *really* good-looking one, right? Oops, sorry Matty."

"Um, yeah, that's him." Good ol' good-looking Neve out on a date with my new breast friend Cecelia.

I mean *best* friend. Best.

Not breast. Shit.

Stacy reaches over and gives my leg another squeeze, her hot pink nails digging into my thighs through my jeans like eagle talons. "I think you're *way* better looking. Want me to prove it? I can eat a mint for you—I have some in my purse. The mint will make your *you-know-what* tingle when I put it in my mouth."

It suddenly occurs to me that my plan…might not go

according to plan.

I'm screwed.

Choking, I press myself into the corner of the driver's side and press down on the accelerator, check my rearview for state patrol, and gun it down the highway.

Cecelia

I stare at myself in the mirror for the millionth time as I wash my hands, relishing the warm tap water and soft melody of electric saxophone that's being piped into the bathroom.

Normally I wouldn't, because seriously, who enjoys *electric* saxophone besides my parents and Kenny G? (To spare you from having to Google him, I'll give you the Wikipedia definition: Kenny G was a famous electric sax player in the 90s. Chicks totally dug him.)

I finish rinsing my hands and grab few pieces of brown paper towel, blotting my hands dry. Leaning forward, I push a few strands of hair away from my face and purse my lips before digging into my thin clutch for the lip gloss Molly shoved in it earlier (NARS gloss in Turkish Delight in case you're wondering—it's awesome).

I'm not wearing anything overtly sexy—in fact, I'm almost all covered up—but as I gaze at myself, I blush a little at my own reflection because I look like myself, only a thousand times better.

Molly did my makeup so I have a full-on smoky eye, and I'm highlighted and contoured within an inch of my life.

Abby, bless her soul, loaned me the top she just wore to her sister's wedding in the Bahamas, a stupidly expensive taupe Diane Von Furstenberg halter-neck tank top. The shirt is sheer and softly drapes in small pleats down the middle, wrapping to tie around my neck in back with a small, elegant, beige satin bow.

Understated.

Sexy.

I'm wearing dark Joe's jeans and high nude patent leather wedges, along with large gold hoop earrings.

My arms are bare and expertly spray-tanned to a light golden brown by Jenna, who, ironically, is a biology major and not in school for cosmetology as one would expect.

I should also mention that in addition to being spray tanned, I've also been brushed with a light dusting of edible body glitter. It's kind of a Jenna's thing—she and Molly kept going *on and on* about how fabulous it is and how guys go wild for it.

At first, I tried to sneak out of the bathroom to get away from them both. I mean, body glitter? On me? I thought they were out of their freaking minds, for several reasons:

1. Have you seen me lately? Hello! Yoga pants and t-shirts are kind of my thing.

2. Um, where are girls *going* these days that a manufacturing company would think we *require* body glitter? Isn't that kind of strictly a...er... strip club thing?

3. Sorry. Just can't imagine myself walking through the mall, seeing body glitter on a shelf, and thinking to myself "Holy crap! Body powder you can eat?! I must own that!" Yeah, *no*.

4. Pretty sure if I was the one licking it off, I would choke on it...*kind* of like how I choke on the powdered sugar at the county fair every time I eat a cream puff. Yeah, choking—*so not a good look for me.*

Nonetheless, I seriously couldn't escape the pair of them. They were way too powerful for me. That Jenna has a crazy strong grip for such a small person. I did try making a run for it once but was quickly grabbed by the collar of my button-down shirt (the one I wore while they did my hair and makeup) and yanked back down into my seat.

In the end, I look pretty damn incredible.

Satisfied, I grab my clutch and push through the bathroom door, holding it open politely for an older woman who's on her way in.

Matthew

I will be the first person to admit: in hindsight, bringing Stacy was a terrible idea. Not only is she clinging to my arm, she hasn't stopped talking since we walked into the restaurant.

My eyes scan the perimeter, the dimly lit reception area obscuring the view into the main dining room. The hostess, standing behind a small wooden podium, smiles politely as we approach and asks us how many are in our party.

"Just two," Stacy promptly replies, running her finger up and down my arm. I curse the fact that I'm wearing short sleeves and that my biceps are so irresistible to women.

It's like I'm cursed.

The hostess looks down at the open book on the podium, adjusts the small lamp attached to it, and chews on the end of a yellow number two pencil. She looks up apologetically. "Do you have a reservation?"

"Did I need one?"

"No, but I'm afraid we're full tonight until…" She looks down again at the book. "7:15. I'm afraid it's going to be about a forty-five to sixty minute wait. Would you like to have a seat at the bar?" She holds up a black buzzer.

Stacy grabs it.

"Um, actually, we have a few friends here. Can we go see if they're already here and say hi?"

"Do you have the name?"

"Uh…I'm guessing it's probably under Lemon Jello. Or you can check the name Underhill."

The hostess furrows her brow at the stupid nicknames Neve thinks are hilarious and uses on a regular basis at hotels and restaurants, but checks the book anyway.

Recognition makes her eyes light up like Christmas trees. "Oh yes, he and his guest are here." She turns to the other hostess, who just walked up with menus. "Can you show these guests to table 24?"

***

The girl staring back at me wide-eyed, fork frozen above her plate in midair, is *not* the same girl I remember from the bar, or from my sister's apartment.

That girl was plain.

Mousy.

Frazzled.

A hot mess.

This girl is just…hot.

Fucking *hot*.

It takes a minute for the recognition to sink in, and we stare at each other…although oddly enough, Cecelia doesn't look *all* that surprised to see me. I mean, maybe I'm just imagining it, but instead of shock across her pretty eyebrows, she just looks amused.

Okay, maybe her eyes are narrowed in a slightly suspicious way, but that's neither here nor there…

Neve, on the other hand, looks stunned, and sets down his knife. "Wakefield, man, what are you doing here?"

Standing to greet me, he pumps my hand as I continue to eye fuck his date as she stares back at me.

"Yeah Wakefield, what are you doing here?" Cecelia's pretty mouth moves sarcastically, and I'm transfixed by the candlelight dancing off her glossy lips.

She looks amazing.

Gorgeous.

Sophisticated. Classy. All the words you would use for beautiful.

I wonder if she smells as good as she looks. My lip tips up and I almost smile at the thought, but I compose myself and clear my throat to speak instead. "I had a date tonight with Stacy here, and this is where she wanted to go."

I give Stacy a little shove.

My trusty sidekick nods her head vigorously beside me, her large boobs shaking beneath her slightly trashy sheer top.

Cecelia rolls her eyes—the light brown eyes she has artfully lined in heavy black coal. Man, there's nothing I love more than a chick wearing lots of makeup. I mean, don't get me wrong, I love the natural look too, and Cecelia is really cute without makeup, but now… She. Is. *Smokin'*.

"What a coincidence." Cecelia smiles crookedly, eyes shining wickedly, and sets down her fork to dab her mouth with the corner of her linen napkin. When she's done, she lays it back down in her lap, cocks her head in my direction, and lifts one of her eyebrows.

Her dark eyes continue boring into me and she licks her lips. Immediately my eyes shift back to her mouth, and I swear she's doing it on purpose.

My dick perks up. You know, like a horny teenager.

Except I'm not a teenager, I'm a man…*ish*.

And sure, perhaps it's time for me to act like one, but it's probably not going to happen today. Or tomorrow.

Or this year, if I'm being honest.

Whatever.

My point is, I'm practically drooling.

Beside me, I get nudged in the ribs by Stacy. "We came to say hi," my decoy charitably puts in. "It's a long wait for our table 'cause Matty didn't make a reservation on account of him only just calling me this afternoon for a date."

Neve lets out a loud, gut-busting laugh, causing my face to get beet red. I'm not sure if he's laughing because he knows my presence here is a crock of shit or because I'm here with a ditz like Stacy.

Let's face it, he knows I have no tolerance for stupidity, even from good-looking chicks, and Stacy could win top prize for village idiot.

"Dude. You can't just show up at this place. I made a rez over a week ago." He winks at Cecelia, who giggles prettily and bats her long, sooty lashes.

Christ, how annoying can two people be?

"How long did you say the wait for a table was?" Neve asks as he dips his head and takes a bite of his dinner, which I can't help noticing is blue cheese-crusted filet and asparagus on a bed of mashed potatoes.

Probably infused with buttery herbs and garlic.

My mouth begins watering.

"Look, I have to use the bathroom. Take a seat but don't eat anything while I'm gone." Neve sets his napkin aside and stands. Ever chivalrous, he smiles cajolingly at my date and crooks his elbow. "Stacy, care to join?"

Cecelia

"So, what are you *really* doing here?"

"What do you mean?" Matthew looks at me innocently from across the table, widening his eyes and giving me another onceover.

He's been doing it since he walked in.

Which, quite honestly, I can't believe he actually did—showed up, I mean. Seriously, what kind of an asshole does that?

I cross my arms. "Oh please. Spare me. You did *not*

drive Miss Mensa thirty miles out of town to come here. Even I'm not that stupid. You'd probably never even heard of this place before tonight."

Matthew doesn't say anything, so I accept this as fact.

"Are you just going to sit there staring at me?" I finally blurt out.

He mirrors my body language by crossing his own arms, and I'm rewarded by the sight of his bulging tan biceps. Shamelessly, I allow my eyes to freely roam his upper body, from the near bursting top button of his straining polo shirt to the veins in his strong arms.

Come on, don't you think I deserve a little peek?

As I continue ogling his masculine upper body (and please, forgive my continuous objectification of him), my eyes eventually roam back up to his face. *Unfortunately* for me, the bastard is smirking arrogantly and spreads his arms wide, gripping the corners of the square table and staring intently at my boobs, then back up at my face.

If I didn't know better, I would think he was mocking me.

Or that he liked it…a bit too much.

Damn him!

"See something you like?" he asks with a low snicker.

Yes!

"Oh *please*," I sputter. "Gag me." I give my long silky hair a toss before leaning back behind my seat to retrieve my purse and proceed to dig through it while I wait for him to respond. He continues to stare as I slowly slick nude gloss across my puckered mouth then lick my lips for good measure before putting the cap back on—you know, since he's my captive audience and all. "So are you gonna tell me what you're doing here or not? Best spit it out quickly, because our dates will be back soon...*friend*."

"Would you knock that shit off," he mutters.

"Knock what off?" I tilt my head curiously, causing my hair to cascade and spill over one shoulder, just like Molly and I practiced before I left the apartment.

"That *friend* bullshit."

"Why? I thought that's what we were."

Matthew's eyes drift to my bare shoulder and he studies my exposed collarbone. "Why is your skin so...sparkly?"

I flick my wrist nonchalantly. "Hmmm? Oh. Edible body glitter." Pleased that he noticed, I slowly trail my index finger up and down my arm. "Jenna insisted on it."

"What the hell does that mean? Edible body glitter."

I roll my eyes at him (which Molly claims he hates). "What do you *think* it means? Use your imagination."

"I'm seriously beginning to question your morals."

I can't stop the snicker that escapes from my sticky lips. "Don't question *mine*, question Molly's. She's always slathering this stuff on. It's Weston's absolute *favvooritee*." I drag the word out and wiggle my newly manicured eyebrows suggestively, then prop my chin up in the palm of my hand. "Actually, you don't slather it on. You brush it on gently with a feather." I sigh lazily. "It feels divine."

"Why would you go and *say* shit like that? Are you purposely trying to get me hard?"

"Because it's more fun than licking my own arm and watching you wet your pants a little."

"Wait, how old are you again?" His eyes are slightly glassy and his pupils are dilated.

"Almost twenty-three." I take a small sip of ice water, and a few beads of perspiration from the glass drip and land on the tablecloth. "So what are you going to do with the rest of your night now that you hauled that deranged drag queen all the way down here? You *do* know she's not going to leave here without a free meal, right?"

He clearly doesn't like me stating the obvious because he replies, "Would you shut up please?"

Shrugging, I smirk. "Hey, I'm just being honest."

"Maybe she would take the hint if she walked out of the bathroom and we were sucking face across the table?"

I flip my hair again. "Gross. Like that would ever happen."

Although, let's face it, I'd *totally* be into sucking face with him.

"Don't look so offended. You might bruise my ego." I give an unladylike snort while Matthew looks around. He cranes his neck and squints toward the front of the restaurant where the restrooms are.

He leans back in his seat and pulls his iPhone out of the back pocket of his jeans.

"Hey, wait a minute—don't you think they've been gone a really long time?"

Matthew

"It's not you, it's me—actually, no, it *is* you." – team-mate Kevin Westerman breaking up with his girl-friend of two weeks

I pull out my phone and check the time. About nineteen minutes have passed since Neve and Stacy left for the restrooms, plenty of time to relieve yourself and come back. Even if Neve had to take a dump, he still should have been back by now.

A knot forms in my stomach and apprehension sets in.

That son of a bitch.

It doesn't take a rocket scientist to conclude that he ditched me here with his date.

I just know it.

I glance toward the entrance once more for any sign of them, then back at Cecelia, who has begun eating her meal again, naively unaware of the fact that she's been ditched. How am I going to break this to her?

Slowly cutting into the filet mignon on her plate with a sharp steak knife, eyes on her plate, Cecelia is the first one to break the suddenly awkward silence. "Are you thinking what I'm thinking?"

I hesitate. "Um..."

"It's okay Matthew, you can say it."

"Fine. I'm pretty sure they're gone."

Cecelia blows her bangs out of her eyes and taps the table with her steak knife, then nods matter-of-factly. "Obviously I'm gonna need a ride..."

"Yup."

"Hitching a ride with you obviously makes more sense than me calling Molly or Abby for a lift, I suppose..."

My chest indignantly puffs out a little. "Hey, you don't have to sound so put out about it. I'll have you know, chicks line up to date me."

Cecelia's face contorts up and now she's staring like I've just admitted to having an STD. "*Yuck.* Your arrogance is only a *small* part of your problem..." Her voice trails off, and instead of nagging, she crosses her arms and huffs, exasperated. Soon, she lets out another sigh and begins cutting another piece of filet. "What a waste of a perfectly good Diane Von Furstenberg top..."

"Excuse me? Von *what?*"

"Never *mind.*" Shaking her head, she sighs again. "So, any idea why they would do this? I mean, obviously *you* came here to ruin my date, but it makes no sense as to why Neve would leave me here with you."

"Believe me, this was *not* the plan."

"I mean, I totally get why Stacy would want to run off

with him. He's *so* hot."

"Uh huh."

"And he is so funny."

"Yup, got it—he's good-looking and funny."

"And he's soooo nice."

"Okay, feel free to stop gushing any time. I hate to be a cold bucket of reality here, but he *did* just ditch you."

"Would you shut up? I would be on a damn date right now if you hadn't shown up. This is *all. Your. Fault.*"

"Whoa, whoa, whoa—you're not the only victim here! My date left too."

"Oh puh-*leez*! Admit it. She wasn't even a real date. No guy would purposefully subject himself to *her* for an entire night—not even you, not even for a quick lay. This, my friend, was a carefully orchestrated move to sabotage my date. I mean, what the hell did you think was going to happen? Or did you not give it any thought? You are *such* a colossal douchebag."

"I resent that."

"But you don't deny it."

"Excuse me, but Stacy's amazing rack is one of her redeeming qualities."

"Oh shut up for once, Matthew." Cecelia juts her bottom lip and her eyes narrow, deep in thought. She sit up straight in her chair and begins tapping the edge of the dinner table with her forefinger. "Actually...something just occurred to me."

"What?"

"Pfft," she scoffs, grinning at me. "Like I'm telling

you. But trust me, you'll find out soon enough."

Definitely not liking the sound of that.

Cecelia

It occurs to me that I could use this whole night as black-mail. Okay, so maybe I wouldn't call it blackmail, *exactly*...

I would consider it more...a future *plan* for *creatively* suggesting Matthew do things for me while holding this evening over his head. Yeah, that has a nice ring to it—much better than blackmail, or extortion, or coercion, or whatever you want to call it.

It would be like an exchange of sorts: in exchange for favors, I won't rat him out to his mother or sister, thus sparing his life from becoming one continuous nagging fa-milial bitch-fest.

Oh, who am I trying to kid—I would never actually do it. Sadly, I'm all talk and no action, although the idea does have merit.

I glance over at Matthew's profile in the dimly lit cabin of his meticulously maintained Tahoe, taking in his chis-eled, slightly scruffy jaw, the nose that looks like it's been broken more than a few times, the scars lining his brow, and the backward baseball cap he threw on as soon as he climbed behind the steering wheel.

The whole truck reeks of male, including the lingering smell of his musty cologne.

It also reeks from a dirty duffle of gym clothes hap-hazardly tossed in the back seat. I noticed them when I first scrambled in, mostly because it freaking reeks, but I'll give him a pass on that since he's an athlete.

Either way, there is no denying it: Matthew Wakefield is all. Guy.

I give his space—and him—one last covert sniff before turning my head to look out the window. I am one hundred percent determined to ignore him.

Except, apparently, he's determined *not* to let me. "Hey." Matthew's deep baritone rises out of the silence. "I'm beginning to feel like a chauffeur. Aren't you gonna talk? Chew my ass out or something?"

I don't respond.

"Can I at least say you l-looked—*look*—great t-to-night? I hardly recognized you at first." He's stuttering a little.

It's so cute.

But hold up. Here's the thing—when someone says they hardly recognized you, is that supposed to be a compliment or something? It's almost like they're saying, *Hey, you looked really ratchet before, but now that you've thrown some makeup on and did your hair, you look so much better! Not nearly as hideous!*

Still, I cut him some slack because I know that's not what he meant, and I'm sick of him thinking I'm complete bitch. So, instead of jumping down his throat, I grin and turn toward him. "Thanks. You look pretty too."

And he does.

His turquoise blue polo shirt brings out the auburn in his mussed up hair, makes his tan skin look darker and his biceps bigger.

Ugh, seriously Cece, again with the biceps.

Sorry, not sorry. Can I help it if his muscles are so big that the shirt strains around his arms and my eyes refuse to look away? It's not like I have any control over it. My body is saying *Take your eyes off his body and I'll cut off all your air flow*, not me.

Matthew Wakefield is quickly becoming my favorite bit o' eye candy, and right now he's looking at me as if I've just become his.

I gulp, feeling like we might be, um…having a moment.

I shiver.

"Are you cold? Why don't you put on your jacket?" His eyes dart to the beige leather jacket I have laying across my lap, which I've been instructed by Molly is for emergency use only. Before I walked out of our apartment, she grabbed me by the shoulders and said (and none too kindly either), *"Now you listen and you listen good Cecelia Carter."* She pointed at me like she was a trial lawyer and I was on the witness stand. *"I busted my ass getting you ready for this date. Do not ruin this outfit by wearing a jacket. This jacket is for emergency. Use. Only. She then gripped the jacket, shaking it at me in her clutched hand with every enunciated word. How do you expect Matthew to lust after you if you cover up your girl bits? Now, I'm going to slowly hand it over, but not willingly…"*

The ironic part is, I seem to recall her telling me about a similar conversation she had with Jenna before her first date with Weston.

In any case, I'm pretty sure Molly was on the verge of slapping me across the face just to make her point. Long story short, I haven't put the jacket on for fear that if I do, she *will* somehow find out about it. I even sent her a Snapchat when Neve went to the bathroom, making sure to display my bare shoulders so I'd have solid proof that I followed through with her command.

Molly. Is. Such. A. Weirdo.

"I'm good, thanks. Just caught a chill."

"I can turn the heat on if you want me to." Matthew reaches forward to hit the heater, but I stop him.

"No, no. If I get cold, I'll put my jacket on."

He eases back into his seat. "Okay. If you're sure."

"I am." I look down and a shiny tube of lipstick in the cup holder catches my eye. Picking it up, I inspect the MAC tube, pull off the cap, and roll my eyes.

Bright red.

Of course.

"I think your friend left this behind." I screw the bottom of the tube and the lipstick rises. "Red, how fitting."

"Throw that thing out the window."

"No way, José. Are you nuts? This lipstick probably cost eighteen bucks and I'm keeping it, assuming she doesn't have herpes."

Matthew laughs, and as he's saying, "Well, I won't be seeing her again—like, *ever*—so do whatever you want with it," my phone chimes.

It's Neve: *There's a perfectly good explanation for my leaving.*

"Well, this is interesting. Neve just texted me, that dickhead."

"Seriously? What did he say?" Matthew is leaning toward me trying to get a look at my cell phone screen, but I tilt my body toward the window so he can't and compose a reply to his friend.

Me: *By all means, give me your best excuse. Hanging on your every word.*

Neve: *I would never NEVER have left under normal circumstances*

Neve: *But I think Matt might be totally into you and was there to pee on his territory*

Neve: *I don't poach on other people's terrain.*

I look over at Matthew, who has his eyes on the road and is pretending not to be interested. I study him anew, assessing him again in a new light. Could it be true? There's no freaking way.

I mean, he couldn't *possibly…*

He glances over at me again, then down at the phone resting in my hand. "What does the douchebag want?"

I fiddle with the zipper on my jacket and bite my lip. How much do I tell him? "You know, just making his excuses." I fumble to put the phone back in my purse, and before I realize it, we're pulling into the parking lot of my apartment complex.

Holy shit, that ride went quick.

Matthew pulls into a handicap parking spot right at the front entrance, cuts the engine, and jogs around the front of the Tahoe to my door—all before I get my seat belt unbuckled.

I gather my things and gingerly place my foot on the running board, stepping down into the cool September evening. Matthew shuts the truck door behind me, and the *blip blip* of the lock indicator echoes in the air.

Awkwardly, we walk toward the front entrance. In the near distance, since it's late night on a weekend, I see several groups of students walking—and stumbling—down the sidewalk, talking loudly and laughing. Off to my right, I watch a few girls fall over themselves in the grass, laughing.

I sigh kind of wistfully as we take the short steps onto the front porch. It's a chilly forty degrees tonight, and I can actually see steam from my breath in the air—not to mention, I've suddenly got goose bumps.

So much for fair fall weather in the Midwest…figures.

Clasping my hands together and hugging my jacket, I shuffle to the large blue door to punch in the keypad code. "Thanks for the ride Matthew. I think I've got it from here."

The keypad blinks green and I push through to the entryway. The long narrow hall stretches bleakly in front of us, the ugly brown carpet that should have been replaced years ago casting a dreary pallor on the walls. There is a yellow glow from the overhead lights that makes the whole corridor look like the hotel from *The Shining*.

So disturbing.

"I'll walk you in. Seriously, I insist."

A slight movement catches my eye. I swear there's a crack in Creepy Writer Guy's door and he's watching us. I nod, conceding to Matthew, and let him lead me to my door because, quite frankly, I'm a tad skeeved out and have no desire to get dragged into CWG's lair.

We silently walk down the hall side by side, and this couldn't be more awkward if it was the ending of an actual date. Fumbling for my keys, we stand in front of my apartment. 24C.

My apartment keys jingle in my hands and I fiddle idly with the patent leather starfish keychain my sister gave me for my birthday last year as we stand there in the dim hall. I don't know if we should be chitchatting or if I should just go in and shut the door on this whole evening.

I look up into Matthews face, and he's staring at me from about a foot away. He's close—so close I can smell the mint from the evergreen gum in his mouth.

Way too close.

I back up, my heel hitting the apartment door. Shoulders sagging a little as I cock my eyebrow at him, I say the first thing that comes to mind. "So, this just got awkward."

He shrugs, his large shoulders moving up…then down lazily. "Ironically, this isn't the most fucked-up date I've ever been on."

I hold my palms up in a *stop* motion. "Whoa buddy, let's not get ahead of ourselves here. This was not a date." Is he out of his freaking mind?

"In a weird way, don't you think it kind of was?" He smiles, his bright white teeth lighting up his entire face, the dimple in his cheek…ugh. *Yum.* So handsome…

Instead, I wrinkle my nose. "Um, no."

He laughs and moves a little closer. "I'm so tempted to kiss you right now."

I gasp and breathe in a whisper, "You wouldn't *dare.*"

He makes a face. "Why do you have to go and say it like *that*?"

I'm not whispering any more. "Because, asshole,

you're the one who ruined my date. Yeah, my real date. *You* don't get a reward for someone else's evening. You are on *crack* if you think I'm kissing that mouth."

"Fine." Matthew stubbornly crosses his arms and pouts, leaning up against the opposite wall.

"Good."

"*Great.*"

We stare at each other, sizing each other up like gunslingers in a showdown. Maybe you think I'm crazy for not letting him lay one on me, but I have a little more self-respect than that, thank you very much. Although, with the looks he's giving me, I'm actually rethinking my resistance…

Just as I'm about to let my guard down and step toward him, the door to my apartment swings open at full force, hitting the wall behind it. Molly stands framed in the doorway, already in her pajamas. She looks at me, and then looks at her brother with an expression of disbelief. "What the hell is *he* doing here?" She directs her question at me, her alert green eyes curious.

Matthew pushes himself away from the wall with his boot and stands straight. He nods toward me. "Her date ditched her and she needed a ride."

Molly's eyes bug out. "*Shut the frick up.* Are you shitting me?"

I roll my eyes and shove my way in past them both, completely irritated. I toss my keys and purse onto the small kitchen table, both Wakefields trailing in after me as I start ranting.

"Gee Molls, that's a really good question. Hmm, did my date ditch me? *Did* my date ditch me? Well, yes and no. This one here"—I pivot on my heel, pointing my finger accusingly at Matthew—"crashed my date, *just as you predicted*, with a drag queen, which I'm sure Neve just *loovvved*…so much so that when they went to the bathroom, they never came back."

Molly turns to her brother and shouts, "Ew! You showed up with a drag queen? What the hell Matthew?!" She shoves him with both hands until he stumbles back, falling onto one of our wobbly kitchen barstools.

"Stacy is *not* a goddamn drag queen!" he shouts back, throwing up his arms in defeat. "And what the hell do you mean I crashed the date as you predicted? Cecelia, what's that all about?"

Matthew

15

"Everything happens for a reason, but sometimes the reason is because you're freaking *stupid*." – Molly Wakefield to her brother

Excuse my language, but this whole evening is turning into one giant clusterfuck.

Word to the wise: never ever crash a girl's date and haul along another girl, especially if the girl whose date you're crashing happens to be your sister's roommate... because when your sister finds out (and believe me, she will), she *will* chew your ass out.

My ears are still ringing from her high-pitched shrieking.

I've never been bitched at so hard in my life, not even the time I was seventeen and my parents took Molly out of town, leaving me alone (huge mistake), and trusting me with their house (huge mistake). Instead of cutting the grass and cleaning the pool like they'd asked me to, I threw a huge kegger (huge mistake). Holy shit did I get my ass chewed out; the fact that my parents continued finding cigarette butts and crushed beer cans for weeks afterward certainly did not help.

Molly, bless her misguided heart, came to Cecelia's defense like a dog fighting over a bone with meat on it, and, being a guy, I didn't see it coming and therefore didn't adequately prepare myself for the assault. My little sister verbally beat me to a pulp—a skill I hadn't realized she possessed—then when she was done, she verbally beat me up again.

Trust me when I say, I've has my ass reamed out plenty, because I've screwed a *lot* of people over…like, a lot of people.

I've never has my ass chewed out like this.

Who knew Molly knew so many vulgar synonyms to call someone an asshole?

Not me, that's who.

Walking into my dark apartment, the first thing I do after chucking my car keys on the granite countertop in the kitchen is stroll to the fridge. The light comes on inside my Sub-Zero and I bend at the waist to peer inside, hungry but not really craving anything, and unimpressed with my dining options.

Leftover pizza.

Leftover Chinese takeout (General Chao's Chicken).

Half a Rubbermaid container of diced cantaloupe.

Leftover steak wrapped in tin foil from my parents' house, from er, two weekends ago…

Are you sensing a trend here?

Sighing, I grab a fork out of the utensil drawer then

retrieve the carton of General Chao's Chicken and take it to the living room. Yeah, that's right—I'm eating it cold.

Newsflash: guys are simple, disgusting, creatures.

After stabbing a decent amount of chicken and shoving the giant forkful into my mouth, I reach for the remote control while I chew and point it at the giant flat screen above the fireplace in my living room, changing the channel from Fox Sports to SportsCenter.

Bored, I half listen and begin texting a few of my buddies while the broadcaster does commentary on a major league baseball team I couldn't give two shits about. Here's the thing about playing for a professional sports team: most of us do not live in the cities we play for. In the offseason, we're spread around the United States, oftentimes in the towns where we grew up and got our start.

I am no exception.

I work in Los Angeles, but live in Wisconsin.

So, even though I'm texting my teammates late on a Saturday night, a handful of them are married, and quite a few of them have kids so chances are, some of them are in bed. One thing is for sure: probably not a single one of them is sitting alone in a dark apartment eating dry, leftover Chinese takeout on their couch.

Depressing, isn't it?

I inhale another forkful, choke a little because it almost goes down the wrong pipe, and wallow in self-pity

Can you fucking believe Cecelia wouldn't kiss me?

I mean, what's up with that? Not to sound like an arrogant prick, but most chicks would give their left nut to kiss these lips—and since I'm on the subject and am feeling irritated, I grab my phone and send her a quick message.

Miss me yet?

I grin at her snarky reply: *Not even close.*

Chuckling, I type out: *I know that's not true. I saw the look you were giving me right before Molly opened your door. ;)*

Cecelia: *Have you had your eyes checked lately? That was scorn, not lust. Huge difference.*

Me: *Come on. I did you a favor tonight.*

Cecelia: *You. Are. Delusional.*

Me: *Nope. Just honest.*

Cecelia: *Ok. FINE. I'll bite: How were you doing me a favor tonight??????????????*

Me: *Whoa, cool it with the question marks. The thing with Neve would never have lasted. He's way too nice for you.*

Cecelia: *Oh my god. You are such a dick!*

Me: *LOL. It's true. You need someone who's gonna tell you how it is. You know, spank you on the ass every once in a while.*

Cecelia

I stare at Matthew's last text, slack-jawed. Of all the boorish, ill-mannered things to say!

Rude!

"That conceited asshole!" I mutter.

"What was that?" Molly asks, passing by and stopping to stick her head in my room. She has a towel wrapped around her hair, blow dryer dangling from her hand. "What are you bitching about in here?"

"Um…nothing."

She snorts. "Please. You can't even look me in the eye." Walking over, she snatches the phone out of my hand before I can yank it out of her reach. "Surprise, surprise. Look who we have here." Her hawk-like gaze misses nothing, and her thumb moves across my phone screen, catching up on all my texts with her brother. Laughing, she hands me my phone back and says, "*Spank your ass once in a while?* What a pig!"

"Er, yeah…"

"Okay, say, *Spanking is nice, but I'd rather be tied up.*"

"What?! NO!"

"Just freaking do it! Trust me—he'll piss himself."

Grumbling, I type out the message with Molly looking over my shoulder. "Make sure you type all that verbatim."

"I got it, you skank."

"Hey now, no need to get nasty."

Me to Matthew: *Spanking is nice, but I'd rather be tied up.*

I hit *send.*

Molly, unable to contain herself, throws herself on top of my bed, shrieking with laughter. "Holy shit, I can*not* believe you actually did it! He is going to *shit* himself. He comes off as such a pervert, but he is *soooo* vanilla."

"What?! Oh my god Molly, I hate you so much right now!" I spit out and launch myself on top of her, fake beating her with a throw pillow. Afterward, we both lay there staring up at the ceiling, choking on our laughter until we're out of breath.

Finally, after what feels like an eternity, my phone pings.

Matthew

Holy fuck buckets.

I stare at Cecelia's message, her words scorching my brain: *Tied up. Tied up. Tied up.*

Seriously, could any two words in the English language have a more powerful impact on my dick?

Here's my dilemma: if I respond with the first thing that comes to mind, she's going to think I'm a *complete* and absolute pervert, *but,* if I ignore her comment and change the subject...well, she might think I'm not interested in tying her up.

Which I am. One hundred percent. On second thought, better make that one hundred *thousand* percent, just in case there's any mistaking my interest.

I mean, normally I'm not into kinky shit, but if she's offering, who am I to deny her? Am I right or am I *right*?

I reach down and grab my hardening package through my jeans as another message from her comes through. Shit, I waited too long to reply. I groan.

Cecelia: *Cat got your tongue?*

Me: *Um...kind of. I'm shocked at you.*

Cecelia: *I wish I could have seen the look on your face. LOL*

Me: *It was pretty damn priceless, I'm sure.*

Me: *Um, just curious…do you really like being tied up?*

Cecelia: *No!!! I don't know. LOL. But since you brought up spanking, it seemed like an appropriate response.*

Me: *I'd slap your ass any ol' day of the week.*

Cecelia: *OMG*

Me: *What?! It's a great ass.*

Cecelia: *I'm not going there with you. I read a Cosmo article once that said sexual banter too soon is a bad idea.*

Me: *Hmmm. Sounds like a TERRIBLE article. Burn that magazine.*

Cecelia: *Actually, I think I framed that page and have it hanging on my wall…*

Me: *I don't doubt that.*

Me: *I should hit the sack. The Lightning play tomorrow and I fly solo as coach.*

Cecelia: *Oh that's right! Good luck!*

Me: *9:30. Ithaca Arena. All pretty fans are encouraged to attend…*

Cecelia

"If you bring me coffee without me having to ask, I just might love you." – *everyone*

What the hell am I doing up at this hour?

Wait—what the hell am I *doing* here? It's the question I've asked myself over and over (and over) since leaving the house this morning at eight o'clock.

On a Sunday morning, for heaven's sake, and I'm not even headed to church.

When Molly caught me trying to sneak out (holding my shoes so I wouldn't make any noise), at first I thought she was going to throw a hissy fit. Instead, she surprised the crap out of me by digging in her purse and pulling out a Starbucks gift card. She handed it to me and said, "Here. He likes a grande nonfat half-caff mocha latte." Then she winked and went back to casually eating her Cinnamon Toast Crunch while reading *US Weekly*, ignoring me completely as I stood there with my mouth gaping. Finally she glanced up at me once more before shooing me out the door.

"Cece, would you *go*? Sheesh. The game starts in forty-five minutes and it's going to take you thirty just to get there." Then she tossed me a pair of mittens. "Here. You're gonna need these."

I. Cannot. Believe. I'm. Doing. This.

Now let me tell you, deciding what to wear today is what really threw me off my game this morning. I mean, what do you wear to a kids hockey game in an ice-filled hockey arena that looks cute but effortless? With an average interior temperature of sixty-three degrees, it's not exactly a tank top kind of event.

A few parents are wearing winter coats, and I wish I had one right now because I have a feeling I might end up freezing my butt off. So, what *am* I wearing, you're asking yourself.

I couldn't look like I tried *too* hard, so after several long internal debates, I finally decided on a light, oversized gray sweater over a long white thermal tank top, dark denim skinny jeans, and gray Frye boots. Wrapped around my neck is a light gray scarf, and to complete my carefully constructed outfit, I donned large silver hoop earrings and artfully piled my hair on top of my head in a messy bun.

Oh yeah, and let's not forget the mittens.

So here I stand, at the top of the Ithaca Arena stairs, clutching two cups of Starbucks—one Americano for me and one grande nonfat half-caff mocha latte in the other for...um, *not me*.

The significance of my gesture is not lost on me, and I

seriously hope it's not lost on Matthew either. The simple fact that I'm even *here* speaks volumes—I mean, I'm really putting myself out there for him considering he acts like a major caveman on most occasions.

But really, what guy doesn't?

Never mind...don't answer that.

Curiously, there isn't much of a crowd. Considering there are about twenty players on each team, there aren't many parents, probably only about eight or nine moms and dads sitting around total. The ones who are here are waiting for the countdown clock to run out and signal the start of the game.

Most of them are ignoring each other, on their smartphones or iPads instead of looking at the ice. I gather from what Molly has told me, it's a scholarship-sponsored team, and most of the boys have everything paid for by donors, kind of like an afterschool boys club program.

So I guess it makes sense that there aren't many people in the stands—if the parents have no money invested, why bother coming?

Kind of sad, really.

I scan the small crowd, biting my lip. The boys are all out on the ice, and Matthew is standing on the sideline with his back to the crowd, clipboard in hand, firm ass clad in dark denim jeans.

A girl could *definitely* get used to this view.

Nice

Slowly, I take the steps one at a time and move toward the bench, glancing at each one as I step down—it won't do to trip and fall flat on my ass, small uninterested audience or not.

Matthew

Eight minutes 'til game time.

I glance down at my clipboard then back up to the ice just in time to see Darnell Pruett take a successful practice slap shot at our goalie. I nod approvingly from my perch.

Good form. Great kid.

There isn't a lot of noise because there aren't a lot of people here, but the sound from the continuously blowing air ducts in the ceiling makes it hard to tell if the boys are talking to each other out on the ice, which is something we've been working on in practice.

They kind of suck at it.

As I reach for the whistle hanging around my neck and place it between my lips (it's easier blowing a whistle than shouting to bring the boys in before a game), a quiet coughing sound catches my attention. It's muffled and not very loud, but still…it causes me to turn.

"Hi." Cecelia greets me with a bashful smile, standing behind the half wall by the benches, two steaming cups of Starbucks in her hands. I look at her face, then down at the coffee, then back at her face, and grin at her like a fucking lame ass.

Say something, Wakefield. I mean, holy shit, I can't believe she showed up. Didn't think she'd have the lady balls, although obviously I can't say that to her. If she were a dude, I probably would.

Dumbly—and with the whistle still clenched between my teeth—I continue grinning. "Hi."

Her face lights up with relief and her cheeks, framed adorably by a light gray scarf, get pink as she extends an all-too-familiar white Starbucks cup. "Grande nonfat half-caff mocha latte."

I spit the whistle out of my mouth, and if possible, my grin gets wider. "Why, are you *stalking* me, Cecelia Carter? Cause that would be *awe*some."

"Shut up and take it." She laughs, a twinkly little laugh that reaches in and pulls at my heart a little.

Oh god, what am I saying? *Pulls at my heart a little*—ugh.

My large hand envelops hers as I grip the cup, our eyes briefly connecting before she looks away, embarrassed. I gesture toward the seating behind me. "Do you, um…want to come sit in here on the bench?"

"Oh gosh! No, that's okay."

"No really, it's cool. Here." I take a few steps toward her, leaning over and unlatching the door that separates the stadium seating from the players, and then I take her hand to help her down the small wooden step.

Behind me the buzzer sounds, and moments later, the box is filled with the fourteen (out of twenty) kids that showed up to play today. Immediately, Mitchell Decker squints at Cecelia through his protective eye gear and asks, "Who's she?"

"Is that your girlfriend?" This from Adam Ruttiger.

"No, she's not my girlfriend. Guys, get your heads in the game."

"Why not? She's hot."

What the hell? "Shut it, Stewart. Seriously."

"It's a legitimate question, Coach. Coach McGrath has a girlfriend, how come *you* don't?" Mitchell shoves his eye gear farther up on his nose with his gloved hand and continues squinting at Cecelia.

"He's probably gay," another voice behind me interjects.

"I am *not* gay."

Charlie Davis, our goalie, shrugs and adjusts his facemask. "Being gay is nothing to be ashamed of, Coach."

"Closets are for clothes," intones another prepubescent voice.

"My sister is a lesbian," Andy Boskowitcz helpfully points out, aimlessly tapping his hockey stick on the cement floor.

"*I am not gay!*" I nearly shout through gritted teeth, causing several parents to turn and look our way. Running a hand down my face, I groan and take a deep, steadying breath. "Oh my god, why am I arguing with all of you? You're not even twelve."

I chance a glance at Cecelia, who is on the bench, barely—just *barely*—containing her laughter. Her shoulders are shaking and she's got her mouth buried so far in her scarf she's practically chewing on it. There's no denying it: the girl is entertained but trying to hide it. If anything is giving her away, it's the damn tears of amusement forming in her eyes and rolling down her cheeks.

Great. She thinks this is fucking hilarious.

The traitor.

"You can jump in at any time here," I point out to her, gesturing to the boys before throwing my arms up in exasperation.

"Why would I do that? You're doing *so well* on your own, Coach."

She takes out her smartphone and snaps a picture of me before wiping her eyes and blinking at me innocently. "What?"

"I swear, if you put that on Instagram, I will *kill* you."

The buzzer sounds again, and I shake my head at her.

Game time.

Cecelia

In a shocking twist, the Lightning won.

The little shits *actually* won.

Now, there isn't much about hockey that I'm an expert on, but judging from what Matthew told me during the game as he tried to help me understand what was going on, he had some serious doubts about their winning—not to mention, to say the boys went into the game incredibly unfocused would be…quite an understatement.

I chuckle at the memory.

Leaning up against the yellow cinder block wall outside of the locker room, I can hear the echo of showers running, lots of shouting, and Matthew occasionally yelling, "Guys, settle down! No running on the wet floors. Nelson, are you *trying* to crack your skull open?"

Actually, he's scolded them about nine times now (I counted) in the twenty-five minutes he's been in the locker room, sounding more exasperated each time.

How cute is that?

I stand here where Matthew asked me to wait for another fifteen minutes before he emerges from the locker room door, looking more than a little frazzled. "Sorry about that," he apologizes, hefting a duffle onto his broad shoulders and running his free hand through his hair. It sticks up in front haphazardly. "Thanks for waiting."

"It's okay. The acoustics in there must be pretty good, because I was able to listen to the entire show and was pretty entertained."

"Uh, yeah..." He scratches his head, grinning. "Sometimes they act like a pack of wild animals, or at least the boys from *Lord of the Flies*."

"Don't you think that's a bit of an exaggeration? Those kids tried killing each other."

"Hell no it's not an exaggeration. They climb all over the benches like monkeys and pick fights with each other. I'd say that's pretty animalistic. No manners what-so-ever."

"You weren't like that when you were eleven?"

"Me? No way. I always took this shit seriously, even at their age."

We get to the glass double doors of the exit and Matthew pushes one open, waiting for me to walk through first. "Plus, if my parents found out I was acting like a little asshole, they wouldn't have let me play. These kids don't really have a lot of mentors modeling good behavior..."

He lets his thoughts and voice trail off as we walk silently to his Tahoe in the parking lot, my navy blue Envoy parked several rows away. Matthew sets the duffle down by his truck before walking me to my car.

"So... " I begin, kicking a stone along the pavement

with the toe of my boot.

"Hey Coach! You're not about to try to *kiss* her, are you?" A kid with glasses is loudly shouting from across the parking lot, heading our way and dragging his equipment bag behind him.

"*Oh my god,*" Matthew groans. "Shoot me now."

The kid continues yelling in a loud, booming voice from several yards away. "Cause that's what it looks like you were about to do, Coach."

"Mind your own business, Mitchell," Matthew yells back at his player.

"I can't Coach."

"Mitchell, *where* are your parents?"

"I'm getting a ride home with Stewart, Coach."

Matthew runs his palm down his face. "Please, *please* stop calling me Coach. I seriously can't take it anymore."

Mitchell finally joins us, out of breath from lugging his giant hockey bag behind him, and proceeds to prop his arm up on my car, leaning into it. A scrawny little guy with thin arms and freckles all over his entire face and arms, Mitchell stares up at me from bottle-thick, horned rimmed glasses.

Oh my gawd, *so* utterly adorable. I could eat him up!

"So. What's your name?" he asks.

"Cecelia."

"Cecelia?"

I chuckle. "Yes."

Mitchell nods. "What are you two doing? Talking about what to do tonight?"

I blink at him, suppressing a smile. "How *old* are you, Mitchell?"

"Eleven."

"Well, Mitchell, my conversation with your coach is *kind of* private."

A kid after my own heart, he rolls his eyes. "So he *wasn't* about to ask you out? That's lame." He adjusts his glasses (yet again) and peers up at us, looking just like that character Squints, the nerdy kid from the movie, *The Sandlot*.

You know the one.

Or maybe you don't, in which case, you're *killing* me, Smalls.

I tilt my head and study Mitchell. "You sure seem awfully curious about what your coach has going on."

Undeterred, the kid pushes on with a shrug. "I have three older sisters, so I kind of know what's going down."

Now Matthew is rolling his eyes. "You should probably go wait for Stewart and his mom over by the doors. It's rude for you to make them wait if they're giving you a ride home."

Instead, Mitchell looks me up and down and says, "It's pizza night at my house if you wanna come. My mom's new boyfriend works at Little Caesars."

Unable to stop myself, I ruffle my fingers through his hair and grin down at him. "Awww, that's okay sweetie. I do have plans later, but thank you for asking."

He hefts his bag up onto his bony shoulder. "Can't knock a guy for tryin." In the distance, a beat-up Buick pulls up to the building. "Oh shit, there's Stu's mom. Gotta go." Mitchell takes off on his little pale bird legs, sprinting as fast as a scrawny kid can sprint while dragging a heavy duffle by the strap across the pavement.

"*Lan*guage Mitchell!" Matthew yells after him.

"Sorry Coach!"

Silently, we watch him run off and climb into the back seat of Stewart's mom's car.

"So…big plans tonight, huh?" Matthew asks.

Um, yeah—if you count finding out what happens next between Lady Mary Crawley and Matthew Crawley on season two of *Downton Abbey* as having plans, then yeah, I have plans—*but let's just keep that little tidbit to ourselves, shall we?*

I shuffle my feet and fiddle with the empty coffee cup still clutched between my hands (which I just realized I forgot to toss in the trash) as we stand next to my car. "Er…kind of."

Kind of, but not really. My neck gets hot and I pull at my scarf. I am such a bad liar.

Matthew studies me intently before slowly nodding, stuffing his hands in the pockets of his fleece vest. "Oh, sure. Yeah, okay. That's too bad."

He's rambling.

Crap. Was he going to ask me out?

Maybe if he reacted in his usual way—you know, like a dick who couldn't care less one way or another if we hung out—I wouldn't feel so bad lying about having plans. Instead, he looks disappointed and rather…dejected.

However, my pride won't let me admit I have a date with the couch tonight, so I say, "Well…thanks for inviting me today. The boys are absolutely adorable, especially that little Mitchell. What a character."

"Oh god, don't ever let them hear you calling them adorable, or cute. Boys hate that." He winks at me. "You know, this was the first game they've won all season… Who knows, maybe you're their lucky charm."

"Oh brother. Don't tell me you're superstitious."

"Aren't *all* athletes?"

I look down at his feet. "I don't know, you tell me. How long has it been since you washed your game socks?"

Matthew scratches his head and pretends to think about it. "Hmm, a few years at *least*."

I laugh and clear my throat. "That's what I thought: superstitious."

"I'm just kidding, of course I wash my socks. Now, my *jock* on the other hand…."

Oh lord, he did *not* just make a reference to his jock-strap.

Let me be honest here for a second: I'm a visual person—and by visual I mean….you say a random word I haven't heard in a while and I'm going to promptly conjure up a visual in my head *of* that word.

Or, depending on where I am and how much time I have, I'll even start a daydream.

For example, I hear the word *jock* and immediately think *strap*. The word *jockstrap* immediately makes me think of Matthew skating toward me in the center of an ice rink wearing nothing but his white athletic supporter, and it's tightly hugging his man bits and hard ass.

Bare thighs. Bare chest.

Bare...everything. All over.

Naked.

Speaking of bare, I bet he has just a light dusting of hair on his inner thighs. And okay, in addition to being entirely naked except for his jockstrap, he might also be wearing skates and firmly clutching his stick. His hockey stick, not his...you know, *stick* stick.

Do you see what I mean about my vivid imagination?! Are you getting the picture here? Ugh, I'm terrible.

So, the last thing I need as we stand side by side in a virtually empty parking lot is a visual of his, um, *junk* swirling precariously through my head, making me hot and itchy.

The fact that I haven't had sex in *months*? Yeah, that's totally not helping. I lick my lips, desperately trying not to glance down and check out his denim clad, um...*package*.

Great. That makes like, five or six references to his penis in less then ten seconds. Oops. I just said penis.

Make that seven.

Or eight—shit, I'm losing count.

Swallowing hard, I force my eyes briefly toward the ice arena as an attempt to refocus. *Get your mind out of the gutter, get your mind out of the gutter, get your mind out of the gutter.*

Would someone please slap me!?

I look back at Matthew, and sure enough, he's watching me, eyes wide and inquisitive with a strange expression across his face. "So, on that note...maybe I should get going? Thanks again for coming today. The guys loved it."

He takes a step forward as if he's about to hug me, but

then he halts, stopping himself short with his arms half raised (so awkwardly) before shoving them in the back pockets of his jeans.

Hello, disappointment? I'm Cece! Nice to meet you!

My lonely arms hang lifelessly at my side. Although… oh my god, can you imagine if he *had* hugged me? It's entirely possible I would have not only wrapped my arms around him, but rubbed my body up and down him a bit, because I want to climb him like a tree.

I would wrap myself around that hard, hot body like a pretzel—you know , act like the hussies he's used to. Oh god. Shit. I have no idea what he just said to me.

Oh yeah, that's right—he has to get going.

"I had a good time, too. So…I guess I'll talk to you later?"

"I'll be around." He winks at me again with a rueful chuckle. "Probably just on my couch."

Oh my god, I am such a soul crusher.

"Bye Cecelia."

He gives a sad little wave before turning and walking across the parking lot back to his Tahoe, his confident gait slow but purposeful.

My eyes slide down to his firm ass.

Biting my lip, I rock back on my heels, debating. If I call him back, is that weak? I do not chase boys—*ever*. On the other hand, if I let him walk away, I'm completely denying us both what we want: to spend the rest of the afternoon together. I mean…it's not like he was asking me to marry him, or even asking me on a date.

I don't think…

Well, technically, he didn't really ask me anything—I kind of shot him down before he could even get to that part. Maybe he was just being polite by asking if I had plans later today…right? Right.

Ugh, why is this so hard? Why do girls overthink every damn thing? I hate myself and my gender right now—I hate my hormones!

I let him get halfway to his Tahoe.

"Matthew!" I half shout.

He turns, eyebrows raised in surprise.

"Wait."

Matthew

"Just shut up and put it in." – overheard (and misunderstood) at Galaxy Golf World on the fifth hole

"I swear, I don't know *how* I let you talk me into this," Cecelia grumbles, crouched over a miniature golf putter, eyeballing the hole at the end of the long astroturf course like she's Tiger Woods during a PGA Tour.

"Like you were going to say no to *all this*," I say, confidently showcasing my manly physique with one of my forefingers like a model from *The Price is Right* then propping my leg on a fake boulder before flexing my biceps a la Mr. Universe.

"You're one sick individual, did you know that," she deadpans.

"Just hit the ball would you, and stop complaining."

"I'm only complaining because I *suck* at this. You brought me here because you wanted to show off."

"Hmm, you may have a point there…" I poke her in the thigh with the butt end of my putter. "Take the shot. There's a group coming up behind us."

Cecelia refocuses, closing one eye and chewing on her lower lip, like those two techniques combined are going to get her a hole in one.

Pfft. *As if.*

She gently takes a few practice swings, pulling back on the putter a few times but not connecting with the ball, all the while wiggling her firm ass. Finally, she taps the small purple orb toward the hole.

It rolls forward, gaining momentum on a tiny slope before rounding a corner, ricochets into a manmade stone (as golf balls often do), and continues at a slow crawl toward the cup in the ground.

Slowly.

Slowly…

Cecelia sucks in her breath, grasping her putter to her chest as the ball continues leisurely rolling toward its final destination before catching on the lip and plopping in.

Cecelia jumps up and down like a lunatic and lets out a loud, "Yes!!! *Woooo hoooo!*" She pumps her fists, shouting, "Did you see that?! Did. You. *See*. That?"

"Um, yeah, and everyone can *hear* you, too."

Sheesh.

For several minutes, I stand there with my arms crossed, waiting patiently as Cecelia struts around like a rooster, leaps in the air a few more times like a cheerleader, throws her arms into a V for victory, and continues loudly whooping for a good solid…oh, I don't know, two or three minutes.

She is utterly ridiculous.

And completely fucking *adorable*.

"Wow" is all I can say when she's done.

"*Ugh*, that felt good." She smoothes down her sweater and straightens the scarf around her neck, glancing up at me with a schooled expression. "Okay. Your turn."

"You are nuts."

Cecelia snorts and walks over to pat my arm. "You're only just figuring that out? Poor guy…" As her hand makes contact with my long-sleeved t-shirt, her hand lingers there a bit too long. Not only that, I *swear* she just squeezed my bicep a little—not that I'm complaining.

Now she's staring up at me with innocent eyes and smirking, a look I've seen on my sister's face a *hundred* times when she's trying not to look guilty. You know the look, don't try denying it: huge doe eyes where you force your eyebrows up into your hairline while you give a blank stare?

Yeah, *that* look, because she's guilty.

"Did you just squeeze my muscles?"

"What?! *No*." She looks away, miffed.

"Bullshit, you did too. Admit it."

Cecelia casts a glance up at me, the big silver hoops in her ears swaying as she shakes her head in denial. "Pfft, no way."

"Why can't you admit you were feeling me up?"

"*Oh. My. God.*"

I give her a long, hard look before tapping my putter

on another fake rock. "Okay, fine." I take the red ball out of my pocket, toss it in the air a few times, and catch it before I drop it on the ground. Glancing back at her, I ask, "Wanna make this interesting?"

Cecelia watches me for a few heartbeats, giving me a onceover from top to bottom before taking her putter and holding it horizontally behind her head with both hands. The motion pulls the fabric of her sweater tight across her chest, and my eyes immediately go to her breasts.

"Even *more* interesting? Please, enlighten me."

I clear my throat, trying not to stare. Sorry, but she's got a great rack.

"You know, like a bet."

"*Ah,* a gamblin' man. I like it. Sure, let's do it. "

"I was hoping you'd say that." I dip my head, pushing the hair out of my eyes before tapping the ball toward the hole.

She laughs. "Yeah, I *bet* you were."

Crap. My ball doesn't go in.

Cecelia coughs into her hand while I walk over and tap it again, missing a second time. "Are you sure you want to do this? Seems risky on your part," she says.

Par three.

"Yu*p*," I respond, enunciating my response with a pop. "What kind of a damn fool doesn't bet on a putt-putt game? In fact, I think it's on the rules sign posted back there on the building." I gesture behind us with my thumb, pointing toward the clubhouse. "Rule number six: *Must place bets.* Besides, I'm gonna win no matter what, so…"

Cecelia lets out an unladylike snort. "Didn't you just

get a par four on a par two?"

"Hello, par three. I'm a professional athlete—your lack of confidence offends me." We walk toward the next course. "Your snorting is a real turn-off too, by the way."

She wrinkles up her nose and glares at me. "Well then it's a good thing I wasn't trying to turn you *on*." She steps around me and places her ball on the ground. "Anyway, you're probably just saying that because Molly's always doing it. I think her snorting may have rubbed off on me."

I shrug. "Yeah, maybe, but still."

"Fine. I'll try not to do it anymore."

Blankly, I stare at her.

"What?" she asks, confused.

"That's it? '*Fine, I'll try not to do it anymore*'?"

She stares at me like I'm a moron. "Well, yeah…"

"You're not going to argue with me?"

"Um…"

"Wow. That's kind of awesome."

"Well, duh—*I'm* kind of awesome. Now close that sexy mouth of yours so I can start kicking your ass."

Cecelia

"Okay, this is it. The. Last. Hole." Matthew hovers over his golf putter, tapping the ball back and forth, waggling his eyebrows suggestively at me.

I shake my head and roll my eyes, looking at everything but him, feigning boredom. "Would you please get on with it already?" The game, while not tied, is close (not that anyone is keeping score), and Matthew keeps stalling.

"Cool your jets, little mama. This shit takes time, and *skill*." He lifts his putter and points it to the small windmill covering the last hole. "See that hole there? When I put this little baby in motion"—he takes his red ball and flippantly tosses it to the ground—"it's going to go into *that* tunnel, fall into *that* hole, and light up *that* siren. Got it? Are you paying attention?"

"Uh huh."

"Good, because this shit's important. Now here's where it gets dicey. I bet"—he wiggles his eyebrows at me again"—that *you* can't make the siren go off."

"Pfft. Please."

"No seriously. I bet you can't do it."

I cross my arms defiantly. "Fine. I bet *you* can't do it either."

"Fine. What will you give me if you don't?" His question comes out husky.

What will I give him?

"I'll…" I look around, thinking, and scrunch up my nose.

Immediately, my thoughts get perverted, thinking about all the things I'd *like* to do to him. Suck on his neck, for one. Lick his dimple, for another. Run my hands all over his bare chest—wait, *scratch that*; I'd rather run my *tongue* all over his bare chest.

Oh god.

As he stands there gazing at me, legs spread in a cocky stance, I'm pretty sure my cheeks get beet red, and I resist the urge to run my hands down my face in frustration. I can even feel my neck and chest getting hot.

Great. Now I can't even look at him.

Worse, I know *he* knows what I'm thinking: something sexual. How do I know this? Easy: the cocky grin on his face, dimple on display to torture me even further. "Well?"

"I don't know," I manage to croak out.

Matthew claps his large hands, rubbing them together. "Isn't it a good thing I've given this some serious thought while kicking your hot little behind?"

Now I feel my ears burning. Burying my face in my scarf and biting my cheek to keep from grinning like an idiot, I force out a sarcastic laugh. "Oh, *this* I gotta hear." I lean on my putter.

"I think you're really gonna like it. I'm a genius."

"Yeah, yeah, yeah, spit it out already."

"When I sink this put and light that lantern, I get to plant one on you."

I roll my eyes. "I figured that's what you were going to say."

"Maybe, but there's a catch!"

"Oh geez."

"I get to plant one on you at any time, in any location, and when I do, I'm going to make it a *good* one."

"What the hell does that mean? Plant one on me, any time, any location?"

"Exactly what you think it means: my mouth, all over you. You won't know when or where it's coming, but I promise, you'll like it." He laughs. "Don't you just love the element of surprise? It will be kind of like a lion stalking its prey."

"*Ummm….*" Seriously, *what does a person say to that?*

"Just say yes. The anticipation will be like foreplay."

Oh dear god. "You are *not* getting in my pants."

Matthew simply shrugs. "Maybe not at first."

"Maybe not *ev-er*."

He looks at me. "You don't seriously believe that, do you? *Ugh*, good god you're cute." He walks over and stands in front of me, getting so far in my personal space I can smell his minty breath. Then the bastard lifts his putter between us, lightly brushing it up against my breasts.

On purpose.

My body, of its own accord, shivers.

Dipping his head down and leaning in, Matthew's breath is on my neck, his nose running lightly along my jaw. "Say yes to the bet, Cecelia." I gulp and he inhales next to my ear then gently runs his tongue along my lobe as he whispers, "Mmm, you smell fucking fantastic, like fresh air and sexual repression."

My eyes briefly flutter closed. He is pure evil.

"How will I know it's about to happen?" I manage to croak out.

"Hmmmm." He hums against my ear, the deep baritone of his vocal cords vibrating against my neck. "I guess we'll need a code word, won't we? When I say it, you will obediently stop whatever it is you're doing and pay your penalty."

"You're pretty cocky for someone who hasn't even taken his last shot yet," I say, tipping my neck back a little so I can look into his eyes. His mouth is millimeters from my mine.

"Confident, not cocky."

"Agree to disagree," I retort cheekily. He's tortured me long enough. "You sure you know what you're getting into by entering into this agreement? One kiss on the mouth is all you're going to get."

He laughs. "I'm pretty sure I can handle it, and trust me, one will be enough."

Er, not sure if I should be insulted by that…

In any case, I lean in until my breasts are firmly plastered to his chest. I wiggle around a little bit, rubbing my naturally round boobs up against the front of his thin cotton t-shirt until his pupils dilate and I can feel him harden in his jeans.

Then I go in for the kill. "Okay. If you're *sure…*"

"Oh, I'm sure," he manages to croak out in a whisper.

"Promise?" I wiggle a little bit more.

His Adam's apple bobs and he gulps, nodding. "Yes."

"One kiss? Then you *never* get to kiss me again."

"Yup."

Hmmm, not sure I like how hastily he keeps agreeing, but I brush it off, reminding myself that he's an arrogant asshole. "Well then, in that case"—I move closer still, my mouth suspended so close to his, there is just the barest whisper of air in between us—"since you're *so* sure you can handle it"—I open my mouth the smallest fraction, and, with a light flicker of my tongue, tease the space directly under his mouth, slowly licking him up to the cupids bow above his upper lip—"*yes Matthew*, I'll take the bet."

His mouth gapes opens and his nostrils flare—all the visible signs that he's one hundred percent turned on. "You…y-you *bitch*." He breathes in a stutter, grabbing at me for all he's worth and trying to slant his mouth over mine. "Forget everything I just said. I want that kiss now."

Little word of advice ladies: do not poke the hornet's nest unless you plan on paying the price.

I push on his chest and quickly shove him away. "Forget it buddy," I say, stepping away with a laugh and smacking him on the back like his buddy would. "We have a deal: *one* kiss—but *only* if you make this shot."

He glares at me, adjusting the bulge in his jeans.

I smirk. "Better make it a good one."

Cecelia

"If thought bubbles appeared over my head, I would be so screwed."

"So...he made the shot."

We're sitting around our small, round kitchen table—Molly, Abby, Jenna, and me—surrounded by various junk foods and a random left over veggie platter from Molly's biology study group. I pick at a piece of broccoli, pulling it apart into tiny sections before eating one nibble at a time.

My roommate half laughs at me, and then shakes her head solemnly. "Of course he made the shot—it's like, what he does for a living, practically."

"Well *obviously* I didn't think he would," I mumble.

"That was your first mistake. Total rookie move." Molly digs through the Jelly Belly bowl on the table, picks through them, selects a few bubblegum flavored ones (her favorite), pops one in her mouth, and begins chewing.

Jenna chimes in. "He plays hockey—for Christ's sake, Cece, it's his *job* to get his puck into a small space." She chuckles at her own joke. "Get it—*puck* into a small *space*?"

"Yeah, yeah, we got it. Your sex puns are *sooo* helpful."

"One could even say he's good at *getting it in*," Jenna chuckles.

"Okay, Jenna, we get it," Molly says dryly.

Abby stares at Jenna, affronted. "Don't be disgusting—that's Molly's *brother*. What is *wrong* with you?"

"Nothing's wrong with me, I'm just stating the obvious. Chill." Jenna shoots Abby a condescending look. Watching them, it's pretty darn obvious there is no love lost between these two. The fact is, they will argue about everything.

The last time they were together in a room (which was just last week), they got into a huge disagreement because Jenna wanted to listen to Pandora, and Abby thought we should be listening to iHeartRadio.

Stupid.

Seriously though, I have trouble finding out where all the animosity stems from. I have a sneaking suspicion that at one point Abby had a small crush on Jenna's ex-boyfriend, Alex, and blamed Jenna for breaking his heart during the breakup.

But whatever, back to *my* problem.

Jenna takes a bag of Skinny Pop and rips it open, sending a few loose popped kernels scattering to the floor. She looks over the edge of the table and gives a weak *Oh shit* before stuffing a handful from the bag into her mouth. "Okay"—*crunch*—"so what I want to know is"—*crunch, crunch*—"how the two of you ended up playing miniature golf in the first place. That is so weird."

"Why is that weird?" I ask, rising from the table to grab a bottle of water from the fridge. "Does anyone else want anything while I'm up?" A chorus of no's fill the room before I shut the door on the fridge and return to the table. "We went to play putt-putt because nothing else was open." I laugh. "Scout's honor."

Abby chimes in, "So...I think we're all wondering the same thing...what's the magic word going to be?"

"Like I'm telling you guys that."

Jenna leans in. "Is it something like...*moist*? Or *gurgle*?"

I roll my eyes.

"Jenna, be serious. My brother would never pick a word like that." Molly rests her chin in the palm of her hand and pops another Jelly Belly into her mouth. "He'd pick something like...snozzberries, or...fucktard."

"Um...what the hell are snozzberries?"

"It was only like, one of his favorite words growing up. Since he wasn't allowed to swear, he'd say snozzberries instead." Molly's voice gets high-pitched and nasally as she does an impression of Matthew as a kid. "*Aw Mom, what do you mean I can't have a new hockey stick? Ugh! Snozzberries!*"

We're all laughing now, including Abby, and Molly continues. "If you think he's a moron now, you should have met him ten years ago. '*Mommmm, Molly took my bike out of the garage and didn't put it back. Mommm, Molly is cop-y-ing meeee."*

"Back then he was way douchier," Jenna agrees. Abby shoots her another exasperated look while I take a sip out of my bottled water and Molly digs through the candy bowl. We are quite the motley crew.

For a few seconds, no one says anything.

But then…

"You *do* know taunting him by licking his face was a *terrible* idea. I mean…it's pretty much the worst thing you could have done."

"Thanks Abby."

"Yeah, but guys love that shit," Jenna interjects with a knowing smile. Out of all of us, she's the most experienced.

My best friend continues. "I mean, licking his lips and walking away? That's like poking a sleeping bear—with a sharp object."

"It was in the heat of the moment."

"At a miniature golf course," Jenna deadpans.

My phone, set in the center of the table, buzzes. Crap. Six eyes bore into me, and I fidget in my seat. Jenna, of course, breaks the silence.

"Aren't you going to see who it is?" Her lips are twitching, and I shit you not, her eyes are actually sparkling mischievously.

"Um….no?

Molly snorts. "Oh please, don't lie—you're dying to look at it."

"Matthew hates it when you snort, by the way. He says it's unladylike."

My roommate just stares at me, her mouth slightly agape. "*Matthew says it's unladylike?* My, my, my, getting real cozy, are we?" Her hand snakes across the table, inches from my phone. "If you're not going to see who it is, I will."

"Molly Wakefield, don't you dare!" shouts my bestie, coming to my defense. Naturally, Abby always has my back.

They're right though—I do want to see who it is.

"Go on. Go ahead…" Abby quietly prompts like she's cajoling a kitten out of a tree, pushing my phone closer with her forefinger. Like a crack addict, my nose twitches and my fingers itch to grab it.

The tiny blue light in the top left-hand corner blinks.

It's him. I just know it.

I unlock the screen and go to my messages. There are three.

Mom: *Don't forget to call Grandma tomorrow. It's her bday*

Mom: *Remind Veronica*

Veronica: *Mom wanted me to remind you to call Nana for her birthday. Plz tell her to stop texting me. It's driving me frickin cray cray.*

"Not him," I say, setting my phone back down, deflated. My shoulders even sag a little. "My mom and my sister."

"That sucks."

I text my sister back: *At least Mom's not following*

YOU on "the Twitter". And please stop saying cray cray

Molly sits back in her chair and studies me. Finally, she says, "Don't you worry your pretty little head. Somewhere out there, my big, dumb, lummox of a brother is plotting his seduction—or assault, whatever you wanna call it." She laughs, popping the last pink bubblegum Jelly Belly in her mouth, chewing slowly and grinning like the Cheshire Cat. "Have no doubt about that."

Oh, don't I know it—he is *definitely* out there plotting.

That's exactly what I'm afraid of, and honestly, what I'm most looking forward to.

Matthew

Just for the record, the word is *canoodle*, and I don't know how the hell I'm going to fit it into a sentence, *especially in public*. Cecelia chose it, and I know she did it on purpose knowing I was going to sound like a fucking idiot saying it out loud, in front of actual people.

I sigh.

It seemed like such a good plan at the time.

Matthew

"Sometimes you just have to knock a motherfucker's teeth out." – overheard in the locker room, post-game

I drum my large hand on the counter in the locker room as I impatiently wait for the boys to finish showering after practice. Out of boredom, I poke my cell with my forefinger so it spins in a circle, round and round it goes, shiny and white on the smooth wooden countertop.

"Don't you have something better to be doing?" Weston asks, coming from around the corner.

"Nope."

"Gee, what a surprise."

"Ha ha, very funny."

"Actually, I *am* surprised. You don't have any tail lined up on a Friday night? Shouldn't you be out pounding a random hoochie into some dirty mattress?"

I shoot him a grimace. "Wow Wes, when you put it that

way, you really make the idea sound *soooo* appealing."

Weston laughs and sets a hockey stick on the counter, examining it carefully for nicks before ripping open a new package of black grip tape.

I nod my head toward the stick. "Who's woody?"

"Ryan's. His mom can't afford to buy him a new one, or new tape." Wes tears a piece of black hockey tape off the roll with his teeth and begins wrapping the handle of the kid's beat-up stick.

"Why isn't he doing this himself?"

"Don't know. Maybe he's embarrassed, maybe he doesn't know how. Anyway, who cares?"

"I do. He should learn to take care of his equipment."

Weston stops for a brief second and glances up at me, a peeved expression across his brow. "Fine. When he comes out here you can tell him yourself, since obviously you're going to be a dick about it. Then *you* can show him how to wrap the blade."

"I'm not being a dick. All I'm saying is, Ryan should learn that depending on how you wrap it, it can feel totally different when you grip it."

Weston stops wrapping and looks up again with both eyebrows raised, the shadow of a black eye still darkening the recesses next to his nose. "I'm not *even* going to comment on that."

"Huh?"

"That sounded *really* lewd and perverted."

"You think that sounded *lewd*? Do you even know what that word means?"

"You forgot perverted. I said you sounded lewd *and*

perverted."

"Jesus Christ, what does my sister even see in you?"

"No, seriously. How about when Ryan comes out here, you explain to him how to hold and wrap his own wood so it feels good when he grips it." As he's saying it, Weston is rocking his hips back and forth, thrusting against the counter.

"Dude, *shut the fuck up*." But it's too late: the douche-bag is laughing and shaking his head as he continues to carefully wrap Ryan's inexpensive Walmart-brand hockey stick like it's a Bauer Vapor APX, completely undeterred. Whatever.

It's annoying the shit out of me that he isn't seeing my point, but is instead making a mockery out of it. Frustrated, I hiss out through gritted teeth, "These kids need to learn responsibility."

In response, Weston tears another long strip off the grip tape roll and continues quickly winding it around the handle of the stick. He spits out a sliver that stuck to his tongue before saying, "I'm not a fucking idiot—I know exactly what you meant, and I respect that, I do, but these kids take forever to do this shit, and I'd rather wrap this myself so I can get the hell out of here. I plan on getting laid tonight. Unlike you, I have a date waiting, so…sorry dude."

He wants to hurry so he can get *laid*? In other words, so he can bang *my* sister. How do I respond to that?

"You're pushing your luck, man."

"Dude, I can't help it if my girlfriend is horny as fuck and likes sex, okay?"

"Jesus Christ, McGrath. What the hell did I tell you

about TMI?"

"Can't help you with that. At some point you're going to have to get over it, bro."

Then, coming from seemingly out of nowhere, a pubescent voice behind us asks, "Hey Coach, what does horny mean?"

Slowly, and with dread—as if facing a guillotine—Weston and I both turn.

Weston clears his throat. "Um, gee... Hey Mitchell. Done with your shower so, um, *soon*?" He's embarrassed and red-faced—serves him right.

"Yes." Mitchell Decker squints at us, his tiny, beady brown eyes magnified by his thick glasses and boring into us both. "What does it mean?"

I fold my arms across my chest and glare at Weston, asking sarcastically, "*Yeah* Coach McGrath, what *does* it mean?"

Weston fidgets. "It means girls who, uh...like to, uh... kiss. You probably shouldn't repeat that word though because girls don't like it."

"But your girlfriend likes it though?"

"Kissing? *Oh yeah* she does." His voice is dripping with innuendo.

"Weston," I warn.

"Why are you getting all mad at Coach McGrath? Are you sore because you don't have a girlfriend and all the guys think you're gay?"

"No Mitchell," I grind out. "I'm mad because Coach is kissing my sister and he won't clam up about it."

Mitchell's eyes get as wide as saucers, and he looks

horrified. "*Ewww, you're kissing his sister?* If one of these guys was dating one of my sisters, I'd probably punch him in the face."

I pat Mitchell—my new favorite player—on the back. "You're a good man, Mitchell Decker. I *knew* there was something about you that I liked…"

Cecelia

It isn't long after I've changed into my favorite pajamas and parked my ass on the sofa before my phone chimes.

Grabbing my cell and a bag of Skinny Pop, my thumb unlocks the screen at the same time my other hand digs into the popcorn bag for a handful.

I shove it in my mouth, chewing, and tap open my new messages.

Matthew: *What's up.*

I look down at my pajamas and sock-covered feet, wincing.

Me: *You know. The usual Friday night stuff.*

Even I roll my eyes at that, and I shove another fistful of popcorn into my mouth. Shit this stuff is addicting.

Matthew: *Are you lying?*

Well this is awkward.

Not sure which approach to take—do I lie, or tell the truth?—I hesitate briefly before replying: *Yes. I'm lying. Why?*

Matthew: *So you must be doing the same thing I'm doing, which is nothing.*

Me: *Pret-ty much.*

Matthew: *So, wanna do nothing together?*

I shit you not, I stare at my phone like it's about to combust into a million little pieces and I'm not sure what to do with it. There might even be an appalled look on my face.

Do I want to hang out with him? Yes.

On the other hand…hell-to-the-*no*.

For several reasons (and obviously I'm about to list them for you):

1. I look like crap, and if there's *one* thing I don't want, it's him seeing me in this state of appearance *yet again*. Granted, he did see me looking amazing on my date, but only after seeing me other times looking…*not* so amazing.

2. Now that I have them on, these pajamas are pretty damn comfortable.

3. No good will come of this. I mean, we just can't seem to behave ourselves when we're together, can we?

4. Seeing him will make me like him even more.

Me: *I'm not sure that's such a good idea…*

Matthew: *Why not? You're home, I'm home, it's Friday night.*

Me: *True…*

Then I add*: I'm comfy and don't want to get dressed…*

Matthew: *What are you wearing?*

Me, glancing down at my pajamas: *Old yoga pants, a giant sweatshirt, fuzzy socks…mud mask*

Matthew: *Wow. You sure know how to turn a guy off.*

Me: *(Shrug) Honesty is the best policy???*

Matthew: *Er, not always. A mud mask? Seriously?*

Me: *How do you think I get my skin to look so dewy? Mother Nature? (SNORT)*

Matthew: *I cannot believe you just snorted via text.*

Me: *Well, it wouldn't be the first time...*

Matthew: *YOU DON'T SAY!!!?*

Me: *Wow. I'm sensing some sarcasm...*

Matthew: *Well that's good, because I was laying it on pretty thick*

Me: *I shrug and snort IRL, so why not in a text message? Just keeping it real.*

Matthew: *...I will never understand females...*

Me: *(Crickets)*

Matthew: *STOP DOING THAT!*

Me: *(Shrug) Stop doing what?*

Matthew: *Putting shit in parentheses like we're having an actual conversation!!!*

Me: *Hmmmmm (scratches chin). Why do you think this bothers you so much?*

Matthew: *What are you, a psych major?*

Me: *First of all, I'm working on my master's. Quit confusing me for an undergrad—I already HAVE a degree in economics, smartass.*

Matthew: *Sorry. I get confused because you live with my KID sister...*

Me: *I guess that's understandable.*

Me: *But...she hardly ACTS like a kid...IF you catch my drift (wink wink)*

Matthew: *You did NOT just do that*

Me: *I'm not sure what you're getting at?????*

Matthew: *"If you catch my drift" – then WINK*

Me: *LOL*

Matthew: *That's something a dude would say. Are you sure you don't have any brothers?*

Me: *Hold on, let me check (looks behind living room couch) Nope. No brothers.*

Matthew: *And you call ME a smartass?*

I'm so tempted to respond with *At least it's a nice, firm one*, but I don't. Instead, I giggle to myself and type: *So, switching gears: Halloween is coming up...*

Matthew: *Ahh, yes. Every skank's favorite holiday. Not sure what the plans are. I'm getting kind of old to be out on State Street, you know...?*

Me: *Yeah, me too. Not into it, never really was. Second year in a row we're going to my friend's house party— much much classier than State Street.*

Matthew: *Who's 'we'?*

Me: *Some of my sorority sisters – another alum owns the house. Beautiful, on Lake Michigan. She's married with a baby, but they've been doing this bash every year.*

Me: *Molly, Weston, Jenna, Abby, and whoever else Wes invites. Some people go in disguise, like a masquerade.*

Matthew: *So, what were you last year? (Please say naughty referee)*

Me: *Um, can you seriously picture me as a naughty*

anything?

Matthew: *Why are you even asking such an absurd question? Of course I can – it's my job as a guy to picture you naked.*

Me: *Well, if you haven't noticed, I'm pretty conservative, so...*

Matthew: *Ok. So what were you? (Please don't say Harry Potter)*

Me: *LOL. No. God no. I was Lara Croft, Tomb Raider.*

Matthew: *Um, that sounds sexier than a naughty referee... I'm going to close my eyes and picture that for a second.*

Me: *STOP IT! LOL. Here's a pic*

I scroll through the gallery of images on my cell phone, find a photo of myself from last year's Halloween party, and attach it. My costume was pretty simple really: tight black tank top, hair in a long side braid, tight brown safari shorts with gun holster garter belts. I looked ready to kick someone's ass, Angelina Jolie style.

Matthew: *Ummmmm. Holy shit. That. Is. Hot.*

Me: *Yup. Hot. That's me (rolling my eyes). You like the gun holsters, huh?*

Matthew: *They pretty much do it for me, yes.*

Uncomfortable with the sexual undertones, I change the subject.

Me: *So what were you last year?*

Matthew: *Something dumb. A group of us went as army men. You know, the plastic toy kind we played with as kids. Huge pain in the ass cause we had these stupid boards strapped on our feet to make us look like toys. It was my friend Scott's girlfriend's dumb idea, which was better than his dumb idea to go as the gang from Scooby Doo.*

Me: *Army men doesn't sound that lame...a pain in the ass maybe, but not lame.*

Matthew: *If you say so...*

Matthew: *So, this classy party isn't a masquerade or anything, is it? (That means you're in a disguise right?)*

Me: *Like, do we have to wear a mask? No. I mean, you can if you WANT to. LOL. It's not like you can't figure out who anyone is, unless you're a complete moron, of course.*

Matthew: *Sounds fun.*

Me: *Yup. Should be interesting.*

Matthew: *Sounds like a good place for a little...you know. Canoodling.*

Me: *DON'T YOU DARE*

Matthew: *No worries, Cecelia.*

Matthew: *You're coming to Sunday dinner this week, right?*

Me: *Um...not willingly.*

Matthew: *You've really got to stop letting Molly manipulate you.*

Me: *POT TO KETTLE*

Matthew: *Actually, family dinner sounds like a good place too, right after you pass me the mashed potatoes...*

Me: *You wouldn't...*

Matthew: *Who knows - maybe you'll want a second helping.*

Me: *I hate you.*

Matthew

"Cherish the time spent at dinner with your family as a reminder of why you moved far, far away from them." – Cecelia Carter

I fix the collar on my polo shirt in my parents' powder room, unbuttoning the top button before giving myself yet another onceover.

Too much chest hair, or not enough?

Hmm. I can't decide.

I mean, it's dinner at my folks' place. If I have my pecs hanging out, Mom and Dad are seriously going to wonder what my problem is, and will probably call me out in front of everyone at the table. On the other hand, I kind of want to drive Cecelia a little bit crazy. After all, I have seen her covertly checking me out a few times and know she's totally into my body.

Even though she won't admit it.

I fiddle with the button a few more times then decide to

leave it. A little skin never hurt anyone.

I wash my hands one more time (eyeing myself in the oval mirror the entire time), dry them on the navy blue towel hanging next to the sink, and smooth a few stray hairs on my head.

Shit. I can't stop primping.

"Matthew honey, I thought you were going to come set the table," my mom's voice carries from the kitchen.

"Just taking a leak, Ma," I call back with a smug grin on my face.

Which immediately gets wiped off when she suddenly appears in the doorway two seconds later, arms crossed and wooden spoon clutched in one hand.

She looks pissed.

Amused, I grin before ducking out around her. "Sorry."

My mom follows me back into the kitchen, sighing. "Can you lose the smart-aleck routine for five whole minutes? And don't forget to set an extra plate for Molly's roommate," she reminds me, picking up a glass pitcher of water and handing it to me. "Take this into the dining room, please."

She's not done lecturing me yet—her voice follows me into the formal dining room as I place the water on the table and start taking place settings out of the sideboard. "Speaking of Molly's roommate, can you be nice tonight and leave the poor girl alone?"

I roll my eyes at the ceiling and mutter to myself, "Poor girl? Hardly."

My mom continues, "She is a *guest* in this house, and Molly's roommate, not one of those icky girls that hangs out at the rink. I expect you to be a gentleman."

Icky girls? Well shit, that's a new one.

"Hey, do you know if Weston is coming?"

"I don't think so? Maybe, but I doubt it. Molly said something about a press conference tonight."

I remember those days of working my ass off every damn day of the week as a college athlete for the Wisconsin Badgers. Not only did I play several games per week during hockey season, the team practiced for hours each day in between, often doing press conferences and junkets just like the pros—*without* the benefit of pay (unless you counted full-ride academic scholarships).

In fact, more than a few of my teammates had agents. Those were the players trying to get drafted before graduation.

However, like myself at his age, Weston has no intention of going pro until he's done with graduation. His degree is his priority, and despite our differences (i.e. him banging my little sister), I respect him for that. Mindlessly, I set the table as my mom flits in and out of the dining room and kitchen, placing dishes on the long mahogany table.

I notice there are indeed mashed potatoes and smirk.

Cecelia

"Are you *sure* you know what you're getting yourself into?" Molly asks as she steers her Jeep into the turn-around at her parents' house, putting the Jeep in park and turning to face me. "Because my brother is going to act like a twelve-year-old having you in the house."

Matthew's Tahoe is parked under the basketball hoop, and the sight of it makes me shiver.

"I'm sure."

With a wide mischievous smile, Molly reaches for the door handle. "Alrighty. Then let's do this."

***

She's right. Matthew is acting like a twelve-year-old.

I'm seated next to Molly and across from Matthew, and the small Wakefield clan is gathered around the large oval table as steaming plates are passed all around.

"Cecelia, I noticed you haven't tried my mom's mashed potatoes." Matthew's statement comes from across the table where he's seated. I look up and suppress an eye roll as he blankly stares at me.

Oh, okay. I get what he's doing.

"Matthew! Don't be rude. Cece, you do *not* have to take any potatoes. Please excuse my son." Mrs. Wakefield's face is bright red.

"Yes, Cece, please excuse my brother. He's never had the best manners." Molly rolls her eyes before reaching for the water pitcher and refilling her glass. "Mom, remember when he used to beg to eat under the table when we'd go out to dinner? What was he, nine?"

Mr. Wakefield chuckles, buttering a dinner roll. "I remember. He kept sliding down in his seat, thinking we wouldn't notice he was inching farther under the table. Little bugger."

"He was *nine*?" I ask incredulously, fork suspended over the ham on my plate.

From Matthew, "*Please stop.*"

"Yeah. And he wasn't a *little* bugger. He was like Baby Huey—nine years old and at least five foot five. I was six, and even I knew better than to eat under the table." Molly looks at her brother with a raised brow. "I mean, what were you *doing* under there, anyway?"

Before he can respond, their mom cuts in. "He wanted to play Transformers." Mrs. Wakefield grins at me as she forks a piece of ham. "He was obsessed with those tiny little dolls."

"*They were not dolls,*" Matthew says, clenching his pearly white teeth and hissing through them. "They were *action* figures."

"See? Obsessed." Molly laughs into her glass, blowing a few bubbles as she takes a sip of water. "You probably still have them, don't you?"

"Shut up, Molly."

She laughs again and slaps her hand down on the table, causing the silverware to rattle. "Ha! I *knew* it. Hey, what was that one doll you slept with? Optimus Slime?"

Matthew is quiet for a few brooding seconds, debating his options as his sister goads him. I can practically see the steam rising from his ears.

His nostrils flare. "*Prime.* His name is Optimus *Prime.*"

"Right." Molly shrugs flippantly. "Remember that time you tried throwing your Warpath doll over the house but it landed on the roof instead?"

"It's not a doll. It's an action figure."

"Whatever." Molly dismisses him with a wave of her hand then scratches her chin as if deep in thought. "Come to think of it, wasn't the Warpath character a vain, loud-mouth showoff? Hmm, kind of sounds like someone else I know."

I look at her, surprised. "How on earth do you remember that?"

"Because, oh my *gawd*, he *never* shut up about it."

"All right kids, that's enough," Mr. Wakefield interjects, clearing his throat and setting down his fork. "Surely we can discuss something our *guest* might enjoy."

He shoots a pointed look at both his children, glancing at me briefly with a wink, his eyes crinkling at the corner and looking just like his son. I notice that, like Molly and Weston, Mr. Wakefield also has a small smattering of freckles across the bridge of his nose and friendly green eyes.

"Maybe I'll take some of those mashed potatoes now," I joke uncomfortably, reaching for the large, steaming bowl of mashers.

"Brown-noser," Molly whispers next to me, jabbing me with her elbow and almost causing me to lose the heaping spoonful of spuds I'm scooping onto my plate.

"Knock it off," I hiss, elbowing her back.

Mrs. Wakefield interrupts our bantering. "So, Cece, Molly says you're almost done with your master's. When do you graduate?"

"I'm actually done this December."

"Business?"

"Yes. I have a real interest in economics as well, which is what my bachelor's is in, so I'm actually looking for an analyst position."

"That's fantastic. So you're moving on then?"

I nod. "Yup. As soon as I find a more professional position, I'll start apartment hunting." I make a frown face at Molly, who lays her head on my shoulder in a mock pout. I put my arm around her, patting her face with my hand. "I know someone who's going to miss me."

Suddenly, Molly's head shoots up and she looks across the table at her brother, who's sitting directly across from me. "*Umm*…dude, did you just run your foot up my leg under the table?"

For a brief moment, Matthew has the decency to look affronted—but then that guilt turns to disbelief. "*What? Why the hell would I run my foot up your leg?*" He hangs his head over his plate, shoveling the food in.

Mr. and Mrs. Wakefield exchange glances.

"No, you were *def*initely playing footsies with me under the table." Molly quickly scoots her chair back a few inches and sticks her head under the table. "I knew it! Why the hell is your shoe off?"

Matthew

Instead of responding, I jam a giant hunk of steak into my mouth, chewing slowly. I also don't blink or bat an eye as Molly stares me down from her side of the table, which is really hard to do with a mouth full of food.

Momentarily, I forget anyone else is at the table, and through narrowed eyes, shoot my most haunting death glare at my loudmouth sister. If she'd shut her big, fat, loud mouth, no one would know I was trying to play footsies with her friend in the first place.

"Matthew, please leave your sister alone. You're twenty-three years old for Pete's sake," my mom lectures. From the slight curve of her lips, I know she is onto me, too.

Molly crosses her arms and studies me. She's quiet for a few minutes, but then says, "Hey Mom, did you know Cece went out on a date with *Neve* last weekend? You should ask her how that turned out."

I could seriously take her out to the backyard and choke her.

My mom sets down her napkin. "Oh really! I didn't know that! How exciting! He's such a handsome young man," my mom gushes. It's nauseating. "Where did he take you?"

I bite the inside of my cheek to prevent myself from clenching my jaw—a dead giveaway to my family that I'm getting pissed. I try forking up a mouthful of mashed potatoes and forcing them into my mouth, which still has meat in it, making swallowing nearly impossible.

"We went to this little French place called Le Petit... Le Petit... Oh, shoot, I can't remember."

Un Petit Goût.

It was Un Petit Goût, which means *a tiny taste*.

Cecelia looks up at me questioningly, as if waiting for me to jump in and fill in her blank, but I don't. I can't just jump in and supply the words for her and incriminate myself in the process, especially since my mom already warned me about leaving Cecelia alone. So instead, I remain silent and shove yet another forkful of food into my mouth.

The potatoes taste dry, like I'm trying to swallow down sandpaper, so I take a chug of water, too. At the rate I'm going, I'll have gorged myself into a coma by the end of dinner.

"Well, it sounds lovely just the same," my mom says. She leans in toward Cecelia, conspiratorily. "So, do you think he'll ask you out again?"

"*Umm*....somehow, I doubt it."

Molly snorts.

Cecelia catches my eye and we grin at each other. I know we're both thinking the same thing: that I can't stand how Molly is always snorting, and how unladylike I think it is.

We *must* be grinning at each other stupidly because a shoe kicks my shin and Molly is shooting me a *knock-it-off* look.

Point taken.

"Well, it's *his* loss," my mom continues. "Anyone would be a fool to let you get away."

Cecelia

"To be fair, if you didn't want stale potato chips and orange juice, then you shouldn't have said '*Whatever*' when I asked what you'd like for dinner." – Matthew's old college roommate, Smitty

I try not to squirm in my seat—really, I do—but it's damn near impossible.

Between constantly getting kicked under the table or elbowed in the ribs by Molly (which is sure to leave some nice bruising), I also have to avoid:

1. The heated looks Matthew is sending me from across the table as he continues shoving food into his mouth *just* to avoid confrontations from his family (what a chickenshit).

2. The confused glances their poor parents keep giving each other because they clearly have no clue what the hell the three of us have going on.

In a way, it's almost like some fucked-up love triangle—minus the love, minus the triangle—and I'm most definitely in the center of it.

I zone out for a second, but then I hear Mrs. Wakefield saying, "Well, it's *his* loss. Anyone would be a fool to let *you* get away."

I shoot another covert look at Matthew—who is downing a glass of water and probably pretending it's something stronger like vodka or a Jagerbomb—and get another small poke in the ribs from my roommate. Clearly, she is enjoying all of this.

The playful banter among Molly, Matthew, and their parents progresses as the night goes on until we're all helping clear the table and bringing everything into the kitchen. Dishes get loaded into the dishwasher, the tablecloth comes off, glasses get washed by hand in the sink, and leftovers get distributed among us kids in plastic containers.

Molly and I are standing at the kitchen sink—her washing drinking glasses, me drying them—when Matthew walks in, letting out a loud sigh.

Without even looking over at him, Molly emits a loud sigh of her own. "What," she deadpans. It's not a question, and it's not a statement.

"Why haven't I been invited to this Halloween party you're going to?"

Molly removes her hands from the soapy sink water and places them on the edge of the sink, turning her body toward me, a disgusted look on her face. "*Seriously?*"

I shrug. "What? He asked what I was doing for Halloween…then one thing led to another…"

"Can't I have *one* night free from this Neanderthal? You *had* to bring up the party? Ugh, I could smack you right now."

Like she hadn't been doing that all night already?

"Jeez, chill. I didn't know it was a *secret*. I thought *ev-eryone* was going. Besides, *I* invited *you*, so you have no room to complain."

Molly slaps a frustrated hand against the counter, caus-ing a small spray of soapy water to cascade and hit the window above the sink. "*Ugh*. Ever since the two of you started emailing each other or *whatever it is you're do-ing*, he's been nothing but a pain in my ass, I swear." As I contemplate strangling her, she goes on. "Cece, you have *got* to quit inviting people. I mean, atop. You keep inviting literally *everyone* under the sun and Amber is going to be pissed." She shoots me a pointed look that says *don't argue with me*.

I give Molly a deranged look because clearly she's lost her damn mind, and Matthew clears his throat. "Hi. I'm still standing right here."

We both ignore him. "I didn't *invite* him, Molly. I just *men*tioned it. Calm down."

"Yeah, so this isn't awkward," Matthew mutters.

"Shut it, Matt." This from Molly.

"You know what your problem is Cece? You're *wayyy* too nice, a freaking bleeding heart."

Matthew snorts (the hypocrite) as Molly grabs a towel to dry her hands, turning to face her brother with a sac-charine sweet smile planted on her face. "Ok. Fine. Matty, would you like to come to a grown-up Halloween party? It's probably much classier than what you're used to, not really your usual scene."

Matthew palms his chin. "Hmm, as tempting as that invitation sounds, I'll have to think about it. Can you text me the details?"

Molly's mouth falls open. "Oh my gawd, I'm going to *kill* you…"

In response, he grabs an orange off the counter and saunters out of the room while chuckling.

Molly turns to me, a shit-eating grin plastered on her face, whispering, "There, happy now? I just did all your dirty work for you. Your little man-crush is coming to the party. Please, hold the applause."

Now it's my mouth that falls open. "*What the hell!?* Were you trying to give me a damn heart attack? I seriously thought you were pissed!"

"Would you keep your voice down? He's probably listening through the heating vent for crying out loud."

"Sorry," I apologize in a staged whisper. "It felt like you were throwing me under the bus."

"Au contraire! I was doing you a favor. *Cece*, you need to make him start working for it a little. Sheesh, my brother always gets whatever he wants—it's so annoying." Then, as she opens a cabinet and grabs a clean wash cloth, she lets out a soft giggle. "Oh my god, did you see the look on his face while we were arguing? Like a sad, confused puppy dog. He *sooo* wants to come to that party."

"How do you know?"

In typical Molly fashion, she snorts. "Puh-*lease*. He couldn't have *been* more obvious. I mean, *hellooo*. He literally came right out and asked to be invited."

"Yeah, I guess…"

"No, not '*I guess.*' Cece, the guy was trying to play footsies with you under the damn table and ended up rubbing my leg instead."

196 | SARA NEY

"Can we *please* not talk about that?"

"He looked like he was going to crap his pants when I called him out on it." We resume washing glasses and silverware, and then Molly glances at me sideways and quietly says, "He needs to just freaking ask you out already. This cat and mouse game is getting ridiculous."

"Yeah but I don't think he really li—"

She shushes me with a loud, obnoxious *Shhh!* "Don't you *dare* start in with that 'I don't think he likes me' self-deprecating crap. It's nauseating."

"Um…you seem angry. I think you've been hanging around Weston a bit too much. You look like you want to body check me."

She ignores me and barrels on. "So now we have our work cut out for us to decide what costume you're going to wear to this party, and we only have a few weeks to do it…"

Oh. Crap.

***

Matthew: *Do you know how much self-control I exercised tonight by not claiming my prize and using the code word? Just sayin*

Me: *I was wondering if you would, but then again, it wouldn't have been much of a surprise.*

Matthew: *True. I am kind of going for shock value.*

Me: *Great. Just great…*

Matthew: *The look on my mom's face would have been*

priceless, tho.

Me: *Yeah. Even more so if I hauled off and slapped you when you tried to kiss me. LOLz*

Matthew: *You wouldn't dare. That wasn't part of the deal*

Me: *The deal was that you got to 'plant one' on me, not that I would LET you... Compliance was NOT part of the discussion.*

Cecelia

"We're all gonna have so much fucking fun, we're going to need plastic surgery to remove our god-damn smiles." – Clark Griswold

There are really no words to describe the parties my friend Amber and her husband Lincoln throw each year—you really *must* see it to believe it—but I'm going to give it my best shot anyway.

At the tender ages of twenty-four and twenty-eight respectively, Amber and Lincoln (a trustfund baby of *epic* proportions) live on a little slice of heaven called Lake Geneva in a house that has been in his family for *generations* (see: trustfund baby), and which Lincoln inherited from his grandfather on his twenty-fifth birthday.

(And really quickly, before I go any further...with a name like *Lincoln*, was it really necessary for me to tell you he comes from money? Yeah, didn't think so.)

Nestled back from the main road and only accessible down a long, winding driveway, the estate sits on several acres of premium lake frontage—a prime location for their third annual Halloween bash.

Invite only and celebrated under a black tent (one normally intended for wedding receptions)—Amber really knows how to throw one hell of a party—this spectacle is like nothing I have ever personally seen (and I've seen some crazy shit).

Under the canopy, in the center of the dance floor, a large, manmade constructed tree stands, seemingly holding up the entire tent. It's lifeless, leafless branches are wrapped in low glowing LED lights, emitting just enough light to be functional.

On both sides of this giant tree, two monstrous black chandeliers hang, their prisms and crystals adding a sophistication to the event, while a large Dracula ice sculpture at the head bar lends an air of fun.

The dance floor is, of course, hardwood, and not one, but *two* DJs are set up on a makeshift stage; their up-tempo music already has the crowd dancing.

A total of four fully stocked bars flank each corner of the tent.

No one is leaving here sober—not on *purpose*, anyway.

Nervously, I run my hand down the smooth corset of my costume, careful not to snag the delicate satin fabric. For weeks I asked myself: what does someone as modest as me wear to a Halloween party? Actually, let me be more specific: what does someone as modest as me wear to a Halloween party when they're trying to impress a guy but *not* wanting to look like they're trying too hard?

Or like a hooker.

Because if I had let my friends have input, I would be

one of the following for Amber's party:

1. Slutty goalie or hockey player
2. Naughty nurse or accountant
3. Trampy waitress or barista
4. Slutty, naughty, trampy (insert word here)

Are you sensing a pattern?

Trust me. I searched high and low for a costume, and even tried coming up with one of my own creation without the help of my Halloween hooker-wannabe friends—you know, the friends that are determined to truss me up like a Thanksgiving turkey and parade me around in front of Matthew like a lamb being led to slaughter.

I mean, what is it about this particular holiday that turns perfectly respectable (and smart) girls into pseudo-sleazeballs?

I *sooo* did not want my boobs hanging out all night.

But, *when in Rome…*

Matthew

My friends and I stand at the entrance of the black reception tent, gawking at the sight before us. At least one hundred and fifty people in costume are mingling around, drinks in hand, many of them swaying or dancing to the music pumping from the speakers placed strategically throughout the canopy.

"Holy. Shit," Neve says beside me, bumping our friend Kevin in the ribs and pointing out some chick dressed like a black widow spider with her tits spilling out of her top—

although I know he's not just in awe of the woman in her costume, but of the sight before us.

It's definitely sensory overload.

"Dude, there are so many fucking people here—how were you planning on finding McGrath and your sister?"

I hold up my cell and wave it in the air. "Molly texted me, dipshit. Says they're standing by one of the bars." I hold the phone at eye level and read the screen out loud. "Walk in tent, turn left. Bar on the far side by wall."

"How come we nevah been to this pahty before?" our friend Bernie, who's dressed like a gynecologist, asks from behind me. "It's wicked awesome."

Bernie is from Boston and says shit like *wicked* and *awesome* and *bubbla* (instead of drinking fountain).

"Because this is a friend of Molly's roommate."

"Right, right…the chick you've got a hahd-on for."

"Shut up Bernard and put your goddamn mask back on."

"Whoops, sorry. I forgot."

Together there are five of us, including friends of mine both from college and the coaching staff with the Badgers, and we're all dressed like some kind of surgeon or doctor (mostly because they're idiots). Bernie, for example, is dressed like a gynecologist, as I mentioned, and Neve is a fertility specialist. Then there's Kevin, wearing scrubs and a sign around his neck advertising free mammograms.

Erik's nametag proclaims him Dr. Long Dong, M.D.

As we walk through the throng of people, we see zombies, fairies, villains, virgins, and every costume of every possible variety—slutty, gory, demonic, and sweet. Some faux Hooters waitresses stand in a cluster near the dance floor not far from us, twerking and flirting with a collection of football players, while nearby, some dude dressed like Dog the Bounty Hunter does body shots off the stomach of a chick decked out in an *I Dream of Genie* costume.

Wading through the crowd is not fun, but relatively easy enough. There *are* a lot of people, but it's not packed like it would be if we'd gone downtown to the bars on State Street. There are maybe a hundred fifty or so guests in this giant tent (which looks awesome, by the way), and thank god, too, because if we were at the bars, I'd be smashing and jostling into people every two feet—or worse, getting drinks spilled on me.

In a way, this party feels like I imagine a Halloween party at the Playboy Mansion would: part classy, part skanky.

In other words, the *perfect* combination.

"One Less Problem" by Ariana Grande comes blasting through the speakers above, and as we shoulder our way through the crowd, the low saxophone backbeat of the music, and whispery *I got one less, one less prob-lem* chorus suddenly has random girls dancing up on us, grinding their asses on my legs like dogs in heat.

Normally I might be down with that, but not tonight. Tonight I am on a mission, not only to find my sister, but to find her roommate.

I have plans for *her*.

Twenty minutes later, after aimlessly wandering through the increasingly dense crowd, we still have not caught sight of Molly, Weston, or their friends. As Snow White awkwardly humps my thigh to the beat of Iggy Azalea, Bernie is behind me shouting, *"This is the best party ever!"* With his Boston accent, it sounds like he's actually yelling, *"This is the best pahhtee evahhhh."* Yeah. He pretty much resembles a teenager who recently got let out of the house for the first time.

I continue scanning the crowd so intently I don't notice anyone step directly in front of me until I find myself colliding into a warm body—a warm body solid enough to cause my beer to freaking spill down the front of my pant leg with a splash and collect in a small puddle under my combat boots.

Just as I'm about to bark out a curse, I glance up from my soaking pant leg with a sneer on my face and almost shit myself—I'm standing in front of Cecelia, and she looks fucking incredible.

It takes me a few seconds to recognize her; she's wearing more makeup than usual, and of course, she's in a costume—a fucking *mermaid* costume.

As I wonder where the hell the outfit came from, I slowly take her in from head to toe. She isn't wearing a wig, but rather, Cecelia's dark brunette hair is curled in lose spirals down her back and around her face. A coronet of pearls circles the crown of her head (don't ask me how I know it's called a coronet), and she has some smaller seed pearls snaking up her lean arms.

Then, being male, my eyes immediately go to her chest.

Her breasts are being pushed together by the nude corset she's wearing, and they're practically spilling over the top. Tiny sea shells and rhinestones are attached to the trim of the corset, and a small starfish rests in the center.

Instead of a mermaid tail, Cecelia is wearing metallic

aqua hot pants. You know the kind of capri legging things Sandra Dee wears at the end of Grease? Those are hot pants, and they look fucking awesome on Cecelia.

With stacked aqua blue stiletto heels on her feet, it's one hell of a mermaid costume—certainly the sexiest goddamn one *I* have ever seen.

Judging by the shocked look on her face, it's obvious she hadn't seen me coming either. Her eyes, rimmed with dark green eyeliner, are wide and expressive. Nude-colored glitter shimmers, highlighting her cheekbones, her collarbone, and her deep cleavage.

Swear to god, it's the most gorgeous cleavage I've seen in my twenty-three years.

"Matthew," she whispers as if she's out of breath. "Hi."

"Hey sexy lady," Kevin interrupts from behind me before I can respond. "You look like quite a tasty *catch*." He chuckles at his own joke while Neve shoulders his way through. "Get it? Mermaid, fish? Catch?"

"Wow Cecelia, you look….amazing, but what else is new." He leans over and greets her with a quick hug.

She looks at me, then glances at my friends, taking in their costumes one by one, and then she looks at me again. "So, lady doctors, eh?" She crosses her arms and props her leg out as she studies us curiously.

I seriously wish she wouldn't, because her boobs look ready to pop out of her top.

I scowl.

"Yup, and my office is open if you need an exam." Bernie laughs and gives his rubber glove a snap.

Never one to be left out in a group setting, Kevin steps

forward to display his sign. "It looks like you could use a hand with those plump mammories of yours. Free of charge," he says with lecherous a wink.

The level of their perversion is actually pretty embarrassing, and before I can stop myself, I practically shout, "What the *fuck*, you guys?"

"Dude, what's your damn problem? We're trying to have fun," Erik complains, scanning the crowd.

Bernie nods in agreement. "If she didn't want us gawking at her *tits*, maybe she shouldn't have them hanging out."

Cecelia's mouth falls open; her look of horror says it all.

I seriously want to punch Bernie in the face.

Neve clears his throat with a forced laugh. "Um, guys, maybe I should introduce you to Cecelia, you know, *Cecelia*." He stresses her name, dragging it out, his dark brows pushed together as he bores holes into our friends. "Molly's friend." He coughs loudly.

Realization spreads across everyone's faces—well, everyone except Kevin, mostly because he's such a fucking tool box.

Erik lets out a loud "*Ahhhhh, Ceceeeliaaa…*" His hands go up, and as he says "Molly's friend", he emphasizes Molly's name with air quotes.

Nice.

Real subtle, asshole.

"Holy shit you're hot," Erik mutters, not really to anyone in particular.

Finally, Kevin makes the connection. "Oh yeah, Molly's roommate. Also known as the chick Matthew has a raging hard-on for?"

"The *fuck*, Kevin?" Neve punches him in the bicep to shut him up, but it doesn't work.

"I'm just going by what McGrath told me—lay off. *Fucking A* Neve," Kevin grumbles, rubbing his sore arm.

This whole time, I notice Cecelia staring at me in a way she's never looked at me before: something that looks like wonderment, fascination, and undisguised interest, and I won't lie—the cock in my pants likes it.

Cecelia

"Trust me, you can dance." – vodka

This is definitely one of those moments that could be categorized as both horrifyingly embarrassing and totally awesome at the same time.

Nothing can compare to the look on Matthew's face right now as his friends continue to shove their feet into their mouths. I've heard guys talk shit before, and trust me, this isn't fazing me one bit.

Okay, *maybe* I was thrown off a *little* when the guy dressed in scrubs declared I was letting my tits fall out on purpose—as if I would do something like that.

That's totally something Jenna would do, not me.

I can't get enough of studying Matthew though half-lidded eyes. He looks good enough to eat, decked out like a preppy pirate—not the Johnny Depp, Captain Jack Sparrow kind, more like the lazy *I didn't put much thought into this costume because I look hot in anything I wear* kind, like he washed up on the shore of a deserted island while he was on a business trip and *had* to become a pirate out of necessity.

Matthew's ripped up white shirt (which artfully exposes most of his extremely muscular chest) is tied off at the waist by a thick red sash. His khakis—which are now soaking wet from the beer he spilled when I smashed into him—are cut off just below the knee and are ripped apart to the point that it looks like he may have run them through a paper shredder.

Messed up hair, black laced-up boots, and—holy shit—black eyeliner.

I've never admitted this to anyone out loud (nor will I ever), but guys wearing eyeliner *totally* turns me on. Just looking at him right now is making me hot.

I would totally let him plunder my treasure chest.

Pretty sure I wouldn't mind if he dragged me out of here by my hair. I mean: pirate and mermaid?! Kind of the perfect pair, right?

Lost in my own thoughts, it takes me a few seconds to realize the guys are still arguing and punching each other like a bunch of middle school adolescents.

The cute guy with the *Free Mammograms* sign hanging around his neck is rubbing his arm and grumbling, "I'm just going by what McGrath told me—lay off. *Fucking A* Neve."

I can tell he has a carefree way about him, and, despite the fact that he's offering to feel girls' boobs at a party (albeit for free), he is giving off a strong *I'm one of the good guys* vibe. I'm guessing he's the guy no one takes seriously but is actually a really good friend.

His earlier ogling of my breasts notwithstanding, I study him a bit longer and finally decide he might be a good match for Jenna tonight. Matthew and Neve both continue glaring at the poor guy, and if looks could kill, he would be dead.

Regardless, they obviously think well enough of him to drag him to an upscale party.

I clear my throat, even though they couldn't possibly hear it over the music, and indicate the place where Molly, Weston, & Co. are holed up on the other side of the room. "I was just going to the bathroom, but if you keep walking that way"—I point in the general direction—"Weston and a few other guys are standing in the corner."

Matthew steps toward me. "I'll walk with you."

Neve raises his eyebrow.

Matthew shrugs innocently. "What? It's dark out."

He places his hands on the small of my back as "Raging Fire" by Phillip Phillips comes blasting out of the sound system. It kind of feels appropriate, and as we walk out of the giant reception tent and into the dark October night, I absorb the words of the song.

Granted, we're walking toward a port-a-potty so I can pee, but still, the girl in me can turn *any* moment into a romantic one.

His hand still resting at the curve near my ass is turning my damn body into a raging fire, and I resist the urge to wiggle it. I don't know if it's being near Matthew, or the song, or the fact that a soft breeze is brushing the naked skin above my corset that's making me think about getting naked, but Matthews fingers are branding my skin in a slow burn, and instincts tell me I'll still be feeling them later—you know, when I'm all *alone* back in my apartment.

Alone again: story of my life.

We reach the bathrooms and thankfully find them all empty.

"I'll wait for you here," Matthew says, his low timbre vibrating in the dark.

I nod and open the bright blue door to the stall, pausing momentarily before stepping in. I survey the area, checking for pee on the floor and trying to determine how much room I have to move around in without touching the small urinal attached to the wall.

Without pride, I turn to Matthew and ask, "Do you mind if I borrow your phone? It's hard to see in there and I don't want to end up in the hole…"

He digs his phone out of his back pocket without hesitating and hands it over.

"Thanks." I take a breath before stepping up into the smelly portable bathroom. "If I don't come out within five minutes, send in a search party."

Matthew

It takes Cecelia approximately two minutes tops to take a pee before the door to the john flies open and she's stepping down onto the grass in her stiletto heels. Her metallic pants shine from some nearby lanterns, which flicker in the dark, lighting a path to the toilets, and when she walks over to the makeshift handwashing station, I check out her ass as she scrubs her palms.

Unlike a lot of chicks in high heels, Cecelia doesn't stumble all over the grass in them like a baby deer learning to walk. She's graceful.

"Oh, I almost forgot," she says, digging into her corset top and pulling out my cell. "Thanks. It was pretty gross in there. I almost wish I couldn't see. Ugh, I hate those port-a-potties." Her body shudders.

"I wouldn't know. I usually just piss in the grass." I give myself a mental slap.

Why do I have to say shit like that?

Cecelia

It's always in the back of my mind that this could be the night Matthew decides to call in the bet, use the code word, and plant one on me like he keeps promising.

Actually, all he'd need to do is ask—no code word required.

We walk back into the chaos of the party to hunt down our friends, who have surely gotten lost in the crowd by now. Matthew is right on my tail, so close I can feel the seams of his shirt brushing against my back, but unfortunately he hasn't laid a hand on me yet.

Within the tent, it's not terribly difficult to navigate to the far end because Amber has plenty of things to see and do in many places on the property, leading her numerous guests to disperse. Yes, tons of them are drinking at the bars inside the tent, dancing and whooping it up, but plenty more are sitting at tables set up around the yard with glowing pumpkin centerpieces while others are stumbling and laughing their way through makeshift graveyards and haunted mazes.

Matthew's breath warms the back of my neck as he leans in close. "Do you want something to drink before we try to find everyone?"

"Um...uh..." I stammer, barely able to function with his lips so close to my neck, and it isn't long before I'm holding a cup of pineapple vodka and Sprite with Matthew's hand back at my waist, lightly guiding me through the crowd.

He leans in again. "Where were you all standing before?"

"This way." I can barely nod toward one of the bars, the one with the totally ridiculous ice sculpture of Dracula.

"Okay, I'll follow your lead."

Matthew

"Whatever, I'll just date myself." – Kevin Westerman

The party is now officially in full swing, and everyone is having a great time. The DJ has been playing tons of great music—some old songs mixed in with the new, essentially making it feel like a high school dance—and so far, no one in our group is sloppy drunk yet.

I'm the designated driver, so that includes me.

I've had one beer, which is fine. I don't need to get drunk to have a good time, and since I'm not (not even close), it gives me a chance to study Cecelia with a more acute senses and keep an eye on my sister at the same time. Best to keep my wits about me when dealing with two alpha females, especially one that is smoking hot and a total magnet for horny slobs.

This party is full of them.

One thing I've noticed about Cecelia: she's not drunk either. In fact, I'm pretty sure she's still holding the same pineapple vodka and Sprite I got her when we first left the bathroom, and that was over an hour ago.

Standing next to Molly (who, by the way, is dressed like a damn deer or some shit) in a cluster of girls, she's doing what they are all doing: shaking her ass and hopping up and down to the music, which is currently "Good Time" by Owl City and Carly Rae Jepson.

I'm tempted to go over and drag her out of here—doesn't she realize how much her boobs are jiggling? I sure as hell do, and I'm standing about twenty feet away, trying not to stare.

Trying…but not really.

Molly catches me watching and rolls her eyes, but not before elbowing Cecelia in the ribcage. I see Cecelia wince and smack Molly in the stomach.

"*Good for you*," I mouth, grinning when she looks over at me, eyes bright and gleaming. The glance is enough to make me swallow hard, and I can feel the Adam's apple bobbing in my dry throat.

As a professional athlete, I have women and girls throwing themselves at me almost on a daily basis. Sorry, as shitty as that sounds, it's true. Some of the chicks are classy, while others are total sluts, giving it up for anyone with a pro title in front of their name—something I've always taken advantage of in the past.

One thing most people might not think about or give much credence to is that professional athletes are full of pent-up aggression and adrenaline. Sex, for the most part, is vital to an athlete's performance, especially before a big game.

I know you're probably sitting there asking yourself why, so I'll do you a solid and explain why sex is vital (to me anyway):

1. Regular sex helps get my lead out, *if you catch my drift.*
2. It can boost my athletic performance.
3. It reduces my anxiety before a game (see: completely sated).
4. It helps me *not* pound the piss out of my opponents.
5. Sex is fucking awesome.

Wait, correct me if I'm wrong, but was number five a bit redundant? Do you see how I used 'sex' and 'fucking' in the same sentence, and they're like…the same thing?

Dammit, why do I have to be so clever *and* good-looking?

As I stare at Cecelia, I wonder if she's ever heard the rumor that hockey players *bang* better than anybody, which could work in my favor. See, it's all in the hips, and we get a lot of practice swiveling and gyrating on the ice—*a lot*. If you don't believe me, I'm sure Kevin would show you…

Someone knocks me on the arm and I'm bumped out of my contemplations and back into reality.

"Jesus Christ, Wakefield. Why don't you just go over there?" Weston asks casually, taking a short sip from his beer bottle.

Erik grins stupidly. "No shit. Watching you eye fuck her is kind of tragic, dude. Even Kevin had the balls to approach the friend, what's-her-face."

Jenna. Kevin was over dancing with Jenna—correction, Kevin was in a corner dry humping my sister's best friend, his tongue so far down her throat he'd probably hit China by now.

"And we all know Kevin has no game."

That isn't true—Kevin actually has more game than all four of us combined, and I'm positive he's getting more action than I am these days. For some reason, chicks love his goofy demeanor; it draws them to him like moths to a flame. So, I'm not about to go knocking him, especially since I personally haven't had sex—or even someone's mouth sucking my dick—in months.

I know for a *fact* Kevin got laid last weekend.

Twice.

How do I know this? Well for one, he wouldn't shut up about it. Secondly, the moron Snapchatted a picture of himself and added it to his story with some chick's dirty-ass thong in his mouth. He captioned the picture *Tapping that ass* and circled her backside, which was sticking high up in the air, in bright red.

I mean, he was piss-ass drunk, but still.

"Know what your problem is, Wakefield? Deep down inside, you're a giant pussy." Weston takes another small sip of beer, watching Molly from the corner of his eye.

"He isn't a giant pussy," Neve jokes. "He *has* a giant pussy."

"Real funny, assholes."

"Seriously though dude, why aren't you over there getting all up in that? Guys have been on her all night. Eventually she's going to hook up with someone else."

I shake my head and make a scoffing sound, like *yeah right*. "She's not going to hook up with anyone else, trust me."

Erik snorts and fiddles with his surgical mask. "How the hell would you know? Aren't all chicks the same—needy and desperate for attention?"

Weston shoots my friend a look. "Geez, bitter much? What cat shit in *your* litter box?"

"Meow." This from Bernie.

"She is not going to hook up with anyone because she already has the hots for me," I say confidently, arching my eyebrows in an authoritative manner and puffing out my chest.

Bernie laughs. "Whatevah dude. If you're so sure, you would have been all ovah that. How long you been chasing that tail anyway?" Since it's so loud in here, he's practically shouting.

"Would you keep your damn voice down?"

"Why? If I lowah my voice you won't be able to hear me tell you how douchie you're being." Bernie takes a swig of his cocktail. "You're twenty-three years old. Quit acting like you're in middle school."

I think about this for a minute. "Well, it's not like I'm just going to just bust over there. She's in a group full of girls, for fuck's sake. It would look too obvious."

Weston grins and hands me his half empty beer bottle as he says, "That, my friend, is where I come in." He sets off in the direction of Molly & Co. and I falter, hesitant to follow him.

Then suddenly I realize: they might be right.

Maybe I *am* a pussy.

Shit.

I swallow the last of my drink then down the rest of Weston's, leaving me no choice but to follow him.

Cecelia

I know he's approaching.

Not because I can see him, but because his friends are so damn loud. Four grown men dressed like lady doctors hooting, hollering, and whistling like a bunch of fraternity boys as Weston and Matthew lead their way through the crowd toward us.

I'm pretty sure I just heard one of them yell, *"Tap that ass!"*

Matthew tails several feet behind Weston, almost hesitantly, as if this wasn't his choice. I covertly watch him from above the rim of my glass (yes…the *same* drink I've been holding the entire time we've been here), taking teeny tiny sips just so I can watch him walking without being obvious.

I cannot take my eyes off his face. The fact that he's wearing eyeliner is getting me so hot and bothered, I accidentally take a giant gulp of my warm pineapple vodka and Sprite, causing me to choke a little and turn beet red.

Molly elbows me (for the fifth time tonight) and leans in. "Brace yourself. Shit is about to get real." Her deer antlers poke me in the side of the head and I swat her away.

"Oh my god, get away with those damn things. Would you stop?" I hiss.

"Seriously though, look at Matthew. It looks like he's about to wet his pants." Molly twitches her nose, which she's painted black, and the little white fawn freckles she's painted on her cheeks catch the light.

She looks pretty darn adorable.

"I should get a picture of this moment for Instagram."

Okay. *Not so adorable.*

Molly smacks the drink away from my mouth as I go to take another gulp. "Stop chugging your drink Cece. Yuck. That thing must be piss warm by now. Here. Take mine and I'll get myself a new one while you and my brother awkwardly make doe eyes at each other." She grabs my cocktail glass and hands me hers. "Get it? *Doe* eyes?" Then Molly turns on her heels, making a beeline toward the bar, the little white tail pinned to her butt wagging.

Weston changes course and goes after her.

As a country song about a girl in a red sundress, pick-up trucks, creeks, and cornfields plays overhead (yes, for real), I paste a smile on my face, hoping it doesn't make me look constipated, and then he's there, standing in front of me.

And…is it just me, or does he look nervous? Molly was right—he does look like he's about to wet his pants.

Surely this cannot be.

"Hi!" I yell over the noise. "Having fun?"

"Totally. Thanks for the invitation."

I cock an eyebrow at him because we both know he invited himself to the party.

He laughs and bumps me with his shoulder. "I'm just teasing. We both know I forced my sister to bring me along."

"Well I think it worked out well for everyone. Molly seems glad you're here. You two don't hang out at the same places very often, do you?"

"No. I mean…I'm only in town for half the year. The other half I'm in California, working."

Well, if that isn't a healthy dose of reality. I look him up and down appraisingly and change the subject. "I don't know if I mentioned this before, but…I really like your costume. Very…rogue-ish."

Matthew plants a hand on his hip and cocks his head at me, grinning. "Rogue-ish? Did you just make that up?"

"Mmmm, I'm pretty sure it's a word, and if it's not, it should be." I smile up at him. Even with me in these heels, he's taller than I am. "Digging the eyeliner in a big way."

He leans in. "I'm sorry, what was that?" He points to his ear. Crap. He can't hear me over the music.

I suck in my breath and move close enough to get a good whiff of him—sweat and cologne, my favorite combination. "I said, 'Digging the eyeliner in a big way'."

"Oh yeah? That's good to know."

"Do you plan on wearing it from now on?"

He pretends to think about it, tapping his chin in thought, and breathes into my ear, "Maybe on special occasions."

"I can't think of any 'special occasions' where eyeliner would be appropriate—unless, of course, you're going to change your everyday look."

I can feel his low chuckle in the pit of my stomach as he replies, "Maybe just to throw off little Mitchell Decker. That kid would piss his pants if I showed up to practice looking like Jack Sparrow."

I nod and my nose accidentally brushes his cheek. "The Johnny Depp look is *hot*…but, on the other hand, it would just reinforce their theories that you're, you know…"

"Chasing the GLAAD rainbow?" He looks over my shoulder and gives a brief nod to someone behind me. "Kevin and Jenna sure seem to be hitting it off."

"Yeah, I figured they would. He's totally her type—quirky and fun."

"Quirky…I guess that's *one* way to describe Kevin…"

We stand there awkwardly, him twirling his beer bottle, me fiddling with my glass. You could cut the sexual tension with a dull knife, *and it's the best kind of tension in the history of mankind.*

I never thought I'd be saying this, but I'm actually relieved to see Molly and Weston weaving their way back toward us, new drinks in hand. Surprisingly, they are each carrying two drinks, and when they reach us, Molly hands me a large frosted glass full of ice and…

"Here. I got us both water with lemon."

How thoughtful—I need to keep my wits about me.

Weston hands a beer to Matthew, then looks in between us. "So, how are you two kids getting along?"

Molly rolls her eyes. "Clearly my brother has no game since they're just standing here staring at each other."

Oh. My. God.

Weston laughs. "You got that right. Babe, wanna show

them how it's done?" He grabs her by the waist and swings her around, grinding his hips against hers to the beat of the music and planting his lips on her neck. It's so painfully awkward standing here watching them grind against each other.

Worse, they've started sucking face to "How Far Do You Want to Go" by Gloriana, which happens to be one of my favorites, and apparently theirs too—it looks as if they want to go pretty damn far.

On the dance floor.

In front of everyone.

It's pretty hot—and revolting, all at the same time. I can actually see their tongues from here as they make out.

They're totally doing it on purpose to torture us.

What's worse? *It's actually working.*

Red-faced (I quickly thank God for all the makeup on my face), I glance at Matthew. His lips are pressed together in a line so tight I can't tell if he's outraged by their behavior or turned on by it. Counting to three in my head, I take a chug of water like it's a shot of liquid courage then set the glass down on a nearby bar table. Before I lose the resolve, I position myself close enough to Matthew that the heat radiating from his large body warms my insides.

Slowly Matthew dips his head to the side, his entire body acknowledging my presence as he lowers his face a fraction so we're eye to eye with our noses almost touching. I'm not sure how long we stand there—it could have been seconds, it could have been minutes—but all we do is stare at each other, our hot breath mingling and our chests beginning to heave up and down like we're trying to bring our heartrates down after a race.

Matthew's clear green eyes are starkly contrasted by the dark charcoal black eyeliner rimming his lids. He gazes unflinchingly, so intently that I lick my lips and nervously bring a hand up to brush a stray hair behind my ear.

He is so close that if I stuck out my tongue, it would end up in his mouth.

He's not holding me or touching me, but I can feel my legs trembling just the same.

Matthew tips his head so his cheek brushes mine, and without saying a word, he gently nuzzles my hair. I can feel him inhaling my scented shampoo as he pushes my locks aside with his nose.

Slowly…excruciatingly slowly…he parts his lips and brushes them along the side of my neck, inhaling and exhaling in short, uneven breaths.

The barely perceptible touch of his lips against my neck feels like a hundred thousand butterfly kisses, and, no longer having control over my own body functions, I tip my head to the side to give him better access.

And because it feels incredible.

My eyes flutter shut.

My body shivers.

Moaning from the easy exploration of his mouth, pleasure zips through my body like an electric shock—I swear, if I didn't know any better, I'd think I was having an orgasm right there in the middle of the dance floor.

I feel greedy and selfish.

My body wants more.

I want more.

I am limp, putty in his capable hands.

With his lips still on my neck, he exhales, his warm breath coming out in a long, drawn-out groan that melts my insides like butter.

Our bodies, of their own accord, move closer still, pressed together but still too far apart. I curse the damn adornments glued to the bodice of this corset because I can't feel him against me, and I cringe inwardly knowing he's probably being stabbed in the pecs by pointy beads and daggers disguised as seashells.

Epic fail. They looked so cute when I was gluing them on...

Matthew, bless his heart, doesn't seem to notice *or* care. Hands reaching up, his strong capable fingers weave gently through my long hair in a caress, resting at the base of my neck. I let out a sigh because he's finally touching me, kissing his way down my neck, nipping my shoulder with his teeth.

I feel his wet tongue on my skin.

On my collarbone.

In my cleavage.

Matthew's strong hands grasp me around the waist, sliding them down to grab my ass cheeks, fingertips flexing over my backside, the tendons in his forearms tense as he battles his willpower, every stroke becoming unbearable for us both.

Roughly, he hauls me against his straining erection and grinds himself into the crotch of my thin hot pants as he simultanesouly dips his tongue into the valley between my breasts. I tip my head back like a wonton trollop, so close...*so so* close to climaxing that my fingers dig into his scalp and I moan loudly into his ear.

"Oh god, Matthew. Mmmm. *Ugh...*"

I'm sure to the casual observer, I look like a little hussy.

Because, well, I'm acting like one.

Roger would be so ashamed.

The only slow song of the night begins. Couples morph into one around us, forming pairs to dance, some grinding sexually, others engaging in drunken make-out sessions, the rest just acting stupid.

The guy's self-control is award-winning. I mean...it takes every ounce of willpower I possess not to rip his shirt open and lick him from top to bottom.

"Cece." Coming up for breath, Matthew's low gravelly voice shudders. "Cece, we have to stop or I'm gonna come in my pants like a twelve-year-old."

Sounds like an okay plan to me, I want to say, but I nod instead. He holds me still, pulling me in so our foreheads and noses are touching, and we sway to the music. My hands begin lightly caressing his muscular back, and I turn to rest my head on his broad shoulder.

I swallow. "Do you have your eyes closed too?" I ask just above a whisper, hoping he can hear me and hoping I don't sound lame.

His nod is barely perceptible.

Yes.

Matthew and I continue to sway, just barely moving at the edge of the makeshift hardwood dance floor. I sigh. Our lips came so close to touching, it was almost painful. The fact that Matthew can't *technically* kiss me until he says the code word gets me even hotter.

It's like...the best foreplay *ever*.

I want him to kiss me, but then again, *I don't.*

My hands continue to roam, lightly sliding low on his lean hips to the curve of his backside. I let my feather-weight fingertips travel briefly over his firm ass before letting them settle around his trim waist.

It is, hands down, the most romantic and erotic moment of my young life, and for a fleeting moment, I find myself thinking this must be what falling in love feels like.

Cecelia

"In alcohol's defense, I'm done some pretty stupid shit while completely sober, too.

"**H**oly shit balls Cecelia. Seriously? You and Matthew looked so hot on the dance floor that Weston and I went and had sex in the woods behind the party tent."

It's two o'clock in the morning and we're sitting on my bed, makeup and costumes off, both of us showered, Weston passed out in her room. I can hear him snoring loudly.

"Okay, first of all, since when do you say things like *holy shit balls*? Second, how can you talk about getting turned on by watching us like it's no big deal? We aren't some random people, you sicko. That's your brother— don't you think it's kind of weird? And perverted?"

Molly flops down on my bed and gazes at me oddly, her freshly scrubbed face appearing far more innocent than it actually is. She blinks at me before responding. "Because Cece, it's *you*. You're my friend and I'm happy for you." She gives me another strange look like *I'm* the crazy one here.

Oh.

Well then.

"And I'm sorry, but I've literally never seen anything hotter than the two of you in my entire flippin life. It was like…soft-core porn up close and personal."

Soft-core porn?! Oh my god, seriously?

I gape at her with my mouth hanging open.

"Anyway, I better get to sleep. I have to work in the morning." She leans over and pulls me in for a hug, planting a kiss on the top of my head with a loud smacking sound. "Good night, kiddo. Don't stay up too long."

"Good night, Mom." I laugh.

Little does she know, sleep won't be happening for me any time soon, because the minute I hear her door softly close, my phone chimes.

I suppress the urge to roll around on my comforter like a giddy school girl and squeal.

Matthew: *Did I tell you how great you looked tonight?*

Me: *Actually, no you did not…*

Matthew: *I meant to. You looked incredible…edible… edible.*

Do you hear an echo?

Me: *Stop it or you'll make me blush.*

Matthew: *I'd also like to point out that you smelled delicious. Good enuff to eat…*

Me: *OMG no I didn't. I smelled like sweat. Wait—you were smelling me?*

Matthew: *Um yeah, totally smelling you. Unlike *some* people, I can admit when I'm sniffing someone.*

Matthew: *And this might be the beer talking, but when I first saw you tonight…*

He doesn't finish his sentence, but instead lets it trail off. I inhale, staring intently at the phone, willing him with mental telepathy to send the rest of the sentence through. A few moments go by, damn him, before my phone chimes again.

Matthew: *Sorry, I'm still driving. Now I'm at a red light.*

Matthew: *I don't think I had the chance to tell you goodbye* ☹

Me: *No. You kinda had your hands full with the four lady molesters.*

Matthew: *Omg I had to haul every one of their asses home. Felt like I was back in college, getting my drunk friends back to the dorms.*

Me: *I'm surprised you weren't drinking*

Matthew: *I had a few*

Me: *You couldn't have had more than 2 or 3 beers*

Matthew: *Kind of at the point in my life where I want to remember what happens on the weekends, KWIM?*

I smile at his reply, typing out: *My sentiments exactly. Weston is passed out in Molly's room snoring like a lumberjack, or something like that. LOL*

Another few minutes go by before he replies.

Matthew: *So...are you wide awake, or just about to fall asleep?*

Me: *Something in between, actually...*

Randomly, I think I hear knocking in the other room like someone is softly tapping on the cheap wooden door. I cock my head to the side, intently listening.

I think my mind must be playing tricks on me, but then I hear the tapping again.

Tap. Tap, tap, tap.

Me: *Omg Matthew. I think someone is at my door. SHIT! What should I do??????????*

Matthew: *DO NOT ANSWER IT. DO. NOT. ANSWER. IT*

Me: *I'm kind of freaking out here!!!!!!!!*

Matthew: *Do you have a baseball bat?*

Me: *No, but I think Molly has a hockey stick in the living room.*

Me: *Wait. Shouldn't I just go wake Molly and Weston up???*

Matthew: *NO! That turd is useless when he's drunk.*

I bite down on my lower lip and hear more tapping at the front door. Shit! Why the hell don't we have a peephole?

Tap, tap, tap.

I stand, tiptoe into the living room, and cautiously grab the purple hockey stick leaning against the back wall, careful not to scratch the paint on it—which is dumb, because *hello!* Clearly there is a *murderer* outside my door.

Clutching the hockey stick in one hand and my cell

phone in the other, I debate my course of action. Several possible scenarios wait for me on the other side of the door, including:

1. Opening the door to be immediately axed to pieces by a raper-slash-murderer.

2. Opening the door to a neighbor in need of assistance.

3. It's Creepy Writer Guy, and he's here for my underwear.

4. It's Creepy Writer Guy, and he's here to rape-slash-murder-slash-axe me into pieces.

I run out of possibilities after number four. I mean... just how many people could it possibly be on the other side of this cheap plywood door?

My phone chimes, and it's Matthew: *DO NOT OPEN YOUR DOOR.*

Shit, shit, shit.

Not only is there a creeper outside my damn door, I am wearing pajamas and look about as opposite of badass as a person could conceivably appear in this situation. They're not just any pajamas, they're skimpy pajamas—I mean, if you classify a cotton camisole and drawstring shorts as *skimpy...*

When faced with certain death, I can't think of a single soul who would want to be slaughtered wearing PJs.

How humiliating.

Tap, tap, tap.

I am so bloody freaked out. I glance toward Molly's door—surely she's still awake. Finally, still white-knuckling the hockey stick, I thumb through my contacts and tap on Matthew's information, hit the *call* button, and hold my breath.

Resting my head against the wall next to my front door while I wait for the phone call to connect, I hold it up to my ear.

It finally starts to ring.

Hey.

Wait a minute.

My head pops up from the wall and I turn my head, pressing my ear firmly against the door. Yup, I definitely hear a ringtone coming from out in the hallway.

The theme song for Star Wars.

That jerk!

Suddenly enraged, I throw down the hockey stick and yank open the door.

Matthew

"You...you asshole!"

The door to Cecelia and Molly's apartment flies open and Cecelia stands in the doorway, chest heaving and bright red with fury. Her long brunette hair flows down her back, still damp from a shower, and her eyes are wild with rage.

Yeah, I *am* an asshole, an insensitive prick, and I prove it by laughing as Cecelia grabs me by the shirt collar then aggressively shoves me with all her might, both palms flat against my chest. I grab her by both wrists as she unsuccessfully attempts to propel me into the wall.

She's breathing hard, face bright red and....so is her half-exposed chest. I force my eyes up and bite my lip to stop another burst of laughter.

She looks so unbelievably infuriated.

"You are such a dickwad," she spits out.

"I'm sorry. I wanted to see you." Loosening the grip on her wrists, she seems to get control of her erratic breathing and looks up at me. I'm still dressed like a pirate, having driven all over town driving my friends home and thus not having been home yet.

"Did you think scaring the living *shit* out of me at two in the morning would be funny?"

"Um…" How do I answer that? I can't say yes—she's obviously super pissed.

Cecelia continues ranting and tries shoving me again. "What an idiotic thing to do, you big jerk off. Why would you do something like this?"

Newsflash: I am a *guy*.

We think *everything* inappropriate is funny—farting, burping, lighting shit on fire, and yeah, scaring the living shit out of girls we like at two o'clock in the morning.

Do you want to know how I *know* men are idiots? Because one time I had an ex-girlfriend who posted a sign on my refrigerator after one of our many knock-down-drag-out fights (note: she was clingy and wanted a commitment) that said, *Men are stupid. If you forget, give them a second. They* will *remind you.*

So yeah, if you need further proof, I have it in writing on my fridge.

At the moment, it appears Bridget (the ex) might have

been right.

Go figure.

"Don't be mad. I didn't think you'd be *that* freaked out." I grin, the lie slipping out easily. With makeup on, Cecelia is beautiful. Without it—damp hair and all—she's absolutely a-*freaking*-dorable.

And do-able. (Haha, see what I did there?)

I pull her in a little closer.

"Why are you *here*? I'm beginning to think you might have a few screws lose.

"My car drove itself here. It's like that car from *Knight Rider*."

"What the hell is a knight rider?"

"It's a TV show from the 90s. Michael Knight's car Kitt was bad ass and drove itself." Cecelia is regarding me like I've lost my mother effing mind. "On second thought, you know what? Never mind…"

"It's past two o'clock," she reminds me again. "This was *kind* of a dick move."

I shuffle my feet, which are still stuffed into the black steel-toed construction boots I borrowed. "Are you mad?"

I can't even flirt without scaring the shit out of a girl— apparently I'm pretty terrible at this relationship crap. Then I recognize the fact I just classified us as *in a relationship*.

I stare down at Cecelia, seeing her in a new way as she bites her lip and stares at the far wall, thinking. "No. I'm not mad."

I let out the breath I didn't realize I was holding. "Good, because I wanted to tell you goodnight."

"You came all the way over here to say goodnight? You need medication."

"Probably. Also…maybe I wanted a peek at you wearing nothing but your jammies." I peer down at her cleavage. Her round breasts are smashed against my chest, pushed together from the contact of our bodies and taking on a Maxim-worthy appearance.

Nice.

"Are you here to call in the bet?" She squints up at me suspiciously. "Because you can't kiss me until you do."

Actually, I hadn't thought about the bet in days…but now that she brought it up…

Laughing, I brush a few stray hairs out of her eyes as an excuse to touch her face. "Do you *want* me to call in the bet?"

"No…but…the bet was that you could kiss *me*. We never said I couldn't kiss *you*."

Cecelia

Matthew's nostrils flare as I say "We never agreed I couldn't kiss you," and his pupils dilate.

I wonder if he'd agree to wear eyeliner for me more often.

It's the sexiest thing I've ever seen.

"I can live with that," Matthew gruffly replies, the low timbre of his voice vibrating against the walls. He runs his large hands up and down my arms, as if trying to warm me up.

236 | SARA NEY

Trust me. It's totally unnecessary—my body is *plenty* warm.

"Just so you know, I'm not kissing you on the lips."

Matthew's eyebrows shoot up and he wiggles them suggestively, then rubs his pelvis against mine. I can feel his erection through his pirate cargo pants. "I'm totally okay with you kissing me other places instead."

"All right pervert, bring it down a notch—and for the record, I don't do blow jobs, ever, so get your mind out of the gutter."

"*Never?*"

"No."

"Have you *ever?*"

"Don't you think this conversation is a bit premature? We aren't even dating."

Matthew cocks his head and studies me. "No, it's not premature. The Millionaire Matchmaker on Bravo! says you should always prequalify someone you want to date. Make sure they don't have any deal breakers."

"I think you watch too much television." I chuckle and tap him playfully on the bicep.

"So wait, you're telling me you would never..." He makes a choking sound in his throat like he's gagging. It's disgusting.

"No."

He pulls away and looks down at me. "I'm sorry, but BJs might be a deal breaker for me."

"Are you shitting me? You cannot seriously be telling me you wouldn't date someone because they don't... won't..." I wave my hand in front of his pants, refusing to say the words *blow job.*

"Because they won't suck my cock? Yeah, I wouldn't."

Holy crap, he's actually serious. "Wow. This conversation sure took a turn for the worse."

"Hey, what the hell are *you* complaining about? I'm the one who hasn't been sucked off in months."

"Oh my god you're a pig." I shove him off and away from me, backing toward my apartment with anger, hurt, and a million other feelings surging inside me.

"Baby, I've been one from the beginning." He postures arrogantly, crossing his arms, and his steely green eyes flash brightly under the black eyeliner, making him look like a menacing asshole.

"I am not your *baby.*"

"See, when you say it like that, all throaty and angry-like, I think maybe you *do* want to blow me."

I cannot believe this is happening. What the hell happened to the nice guy I was coming to know and…and…

My bottom lip trembles. *Don't let him see you cry Cecelia. Don't let him see you cry, don't let him see you cry…*

"Go fuck yourself, Matthew."

He gives a short, sardonic laugh. "Not necessary, *baby.* I can find plenty of girls who will do it for me. In fact, I can think of a cheap dozen to call right now and finish what we started."

I step back into my apartment and slam the door in his face so violently the frame shakes.

Leaning against the living room wall for support, I close my eyes, squeezing them so tightly the salty tears behind my quaking lids are unable to escape. The unshed sobs burn inside my chest, and I'm only able to control my breathing by slowly inhaling through my nose, and then slowly breathing out through my mouth.

Several minutes pass before I hear the footfalls of Matthew's retreating form.

Only then do I let my body collapse to the floor, weeping.

Matthew

"The best way not to get your heart broken is to pretend you don't have one." – Charlie Sheen

"**W**ow. You really are a heartless bastard." Weston stares at me from across the tiny table at Starbucks, sipping from the straw of a venti iced tea lemonade. In front of him are a plate of pastries (two small muffins and one blueberry scone), a plastic container of yogurt, and a slice of pumpkin pound cake. "I mean…I kind of thought the whole douchebag thing was just an act. Guess not."

"I couldn't help myself. It just came spilling out." I shift uneasily in my seat as he silently observes me, unwrapping his utensils from their little plastic baggie and stabbing the spoon into the yogurt to stir it. "Like verbal diarrhea."

"Only worse?" Weston asks, slurping a big blob of strawberry yogurt off his spoon, then adds, "You know she's eventually going to tell Molly, right? You're pretty much screwed."

"Thank you Captain Obvious." I unenthusiastically poke at my caramel cake with a plastic fork, deciding I don't have the appetite for it anymore. "You know, this is the reason I've never dated Molly's friends."

"Oh really? It's because none of them will let you shove your dick in their mouth?" He laughs to himself and takes another drink of lemonade, draining the cup then taking the top off to shake ice into his mouth. Chewing noisily on ice chips, he says, "I will say this: you royally fucked up your chances with Cece."

"Seriously dude?"

"What? You can't handle the truth? Cece is probably at home right now stabbing pins into the teeny tiny dick part of a Matthew voodoo doll." He tips his cup back again, shaking more ice into his mouth and chewing. "The likelihood of you getting back into her good graces: slim to none."

The ice in his mouth crunches loudly, and the sound is grating on my nerves worse than nails on a chalk board. The worst part is, I know for a fact he fucking chews ice at the movies, too.

Drives me nuts.

Despite my scowl, Weston continues. "In an ironic twist, I bet she goes and screws some random dude at a party just to spite you." He laughs ruefully and picks up the blueberry muffin, muttering, "That would be a classic chick move," as he peels back the muffin wrapper.

"I swear to god I hate you."

"Bro, is that a nice thing to say to your probably future brother-in-law?" His eyes linger over my caramel cake, setting his muffin back on its plate. "Are you gonna eat that?"

Irritated, I push the cake forward. "Just take the damn thing."

"You're so charming. I don't know how the ladies can resist you."

"Fuck you."

"No thanks. I'm fucking your sister." Weston casually takes a bite of my cake.

"What the hell did I tell you about saying shit like that?"

"Sorry. You're right. Molly prefers the term *making love*." He shoves the caramel cake in his big fat mouth whole, chewing slowly. Crumbs fall out in chunks and land on the table, his t-shirt, and the floor.

"Are you always such a slob?"

"Would you stop deflecting your issues onto me? I'm not the one throwing a bitch fit because I treated the girl I'm falling in love with like a damn groupie." He wipes his stupid face with a paper napkin and points a calloused finger at me. "Last time I checked, that would be *you*."

"Um…"

I glare at him but he continues, spreading his hands out on the table. "If you wanted to make her feel like a cheap whore, I'm sure you succeeded. Congratulations."

Frustrated, I run my fingers through my hair. "You know that wasn't my intention. She and I have been tip-toeing around each other for weeks now, and I'm…I'm so horny I can't even *see* straight, dude. I want to fuck her so bad."

"So is this all that is to you? A quick lay?"

"*No…*no."

"Then maybe you should try telling her how you feel and start being honest." I might be imagining it, but I swear he mumbles *for once in your life*.

"What the hell do I look like? Some kind of pussy?" Weston gives me a pointed look that says *yes you do* and in return, I shoot him a glare. "Don't you dare answer that."

"I just think it's fucked up that you think sharing your feelings makes you a vagina. When were you born, the fifties?"

"Actually, I think *you're* starting to sound like a vagina. My sister sure did a number on you with all this feelings bullshit, didn't she?"

He shrugs. "Whatever dude. I'm the one getting laid, so…"

"So you keep saying," I complain as I begin shredding a napkin. "It's not like I actually wanted a relationship with her."

Weston slams his fist down on the table, startling me and a few nearby patrons, some of whom glance over at us, worry etched on their faces. "If you don't give a shit, then *enough* already. Let it go. You've treated Cece like shit from the beginning, and now she thinks you're a dick. If you want to get laid so goddamn bad and you don't care who it's with, go. Go fuck a groupie. Be my guest, but then don't waste my time with all this…whatever *this* bullshit is." He stuffs a muffin into his mouth then says through a mouthful, "And let's not forget, you called *me* to talk, not the other way around."

I stare at him, a passive expression pasted on my face.

He rolls his eyes. "Cut the crap. Do you want to say *fuck it* or do you want to fix it?"

A loud clearing of the throat from the next table interrupts us, and we both turn in our seats to acknowledge the older, gray-haired woman sitting directly next to us. She looks old enough to be my grandmother and is glaring at us through narrowed eyes. "Excuse me, young men. I've been sitting here since you sat down and I must say, the amount of cursing coming from this table has *ruined* my morning coffee."

"Sorry ma'am."

"Don't apologize to me, young man. Apologize to whatever young lady the two of you are yammering on about. If you ask me, she would be lucky to be rid of you. If you were my grandson, I would be ashamed of your behavior. Appalling." She stands, grabs her giant satchel of a purse and her coffee, and huffs at us before waddling off, murmuring, "*Kids these days.*"

Embarrassed, shocked, and horrified (take your pick), neither Weston nor I say anything long after she's departed. Instead, I pick at a straw wrapper and Weston stares blankly out the window, watching the old woman slowly hobble to her green '95 Cadillac sedan.

"I hate to be the one to say this, but…that old bag made a really good point."

"*Which is?*"

"Maybe Cece is lucky to be rid of you."

"Seriously dude, whose side are you on?"

Weston shrugs, his broad shoulders moving up and down faintly as if he's not committed to the task of his forthcoming lecture. "Look, you start training camp in

California in a few short weeks. A relationship wouldn't have worked between the two of you anyway unless she was willing to move."

"I know, but…"

Weston silences me with his stare and I clamp my mouth shut, watching as he studies me, and then nods. "Okay. We'll figure something out. In the meantime, let me handle your sister."

He winks.

Oh Christ.

Cecelia

Over the next few days, I pour myself into my thesis work, taking refuge in the university's library, hardly coming up for air. At this point, I'm so close to being done with my master's, I can *taste* it.

Thirty-eight more days.

But who's counting?

Not only is it necessary for me to buckle down and get my final paper done, but I honestly need to keep my mind off Matthew Wakefield, AKA *Mr. Desperately Seeking Blow Job.*

Besides, I heard through the grapevine that he's leaving for training camp in California at the end of December, and the last thing I need to do is get wrapped up in a guy who isn't even going to stick around.

Long-distance relationships have never been my thing.

Even casually.

I tried it once when I was a sophomore, after a guy I'd been dating since my freshman year at Madison transferred to Purdue. He was a really nice guy—funny, smart, good-looking with lots of potential—but you know, after only a few weeks of texting and Skyping, we finally agreed a technology-based relationship just...well...

Sucked.

I mean, what's the point of being with someone you can't physically touch, kiss, or hold? And pardon me for saying so, but sex is *way* too important in a relationship to put on hold for weeks—sometimes months—at a time.

Oh shit.

The thought makes me pause, pen poised above my notebook. Sex is way too important in a relationship to put on hold for weeks...*way too important in a relationship to put on hold for weeks.* For one nanosecond, it becomes clear to me why Matthew might have been so pissed off.

I wasn't born yesterday; I know sexual frustration when I see it, and Matthew Wakefield has a classic case of blue balls (Jenna's words, not mine). I mean, I haven't even let him kiss me yet. Instead (as my mother would put it), I've led him on a merry chase, practically making him pant after me like we're on a middle school playground.

No wonder he has that crazy look in his eyes half the time...

I groan at my own stupidity as regret and embarrassment twist in the pit of my stomach. I run a hand over my face, then think better of my own insecurities and stiffen my spine.

Nonetheless, I think we can all agree he was completely out of line speaking to me the way he did.

"Forget it," I say out loud to myself. "I am not letting that jerk off the hook for the way he treated me."

I mean, talk about a guy acting like a colossal douche-bag.

And I think that's putting it mildly...don't you?

***

Matthew: *Do you hate me?*

Me: *So many ways to respond, so little time*

Matthew: *Well, at least you replied. That's saying something.*

Me: *[blank stare]*

Matthew: *I guess I deserve that.*

Me: *[blank stare]*

Matthew: *Know what I find sexiest about you? Your blank stare.*

Damn him.

I stare down at the screen of my phone, thumbs hovering over the keypad, and despite myself, a smile plays at the corner of my lips. Thank god he can't see me right now, or I'd be a goner.

Matthew

"Despite being a huge pain in the ass and a total prick, you have to admit, I still bring a *lot* to the table." – Matthew Wakefield with a grin

One week.

One week and she's barely speaking to me.

On one hand, I should be glad—she drives me absolutely nuts most of the time, and on a positive note, her nagging and bitching have stopped.

On the other hand, *she knows what happened between Cecelia and me.*

My sister glowers at me from across our parents' dining room table. Her arms are crossed, and I can't see it, but I know she's bouncing her crossed leg under the table. It's one of her quirks when she's nervous or pissed off, and if looks could kill, I would be a dead man. In fact, judging from the look on her face, she's plotting my imminent death as we speak and deciding which weapons to use.

I hiss at her, "Would you please knock it off? Mom and Dad are going to think something's up."

Our parents are out of earshot in the kitchen preparing au jus for the roasted tenderloin they're serving for Sunday dinner, and I'm grateful they aren't in the room. The last thing I need is my parents breathing down my neck too. Molly's doing a fine job hating on me enough for the entire family.

She narrows her eyes and gapes at me incredulously. "Something *is* up, dick wad. You are a disgusting slob."

Those are the first words she's spoken to me since the Halloween party, and quite honestly, I'm a little taken aback—Molly hardly ever swears. Plus, we may have had our differences in the past, but she's never given me the silent treatment for so long.

I sit back in the stiff wooden chair, palms flat across the table. "Would you believe me if I said it was an *accident*?"

"An accident," Molly deadpans. "Your arrogance never fails to astound me."

"Seriously Molly, I'm serious."

"*Seriously Molly, I'm serious,*" she mimics me in a whiney voice, sarcasm dripping from her pretty mouth like honey. "No Matthew, *I'm* serious. When are you going to grow up and stop acting like an immature prick? I'm so freaking embarrassed by you. That is my *roommate* we're talking about, you asshole."

"Um, I thought I *had* stopped acting immature..."

"Oh my gawd." Molly throws her hands in the air, and they land on the table with a thud. "I can't even..."

"I can't believe you have the nerve to sit here and judge me when your relationship got off to the same start."

"Um, *excuse* me, it's hardly the same thing—we were in *high school*. Weston wasn't a grown ass *man*. You are." She's enunciating every word like I'm a simpleton.

"No, but he said a bunch of stupid shit that pissed you off too, and you forgave him eventually. Now look at the two of you—you have a great relationship. Why is it so hard to believe that I might finally want that too?"

My sister purses her lips, thinking. I know I'm wearing her down. "Molly, can I tell you something? It's going to sound totally fucked up when I say it, but I swear to god it's the truth."

My sister glances toward the kitchen, where the sound of utensils and pans clanging and being set on the granite counter can be heard. "Okay," my sister says slowly, leaning in. "I'm listening…"

Our mother, of course, chooses that exact moment to reenter the dining room, setting a steaming bowl of broccoli and cauliflower in the center of the table. Steam rises from the bowl as my mom lifts the lid to stick a spoon in it then stirs the hot veggies.

Glancing up, she looks back and forth between the two of us. "All right, what's going on in here?"

"Nothing," Molly and I reply at the same time, then glare at each other for the jinx.

Shit. Now our mom's going to be suspicious. She's narrowing her eyes at both of us, leaning against the table with a hand on her hip. "Hmmm," she mumbles before walking back into the kitchen.

"Way to go, idiot," Molly hisses at me.

"Why is that my fault? You know what, never mind. We don't have time for this. Look. I know I fucked up, *you* know I fucked up, everyone on the bloody planet knows I fucked up, okay? Can we please move on?"

My sister stares at me.

I push on, tapping my forefinger on the table impatiently. "She still owes me, you know."

Molly arches one perfectly plucked eyebrow, nonplussed, and I can tell that under the table she's impatiently bouncing her crossed leg. "Cece doesn't owe you squat and we both know it."

"Do you think if I called in the bet, our angry make-up sex would be far better than regular sex?"

Molly curls her lip at me, barring her teeth, repulsed. I realize at this point, I'm going to have to change my approach, and I roll my eyes at her. "I'm kidding. *Jeez*. First I have to get her to kiss me."

She's not amused.

"Fine. You win." I stop fidgeting and spread my hands out on the table, beseeching. "Please Molly. Just...help me."

Cecelia

I fidget with the hemline of my low-cut top, tugging it up, turning this way and that in front of the full-length mirror, eyeing Jenna and Molly—who are standing behind me—skeptically.

"Er...I don't know Molls. This seems a bit...risqué."

Jenna lets out a sniff of disapproval at my protest. "You only feel self-conscious because you're not used to having your ta-tas out for all of mankind to enjoy. I mean, if you want to go put on something boring and put your date to sleep, by all means, be my guest."

I take another look in the mirror in the hallway, pulling the hemline down on the Band-Aid sized skirt wrapped around my waist. It barely covers my crotch. "It's just... *so* not me."

"Um yeah, and that's a good thing," Jenna says with a smirk, arms crossed as she leans against the wall, studying me like a science fair project. All this is easy for her to say—she's used to dressing like a crazy person. Take right now for example: she's wearing stone-washed denim jeans straight out of the 80s and a loose yellow sweatshirt. Her wavy blonde hair, which she occasionally dip dyes, is piled loosely on her head, all wrapped conveniently in a knotted up neon yellow and hot pink floral scarf.

No Jenna ensemble would be complete without a pair of the wild (sometimes ginormous) earrings we all know and love; today's selection: giant silver hoops large enough to be bracelets.

"I'm sorry you guys, but not everyone can pull off this look. I kind of look like a...giant ho-bag."

"Says the girl who lives in yoga pants," Molly mutters under her breath. I'm shocked she manages not to roll her eyes.

"I heard that," I say with a sigh. "Besides, you know I wear jeans most days, so kiss my butt, and stop trying to get a rise out of me."

"Fine, let's vote on whether or not you can change your outfit," Jenna says.

"You just said I could put on something boring if I

wanted to! And I want to!" I shout, throwing my arms up in frustration.

"Not so fast. This is a committee, and as such, we must vote on anything affecting the common good of the group. Majority rules, sorry."

"But a tank top and a mini skirt in November...? Seriously you guys, this is bad."

"This is nowhere near as bad as some of the outfits she's made *me* wear. You're getting off easy," Molly objects calmly, studying her fingernails intently. "Besides, it isn't about what you want."

"That is so rude. I feel like I'm being held against my will in a very whorish outfit." I glare at Jenna and cross my arms in a huff, pouting. "If Abby were here, *she'd* let me change." And she'd probably let me wear a turtleneck, too, but I keep that gripe to myself.

"Well she's not, so deal with it."

I stand quietly for a few moments, wracking my brain for an out, and then try again. "If I can take this off, I will keep on the next outfit you guys pick out for me. I promise."

Jenna and Molly exchange conspiratory glances then put their heads together in a small huddle, whispering and gesturing frantically. Moments later, their heads pop up.

"Okay. Agreed. Give us a minute to plan this next look."

"Um...can I make a suggestion?"

Jenna's mouth, covered in frosty pink lipstick, falls open. "Are you serious? After this concession you want to make a sug*ges*tion? No. Get your butt in the kitchen while we look through the closet again."

Jeez, Jenna is so rude. How has Molly put up with her all these years?

Matthew

"She's *what*?!" I shout.

"You heard me," my sister says calmly, her legs crossed at my dining room table. "I didn't stutter."

"*Yeah*, I heard you." My tone is low and sarcastic. "But I want you to repeat yourself anyway, just in case I misunderstood."

Molly looks up from the magazine she has her nose stuck in and looks me straight in the eye. "Cece. Is. On. A. Date. With. Neve. Can I go back to reading my Cosmo now? Sheesh."

"Where the fuck did he take her?"

"Tsk, tsk. *Language*."

"Molly, I swear if you don't tell me—"

"*Puh*-lease, like I'm going to tell you. You've already ruined one of her dates with him; I'm not going to let you ruin another. Besides, I don't take kindly to threats."

I swear on all that is holy she does this shit *just* to piss me off. "Did you come here just so you could drop this bomb on me?"

Molly shrugs, barely managing to suppress a grin. "Maybe, maybe not."

"You're going to sit here, at *my* table, eating *my* food, and say that shit to me? You're my *sister*." Her hand, hovering over a container of orange sweet 'n' sour sauce, holds a warm crab rangoon from the Chinese restaurant down the block from my house. She blinks at me, a guilty expression passing over her features so quickly I would have missed it had I not been studying the little traitor's face.

I shake my head sadly. "My own family."

"Oh gawd Matthew. You make it sound like we're the mob."

"I wish we were, 'cause then I'd bury you in concrete and no one would think twice about hunting down your dead, lifeless body."

"So rude. You almost hurt my feelings." She dips her rangoon and licks some sauce off. "Almost. Not quite."

"No double dipping," I grumble like a sullen child.

Molly stabs her rangoon back into the sauce out of spite, licking her fingers clean when she dunks too far in. "How about you worry about something else, hmm?"

"Something like, oh, I don't know, your *betrayal*?"

Molly sits up straight and snaps the fingers on her clean hand. "Oh I get it! You're going to blame me for this, eh? Typical." She stuffs part of an eggroll in her mouth, chewing slowly before swallowing. "Remember that time you tried to make me do your science fair project and then got pissed at me when you didn't win a ribbon?"

"Ex*cuse* me, you said you would help."

My sister laughs, throwing her head back. "Operative word being *help*. You wanted me to do the whole dang thing. Besides, I was in what, like *third* grade? What the heck did I know about diagramming combustible atoms? Jack squat, that's what."

I glare at her, but she continues like she's ticking off

a list in her head that she's been waiting years to recite. "Then there was the time Mom and Dad let you babysit, but instead of watching me you rode your bike to Jonathan Steger's house and left me alone. You got your ass chewed out because when they got home, I had cut up Mom's antique quilt and made a bunch of Barbie clothes with it."

They were no-sew Barbie ponchos to be exact, but who's keeping track…

"You were ten. That was *not* my fault," I dispute through gritted teeth.

"But my point is, you were supposed to be watching me." Molly flips a page over in her Cosmo magazine and leisurely glances down. "Do you see what I'm getting at here? You do shit without thinking of the consequences, then blame someone else."

"I'm still not sure I see your point."

"That's because you're a Neanderthal. Look Matthew, if you—no, don't look out the window, look at me. *Look at my face!* Matthew! Ugh, I swear…"

"*Okay*, okay."

"Correct me if I'm wrong: you like Cece, but you treated her like shit. She goes out with someone else, you get mad. Do I have the general gist?"

I mumble under my breath.

"She's not a game to win, Matthew. You can't treat her like a competition and then when you win, forget the trophy because the thrill of the chase is gone."

"Even though that is a *terrible* analogy, it's not like that—*at all*."

"Then what is it?"

"It's like I told you at Mom and Dad's house: when I was angrily rambling off all that stupid shit about blow jobs and sucking my, um…"

"Weiner?"

"*Oh my god.*"

"Weiner is pretty tame compared to the words I heard you were throwing out at Cecelia. Cock. Dick. *Suck…*" Her face remains perfectly impassive as she recites all the vulgar synonyms a guy could use for his…*package*, as if she says them every day.

"This is not happening right now."

"Would you grow up? Keep talking or I'm not going to stop."

Molly looks at me and waves her hand around in a circle as if to say, *Move it along, buddy.*

"I didn't mean any of it. It was *literally* some of the dumbest shit that's ever come out of my mouth."

"And we all know you've said some really stupid shit."

"Shut up." I grin. "But yeah, basically. First it was just playing off of words, then I just…" I stuck my finger inside my mouth, making an exaggerated puking sound. "Word vomit."

Molly wrinkles her nose, disgusted. "Gross. Go wash your hands." Then, "If you like her so much, maybe you should say you're sorry for talking out of your ass."

"Fuck that. I am *not* saying sorry."

She levels me with a stare that clearly says, *Seriously Matthew?*

"*Fine.* I guess I'll *think* about it…"

"Good boy."

"Molls, I…I don't just like her. I *like* her, like her."

She rolls her eyes at me then mutters, "Ugh, guys really do mature years behind females. Look, I know at Mom and Dad's house you said you wanted to make it work with her, but you can*not* be mad she has a date."

"Yes I can."

Molly throws her head back to laugh then lifts her magazine, studying one of the pages. Without looking up she says, "Then maybe you should have staked your claim a little sooner."

Cecelia

"You want me to list the benefits of dating Neve? Well *duh*, you'd be dating *Neve*. I rest my case." – Jenna

*S*hortly after my hand pulls open the gold hardware handle adorning the front door of Un Petit Goût (yes, the scene of my first date with Neve), I'm being escorted by the maître d' toward the small round table where he sits, waiting,

He stands as I approach, a big smile spreading across his gorgeous face. Dressed in a baby blue, long-sleeved button-down shirt and dark wash jeans, he looks strikingly handsome under the dim lights and candlelight in the restaurant. Attractive, strong, masculine—all wrapped into one delectable package and mine for the taking.

I wait for the flutters in my stomach to appear, and when they don't, I kick back the disappointment, stifling the feeling with the heel of my black patent leather wedges.

Um…*metaphorically speaking, of course.*

Confidently I stride forward in my second outfit of the evening, which I must admit, is one hundred percent better than the first travesty (see: train wreck). As Neve leans in to kiss my cheek in greeting, I silently thank my lucky stars I put up a stink and insisted on changing.

Instead of the microscopic mini-skirt, I traded up for a pair of black high-waisted shorts and sheer black tights. The shorts are amazing and have two rows of petite silver buttons lining the pockets, and they also make my legs go on for miles. A plain, crisp, cap-sleeve white t-shirt is tucked snuggly into the shorts and is set off by a spray tan and bright pink statement necklace hanging in the scoop neck.

I do have a black cropped jacket, but you know Jenna's ridiculous rules about covering up "the sexy":

1. Only in case of emergency.
2. Emergency = temperatures that are freezing.
3. Freezing = thirty degrees or below.

This outfit is smokin' and classy at the same time, very fashion-forward and not really...*me*. However, I can see by the look on Neve's face that he's appreciating the view *and* the effort. I flip my artfully tussled wavy hair over my shoulder and sit, hanging Molly's borrowed purse on the back of my chair and folding the linen napkin across my lap.

"*Wowza*. Who knew a woman could look so damn sexy with none of her cash and prizes showing," my date says with a grin.

"Oh brother," I say with a laugh, quickly taking a sip of the water glass already at my place setting.

"I'm actually really surprised you agreed to come on

this date with me."

I cock my head to the side, already knowing the answer. "How is that?"

Neve shrugs, picking up his knife and tapping it on the table impatiently. "You *know*."

"Please, spell it out for me."

"Fine, I'll be direct, since you're obviously going to make me say it. Molly called me." His bright hooded eyes intently assess me from across the table, and I force myself not to squirm in my seat.

Damn he's good-looking.

It's actually kind of depressing that he does nothing for my libido.

Instead of squirming, I stare at him, eyes bugging out of my head. If I had been chewing food, I would have probably spit it out at him. "Molly *called* you? *Why?*"

The waitress comes before Neve can respond, setting menus on our charger plates, taking our drink orders (glass of moscato for me, thanks), and regurgitating the chef's specials (I don't know about you, but despite the fact that I've completely lost my appetite, gorgonzola-crusted filet mignon with red potatoes and asparagus sounds divine). We wait patiently for her to finish and walk off before we return to staring each other down, each staring for different reasons.

I'm the first to break the silence and fold my hands in my lap. "So…let me guess, this isn't really a date." It's not a question.

Neve has the decency to look guilty. "Please don't get me wrong. I like you, and I'm *really* attracted to you, but… Matthew cares for you more than I've ever seen him care about anyone, and it would be really shitty for me to pursue you."

I mull over this new piece of information while I chew on a slice of the sourdough bread the waitress kindly set on our table. "I don't get it. If he's as 'into me' as you *claim* he is, then why hasn't he said anything to me about it?"

"Are you serious? First of all, he's a guy. Guys don't talk about their feelings. Second—and most importantly—this is Matthew Wakefield we're talking about here, not some normal twenty-three-year-old kid. The guy has *no* idea how to be in a relationship." Neve reaches into the basket of warm bread, ripping off a chunk from the loaf and cramming it into his mouth. "And that includes relationships with his friends. I mean, sometimes the dude is such a prick." As he talks and chews, he spreads butter on another piece of bread with a knife. "I'm not going to put words into his mouth about how he feels about you, but yeah, you're all he can think about. It's driving him crazy. Hell, it's driving *us* crazy. He's been a real bitch since your fight."

My eyes get real wide as I listen to Neve go on (and on) about Matthew; this is the most I've ever heard this guy talk. "Besides Cece, you think he's an asshole *now*? He's been a virtual pussy cat compared to how he was acting just a few short weeks ago."

He stops (finally) and looks up at me as if he's forgotten I'm sitting here. "Whatever did happen between the two of you, by the way?" There is no trace of a clue on his handsome face.

"Um...are you kidding me right now?" Neve stares back at me blankly and I almost slap my forehead. "Oh jeez, no one told you?"

"Trust me, I'm always the last one—" He stops talking abruptly as the waitress walks up to set down our drinks and take our dinner order. Neve and I both order steak, medium rare (sorry to all you vegans out there). When she walks off, he continues. "As I was saying, I'm always the last one to know stuff, and it's not like Matt's gonna tell me anything." Neve eyeballs me with a raised brow. "Why? What did he do?"

I roll my eyes and sigh, loudly. "It's not what he did, it's what he said. *So* out of line." I take a sip of wine. "Are you ready for this one? Get comfortable, 'cause it's a doozy."

It takes me a while, but I'm able to give him the entire five-and-dime version of *Blow-Job-Gate 2014*, otherwise known as *The Incident That Ended Our Friendship*, before the waitress comes and sets down our entrees. I must admit to feeling somewhat mollified—and vindicated—by the reaction I'm receiving from my date.

"Wait, he *said* all that shit? To. Your. *Face*?!"

I nod, taking a sip of wine.

"No way. Nuh uh."

"Yup." I take another sip, chuckling as my lips hit the rim of the glass.

"To your face."

"Yes."

"Wow. Just…wow." Neve shakes his head and cuts his steak. "And you didn't slap him?"

"No, but I wanted to." We both laugh.

"Well shit. No wonder you're ignoring him. What a d-bag."

"Mmmhmmm," I murmur absently into my wine glass.

"But you *like* him."

I fiddle with the stem of my wine glass, refusing to look up, and heave a deep sigh.

"So I guess the question is: what are we going to do about it?"

Matthew

"Are you sure they're going to be here?" I ask Molly for the fifth time, glancing toward the front entrance door of Lone Rangers. "This doesn't seem like a place Neve would bring her after a date."

He has way more class than that—*unfortunately*.

Molly checks her phone and glances up at me. "Oh my gawd, would you chill out? I've got the situation under control. By the way, you're going to owe me a favor, and *I* get to decide what it is."

I glare at my sister, because there is a lot riding on Cecelia showing up tonight. I have a few things I plan on accomplishing when she does, none of which will happen if Neve doesn't bother to bring her, and they are, in no particular order:

1. Get Cecelia to kiss me.
2. Get Cecelia to accept my apology.
3. Get Cecelia to date me.
4. *Repeat.*

Tonight is kind of a big deal for me.

I don't normally lay it all on the line like this, and never in front of other people. My longest relationship was with Shelly Connors in seventh grade math class and was extremely one-sided, as in, I copied off of Shelly and she remained blissfully unaware. That relationship ended when our teacher, Mrs. Rettler, reassigned the class seating midyear, so…yeah.

My buddy Kevin appears from behind me and claps a hand on my shoulder, squeezing it tight. "Dude, don't you feel even the slightest bit demoralized that we're all here to witness your potentially *public* rejection?"

A low growl sounds from behind Molly, and Jenna emerges to bark at Kevin. "Oh my god, would you shut up?" Her eyes flare at him, alive with interest as she fumes. "Ugh. I can't believe *you* know a word like de*moral*ized."

"You better watch that sassy little mouth of yours before I stick my tongue down your throat to shut you up," Kevin retorts, drinking in her colorful outfit appraisingly from head to toe. I don't know what it is about this girl, but she's always dressed like an exhibit in an art gallery. All she needs to complete her ensemble is a neon sign above her blinking *Look at me!*

"You. Are. Dis*gus*ting," Jenna spits out, breathing hard and clearly getting turned on by his dirty talk.

Kevin moves closer to Jenna, smirking. "You like it, you little slut."

Jenna gasps and whispers in mock horror, "How *dare* you."

Molly throws her arms up in the air, cutting off their foreplay with a referee's time-out hand signal. "*Okay, okay* you two. Jiminy Cricket. Take your hate filled eye orgy out to the dance floor or a dark corner, would'ja?" She tosses her long auburn ponytail over her shoulder.

Our friends are ridiculous, and the thought of Cecelia walking into this den of crazy has my stomach turning in knots. "Um, maybe you should all just go…far, far away."

Weston snickers. "Matt, buddy, do you really want us to leave you here to fend for yourself? We *allll* know how it worked out the last time you tried navigating this shit on your own."

He looks rather pleased with himself, the sarcastic little bastard.

"*Whoaaa*, have you always been this snarky?"

My sister cocks her head at me and narrows her green eyes. "Is that a serious question, or are you being sarcastic?"

Her phone beeps and she checks it, smiling, then slides it into the back pocket of her jeans. "Why don't you take Weston up to the bar and wait? You're starting to drive me bat-shit crazy." Molly gives me a shove and scoots us away with her hands. "Shoo. Go. Get the heck out of here."

Cecelia

Neve and I walk into Lone Rangers, one of his large hands curled around my waist, his thumb hooked into the waistband of my shorts, guiding me as we weave our way through the bar near the back wall. I glance up at him and he pulls me in tighter, running the thumb tucked into my shorts back and forth along the bare skin under my shirt.

I grit my teeth and jab him in the ribs, hissing. "Would you knock that off?"

"Sorry, it was an impulse."

He does not look one bit remorseful.

"Ugh. Your impulses are going to get you in trouble, mister."

He grins down at me and kisses my hair, whispering in my ear, "I like you Ceceila Carter. Are you sure you want to go through with this? We can ditch this place and go somewhere else to get to know each other better." Neve flashes me his pearly whites, a lock of shocking black hair falling in his dark blue eyes.

"Um, yeah, I'm sure. Let's just get this over with."

"You don't *sound* sure." He wiggles his eyebrows then shrugs it off. "Okay, fine. Whatever. Can you at least do me a favor and try not to get me punched in the face tonight?"

"I can't make you any promises. After all, a favor is what got me into this whole mess in the first place…"

Matthew

She's here.

Regrettably, she's not alone.

They come through the crowd together, attached at the hip , and before I can even give Cecelia a proper onceover, my eyes go immediately to Neve's giant paw in the waistband of her shorts. Immediately seeing red, my nostrils flare and I turn away to prevent myself from glaring, count from one to ten in a futile attempt to calm myself, then loudly slam my beer bottle down onto the bar top.

The sound of the glass bottle hitting the wooden counter clangs in my eardrums, and as I grip the long neck of it like a lifeline, I repeat, *I deserve this. I deserve this and I brought this on myself,* over and over in my head.

Or maybe not in my head…

Weston gives me a look like I've sprouted three heads. "Dude, do you realize you're saying that shit out loud? Christ, you sound like a wacko." He gives his head a quick nod. "Heads up, they're approaching to the left."

Still facing the bar, I take a swig of beer, relishing the cold liquid pouring down my throat, swallowing hard and kind of wishing I was piss-ass drunk, especially when Kevin loudly announces, "Looky looky what the cat dragged in! It's our favorite new couple."

I almost spit my beer out and swear if looks could kill, my boy Kevin would be a *dead* man.

I'm too sober and way way too old for this shit.

Weston claps me on the shoulder, letting his hand rest there as a warning to chill the fuck out, and I turn toward the group, fake smile pasted across my lips. My eyes settle on Cecelia, and seeing her is like a drink of water to my parched soul. *Holy shit balls* did that sound cheesy— cheesy but…mostly true. My tired eyes haven't set on her in what, days? A week? Two weeks? All I know for sure is it's been too long, and time seems indistinguishable. It hardly matters now that she's here.

Now here I am waxing poetic about a girl who:

1. I'm not even technically dating.
2. I haven't even kissed.
3. Thinks I'm a complete prick.
4. Is here on a date with one of my best friends, who is admittedly probably a better match for her than I am.

Need I go on?

I only have myself to blame.

As Molly hands Cecelia a cocktail glass, I see her covertly watching me from the corner of her eye above the rim as she takes a long sip, a maneuver I've discovered she's honed well; it means she can stare at me without being obvious.

I take her perusal of me as a sign—a very *good* sign.

On the other hand, Neve's hand is still tucked into her goddamn shorts. "Have you guys been here long?" he asks no one in particular.

Jenna flips her long, wavy, blonde and lavender hair, giggling at him flirtatiously, dimples denting her smooth cheeks. "Only for about twenty minutes. You know how it is, no one wants to get here before eleven o'clock and be the first ones out."

I try not to bare my teeth as Neve somewhat reluctantly removes his hand from the waistband of Cecelia's shorts *just* long enough to step forward and bump my fist in way of a greeting. At this moment I would seriously rather *crush* the bones in his knuckles *with* my fist than bump them.

Does that seem harsh?

I mean come on, what the fuck is he doing with my girl? All right, all right, fine—go ahead and argue that she and I really don't have anything going on, and that she isn't *really* my girlfriend, but so what? Neve knows I like her. Weston knows I like her. *Everyone fucking knows I like her.*

Don't they…?

So the question is: what the hell is *he* doing taking her out on another date? It's shady and it's pissing me off. Honestly, he really is lucky I don't deck him. This totally goes against bro code, and judging by the smug look plastered on his arrogant face, he damn well knows it.

He also knows I'm not going to do anything about it, which pisses me off even more.

Molly hovers nearby, sipping her drink but on high alert, like a referee in a game on the ice, waiting to step in if the players start roughhousing. She looks weary and tired, and I wouldn't exactly say I felt guilty for putting her in the middle, but…it's her damn fault for having a witty and gorgeous roommate to begin with.

Weston breaks through the awkward silence. "The two of you look way too dressed up for this place."

Okay, so much for breaking the ice and making it less awkward.

"Well, we weren't going to stop in but Kevin kept bugging me, so…here we are." Neve flashes his teeth, corralling Cecelia closer to the bar and getting out his wallet. Leaning against the counter with a twenty-dollar bill extended, he makes the money into a little tent and lays it on the bar top. He plants a kiss on the side of Cecelia's face, putting an arm around her shoulder and giving her an affectionate squeeze. "Our original plan was to go parking, wasn't it love muffin?"

Cecelia

"This shot of Jager tastes like I'll be drunk texting you later." – Bernie

*O*h my god, *love muffin?*

Seriously? *Seriously?!* Come on!

I groan inwardly and secretly want to both vomit in my mouth *and* elbow Neve in the gut (hard), but can't get my arm loose enough to do it since he's draped all over me like a wet washrag. He's starting to annoy the shit out of me, even though I know he's only doing it to irritate Matthew.

I mean, I want to *annoy* Matthew, *not* make him think I'm a man-hopper, if you know what I mean. If you don't, well, a man-hopper is exactly what it sounds like: the kind of girl that goes from one guy to another—in other words, *a slut.*

I force a smile and, through clenched teeth, mutter sarcastically, "Right. Parking. Up at Walker's Point. You all know how I loooove a good make-out sesh."

Everyone except Neve shifts uncomfortably, their eyes roaming between Matthew and me like they're watching a telenovela unfold before their eyes.

In a way, it kind of is.

Unable to stand it any longer, I peel Neve off of me and excuse myself to run to the ladies room, the privacy a welcome diversion. I lean against the dirty metal stall, staring up at the moldy ceiling, and exhale. My body sags and I dig into my Molly's handbag to check my cell.

The little blue light blinks: one new message.

Matthew: *I know it's not my place, but you look beautiful tonight.*

I stare at the text, slack-jawed. Damn right it's not his place. And yet...

Me: *So complimentary all of a sudden. Gee, I wonder why...*

Matthew: *Learning from my mistakes?*

Me: *Well, at least when you make mistakes, they're not hard to miss. Have you re-evaluated your stance on blowies?*

Matthew: *Have you?*

Me: *OH...MY...GOD*

Matthew: *I'M KIDDING. I'M JUST KIDDING. See? I am a complete idiot. I NEED someone like you to teach me how not to be an asshole.*

Me: *Probably, but you know what they say: can't teach an old dog new tricks. And YOU are definitely a* dog. *Woof woof.*

Matthew: *Wow, you go straight for the jugular, don't you?*

Me: *I call it like I see it. You're not the right guy for me, Matthew, and I don't do casual flings. Sorry.*

Matthew: *I know you're starting to like me, Cecelia. Admit it.*

Me: *I won't admit anything. And if I did, it's too late anyway. You leave in a month for California.*

Matthew: *Why did you have to go and bring that up??????*

Me: *Look. I can't stay holed up in the bathroom texting you. At some point I have to come back out to my DATE.*

Matthew: *Suit yourself. But you should know I still plan on cashing in...*

Me: *Fat chance.*

Matthew: *You know you're going to have to lay one on me at some point. Be a woman of your word.*

Me: *I'm not kissing you. Get over yourself.*

Matthew: *Over myself? I'd rather have you under my-self... Haha.*

Me: *I know this will be difficult for you to comprehend, but when I walk back out, could you please try to behave like a mature adult?*

Matthew: *That just proves you don't know me at all. LOL. Why would I start behaving like an adult now?*

Why indeed.

I lock my cell and stuff it back into my purse, balancing myself on the small single sink in the bathroom by the forearms, staring at myself in the mirror. My deceitful, traitorous-self stares back.

I say I want nothing to do with Matthew Wakefield, that I don't want him touching me, don't want to kiss him, but it's all just one, big, fat lie and I know it.

He knows it.

I sigh.

Man, *I am so screwed.*

Matthew

Normally, I'm not the kind of guy that tries forcing himself on people, especially women—I typically don't have to. But tonight, I find myself zoning in and out of the conversation unfolding in front of me in favor of plotting the seduction of one Cecelia Carter.

Out on the dance floor, Molly, Jenna, and Cecelia buckle over in laughter as they grab each other's hips, swaying and dancing to the house band in what looks like an attempt to *mock* the music. One thing is for sure: they're not taking themselves seriously.

"Dude, it's rude to stare at my date right in front of me," Neve points out, poking me to get my attention.

"Dude, it's rude to bring *my* girl on a date right in front of me."

Everyone laughs at my audacity. "Yeah, I guess it is, but...*oh well.* Shouldn't have acted like a pig, I guess."

"Cut the crap, all right? We all know this whole date is horse shit. What's it going to take to get you to leave?" I cross my arms defensively.

Neve mirrors my stance. "Nothing. I gave you one shot with her the first time I took her out, and I'm not giving you another one. If she didn't want to be here with me, she wouldn't have come, so back off."

"You're seriously doing this to me right now?"

"I think she's worth it, don't you?"

Shit. He makes a good point.

She *is* worth it.

Neve doesn't stop there and prattles on like a gushing school girl. "Smart, pretty…and *man* is she funny. We laughed our asses off through dinner. Hey, did you know she really *does* have a black belt? It's not bullshit. She's had it since she was twelve. Crazy isn't it?" He laughs. "Promised she'd show me how to toss someone over my shoulder."

No, I didn't realize she was actually a black belt; I just assumed she was full of shit and false bravado when she'd said it. It never occurred to me that she would have been telling the truth that morning she was trying to kick me out of her apartment the day we first met.

Now I'm realizing I've never really asked her about herself. Jeez, I really am a selfish prick—no wonder she wants nothing to do with me.

"Her sister, too. Says it's because her dad traveled a lot when she was growing up and her parents wanted the girls to be able to defend themselves."

Kevin leans in intently. "That's so fucking hot. What else did she tell you?"

Neve takes a drag from his pilsner glass and licks the foam from his upper lip. "Well, she went skydiving for her eighteenth birthday and to Ireland alone for her twenty-first. Definitely not afraid to do anything solo." He taps his chin in thought. "Hmm, let's see, what else… "

Suddenly, I can't listen to any more. Cupping my hands around my mouth to create a makeshift megaphone, I shout, "Hey Cece!" She stops dancing and looks my way, surprised—I've never called her Cece before. "Canoodle." The word slips past my tongue and I stare at her hard, harder than I've ever stared at anyone before.

It doesn't take long before Cecelia is stomping over, Jenna and Molly nipping at her heels. Angrily, she grabs me by the arm.

"What the hell Matthew," she hisses, giving my bicep an aggressive squeeze. "Why are you doing this?"

"Hey, more importantly, what the hell is a *canoodle*?" Jenna interrupts, her face twisted into a contorted, confused expression.

"It's an old term that means to kiss and cuddle," Molly answers wryly, raising her brows at me.

"Sounds like some kind of donut." Kevin laughs.

"You *would* think it was a donut, you fucking moron," Weston says, checking Kevin with his hip.

"Hey watch it. I almost spilled my drink—that's alcohol abuse," our friend mutters, clutching his beer glass with both fists and holding it tight against his body to protect it.

Jenna clicks her tongue and watches as I cross my arms and repeat myself, only louder this time. "Ceceila Carter, I said *canoodle*."

She shakes her head defiantly. "No."

"Why the heck do you keep saying canoo—" Molly

stops herself abruptly, her pretty face lighting up as her best friend continues babbling beside her.

"Seriously, ca*noodle*? Why not car? Or cardigan. Or cavity. Or cadaver...." Jenna mutters. "Those would all make more sense than just randomly..." She pauses. "Wait, is that the... Oh my gawd, it *is*. Holy crap, that's the code word from your bet at putt-putt, isn't it?"

I stare at Cecelia, who continues glaring at me, feet glued to the floor. "You bet your sweet ass it is."

Cecelia

Low. Blow.

What kind of a colossal asshole would call in a bet for a *kiss* while I am on a date *with another guy*?

I'll tell you what freaking kind: the Matthew Wakefield kind.

Slack-jawed, I stare at him, wanting to walk over and slap him hard across the face. I mean, seriously, the *nerve* of him. I feel Neve's fingers playing along the seam in the back of my shirt and want to smack him, too.

Stupid boys.

"Why are you doing this?" I hiss at Matthew, our friends (including Neve) looking back and forth between us in stunned fascination. I swear if this was the movies, they would all be eating popcorn and Milk Duds.

"You even have to ask? This is a game we started, and I plan on finishing it, even if *you* don't."

Well shit, of course he plans on finishing it. I should

have *known* when we made the stupid bet that Matthew wasn't going to back down or forget about it like a decent human being with some compassion. Nope. He's too competitive for that.

"What are you trying to say Matthew? That if I don't walk over there and kiss you, you're going to…what? What are you going to do about it?" I lip off, hands on my jutted out hips, unable to stop the words from bitterly spilling out of my mouth. "You can't make me like you, so stop trying. And you can't make me kiss you."

Matthew shakes his head at me, feigning disappointment. "Cecelia, Cecelia…you're testing my patience."

He looks me up and down, grinning like the Cheshire Cat, and I return the favor. His green eyes are bright, interested, and staring right into my soul. His dark auburn hair is disheveled, like he's run his fingers through it a million times already tonight. He dressed up a little, and his tall frame looks utterly delicious in his light sage pinstripe dress shirt, the top two buttons undone and untucked over dark wash, low-slung jeans.

I glance down at his feet (because it's in my nature to not just size him up, but to do it thoroughly) to find navy and white Sperry Top-Sider boat shoes.

Damn him. Damn him and his fine ass.

Nevertheless, I cross my arms, unrelenting, and purse my lips before tipping my chin up and refusing to look directly at him. If he wants to call in the damn bet, he's going to have to kiss me first.

"Cece, maybe you should just get it over with," Jenna calls from only a few feet away, trying to be helpful.

"A canoodle is a canoodle, Cecelia, and might I remind

you, you chose the word." Matthew laughs, spreading his arms wide, inviting me in. "Want me to come over there?" He gives his fingers a little *come hither* wiggle.

"I still think canoodle sounds like a donut." I'm close enough to hear Matthew's friend Kevin mutter this insightful comment, and to see Jenna pinch him in the forearm. "Ouch! What?"

God this is embarrassing.

I glance over at my date, only to find him chatting up a scantily clad female bartender, his back completely turned to Matthew and me, apparently uninterested in the unfolding drama even though we *agreed* and discussed that he was going to pretend to be into me to make Matthew jealous (I know, I know, it's a stupid thing to do) and to make him suffer a little bit longer before I finally gave in and admitted to liking him, too.

Well, there goes that plan. Thanks a-freaking-lot, Neve.

Ugh, flippin guys. Not to sound bitter, but why can't they just do what they're told? Or for that matter, what they say they're going to do. That would sure make life easier. Instead of getting involved with an *alpha* male, maybe I should start looking for someone a little easier to boss around.

Sigh.

Yeah, I know, you're right—who am I trying to kid? Matthew's bossy, overbearing nature is what attracted me to him in the first place, and I'm confident that's what attracted *him* to *me*, too—my sass, spunk, and sometimes overconfident disposition.

I get jostled by a passing bar patron crossing behind me and lurch forward a few feet, stumbling toward Matthew so that I'm standing even closer—close enough to touch, actually. I blow the hair out of my eyes, grateful that I'm not carrying a glass—which reminds me, why the *hell* don't have a drink in my hand?

I need one now more than I did before.

I turn my head and mouth to Molly (who's watching us as intently as she watches *Pretty Little Liars*), "*Get me another drink*," then tip my head back and make the universal sign for *chugging a drink* with my hand. She rolls her eyes but turns toward the bar, giving a shrill whistle to catch the bartender's attention.

Man, she sure is pushy when she wants to be—must run in the family.

Matthew eyes me up and down, beginning with my stocking-clad toes. He takes in my sheer black panty hose, which elongate my legs, and my feet, which are buckled into black strappy wedges. Those bright green eyes of his travel up slowly…ever so slowly…hitting my thighs, resting briefly on the hem of my high-waisted shorts before leisurely roaming over my tight white shirt, lingering on my breasts, then bare arms.

There isn't a piece of me he doesn't concentrate on.

It would be a tad dramatic to say I feel exposed, but… there it is in a nutshell: him stripping me bare, in public, in front of all our friends.

Our eyes meet and his lips tip into a crooked smile. "How many times are you going to make me say it?"

I plant my hands firmly on my hips and smile back. "If you wanted to kiss me so bad, why did you have to invent a reason to do it? *Jeezus*. You are *twenty*-three years old— aren't we a bit old for games?"

"So you're telling me I should have just *done* it?"

Jenna snorts behind me. "*Duh.*"

Matthew

I hate to be the bearer of bad news, but…sometimes guys (*especially* twenty-three-year-old ones) need to be told what to do and given the green light to make a move. I thought for sure after miniature golf at Galaxy Golf World, Cecelia had friend-zoned me.

It also doesn't help that she hasn't been throwing out signals (like most girls I knew); she hasn't been throwing herself at me, and she hasn't been coy. She's been being her bratty, sarcastic self, and it's throwing me off my game. How do I know she won't knock a gap in my teeth when I make a move?

And come on, what was with all the high-fives and fist bumps that night?

I have no idea where I stand with her, especially after the whole *BJ* thing no one is going to let me forget. Call me insecure, but no matter what any guy tells you, guys do need to know they're not going to be rejected (see: shot down).

If Cecelia had a little green *go* flag, now would probably be a good time for her to wave it around a little bit…

Cecelia has her hands planted on her hips and a smile pasted on her glossy lips. "If you wanted to kiss me so bad, why did you have to invent a reason to do it? *Jeezus*. You are *twenty*-three years old—aren't we a bit old for games?"

"So you're telling me I should have just *done* it?"

Jenna snorts behind her. "*Duh.*"

"So what are you saying?" I ask slowly, confused.

Yes, I'm an idiot. Sue me.

Neve is behind Weston, his head bowed in disappointment, and Kevin has his lip curled at me like he's just swallowed something sour.

Cecelia throws her hands up. "I'm saying what I'm saying!"

"Um…"

"You didn't have to make a bet with me or make up an excuse to get a kiss from me."

I fight the urge to scratch my head. "So what you're saying is…?"

"Oh my fucking god man, shut the fuck up and just kiss her already!" We all turn our heads to see some random guy shouting at me. Around five foot seven, he's wearing a white wife beater and jeans, waiting in line at the bar. He's glaring at me, looking flagrantly disgusted. "I have completely lost faith in an athlete's ability to get laid. You are a total disappointment, bro."

Shaking his head, he pushes through the crowd and stalks off without even getting a drink.

There is a delayed reaction before everyone begins cracking up. Kevin hunches over, his loud, boisterous laugh echoing throughout the bar while Neve grabs the wooden bartop to hold himself upright. Molly and Weston are, of course, laughing too, and Cecelia has tears streaming down her face.

"Oh my god," Cecelia gasps, clutching her stomach.

"You should see the look on your face right now." More breathless laughter. "Oh man, Matthew. I should take a picture. I'm dying."

Crossing my arms and giving them all the evil eye, I complain, "Yeah, that was real funny guys. Stop pointing your finger at me Kevin, it's rude." This starts another fit of raucous laughter, and they're almost all keeled over, falling all over themselves in hysterical fits, still pointing at me.

Bunch of assholes.

Cecelia wipes her eyes with the back of her hand and reaches up to pat my shoulder. "I'm sorry, but even *you* have to admit that was hilarious." She bites her lip like she wants to add something else, but instead just says, "How random *was* that guy?"

"So random," I deadpan, not even remotely amused. "Okay you dipshits, that's enough," I add, using one hand to shove Weston into a barstool, which isn't nice, but so what? It makes me feel better.

After everyone is done making the loud sighing noises you make when you're just *so* utterly amused you can't *stand* it, they finally get control of their wits ten minutes later. Bout damn time.

Cecelia

At some point, a little voice inside your head (or maybe it's the devil on your shoulder) whispers, *What are you fighting this for? You want him to kiss you, admit it. Just let him do it already.*

Then there's the intelligent voice shouting, *Are you crazy? This guy is a dick. Do not let him touch your lips. He is moving away for six months!*

Regardless of the conflicting feelings I'm having, one thing seems certain: at some point, I'm going to cave. It's inevitable…

I mean, what's the worst thing that can happen if I do?

Standing not two feet away, assessing me, is Matthew Wakefield, a guy who just will not go away, who drives me absolutely up the wall with his constant profanity, vulgarity, and yeah, his amateur stalking tendencies.

A guy who has, in a weird, twisted, messed up way, actually become a *friend.*

Yes, it's true: he has made me cry. He has embarrassed me. He drives me up the wall…but he also makes me laugh. And blush. And just a look from him sends shivers up my spine. He's big and imposing, and he makes me feel safe.

In a way, Matthew has wooed me with sweet emails and text messages, sort of like my own modern day Cyrano de Bergerac.

All right. *Fine.* The emails and texts were not sweet in the least—in fact, they're demanding, sarcastic, and wry—but they're *mine.* They're mine, and Matthew sent them, and they…they make me *feel* something, something that's not a thesis paper, doesn't have a deadline—something that makes my heart race. Something real.

If those emails and texts had been written on actual paper, I'd probably save them, fold them up like people did in the 90s (before they had cellphones) and store the notes in a shoe box on a shelf in the back of my closet so I could bring them out years later and reread them over and over.

Cause that wouldn't be weird at all…

So honestly, don't you think all the things about him that make me feel good outweigh the bad? The fact that he's leaving for training camp? I mean…it's not like he has a choice; it's his job.

I'm almost twenty-three years old for crying out loud; I'm *pretty* sure I can handle a short-term relationship, or friendship… whatever kind of *ship* it is that we're in… can't I?

I set down the apple martini Molly handed me earlier and step forward, spreading my arms wide. "All right Matthew, you want me? You got me. Lay one on me."

Matthew

"When I see lovers' names carved on trees, I never think it's cute. I always just think, *How strange that someone would bring a knife on a date.*" – Abby, via a witticism she saw on the internet

L ay one on her?

"That wasn't the deal," I stubbornly persist.

Cecelia crosses the arms that were just spread wide. "If you want me, you're going to have to kiss me first. That's the newly minted deal."

"Fine," I agree.

"Good."

"Okay then." I step forward.

"Super."

"*Oh my god, here we go again...*" Someone groans. It sounds like my sister, but I don't turn around. Someone else agrees, saying, "*This is painful.*"

"Dude, if you don't kiss her within the next five seconds, I'll do it for you," Kevin half jokes, shoving me into Cecelia from behind. I feel like a freaking eighth grader at a school dance.

"Well?" Cecelia taunts me.

She can't fool me. I can tell by the gleam in her eye that she's excited as she stares me down, not a self-conscious bone in her body.

A few more inches and our noses will be touching. "I'm giving you one more chance to be woman of your word, Cecelia Carter. It's now or never. So, I'll say it one more time…canoodle."

Cecelia moves a centimeter closer and leans in to whisper in my ear. "Canoodle. That is the single *dumbest* word I've ever heard coming out of a person's mouth." Her warm breath tickles my neck as she pulls away to look at me, one eyebrow raised defiantly.

"It's your fault," I whisper back, inching closer. "I personally would have chosen something like *dipstic* or… or…"

"Snozzberries?" she finishes with a light giggle.

My jaw drops and I put a hand to my heart. "Dear lord, are no memories sacred between me and my sister?"

Cecelia taps her chin, pretending to think about it. "Mmm, 'fraid not."

I shoot Molly a hard glare. She obliviously stares back and gives me a *what did I do now* shrug of the shoulders. "That little traitor, always double-crossing me."

"Hey." Cecelia nudges me. "Let's get this over with. Everyone is waiting for some action; we're like a sideshow in a circus."

Slowly I reach for her, gingerly resting my hands on her shoulders before cautiously caressing sun-kissed skin, the pads of my fingertips lightly skimming her bare arms, causing goose bumps to rise. My large hands snake their way over her ribcage, under her armpits, and pull her in closer. I lean down so my nose is nestled in her thick hair, drawing in a breath and relishing the close contact of our bodies pressed together. Sweat, fruity shampoo, and a soft musky cologne assault my senses—but in a good way.

Reaching around to brush a stray tendril away from her eyes, I cautiously bring my face down and brush my lips across her temple. "There," I murmur, satisfied, backing away.

"What the...hell?" Cecelia mutters.

I can't help it. I bust out laughing. "You said you wanted me to kiss you first. Doesn't that satisfy the requirement?"

"You are a *jackass*," Cecelia hisses, shoving me hard, though not hard enough to budge me.

I am a fortress of steel.

"*Seriously bro? That's the best you got?*" Weston heckles like a spectator on the sidelines while Neve cups his hands around his mouth and shouts, "*Weak! So weak!*"

"I've about had it *up to here* with you, Matthew Wakefield," Cecelia seethes through clenched teeth, trying to break out of my embrace in a huff.

How cute is she when she's all pissy?

So adorable.

Undaunted, my arms are around her in a vice, hands clasped behind her back. I give her a good yank, slamming her retreating figure into my solid body, and plant an open-

288 | SARA NEY

mouth kiss square on her surprised mouth.

Cecelia's expressive brown eyes widen in shocked desire as my teeth nip at her lower lip before forcing her mouth open with my tongue, and I feel victory when her hands flirt with the waistband of my jeans, tugging the hem of my t-shirt up to slide her hands underneath.

"Asshole," she hisses even as her fingertips graze the skin of my abs.

"Shrew," I counter, a deep rumble coming from my chest.

Then, in an apparent decision to throw all caution to the wind, Cecelia slants her head and locks her full glossy lips against mine, both of us emitting low moans of pleasure and pain and relief that this is finally happening. Wasting no time, I reach down to haul Cecelia up against my groin, squeezing her ass cheeks with both hands before reluctantly settling them at her trim waist. Suddenly we're making out like it's our job, sucking face and tonguing each other's mouths like we're starving refugees and our lives depend on it.

Music blares above us through pounding speakers. Cecelia's fingers somehow wind up in my hair, raking through the locks at the base of my neck and pulling me closer. I oblige, bending slightly at the knees, aligning our pelvises and grinding into her, giving zero fucks that we have an audience.

Someone might have yelled, *"Holy shit that's turning me on,"* while another declared, *"This is better than porn!"*

Then, somewhere in the recesses of my mind, I hear my sister loudly announce, *"I am leaving! I thought I'd be able to handle this, but dear god, I cannot watch. Help!*

People, my retinas are burning!"

Cecelia

A few things are going through my head as Matthew's hands cup my ass through my thin shorts, hauling me firmly against the bulge in his jeans, and I can't stop thinking:

1. His mouth and hands feel amazing.
2. His silky tongue feels even *better*.
3. Why did we wait so long for this moment?
4. I wish like hell we were alone.

Pressed against Matthew's hard, muscular chest, it's easy to get carried away, despite the room full of people—possibly *because* of the room full of people. I've never been into exhibitionism—or voyeurism for that matter—but make no mistake, I am getting a cheap thrill from being so thoroughly kissed in public.

The music from the speakers blasts into the bar, coupled with all the colliding voices in the room fighting to be heard, creating almost a white noise. The base beat adds to the vibrations already coursing through my loins, and I have to suppress another throaty moan. It wouldn't be seemly to melt into a mushy puddle at Matthew's feet in front of my actual *date*, whom I've utterly forgotten about.

There are so many people in this bar, Matthew and I are all but forcibly thrust together, the patrons around us forming a solid wall.

We kiss for a few more seconds before I pull my hands out from under his shirt, dizzy from the blood surging through places I didn't know existed—or that were just dormant for too long (I won't mention *where*, but the place is *downtown* in my nether region and starts with the letter *V*).

I reach out for him once more, craving more of his body heat, running my palms up his bare arms, lightly tracing the ripples of taunt biceps, before someone clears their throat and I snap out of my sexually intoxicated state.

And then—just like in every kissing scene, in every cliché romance novel—after I pull away from Matthew, my fingers automatically reach up to touch my lips. They're swollen and completely void of the Tahitian lip gloss I so carefully applied earlier.

At this point, it's safe to declare myself thoroughly and properly kissed.

Wiping my damp mouth with a forefinger as if I'm dabbing away crumbs from an indulgent, messy snack I just ate (which I kind of just did), I take a step back, as far as I can go without bumping into the person behind me, and gaze up at Matthew shyly from under onyx eyelashes. He eyes me expectantly, somewhat tenderly, even…

The look on his face surprises me; his eyes have softened around the edges, and his normally sarcastic mouth is relaxed. As we drink each other in from head to toe, a blush creeps up the tendons in his neck, resting on the planes of his cheekbones. It's then I realize we're both seeing each other in a completely different way.

Good different. Exciting different. *Special* different.

They say a single word can change a life, change *everything*: in this case it's a single stare doing the changing.

Making us fall—*and fall hard.*

Then another thought occurs to me as we stand there

breathing heavily from our heated, public, make-out session: what do we do now?

Where do we go from here?

Matthew

There's much to be said for traveling in large groups: after my make-out session with Cecelia, the guys pretty much save me from making a *bigger* ass of myself by dragging me out of Lone Rangers before I could drag *Cecelia* out— you know, like the uncivilized caveman she believes me to be.

It's late—almost 2:00 a.m.—but I'm sober enough to send a text that isn't going to sound like a sexually fueled booty call.

At least, I hope it won't sound like one. I mean, what the hell do I know—didn't I just tell you it's two in the morning?

Here's hoping.

Me: *You awake?*

It takes a few minutes, but she finally responds.

Cecelia: *Of course.*

Me: *Sorry I left so fast. I hope you didn't take it personally*

Cecelia: *Take it personally? You were basically kidnapped by those heathen friends of yours. I'm surprised you were able get out of the headlock Kevin put you in. LOL. Impressive.*

Me: *Kevin is an idiot.*

Cecelia: *(shrug) He was just trying to help.*

Me: *By going all MMA on my ass? Um…no.*

Cecelia: *Come on, the guy's got moves. Jenna and the girls were impressed, even if you weren't.*

Me: *I will admit, the look of horror on your face may have been worth having my head vice-gripped into Kevin's stinky armpit…*

Cecelia: *Yeah. You've been impressing me since the beginning (patting mouth and yawning).*

Me: *You couldn't wait to send me that first email back in September, could you?*

Cecelia: *Are you nuts? Molly basically forced me to send it. Besides, you didn't even know the email was from me.*

Me: *Of course I knew it was you, goofball.*

Cecelia: *Seriously???*

Me: *Are you kidding? No one forgets the girl who threatens to mace them and kick their ass. Of course I knew it was you, I was just been messing with you. LOL. Remember when I ate your trail mix? You were so pissed.*

Cecelia: *Yes, I was, but in my defense, you were acting like a savage. Digging through my stuff – so rude. LOL*

Me: *Can't you just admit the feigned rage was just your futile attempt to resist me? You secretly WANTED me to eat your food. Why else would you have dumped it on to the couch?*

Cecelia: *Um, so I could have my hands free when I rescued your sister from the evil guy invading our apartment, that's why!!!*

Me: *Okay, fine, but for the record, I thought you were*

cute even when you were trying to shove me out the door

Cecelia: *Awwww, really?*

Me: *HELL NO! I thought you were a raving lunatic lololol*

Cecelia: *blah blah blah (crosses arms, pouting)*

Me: *So. I guess I'll stop beating around the bush and just come out and say it...*

Cecelia: *...?*

Me: *Would you like to go on a date? With me, specifically.*

There is a pause before her reply, and I look at the time stamp: three minutes have passed since I sent the message. Crap.

I blew it.

Me: *Um... What do you say?*

Cecelia: *I'm sorry, I might have just passed out from shock. What do I say? I say, it took you long enough to ask.*

Me: *Okay. So, just to clarify, is that a yes?*

Cecelia: *That's a yes.*

Cecelia

"I'd rather go freaking *blind* than go on a blind date."
– Jenna

"**I** feel like the only thing we do these days is primp you to see my brother. I'm not sure how I feel about this whole thing, to be honest. I mean, I'm seriously questioning your judgment in men," Molly remarks, standing behind me and watching me through the bathroom mirror, one hand holding a chunk of my long hair, the other wielding a purple ceramic curling iron.

"She can't help who she falls in love with, Molly. Some things are just meant to be," Abby firmly counters from the doorway, winking at me.

"Who says she's in love with him?" Jenna, who is mixing brownie batter in the kitchen, hollers. Her curious face peeks into the bathroom moments later to ask, "Wait, you're not in *love* with him, are you?"

The room quiets as everyone waits for my response, three wide-eyed reflections staring back at me expectantly. Molly's eyes are filled with wonder, as if the possibility of my loving her brother hadn't occurred to her before.

When I hesitate, she gives my hair a sharp tug, prodding me to speak. I gulp and avert my eyes, forcing out an unconvincing laugh. "Love him? Come on you guys, you know me better than that."

"The heart wants what the heart wants," Jenna says with a shrug. "I fell in love with Billy Rutley after only one date."

Molly snorts. "Yeah. Then you broke up with him after three."

"*What*ever. My point is, just because she hasn't known him forever doesn't mean she can't be in love with him." She shoves her chocolate-coated wooden mixing spoon at Abby. "Wanna lick?"

Abby rolls her eyes. "Get that thing out of my face."

"*That's what she said*," Jenna singsongs as she walks back to the kitchen with Abby following her, chastising the entire way.

"Those two, I swear." I laugh, shaking my head a little.

"Don't move your head," Molly scolds, holding up a large lock of hair, spraying it, then wrapping it around the barrel of her large curling iron. As she waits for the curl to set, she looks at me hard in the mirror. "Well?"

Not wanting to meet her intense stare, I look down at my freshly painted nails, studying the pale, nude polish before whispering, "I don't know. Maybe?"

Slowly, she unwraps the curl and holds it in place with a bobby pin so it can cool. Molly sets the curling iron on the counter and rests both hands on my shoulders, giving them a small shake. "Hey, look at me."

I look up and meet her eyes.

"I'm glad."

"You...are?"

"Hello! What do you think all my hard work has been for?" I scrunch my face and must look completely confused, because she begins laughing. "Cece, think about it. Go back to the beginning... Do you *really* think I couldn't have gotten ahold of my very own brother when I didn't have a phone? And who the heck sends emails these days? It was almost too easy. Let me see, what else...he knew where your first date with Neve was. He shows up at a Halloween party thrown by your friend. We're all there when he calls in your bet and kisses you senseless."

"But...why?"

"Why? Are you kidding me right now? Matthew is exactly what you need."

"Exactly what *I* need? Please. What about what *he* needs? That guy—no offense—needs a caretaker."

"See, that's *exactly* what I meant: *perfect* for each other."

"You are crazy."

"Well I guess that's one thing Matthew and I have in common—we're both crazy about *you*."

"Okay, now that's just weird."

"I didn't mean it like *that*." She laughs, tapping me on the head with a wide-tooth comb and staring at me thoughtfully. "Do you want your hair up or down?"

We both study my reflection, Molly tipping her head

this way and that as she contemplates how to style my long hair.

"I'm thinking…down?"

She nods her head in agreement. "Yeah, that will look good with the shirt we picked out." She picks up the curling iron again. "Let's get this done so Jenna can do your makeup. It sounds like those two are about to get into another argument."

"It's a love-hate thing. They love to hate each other."

Molly chuckles. "Pretty much. Kind of reminds me of Weston and Matthew, don'cha think?"

"Totally! I never thought of it like that…"

"They pretend they can't stand each other, but I think they act more like brothers…well, except that one time they had a game in Indiana and Matthew 'forgot' to bring Weston home from the airport."

I grin as she begins parting my hair into sections. "Hey, at least they can laugh about it now, right?"

"Um, yeah, *no*. They most definitely do not laugh about it. Well, I shouldn't say that—*Matthew* does."

"*He* would."

"Yes. One could never accuse my brother of not having a sense of humor, as twisted as his is."

"But…he's *so* cute." I sigh wistfully, letting out a rush of air. "And his body is so firm. *I could rub his arms up and down all day.*" Horrified, I look up and meet Molly's surprised eyes in the mirror. "Holy shit. Did I say that out loud?"

"Whoa. That's like, the first time you've ever admitted you think he's hot!"

"Well it's not like I'm going to talk about that stuff with you—it's too weird. Going on and on about your brother's hot body? Um, no thanks."

Molly lets out a loud laugh, then leans in to press her cheek to mine, speaking in a commiserating tone. "In that case, let's get you ready, because you know you're going to be pressed up against it later."

Like I needed a reminder?

Matthew

As the forward for a professional hockey team, I shouldn't theoretically be nervous about this date; after all, I've been in much more stressful situations, such as performing in a packed arena of twenty thousand plus people and being in the spotlight during the televised National Hockey League draft at twenty-one years old. I mean, I get my face bashed in by hockey sticks on national television on a weekly basis, for Christ's sake.

And yet, here I am with goddamn butterflies in my stomach.

Damn inconvenient is what it is.

I wasn't even this nervous when I got laid for the first time at the ripe old age of fifteen and had no clue which parts of my anatomy went where. Granted, my slutty junior date sure knew where to put my dick, but still…

I grab the keys off the table in my condo's small foyer, flip the lights off, and before I know it, I'm pulling into Cecelia and Molly's apartment complex. It's now November, so the air is frigid and the trees are almost devoid of leaves.

In the sky, the moon struggles to rise in the horizon, even though it's not quite dark enough to stand out against the setting sun.

I saunter up the walkway, trying to find my swagger, and with all the anticipation surrounding this evening, I feel like I'm picking up a prom date.

The door whips open before I can even knock, and Weston stands in the doorway, a cocky grin on his face. My sister peeks out from behind him.

"How did you know I was coming? There isn't even a peephole."

Weston's narrow eyes rake me up and down, like I'm some shady teenager there to molest his precious teenage daughter. "Hey, how about you not worry how I knew you were coming. How about you just worry about yourself."

I find this hilarious and smack him on the shoulder. "That's funny. Is Cecelia ready yet?" I glance around the small apartment, no trace of her readiness lingering any-where.

Molly purses her lips. "Brother, why don't you have a seat on the couch while Weston cleans off his shotgun. *Hardy har*."

They're acting like protective parents.

It's really kind of annoying. "Would you two knock it off?" I pull out a kitchen barstool, but don't sit on it.

"I know what boys like *you* want." Molly grins sugges-tively. "And our Cece is a good girl, so no funny business. Keep your hands to yourself."

"Um, yeah. *That's* not gonna happen." I laugh as Weston punches my upper bicep. "Ouch! What the hell was that for? I was kidding."

Only I wasn't, not really.

"Chill, I'm taking her to the Pee-Wee Hockey Expo and then for hot chocolate or something. There isn't going to be a lot of opportunity for groping—although, there's always the locker room…"

Except, the sarcastic words I'm about to say falter in my throat when Cecelia choses that moment to come out of her bedroom, looking fresh faced and casual in a tight, short-sleeved gray t-shirt, dark skinny jeans, and tall tan equestrian boots.

Smiling, she slips her arms into the red, tartan plaid button-down flannel shirt she's holding, quickly buttons the two buttons in the center, pulls on a tweed puffy vest, and stuffs a gray knit hat into the pocket.

I take her in from head to toe, drinking in every delectable ounce of her; to say she looks cute is a gross understatement.

"What? You told me to dress warm," she jokes. "I wanna be prepared."

Um, yeah, I definitely have no intention of keeping my hands to myself, not after waiting for so long, and sure as shit not after that heated first kiss Cecelia and I shared at the Lone Rangers a few nights ago.

No way.

Weston catches me staring and punches my arm again, shooting daggers at me.

I shrug.

Sorry dude, the hands-off thing is *so* not going to happen.

Cecelia

"So, where are you taking me?" I ask my date, giving him a sideways glance. His eyes are intent on the road, so I'm able to freely linger (see also: ogle) on every sharp curve of his face every time an oncoming car passes and headlights illuminate the cab, making my perusal easier. Every plane of Matthew's strong, freshly shaved jaw is sharper in the dark, as is the small bump *just* at the bridge of his nose, and the scar near his temple.

His hair is still slightly damp from his shower, the thick tresses combed back but still somehow unkempt, black sunglasses propped on his head even though the sun has long since disappeared over the horizon.

I find both Matthew and our close bodily contact all mildly erotic, and I clear my throat to hide the onslaught of discomfort. I glance around the cab of his Tahoe and am surprised to find it has been detailed. The garbage is gone. No gym bag, no hockey equipment, no crusty dirt or gravel stuck to the floor mats.

"You didn't go and get your car cleaned for little ol' me, did you?" I tease.

He glances over for a heartbeat, dimple softly denting his cheek. "Guilty as charged."

"You seriously went and had your car detailed for our date?" I'm stupefied.

Matthew wrinkles his nose. "Um, yeah? I mean… didn't it stink the last time you were in it?"

"Well, yeah, it was pretty rank if I recall, but at the time I thought it'd be rude to mention it."

My date throws his head back against the headrest and lets out a loud burst of laughter. Of course, I can't help but admire the thick, straining cords of his neck column, and the dark stubble of five o'clock shadow disappearing into the collar of his button-down shirt.

He catches me studying him and arches an eyebrow.

I clear my throat. "So...you like the color blue, huh?" I ask, referring to the light blue of his shirt. To be honest, it's *barely* blue. It is embroidered with a delicate paisley pattern in the same hue, modern cut with long sleeves, which Matthew has rolled to his elbows, exposing his broad, muscular forearms.

Very sharp.

Very dapper.

Muy delicioso.

He looks over and studies me back. "What makes you say that?"

"Nothing. I just noticed you wear blue a lot. You look very handsome tonight, by the way."

"Thanks, you do too—not handsome. Ugh, that's not what I meant. Pretty. You look amazing, is what I meant. Oh my god, I've turned into an idiot." He laughs. "You can shut up any time now Matthew," he adds, mocking himself in a low, grumbling voice. His laughter is soft but deep, and fills the cab of the Tahoe in a way that makes the space feel small.

Intimate.

Phew, is it hot in here? Maybe it's time to crack the window and let some fresh air in!

I could easily reach over and touch him if I wanted to,

but instead, I clear my throat. *Again*. We've been driving for a while, and I am dying to know where we're headed without having to ask outright.

But if I've learned anything about guys, it's that:

1. They do not take hints very well.
2. Often, they need things spelled out for them.
3. Subtlety is *use*less.

Once when I was younger, I wanted to go to the mall with my friends, and I wanted my dad to give me spending money. I tried to get him to get it for an entire day, dropping hints and being an overly dramatic teen. Finally, my dad stopped me and said, "If there's something you're trying to tell me by moping around, you better come out with it because, I have no idea what's happening right now. Men aren't mind-readers Cecelia."

So take my advice: come out and ask if you want something because a guy, no matter how smart, will *never* get the hint.

He. Just. Won't.

Ever.

Besides, don't you agree that beating around the bush is just a different form of game playing?

"Where are we going?" I cut to the chase, direct without sounding overly anxious.

"Nosey little thing, aren't you?" Smiling, Matthew reaches across the center console to grasp my hand, interlocking our fingers. I look down at our joined hands, marveling at the difference in their size, shape, and feel. While my hands are silky smooth from pampering and manicures, his are dry, rough and calloused, a hardworking man's hands, utterly masculine.

There is a dusting of dark hair on his knuckles that actually makes me swallow a lump in my throat. Seriously, the hair on his knuckles is turning me on? Clearly I have issues.

I can't stop staring at his thumb caressing my pale skin; the sensation feels both foreign and intimate, not necessarily a bad different, just...different.

"I'm sorry, is this too weird for you?" Matthew asks as if reading my mind—or my face. He's probably noticed that my cheeks are on fire. In any case, I glance away from his heated, piercing green eyes and tilt my chin up.

"If you're trying to distract me so you don't have to reveal our destination, it's *not* going to work."

Matthew snickers and squeezes my hand twice. "Maybe you should let yourself be surprised."

"You can't blame me for being curious," I mumble, face turned toward the window. For a brief few moments, I quietly watch the landscape go by. A farm in the distance, windmills, and a small shopping center zoom past before we pass a Target and a home improvement giant. I cannot imagine for the life of me where we could possibly be headed. "Can't you just tell me?"

"You're almost as bad as Molly," Matthew observes. "She cannot *stand* not knowing anything. Once, I think for her twelfth birthday, Jenna tried throwing her a surprise pool party for her birthday at our parents' house, but Molly was *so* suspicious that when the day of the party finally arrived, they couldn't get her into the back yard for the actual surprise. Jenna had to drag her by the arm, and by the time they made it out there, Molly was so pissed off and embarrassed, she spent the first twenty minutes of her party in the house pouting before she'd put her swimsuit on."

Yeah, I could totally see my roommate doing that.

"My mom was so pissed that she was being such a little brat. I was convinced they'd ban her from having any more birthday parties." Matthew chuckles at the memory. "Everything turned out fine, of course, but if Molly hadn't been so damn *suspicious* leading up to the party, she would have had a ton more fun—and wouldn't have gotten her ass chewed out in the process."

I give him a sideways glance. "I'm not sure I get what your point is here and how that relates to me. That story is an *atrocious* comparison."

Matthew snorts. "My point is, just enjoy the ride. Don't be so uptight."

Uptight? *Me*? Pfft.

We ride in silence for a few more miles before turning into the well-lit parking lot of an ice arena.

So not what I was expecting.

Matthew

"Girlfriend? That's a funny way to pronounce Netf-lix." – Rachel Sinclair, Molly's occasional (and always sarcastic) study partner

"**M**an, am I glad I brought these babies," Cecelia croons beside me, referring to the hat and mittens she's just donned and looking absolutely adorable and delicious in both. Her long wavy hair spills out the bottom of the gray cable-knit cap, framing her flushed cheeks and highlighting her finely arched eyebrows and the cupid's bow of her pert lips.

Okay, okay, I'm probably waxing poetic a little too freely, and it's probably not the warm-weather clothing so much as the fact that I can't stop staring and admiring her many fine features.

We're seated in the stands of Madison Ice Arena North, a low-rent facility on the edge of town, closer to the ghetto than I'm used to, and about a thirty-minute drive from the rink where my kids normally play.

They don't have a game tonight; it's actually an exhibition of leagues and kids that have split into smaller teams to play in three-on-three tournament brackets. I don't have any of my students participating this year—at one hundred twenty-five bucks a pop, the astronomical entry fees alone keep them at bay—but I still come year after year to watch the younger generations of kids play, especially the pee-wees.

The arena is cold—really freaking cold—and Cecelia hunkers down next to me on the wooden bench, sidling up close and clutching a hot chocolate in her gloved hands.

"Brrrr." She shivers and takes a loud sip as steam rises from the small gap in the top. She lifts the cup and studies the steaming hole with one eye. "How come, do you suppose, the hot chocolate at these things is always just made from water and cocoa mix? Yucko."

"Because it's cheap," I hypothesize. "Plus, it's cheap."

Cecelia laughs into her cup and eyes someone above the rim. "But maybe not as cheap as that chick over there." She nods toward the ice, where someone's mother stands next to the boards wearing a short skirt, heels, and a sweater—not exactly ice rink appropriate apparel. I mean, it's bleeding fifty-five degrees in here, tops.

"Please don't let me out of your sights tonight, not with that one running loose," I say as a horrified chuckle escapes my lips, only half joking. Those rink bunnies (who show up everywhere) can spot a meal ticket from one hundred yards away, and I don't want her smelling me. "I don't even want you leaving to go to the bathroom…haha."

"You better be nice to me then." Cecelia playfully bumps me with her shoulder. "Otherwise, I'll flag her down with my hat and offer you up on a platter."

I lean in close. *"You wouldn't dare."*

She leans in, unflinching, and purses her glossy lips. "Try me."

Just a few centimeters closer and I peck her lips, sending a surprised and embarrassed blush to her already flushed cheeks. With a gloved hand, she reaches up and touches her mouth, smiling. "Okay, well, *that* definitely earned you brownie points."

"I hope so, because your lips taste like hot chocolate and coconut, and coconut just became my new favorite thing of all time."

"That's funny, I remember Weston saying the same thing when he discovered your sister wore edible body glitter."

I stare at her for a second. "What is it with you people? Why does everyone have to constantly remind me that my sister is 'doing it' with that guy? You just killed my buzz."

Cecelia arches her eyebrow and digs in her bag, pulling out a tube of clear lip gloss. She turns it toward me and I read the label: coconut. "I know how I can make it better…"

"Um, okay, yeah…that might help me feel a little better." I watch, somewhat spellbound, as she slowly unscrews the cap and begins swiping it back and forth across her full lips before rubbing them together. Then, I utter a phrase I've heard my dad say to my mom a million times. "Come here and give me some of that sugar."

It's cheesy, but it works—she leans into me with a big grin on her face and presses her body against mine on the cold bench. Her large, expressive brown eyes are lined with dark liner, and her lashes look a mile long. For the first time, I notice she has a few rogue freckles next to her nose and I reach up to touch one, connecting each dot with the tip of my finger. She smiles and kisses my palm, nuzzling her cheek into my hand. I immediately bring my other hand up to cup her face, marveling at the soft, blemish-free skin under my calloused finger.

We both lean closer still, until there's no room between our bodies, and I pucker my lips dramatically, causing Cecelia to giggle before our eyes slide shut for our impending kiss.

Our lips are a breath away before I hear a loud *Hey Coach!* somewhere off in the distance. I can't tell where it's coming from, but it's an oddly familiar voice and makes me pause long enough to crack my eyes open.

"Coach! Coach, down here!"

Cecelia

Groaning (*not* from pleasure), Matthew lifts his head—though not before stealing another quick kiss. He stares out into the crowd in search of the small voice that is certainly shouting at him.

He doesn't have to search long, for down at the bottom of the bleachers, wearing jeans and a red hooded *Madison Lightning* sweatshirt is none other than a waving, enthusiastic Andy Boskowitz, and he's standing next to a grinning Mitchell Decker and that kid Stew. Stewart. The proverbial three musketeers, they're all holding popcorn and soda and are headed up the stairs in our direction.

"Ah shit," Matthew mumbles. "Brace yourself."

The boys continue climbing toward us, with Mitchell tripping on one of the steps and almost spilling his popcorn. He pauses to reposition his glasses, not once losing his cheeky grin.

"Oh my god, they are *so* freaking cute," I gush as the trio awkwardly lumbers forward. "I can't even stand it."

Matthew casts a glance over and looks at me like I've turned blue and sprouted two heads. "Are you nuts? Our whole night is about to be *ruined*."

I laugh, despite the serious expression on his face—or perhaps because of it. "Seriously? How could they *possibly* ruin this romantic atmosphere you've planned for us? Look around you. If anything, they're about to enhance it with their shenanigans…"

"Shenanigans is one of my favorite words," Andy Boskowitz proclaims as he plunks himself down next to Matthew. "My brother watches *Super Troopers* all the time so that's how I know that word."

As if that explains everything.

"Hey Coach. I thought you said she wasn't your girlfriend," Mitchell says, sandwiching himself between Matthew and myself without ceremony or permission. He fists a handful of popcorn into his mouth, staring up at Matthew through his thick eyeglasses. "Well?"

Yeah…*well*?

Inquiring minds want to know.

"Do you remember what I told you in the parking lot after practice last week Mitchell? About some things being private?" Matthew looks down at him, stern look on his face.

"Nope, you didn't say that," Mitchell says obliviously

as Matthew gives him a hard stare. "I would remember." He taps his skull for emphasis.

Before Matthew can give a rebuttal, Stewart cuts in from the bench behind us. He has his elbow resting on Matthew's shoulders, casually hovering over him. "Hey Coach, do you think next year we can enter this tournament? The three-on-three scrimmage looks cool."

"I don't know, Stew, it's pretty expensive. We'd probably have to do some fundraising to raise the money, and that takes up a lot of time." Stewart takes a drag off his soda straw, the ice cubes sloshing in the sweating cup. Some of the drops fall on Matthew's shoulder, creating a damp spot, and he sighs. "If it's something you guys really want to do, I'll talk to Coach McGrath and maybe we can figure something out, but no promises. How does that sound?"

"Cool. Hey Coach, do you think your girlfriend here would want to be our team manager?"

"We don't need a team manager, Stewart."

Mitchell's arm shoots up and thrusts his fist in the air, finger pointing straight up, a la Sherlock Holms just having solved a mystery. "*Ah ha!* So you admit she's your girlfriend."

"I was *not* admitting she's my girlfriend."

"But you also didn't deny it."

Matthew shoots me a beseeching look. "Would you help me out here, please?"

I cross my arms and lean back, resting against the seat behind me. "Why would I do that when this is *so* entertaining?"

"Because I'm being ambushed by a pack of eleven-year-olds. They're like the hyenas in *The Lion King*."

"What's in it for me?"

Before he can respond, one of the boys interrupts. "Hey Coach, what are you doing here, anyway?"

"I'm on a date, Andy." He says this through gritted teeth, jaw clenched.

"Whoa, no need to get snippy, Coach." Andy Boskowitz looks around. "A date with who?"

"With me," I finally chime in, plucking a few kernels of popcorn from Mitchell's popcorn bag. I chew it noisily.

For a second, all three boys look confused, until Andy, who begins unwrapping his hot dog, says, "Oh, so you were being serious when you said you weren't gay. I get it now."

I laugh and ruffle his shaggy hair. "No, luckily for me, Coach Wakefield is not gay—at least, I don't think he is…" I wink at Matthew, but he isn't amused.

"If you're on a date, then why are you *here*?" Mitchell asks. "My sister would be so pissed—sorry, I mean *mad*— if her boyfriend brought her here for a date. I mean, she has some pretty low standards, but still…" He shoves more popcorn into his mouth. "Even *she* wouldn't wanna come here."

"Yeah, Coach. This place is a dump," Andy throws in helpfully.

"Gee, thanks guys," Matthew deadpans. Unfortunately for him, the sarcasm flies right over their eleven-year-old heads.

"You shouldn't be *thanking* us, Coach. Seriously, this place is a shithole. Did you see the bathrooms? I think someone wiped their crap on one of the stall doors." Andy Boskowitz is clearly wise beyond his years, and he gives me a pitying look. "Right where it says 'Gretchen G is a Slut'."

Stewart, in the spirit of the conversation, perks up. "You know what would have been a better choice, Coach? A fancy dinner and maybe bowling. That new Super Alley is *awe*some. You can bowl *and* play video games if you get bored."

Mitchell agrees. "Yeah! Did you see the Mortal Kombat game they just got? It's so cool. I was the *fifth* highest score last time I was there!" Mitchell and Stewart bump fists then make exploding sounds, and as they do, a few particles of popcorn fly out of Mitchell's mouth and onto Stewart's jacket.

"Hey! Watch it!" Steward scolds, clearly disgusted and disgruntled by his friend's flying chunks.

I steal a glance at Matthew, who is rolling his eyes and shaking his head ruefully in my direction, finally casting a glance at me over Mitchell's head and mouthing, "*I told you so.*"

***

"Ugh, I told you that would happen." Matthew pouts in the parking lot an hour later as he blindly tries jamming his keys into the ignition. "I should have known that of all the kids to run into, of course it would be those three."

"Actually I would say it went pretty well." At his frown I add, "Just being honest. What's that saying you threw out at me once? Don't shoot the messenger...?"

"You have a warped sense of humor, Miss Carter."

I shrug into my warm jacket, hunkering down as the wind blows frantically around the car, bending trees like twigs along the road and causing the Tahoe to skip from its weight. It's cold and damp and cozy—the perfect kind of weather.

It's also the perfect weather for another hot chocolate or tea, which is what we were pulling into the Starbucks parking lot to get.

I shiver again as I hop out of the truck, Matthew beating me to the door and holding it open. We step inside, side by side, and shuffle up to the counter. It's getting late, but there are still plenty of people loitering. A man sits with his laptop at one of the pedestal tables with a grande cup of... *something* in front of him. In a large, overstuffed leather chair, a dark-haired woman with dreadlocks seems fully immersed in a paperback—until she glances up and our eyes make contact, both of us smiling in acknowledgement before she buries her face back in her novel.

Near the barista's counter, two older teenagers sit together at a high table, textbooks open in front of them. One is frantically typing away on her phone, and the other has ear buds planted, head bobbing, and is copying notes from his book to a steno pad.

There is a large fireplace dividing the entire store, the dimly lit space brightened by the crackling, orange flames as they cast a warm heat throughout. Two large, worn leather chairs and a coffee table flank the tile hearth. I walk over and set my purse down on one of the chairs, claiming it before we order at the counter and take our seats again.

We sit idly before speaking, both of us sipping our hot beverages and listening to the mellow soundtrack of instrumental music, both of us seemingly captivated by the open flames in front of us.

Matthew is the first to speak, setting down his grande nonfat half-caff mocha latte before adjusting in his seat, twisting his large body so he can face me properly.

"Okay, fine, I admit it. This evening with the boys might have been a teensy-weensy bit of fun." He holds his fingers up in measurement, thumb and forefinger indicating our level of fun.

It's about three centimeters worth.

Ha ha.

I lean back and smack my thigh gleefully, the sound echoing off my jeans, then point at him like he's a witch at the Salem trial. "See! Didn't I tell you?" He regards me then with a grin, his eyes crinkling at the corners, and I study him for a few heartbeats, noting the stubble of a day's growth at his jaw and the way his green eyes watch me. Always, always watching me. "The way those little boys look at you…"

…*is the same way you look at me.*

The words almost pass my lips.

I want to say it.

But I don't.

Instead, I avoid his questing gaze and take a sip from my cup of the frothy hazelnut chai latte steaming from my cup, clutching it with both hands as if I'm out in the cold and need to stay warm.

"How do they look at me?" Matthew asks, cocking his head at me like a curious puppy.

"You know, they look up to you. They watch you like

you're Captain America, wielding a golden hockey stick and covered in video games."

A pretty lame analogy, but it *does* manage to have the desired effect.

"No shit. Really?" I nod. "Huh, I guess hadn't realized…"

"Well, it's like you said that day I was at the boys' practice: they don't have many positive role models where they come from. I don't think you realized when you were telling me that that *you* are that positive influence they need. You and Weston, you're their role models."

"That's some scary ass shit," he jokes then gets quiet. Matthew shifts in his seat and I can see the wheels turning in his head. Slowly he begins, "I know that being, you know, a professional athlete, people look up to us. We get hounded and some of us even get stalked—not me, but I've heard stories." He takes a drag from his latte before continuing, and I watch the muscles in his throat contract as he swallows. "Anyway, the team's public relations people and our agents handle most of the public image and community service stuff, so it's easy to forget about the little kids you actually build a relationship with giving you a hero complex. Everyone else…they don't even know you. They just see you on television and assume you're decent, when some of the guys, you know…aren't."

I nod for him to continue.

"It's not easy having the public watching everything we do. That's why I come home. I can't stand being in Los Angeles—no offense to LA, of course, but…it's turned me into a total homebody. I don't go out, I don't really know anyone besides my teammates, and a bunch of them are married. So, when I hang out with John Tamaso, for example, it's at his house with his wife and four kids, or Brady Chandler will bring his family over, and it's them and me barbequing by the pool at the Tamasos' rental house." Matthew rests his head back against the leather chair and sighs. "You don't even want to know how the single guys on the team act on our off days. It's a wonder we win any games." He's quiet for a few seconds, closing his eyes. "I already let my agent know I'm looking for a trade. Any place is better than Anaheim."

He sits like this for another eight minutes or so—head back, eyes closed—and you know me…ogling him every chance I get without being obvious. I look my fill, staring intently at his lips (my favorite part of his face), trying to remember what they felt like pressed against mine.

I study the shape of them, and the way he has them pursed, the sharp indent at the bow, well defined and full, his lower lip slightly pouty.

Without thinking, I touch the tips of my fingers to my mouth, running my index finger back and forth across the bottom of my lip as my gaze moves lower to the gap at the collar of his shirt where he's left the top unbuttoned.

I imagine trailing my hands across the cords of his neck, slowly unbuttoning his dress shirt down to his navel and running my soft hands across his pecs. I wonder briefly if he has a hairy chest, or if it's bare, and then my mind (and eyes) wanders farther south to his happy trail… and just as I'm getting a visual of what it looks like in my mind—

"Are you staring at me?" Matthew opens one eye and looks over at me.

"Um, no. Pfft, why would you ask that?" I fidget with the plastic cover on my latte and glance up at the ceiling, puckering my lips in a move that has gotten me busted numerous times in the past. My face heats up considerably and I'm certain my cheeks are a shade of fuchsia. "I had something in my eye."

He opens both eyes and stretches out, feet splayed broadly apart, hands going up behind his head, as if inviting me to gawk. "Go ahead, look your fill. Really, I don't mind." He spreads his legs wider still, the denim of his jeans pulling taunt against his impressive...um...*you know*.

Oh my god—I'll be twenty-three in May and I can't even say it.

"Thanks, I'm good."

"Cecelia, you were staring so hard I could feel it, even with my eyes closed. Admit it, you were undressing me in your mind." He extracts himself from the chair and bends forward, resting his elbows on his knees and chin in his hands. "I could even feel it in my..." His eyes cast downward then up at me, going back and forth a few times as he wiggles his eyebrows suggestively.

I lean over and give him a playful shove, letting my now sexually charged fingers linger on his solid bicep. He grabs that hand, then the other, dragging me and the chair I'm sitting in to the apex of his thighs until we're face to face, just inches apart.

Matthew raises my hands to his mouth, turning them both over and planting open-mouth kisses to my sensitive palms and up my exposed wrists. His nose inhales the smell of my perfume, and as he nuzzles my wrists, I shamelessly watch, spellbound.

His hands work their way up my arms, grazing my

shoulders briefly before resting around the column of my slim neck. Matthew's thumbs caress the underside of my jaw softly, the calloused pads branding me.

Involuntarily, my lips part. He leans forward, brushing his mouth against mine, our eyes closing. I breathe him in before our tongues mingle, my teeth nipping his pouty lower lip.

"Stop it Matt, we can't do this here."

"Do what? This?" He buries his nose in my temple, and I chuckle softly when he kisses the tender skin at the corner of each eye. "Why not?"

"You're insane. People are starting to stare."

"Fine. Then come home with me so we can be alone."

Mayday, mayday!!!! Code red!

I hesitate, panicking a little.

This is only our first date and I am *soooo* not a hussy. I swear the guy is a mind reader because he says, "Cecelia, I... This might be our first official date, but...I've been courting you for weeks. Admit it—we've been dating since the day I stole your shitty, generic trail mix."

Love and loathing.

"We're both adults, and I think it's safe to say..." He doesn't finish his sentence.

"Safe to say...what?"

Matthew clears his throat, mildly uncomfortable with whatever it is he's about to say. Actually, he looks slightly pale and constipated. "That we're, um...going to be, um... committed to each other...or am I reading you wrong?"

Committed. Did he just say that out loud?

Although my heart is beating wildly in my chest, I still manage to eye him skeptically, brows raised. "Are you just saying that to get in my pants?" *Because it's working.*

He looks affronted, clutching his chest. "Why do you always ask me that?"

"Oh come on, I've only ever asked you that twice…"

"Okay but, why are you asking me to begin with? I think you'd know me well enough by now."

Honestly, we know there are several good reasons I'm not hastening to hop into Matthew's truck and ride off into the sunset with him, and they are:

1. He's leaving for California soon.
2. Technically, we just started dating.
3. He's leaving for California soon.

Those are my thoughts in a nutshell, and I have a sneaking suspicion he already knows this. In any case, it would be foolish of me to jump feet first into a physical relationship that's only going to end in heartache—namely, mine.

We watch each other, my face still cradled in his hands, his thumbs still stroking the underside of chin. I tip my head to the side, marveling at the delicate touches his strong hands are capable of and the feel of them on my skin.

We probably look like lovesick fools…and perhaps maybe we are.

"Cecelia. Tell me what's wrong—and don't say *nothing.*" Matthew's sharp gaze searches my face for a sign of… something; this giant guy's guy who, not so many weeks ago, I didn't think was even capable of human feelings, let alone talking about them. Quite honestly, it's freaking me out a bit, this bizarre parallel universe we've entered where the guy is throwing out words like *committed* and voluntarily talking about his feelings...*on purpose.*

Macho.

Stubborn.

Conceited.

Arrogant. Prideful. Sarcastic. All words I'd use to categorize Matthew Wakefield. I've had them filed away for so long, using them as an excuse to not get attached, that sensitive, caring, and faithful haven't registered with me.

Until now.

"Hello, earth to Cecelia." His head dips. "Babe. *Cece?*"

Startled, the sound of my nickname slipping off his tongue causes me to blink rapidly and refocus. "Sorry, I was thinking."

"You know what sweetie, forget I said anything. Let's just sit here for a bit and enjoy the fire, okay?" He says it softly, reassuringly as he presses his full lips down on mine one last time, softly but firmly, before releasing my face and settling back into his seat.

Oh shit. He used an endearment—and not just one, but two.

Babe. Sweetie.

Now, I know there are a lot of girls out there who cannot stand endearments or nicknames. To some, the sound of an endearment is like nails on a chalkboard and cannot be tolerated. I, however, am not one of those people. The inner romantic inside me *freaking loves it.* Sweetheart, baby, honey—shit, I'd even settle for being called muffin.

Yup. I said it.

Muffin.

Disgusting, right?

If my heart was locked and protected before this moment, Matthew just unknowingly produced the key.

Matthew

"I found the key to my own happiness: stay the hell away from assholes." – wisdom that's easier said than done

Holy crap.

Cecelia is in my condo.

In the bathroom, if you want to get technical.

Have you ever read a romance novel, and the main male lead says some lame bullshit line to the heroine that goes something like, *Trust me, you're the first girl I've ever brought back to my place.* Um yeah, that is not the case for me. I *have* brought random hookups back to my place, I won't lie. Random women. Random faces. Not all of them were classically beautiful in the way you're probably thinking, nor has beauty ever been a prerequisite. In fact, it's more accurate to say…I don't really *have* a type. You don't have to be a size two blonde bombshell with silicon breasts to turn me on.

You can be flat chested for all I care.

Don't get me wrong—I'm not saying I haven't had my fair share of plastic, made-up Barbie doll types; a lot of them *have* been total skanks (for example, the prostitute Kevin hired for my birthday). But I've also bagged my share of *nice* girls, probably from *nice*, decent families, educated even.

In fact, one chick I banged was a Harvard Law student.

I've never been a saint, and I sure as hell ain't ever been a monk.

My point is, having Cecelia in my house for the first time somehow feels infinitely different than all the others that have been here before her. I'm not going to put a label on it, but if the way my stomach is doing backflips is any indication, I would definitely say I'm nervous.

Huh, who would have thought?

Certainly not me.

I take my shoes off by the front entry, putter to the kitchen while I wait for Cecelia to finish up in the bathroom, and pour us both a glass of a 2010 moscato riesling mix. Setting the bottle on the granite kitchen counter, I walk the glasses into the living room and…

Stand there.

Glancing around my condo, I'm not really sure what to do now or how to proceed. Do I sit on the couch, casually chilling with my arm up on the backrest? Should stay standing and lean against the doorframe to the kitchen instead? Do I turn on the stereo, get a little Marvin Gaye action going? You know, *set the mood…*

Shit. I can't just stand here awkwardly holding these two wine glasses in the middle of the room, that's for damn sure. I look like the fucking butler.

I hear the powder room sink turn off down the hall and decide to walk back into the kitchen, wait a few moments, then walk back out into the living room. It's all so very amateurish, but my timing is perfect; Cecelia is just coming out of the bathroom when I reenter. I extend my arm, offering her a wine glass and a seat.

She smiles demurely and takes the glass, our fingers touching in a *two hands in the popcorn bucket* moment, the chemistry between us tangible and sizzling in the air. Cecelia has removed her puffy vest, and after resting her wine on the coffee table, begins undoing the few buttons on her plaid shirt that are done up, shrugging it off and laying it on the back of the couch.

Standing in a gray cap-sleeve t-shirt, she gives me another shy smile before plopping down on the couch, careful not to spill any wine.

I study her there, on my couch, like she's a foreign object that's been plucked from obscurity and dropped there.

"What?" she asks.

"Nothing. It's just…"

"Just what?"

"It's just… you look so damn *good* sitting in my living room."

"I…it feels good *being* in your living room." She laughs nervously and pats the cushioned seat next to her, staring up at me and giving her head a little shake. "You're so cute."

"I'm cute? Wait, did you somehow become drunk?"

Cecelia

Did I somehow become drunk?

What?

Matthew looks so confused that I just called him *cute* that he glances around the room, as if expecting someone else to pop out of the shadows and join us. Great, just great. Now I actually feel *guilty* that I've never sincerely complimented him before. How terrible is that? Sure, I flirt with him regularly, but that's not really the same thing. I mean, aren't compliments fuel for the male ego?

Do you have a pen, because you might want to write down these words of advice: *the way to a guy's heart is not through his stomach, it's through his ego.* Inflate it with praise and you, my friend, are golden.

That. Is. A. Fact.

Trust me on this.

I gulp down a large sip of wine (call it liquid courage if you want), finishing the glass in one, long chug (classy, I know), and set the now empty glass down on the coffee table, dab at my moist upper lip, and smile convincingly as Matthew stands in the middle of the room, staring at me like I've sprouted two heads.

"Are you going to come sit by me, or did you only lure me here and ply me with alcohol so you could gape at me without any distractions," I tease.

"Sounds about right," Matthew volleys back cheerfully, making his way around the coffee table with a smug smile on his face and settling onto the sofa. His right arm goes up behind my head, on the back of the couch, and the hairs on the back of my neck prickle from his close proximity. "Any chance to ogle you is all right with me. Plus, you smell amazing—an intoxicating blend of hockey ice and perfume." To illustrate his point, he leans in and sniffs my neck, loudly inhaling and coming away with a satisfied *ahhhhhh*.

I give him a smack on the arm, giggling nervously. "Ha ha, very funny."

"Truthfully though, you could smell like shit from a barn and I'd still be attracted to you," Matthew jokes as he casually brushes his fingers through my long hair.

I lean in toward him and tenderly but firmly brush my smiling lips against his. "That was such a sweet thing to say."

"I know how to charm the ladies." He grins, leaning in for another kiss. We stay like this for a good fifteen minutes, softly kissing each other, lavishing each other with affection in the most primal yet innocent of ways.

It makes me feel thirteen again, back when I was young, innocent, and still thought boys were good and honest and decent—back when I had no idea about erections and "bases" and sex stuff.

Right now, at this moment, we have all the time in the world. There is no rush to talk of our next date, nor is there a rush to Matthew's bedroom, which is just down the hall across from the bathroom (and I would know, because I peeked into it when I was using the powder room earlier).

It's just us and our lips, and it's…amazing.

A faint buzzing from inside Matthew's front jeans pocket interrupts us.

"You can see who that is," I say, wiping my mouth

when the phone begins buzzing for a second time. "It could be important."

"Or it could be my nosey sister," he deadpans as he pulls his phone out, swiping the screen. He holds it up for me to see, and he's right, it is Molly. "See? Told you."

"How come she isn't text bombing me?" I ask indignantly, pretending to be insulted.

"Because you're way meaner than I am," he teases. "Should we send her a selfie?"

I bounce up and down. "Yeah! Good idea."

"Should I have my hands on your boobs?"

I smack him in the chest. "Ha ha, very funny."

"What? I think it's a terrific idea. Give it some more thought before rejecting it completely."

"You know, we can have fun with her without you fondling my breasts. Get your mind out of the gutter."

Matthew rolls his eyes. "Well *that's* no fun. Can we be kissing or something in the picture?" He pokes at his screen a few times and opens Snapchat.

I don't question the *or something* part of his statement, instead sighing in resignation. "Sure, why not."

"Oh goodie. Here, get closer," Matthew instructs as grabs my hips and pulls me across his lap, holding his cell phone out in front of us with one arm, the other holding me firmly around the waist.

He gives me a sidelong glance. "Pucker your pretty lips."

I pucker my lips and giggle.

"Last chance on the breast fondling. Going once...

twice…"

"Would you just take the damn picture?" I say as I burst out laughing.

His face is next to mine, and I can feel his breath on my neck. "You always were so impatient," he murmurs. "What else are you impatient for?"

At his sexual innuendo, I tilt my head to glare at him and it's that moment he leans forward and plants one square on my lips, a full-on, every centimeter of our lips pressed together, no room for air kind of kiss. My eyes flutter closed involuntarily, and the click of the camera barely registers in my subconscious as my lips part and his tongue slips into my mouth.

He lowers his picture-taking arm, dropping his phone to the rug before both hands grip my waist. Then his hands snake around to my back, running them up and down my spine, his fingers kneading each vertebra and melting my insides like cheap, pliant, putty in his masculine hands.

He buries his nose in my neck, planting kisses inside the open collar of my flannel shirt and inhaling the smell of me at the same time. *I guess he really wasn't joking when he said he loved the way I smelled…*

My hands roam his upper torso and I run them up inside then under the arm holes of his soft gray t-shirt, squeezing and memorizing every cord of his firm shoulders and brawny biceps. He flexes them as I run my smooth palms over his skin farther into his shirt and groans when my warm fingers graze his collarbone.

Innocently.

Sensually.

Both at the same time.

330 | Sara Ney

Leaning down, I lavish kisses on his temples where his sideburns and freshly shaved face meet. He tips his head like a kitten still wanting to be petted, and I oblige him by trailing my lips along his jaw and nipping his ear with my teeth.

He practically purrs his approval and returns the favor by nudging my chin and giving my jaw a few flirty licks. They're not the wet sloppy licking you're probably envisioning; no. Matthew's tongue playfully slides along my skin like a wave on the water—smooth and leaving ripples in its wake. It's teasing and gentle, and it's driving me *mad* with desire.

I didn't think it was possible, but maybe I have a little kink in me after all...not that what we're doing is *Fifty Shades of Grey* kind of stuff, but under normal circumstances, I wouldn't let some guy lick my neck. It's just not my style, and if it were anyone else doing it to me, I might feel weird or gross.

But the fact that Matthew Wakefield has his glorious tongue on me? Great Jesus, Mary, and Joseph, I've died and gone to heaven, raging hormones be damned.

My hands work their way from his biceps, to his forearms, to his washboard abs. He sucks in a breath as my fingers skim the waistband of his well-worn jeans, the anticipation palpable. Unfortunately, grabbing a guy's *junk* isn't exactly my style either, so my hands reach down between us, bypassing his erection and heading for his inner thighs instead. I rest them there, kneading his quads through the denim, marveling that, even at rest, his physical strength is evident.

I bet he could bench press me, and I bet that I'd let him. I'd also bet that I'd squeal with delight.

There is no sound in the room except for our heavy breathing—no radio, no cell phones beeping, no sounds from the traffic outside. Even if there were, I wouldn't have registered it anyway—my brain is mush.

Apparently Matthew's isn't, because before I realize he's lifting me up, he's carrying me down the hallway to his bedroom and plopping me in the center of his bed. I fall flat on my back, hair fanned out (attractively, I'm sure), knees bent, and cheeks flushed.

For a moment, he does nothing but stand next to the bed, staring down at me shamelessly as if deciding his next move; unabashed, I stare back. Mind made up, Matthew crawls onto the bed and sidles up next to me, pulling me into his body and propping his head in his hands, looking down at me before planting a kiss on my forehead.

Then another.

He reaches over, brushing the hair away from my temples, before planting a kiss there as well.

One kiss…two.

I reach up and capture the back of his head, pulling it down toward my mouth. Our lips and tongues meet, re-introducing themselves like two long-lost friends, never having missed a beat.

My fingers stroke the back of his head, weaving through his thick, silky hair, pulling and tugging him closer. His large hands cup my neck, stroking my collarbone through my flannel shirt until his index finger finds and fiddles with the top button.

"Can we take this shirt off?" he asks, his teeth raking my lower lip. "It's in my way." Wordlessly I comply, facilitating the task of unbuttoning it until Matthew abandons the project completely, leaving me to go at it alone so his hands can explore my skin, which I am *one hundred thousand percent* okay with.

My shirts spreads open, my skin is exposed, and his hands tangle with my bra. His head bends, and his wet mouth covers me with more kisses, this time on my stomach, ribcage, and breasts.

Call me lazy, but I lay there like a tart, unmoving, letting him lavish me with attention.

Soon *his* shirt disappears, followed by my bra…lots of panting and moaning…roaming hands…and then our underwear and pants.

Everything lands on the floor, clothes tossed haphazardly about the room. The only light is streaming in from outside, casting shadows on our entwined, naked bodies.

One of us has the good sense to put on a condom—I'm assuming it was him, but I may have helped)—and now he's on top of me, his beautiful pelvis hard at work, forearms flexed and braced on each side of my head.

I let out a gasp, then a moan—he feels so good and it's been *so* so long. Matthew dips his head, seeking out my aching lips in the dark, sucking on my bottom lip and grinding his hips into me at the same time.

He gasps my name in a long, anguished sigh.

I can't tell yet if we're just having sex or if we're making love, but raw emotions are taking over in depths of my soul that I've never explored, so it's no surprise I feel tears escape from the corner of my eyes. I thank God it's dark in here (although I'm not sure I should be praying during this particular activity, if you know what I'm saying). It's on the tip of my tongue to blurt out *I love you*, but sex I love yous can have absolutely catastrophic effects, so I keep it to myself.

A few more moans, more gasping, and soon we're laying side by side, chests heaving from the exertion. Matthew reaches down and pulls the covers up and over us, reaching for my hand and bringing it up to his mouth. He kisses my palm before laying it on his still heaving chest.

Hope blossoms in my heart, and I snuggle up next to him. We don't talk, but we don't fall asleep either (like so many romance novels like to depict when a couple finally 'does the deed'). I mean, it's not like it's two in the morning or something; it's only eleven o'clock for crying out loud.

"Sweetie, don't get too comfortable. I have to go get rid of this thing," Matthew whispers in the dark, sliding out of bed and disappearing into the master bathroom. A few seconds later I hear the toilet flush and the sink run, and then he's climbing back into his big, comfortable bed.

He slides in next to me, planting a kiss on my naked shoulder, and I shiver before he pulls the covers back up over both of us. Like he did earlier in the evening, he buries his nose in my hair and takes a whiff. "I'm not really tired." He chuckles. "Are you?"

My mind is reeling. Honestly, I hardly know what to say or how to proceed. I mean, I just had sex—really, *really* incredibly amazing sex—with Matthew Wakefield, and now we're lying naked in his bed and he's talking to me like we're discussing the weather.

Or like…the casual banter you'd have with a boyfriend or girlfriend after just having had sex with them.

I let my head fall against a pillow and sigh, throwing

my arms up behind my head. The motion pulls the covers down, and the cold air of his bedroom hits my exposed breasts. I giggle nervously, quickly pulling the covers back up—I'm *comfortable* with him, but not comfortable enough to have *the girls* exposed to his roving eyes, even if it is dark.

As if he can read my thoughts, I can hear him smirking in the dark, and his hand moves under the covers to graze my stomach, roaming gently and hitting all my sensitive spots. "I could stare at your boobs all day," he teases before palming one lazily, then the other. I have to bite my bottom lip and concentrate to stop myself from moaning out loud. "Hell, I could stare at *you* all day...if you'd let me."

Oh lord.

Matthew

"Sometimes I miss him, but then I remember what a douche he was and how awesome I am." – Jenna when asked about her ex-boyfriend Aaron

Even sitting in just her plaid flannel shirt, Cecelia is sexy. Cross-legged on my couch and clutching a white carton of Chinese takeout leftovers in one hand, she has my remote control in the other.

"Anything look appealing?" she asks, flipping past CSPAN, CNN, and ESPN, her head bent at a cute little angle as she studies the screen over my fireplace. "There isn't shit on," she grumbles. Her eyes get real wide and she looks at me, apparently feeling guilty about her vulgar slip. "Um, sorry?"

"I see something appealing, all right." I cross the room and plop down on the couch next to her, plucking the carton and remote from her hands. "It's wearing a cute little button-down shirt and nothing else, and it screams my name when it comes."

"Oh my god." Her cheeks get bright red and she grabs a pillow, burying her face completely in it. After a few seconds, she raises her head, narrowing her eyes at me. "I do *not* scream."

I wave my hand airily. "Semantics. Moaning, screaming—whatever you want to call it."

"*Why* are we having this conversation? You said you wanted food."

"I *did* want food, but you're just so damn cute sitting there all…post-coital. It's turning me on again. Come on, let's do it on the couch." I reach for her, but she slaps my hands away, laughing.

"I'm *not* doing it with you on the couch. Try again later. Give me back that bok choy."

I'm undeterred (perseverance is one of my best qualities) and try again. "So, you're not necessarily saying no to the couch sex…?"

She pins me down with a stare—okay, it's more of a glare—but doesn't say anything for a moment. Then she asks, "Did you send that Snapchat that you took before to Molly?"

"No. It was pretty racy. I think I'll keep it for myself and jerk off to it when I'm out of town." She stares again, this time with her mouth hanging open. "Shit, did I say that out loud?"

Newsflash: *I'm always saying shit like that out loud.*

I ignore her look of horror and forge on. "Want to take another one? We can pretend we have all our clothes on." I wink at her, earning yet another blush for the evening.

"Okay, but this time you come sit on *my* lap." Cecelia pats her legs, which I can't help noticing are tan and smooth…which makes me *really* want to touch them, idly run my palms up in between them…

Crap. I can't stop the dirty thoughts and lick my lips, which causes Cecelia to snap her fingers in front of my face. "Hey buddy, stop daydreaming. Eyes up here."

Gee. I guess we know who's going to wear the pants in *this* relationship, and it's not me.

At this point she could tell me to get on the floor, roll around, and bark like a dog, and I would do it—not that I'm going to be divulging that information to her. *No.* No guy wants a woman to know how much control she has over him, but…you know. Just saying.

Cecelia is amazing.

Sexy. Smart. Funny. Beautiful inside and out.

And the most attractive quality of all: she puts up with my bullshit. Have I mentioned this before? Well, even if I have, so what?

She's not perfect, but she's mine—or more accurately, I'm hers.

Looking at her now, curled up on my couch patting her lean legs, I want her to curl up on *me*. Instead, she takes the carton of bok choy off the coffee table and sucks a long noodle through her pursed lips, the juice making a messy sucking sound as she inhales it, not looking one bit appalled by her lack of table manners. She looks at me and shrugs, as if to say *oops, sorry* before wrapping another long noodle around the fork.

"I'm not kidding Cecelia. I can't sit here and watch you eat that shit without wanting to peel that shirt off you and drag you back to the bedroom."

"Are you *nuts*? You're either *blind* or a complete lunatic. I have my mouth stuffed with noodles. How can you *possibly* be turned on right now?" she asks sarcastically as she swallows, rolling her eyes at the ceiling.

Um, maybe it's because I can see her nipples through the gaps in her shirt when she moves her arms; I decide not to mention this fact in case she decides to alter that situation. "*Trust* me, it's possible."

She tosses her long, mussed-up sex hair over one shoulder and sasses, "Well you're *just* going to have to wait."

"How can I convince you?" I ask, whining a little bit and trying to look pathetic, hoping maybe she'll take pity on me and rip off her panties.

Cecelia takes another long drag of bok choy and tips her chin at an indignant angle, sighing. "You can't."

"Fine. Then let's at least take a Snap and send it to my sister."

I move closer to her on the couch, grabbing my phone and opening the app.

Cecelia gulps, eyeing my chest nervously. "Um, aren't you going to at least put your shirt back on?"

"Hell no. My sister deserves to be frazzled by our after-sex selfie. It'll serve her right for being so damn nosy. Now get closer." I take the noodles from her again, setting them back on the table, and put my arm around her—and since I'm a head taller, I try to look down her shirt.

What?! *I'm a guy*, it's what we do…

I hold the phone out in front of us as Cecelia slowly wraps her arms around my waist, her fingers tickling my ribcage and spine.

"Hey, are you trying to molest me or give me a hug?

Make up your damn mind," I tease.

"Both," she smarts back, earning herself a smack on the lips. I let my mouth linger on hers before pulling away, sucking on her tongue before releasing her to clear my throat and get back to the task at hand.

"Okay. On three. One… two…ten."

I snap the picture, and afterward, we put our heads together to study the image on my phone.

Wow, is all I can say. Just…wow.

Cecelia

We look…so…

Well, okay, honestly we look like we've just had raucous sex. My hair is a rat's nest, and it's pretty obvious my shirt has been hastily rebuttoned (and not very well). I have slight beard rash on my chin from Matthew's five o'clock shadow, and my lips are slightly puffy and swollen. Even from the profile, you can tell I've been thoroughly kissed.

Matthew, for his part, looks cocky and well…perpetually horny, like he's just bagged a conquest and is damn proud of it. His lips are twisted in a sardonic smile, but it's his *eyes* that give him away. Rather than the arrogant look I'm *sure* he was going for, they look oddly…content.

In the quickly snapped picture, I'm placing an open-mouth kiss on his collarbone with my eyes closed, and while Matthew has his eyes open and is staring straight into the camera lens, his fingers are curled around my neck almost possessively and his smiling lips are buried in my hair.

Sweet jeezuz do we look sexy.

On top of that, we look so blissfully...*happy*.

***

Later that next day, when I'm alone in my bedroom, I get a text.

Matthew: *What are you up to?*

I cram a few books, a notepad, and my ear buds into a Vera tote before tapping out a reply.

Me: *Getting ready to go write one last paper! You?*

Matthew: *Trying to be so irresistible you won't be able to find an excuse not to see me tonight. I'll let you know when I come up with something...*

This makes me smile.

Me: *You're headed in the right direction*

Matthew: *Wow. You're surprisingly easy.*

Me: *Awww, that's what all the boys say ;)*

Matthew: *Wait, what?*

Me: *LOL*

The phone pings again, but I'm interrupted by a knocking on my doorframe, and I glance up to see Molly standing in the doorway of my bedroom, arms crossed and tapping her foot impatiently.

"Do you have something you want to say to me?" she asks, stepping over the threshold, crossing the room to my desk, and plopping herself down in the rolling chair. She swivels it around to face me, raising her eyebrow expectantly.

"Um…I'm not sure what you're…um…." I let my thought trail off, not sure what to offer up to her. I certainly can't blurt out that I had sex with her brother last night, or that I spent the night at his condo, or that he's quite possibly becoming my best friend. The phone on my bed pings again, breaking the silence but also making it more awkward because Molly and I both know who the pinging is.

She pulls her cell out of her back pocket, taps it a few times, and holds it out.

Not surprisingly, it's the Snapchat photo of Matthew and me. My face heats up and I look away, embarrassed.

"Molly, um…."

"This is on his Snap *story*, Cece. *His story*."

I freeze and my body tenses up. "What?"

"Haven't you looked at it?"

"Well, I mean…after we took it."

Molly nonchalantly studies her nails and swivels back and forth in the desk chair. "If I were you, I'd take a look at it." Without looking up at me, she thrusts her cell in my general direction.

I grab the phone and find Matthew's name in the story list, the little pie chart indicating one story. Tapping it twice, I hold his name down and our photo pops up, along with the tag line *Off the market* and a few heart emojis.

My mouth falls open and Molly continues. "That's not even the best part. Have you been online today?"

Unable to speak, I shake my head.

"The picture and an article have been picked up by

ESPN."

"Wh…what?"

"You heard me." She stands up and straightens her shirt, pulling it down and dusting off invisible lint before casually strolling out of my bedroom, waving a hand over her shoulder. "Toodles!"

I grab my phone, reading and rereading Matthew's last messages.

Matthew: *So is that a yes for tonight?*

Matthew: *This time I promise not to take you to an ice rink. ;)*

I'll be honest—I panic a little. Now I don't know if I should be seen with him in public. I mean, he's a public figure, for crying out loud. Now that our private picture is out there for world to see… Oh my god, what if his parents have seen it? *Oh my god*, what if *my* parents have seen it?

Holy shit, I'm freaking out. I don't know if I can handle this.

Get it together Cecelia. I shake my head, hair swishing around my shoulders, and take a deep, cleansing breath.

Wait, what am I saying? Of *course* I can handle this! I'm a strong, independent woman with two college degrees, not to mention my impending master's. I should be *happy* that's he's declared himself in a relationship to the world—ecstatic, even!

But…he hasn't declared himself to *me*, and isn't that what matters?

I sit on the edge of my bed, clutching my cell phone in my now trembling hands.

It pings again, and I tip it up to see my sister's text light up the screen.

Veronica: *Good morning, you dirty slut. Anything you want to tell us?*

A laugh bursts out of me before I can stop it, and smiling, I reply: *You know I've always had a thing for athletes...*

Veronica: *That's the understatement of the year. Roger is planning the wedding, btdubbs. He's very excited about his professional hockey player son-in-law. Mom is reeling because u clearly have loose morals.*

Me: *Obviously.*

Veronica: *So...seriously tho, is it serious? Is this a real thing? No bullshitting a bullshitter.*

I hesitate, thinking.

Is this a real thing? I can't answer for Matthew, so instead I tell her what's in my heart.

Me: *Yes, I think so. Yes. It's the real deal.*

Veronica: *Well then. You better get his fine ass to Mom and Dad's before Mom has a stroke.*

Me: *(Groan)*

Then to Matthew, I reply: *It's a yes for tonight*

It's a yes because he doesn't know it yet, but we seriously need to talk.

Matthew

"Let me put it to you this way: you hurt my best friend, I'll make your death look like an accident" – the only hostile words Abby has ever uttered

"**S**o, I'm just going to put this out there: my parents want to meet you," Cecelia says from across the table, legs crossed but bouncing nervously, looking slightly agitated.

All right, that's not accurate; she doesn't look agitated—she looks pissed about something.

I lean back in my chair and watch her, taking a drink from my latte. "Okay."

She raises her eyebrow skeptically. "*Okay?*"

I nod. "Yeah. Okay."

"You're not going to ask me *why* they want to meet you?"

Sorry, but I laugh at her. She's clearly affronted, but it's *so* cute. "I have my suspicions, but fine, I'll bite. Cecelia, *why* do your parents want to meet me?"

"Because, you colossal jackass, you posted that picture of us on Snap and my bloody dad saw it online." She crosses her arms and huffs, flouncing back in her overstuffed chair dramatically. "Now they think I'm hiding a boyfriend."

We're sitting at Starbucks, which seems to have officially become our spot, noshing on coffee and warm buttered croissants. *Yum.*

"I'm confused. Why is that a *bad* thing?"

Cecelia stares at me like I've sprouted ten spitting alien heads, and her lip curls up. Leaning forward in her chair once again and holding up her left hand, she begins ticking off reasons that, apparently, justify her pissy attitude. "Let's see, for starters, we're both half naked in the picture that was supposed to be *private*! *Private* Matthew. Secondly, and thirdly, you posted it on your story—your *story*!—and it got picked up by a freaking sports network. Fourth, you announced we're a thing, and we"—her hands move back and forth between us—"*we* haven't even discussed it yet. You're freaking leaving for Cali*for*nia Matthew. *California*."

"Babe, please, you've got to stop repeating yourself. You sound like an echo."

"Did you listen to a thing I just said?" She looks at me like I'm an idiot—and hey, I probably am.

"Yeah. You're mad."

She throws herself back in a huff, lips pursed. She crosses her arms and glares at me.

"Wait, are we fighting?" I ask innocently, because honestly, I have no idea what is happening right now.

Cecelia blows out a puff of air, and her long bangs wisp

around her face. Her arms land with a thump on the arms of her leather chair, and she slouches before sighing like she's given up. "*No*, we're not fighting." A smile plays at the corner of her lips. "I think your brains are addled from being bashed with too many hockey sticks."

I pull her chair toward mine and rest my palms on her thighs. "I thought you'd be happy."

Her eyes are on my hands, and she studies them for a few moments in silent contemplation. I can tell she's thinking hard, and when she finally lifts her head, I'm not sure I like what I'm seeing.

She looks guarded and unsure. Biting her lower lip, she glances around the coffee shop. "Matthew, you're... leaving."

"So?"

"So? How can you be so...blasé about it? You're going to be two thousand miles away." She says this in a *like, duh* tone of voice, as if it explains everything.

"Actually, it's only nineteen hundred and seventy."

"Huh?"

"Miles. There are only nineteen hundred miles between Madison and Los Angeles."

"Oh my god, stop being so damn literal like it's no big deal to you. What am I supposed to do while you're gone? Languish here while you go traipsing about your business in California?"

"Um, *no*... Cecelia, the season is only like, five months long. If we don't go to the Stanley Cup, it's even shorter. You can fly home and see your family every weekend if you want to." I take a drink from my latte and lean back again, reluctantly removing my hands from her body, then take a bite of the croissant that's been sitting forgotten on my plate. Taking a bite, I chew, wipe a crumb off my chin, and add, "Sometimes I'll be able to come with you."

She shakes her head and stares at me, brown eyes gone huge. "*What*?"

"The season is only five months long—"

"I *heard* what you said."

"Then why did you—"

"Would you *shut up* for a second? I need to think." Her hands go up to knead her temples and she leans forward, resting her elbows on her knees.

I shut up for a second.

Then she raises her head and looks at me, her eyes searching. "I don't get it."

I cock my head, confused. "What don't you get?"

"I don't understand what you're saying. Actually, I think it's *you* who doesn't understand what you're saying."

Cecelia

He must be crazy. There can be no other explanation for him wanting me to follow him to California. I mean…it's only been a few weeks. Plus, I'm in my master's program; true, I'm almost done, but…still. There's job hunting, and new apartments, and…and…

He cocks his head again, staring at me with those bright green eyes. "I thought it would make you happy to be with me," he says, crossing his legs and leaning back in the big leather chair.

"But we haven't even discussed it," I argue, determined.

Those eyes bore into me further. "We're discussing it now," he points out.

I roll my eyes and cross my arms, glancing out the window to the dark parking lot outside. "First you announce that we're in a relationship, then you drop the California bomb on me. It just seems a bit...*rushed* for a twenty-four hour period."

"I'm sorry you feel that way, but, well, it's not like we have a lot of time. I leave in three weeks and won't be back until Christmas, and that will only be for two days. Do you really want a long-distance relationship? Because I sure as hell don't. They suck. I watch them play out with my teammates and they always crash and burn." He pauses to take a deep breath. "I'm going to lay it out there for you, okay? Plain and simple, I don't want to leave without you by my side."

The logical Cecelia that overanalyzes everything wants to argue with him, point out all the flaws in his logic, all the reasons it would never work having me with him. My heart, however, just about burst inside my chest when he said he didn't want to leave here without me by his side, and the thought of waking up in bed with him every morning? Um, *hello*!

I mean, holy *swoon*, right?

My mouth gapes briefly before I snap it shut. "Matthew, I have a degree to finish, papers to write, a job to find..."

Now he's rolling his eyes. "I'm not discounting your priorities, babe, but let's be honest here: you're days away from getting your degree. You don't have any classes to attend, and as far as jobs go…what difference does it make if it's here or in California? Or if you wait until you get back? Or if you take a job and work from home?"

Hmmm, all very valid points.

There really isn't anything tying me down, not technically, and I'm not even from Wisconsin to begin with. My family is in Illinois, but flying home really wouldn't be an issue.

"It's possible that we'll drive each other nuts," I point out with authority.

"It's possible that we *won't*," he counters with a raised eyebrow. "Besides, we'll be back in the Midwest within a few months, and don't forget, my agent is shopping me around for a trade. I could end up here in the long run." He takes another casual drink of his latte, before smugly adding, "I'm good enough to play for the Blackhawks, you know."

The Blackhawks are Chicago's professional hockey team, and his mention of them almost makes me spit out the coffee I just took a drink of—not to mention, his continued use of the word *we* is making my head spin. Not to be overly dramatic, but it's almost information overload.

I knew Matthew Wakefield was intense, but this is overkill.

"Maybe you should come over here and sit in my lap. That might make your decision easier." He laughs, patting his slightly parted thighs.

I gulp and shake my head, giggling. "That is *so* not what I need right now."

"So maybe I should take you back to my place and

convince you."

***

"He said what?!" Jenna shouts at me, her palms slapping the table and making the whole thing shake. "Say that one more time so I can process it."

I've just recounted the Starbucks exchange to the girls, who were already gathered in my kitchen when I got home. I kind of felt guilty spilling the beans to the entire group before talking about it privately with Molly first, but… Jenna was so persistent when I walked in the door that I really didn't have much of a choice.

"He said he didn't want to leave here without me."

"Without you. *By. His. Side,*" Jenna says slowly, emphasizing each word. "Let's all take a moment of silence to let that sink in, shall we? No one say anything. In fact, maybe we should all bow our heads."

We all look around at each other, smirking as Jenna bows her head, long earrings grazing her collarbone. She squishes her eyes shut then opens one to make sure we're all observing the ritual.

"Come on you guys, this is a momentous occasion! Give it the respect it deserves!"

Abby snorts. "I am *not* bowing my head, you weirdo."

"Hey, just be glad she didn't make us all hold hands," Molly intones dryly. "But seriously Cecelia, what are you going to do?"

I throw up my arms, exasperated. "Nothing. I mean,

it's crazy. I can't move to California! I hate California! Besides, I don't even know if we're dating. I mean, it's crazy, right? I'd be nuts to consider it." I scoff, making a few *pfft* sounds. Everyone is staring at me like I've gone off the deep end, but I'm on a roll and can't stop the verbal diarrhea. "I barely know him. We've been out once. It's nineteen hundred miles. I can't leave my family to follow a guy! That's what I'd be doing, right? Following a guy? It's pathetic, who does that? I can't stand girls who do that. Get a backbone! Anyway, it's crazy. My parents would kill me! I'm a grown woman for crap's sake. I can't *move*. I have a life here." I stop rambling and look around the table at Molly, Abby, and Jenna's smug faces. "What?"

"Do you know what you sound like?" Abby asks, crossing her arms.

"Um…what?"

"Like you're trying to convince yourself it's a bad idea."

"It *is* a bad idea," I shout, latching onto the concept. "My cousin Stephanie moved with a guy to Florida once. He ditched her as soon as they got there, locked her out of their apartment, and she had to take a bus home. So there."

"Yeah, but wasn't the guy in some grunge band who, like, cheated on her constantly to begin with?" Abby asks skeptically.

"Whose side are you on?" My brown eyes narrow at her.

"No one's. I'm just saying, it's not like Matthew has a normal job. If he wants to be with you, he has to ask you to go with him, Cece. Think about it. He's a freaking professional athlete, not some normal twenty-five-year-old trying to make it in an entry-level job. He travels for a living."

"*Thank* you, Abby," Molly says, smiling. "That's exactly what I was going to say." Then she turns her attention on me. "Cece, I'm *all* about you doing what you think is best, but what Abby's saying is Matthew isn't *normal*, and dating him isn't going to be *normal*, and…it is what it is. I'm sorry, but this brand of crazy is how it's got to be. He needs someone who's a definite in or out. When Weston gets drafted—God willing—if he's going to be in my life, I'm going to have to make the same sacrifice all partners of pro athletes make. You move. You hop on a plane and go. It's a lonely life for them on the road. Their bodies get beat up, fans go crazy. They get traded to one city after the next. They need someone stable in their hectic, messed up lives."

"The fact that we're even having this conversation is fucked up," I say, the curse slipping out before I can censor myself. "Is everyone *forgetting* the fact that we barely know each other?"

Jenna rolls her eyes. "Oh give me a break. The two of you have been going at it since the day you met. We know it, Matthew knows it, and you know it, so stop fooling yourself because you're scared."

"So what if I'm scared?" I throw back. "In fact, I'm scared shitless! What if I move and he doesn't want me anymore? What if all we do is fight? What if I can't find a job and I sit home like some housewife, twiddling my thumbs and staring at the door every night waiting for him to come home? What if I can't handle the groupies?"

I hold my shaking hands out in front of me for everyone to see, oblivious to the tears streaming down my cheeks.

Abby stands up and comes to my side of the table, pulling me into a side hug. "Honey, oh honey. Don't cry. You don't have to decide now."

"Men are *such* bastards," Jenna says gravely, causing Molly to roll her eyes for the second time in a matter of minutes.

"Ignore her," my roommate consoles. "It's okay. No matter what, it's going to be okay. If you want to stay with me, stay here in our apartment, go on with your life, and only see him when he has bye weekends, that will be okay, too. He'll understand. That's just how his life is."

"Maybe you could insist on separate bedrooms," Abby suggests helpfully.

"You did *not* just say that." Jenna laughs loudly, cackling like a maniac. "Separate bedrooms!? The whole point of moving in with someone is so you can screw any time you want. God, sometimes I wonder about you…"

Molly holds her hand up in front of Jenna's face. "I'm going to pretend you didn't just insinuate my brother would go through all the trouble of moving her across country just so he can screw her."

Jenna, who has never been one to take a hint, continues. "In fact, I can't believe you and Weston aren't living together yet, the way you two go at it."

"First of all, we are *not* always going at it. I'm insulted you'd even say that. Secondly, unless we get officially engaged, we can't live together. Parents' rules, and they pay the rent, so…"

"Plus, you're only twenty," Abby puts in. "Way too young to be shacking up."

"Says the nun," Jenna murmurs.

"Since when is it a crime not to have sex with every

guy I come in contact with?" Abby asks, hands propped defensively on her hips. "At least I have a little self-respect."

"You guys *stop*," Molly interjects, putting both her hands up to halt the conversation. "Why are you two always arguing? Enough! We're here to help Cece, not fight. If you can't get along, then I hate to say it, but maybe you should leave."

"Yeah, *Abby*. Maybe you should leave."

"You know what? I'm going to my room," I say, my head suddenly throbbing. Before shutting my door and throwing myself on my bed, I pop three ibuprofen and drink an entire glass of water from the bathroom sink, which is kind of rank, but at least it's cold.

I can hear Jenna and Abby still bickering in the kitchen as I sit on the edge of my bed and let myself fall back into the center of it. Staring up at the ceiling, it's not long before I hear the sound of the door creaking open then clicking closed, and then my mattress dips as Molly slowly lowers herself down beside me.

She doesn't say anything; instead, she starts finger combing my hair and staring off at the wall, probably contemplating what words of wisdom she wants to impart on me.

We sit like this for a long time, only the sound of our two friends arguing in the other room filling the air. Finally, I roll over on my side, facing Molly and looking up at her.

She continues playing with my hair, but quietly says, "You know, you can't avoid it forever. It's not going to go away."

As if I didn't already know that.

"Why does life have to be so complicated?" I finally ask, barely above a whisper.

Molly laughs softly under her breath, tussling my hair, then bends softly to whisper in my ear. "Silly, silly girl. If love was easy, it wouldn't be worth it."

Matthew

"I have no idea what I'm doing when it comes to women, and that's kind of how I like it." – Bernie

"Repeat that last part for me. I don't think I heard you correctly," Weston says, skating a circle around me on the ice, his hockey stick tapping the ice in a repetitive motion.

"You heard me just fine the first time," I grit out, irritated.

"Yeah, but I want to hear you say it again. I want to make sure I have all the details correct when I repeat it later." He skates away from me backward and sticks the tip of his tongue between his teeth, making me wonder how exactly I'm able to put up with his bullshit.

My hockey stick slices the puck to him in a fluid motion (I don't mention the fact that I'm aiming for his head), and his eyes widen as it flies toward him through the air.

His stick goes up, breaking the puck's path mid-flight, and it lands with a smack down on the ice.

"You know Matt, I always knew this day would come."

"You know Wes, this is why I aim pucks at your cocky ass face."

He gasps in protest and lifts his glove to his chin. "You would purposely mar this beautiful face? Matthew, how could you?"

My only response is to skate around him, easily stealing the puck resting between his skates. Weston responds with a muttered *sonofabitch*, chasing me in earnest in an attempt to steal it back.

We skate down the center and I check him with my elbow, grinning broadly. "Try to keep up, son."

I change directions, heading back toward the opposing goal, the small round puck slicing back and forth in front of me in the precise, clipped, rhythmic motion that's made me famous.

We cat-and-mouse like this until we're both breathing hard, and I feel a sense of superiority that he hasn't managed to steal the puck away. Leaning up against the boards by one of the penalty boxes, I take off my glove, grab a water bottle, and squirt the cold water down my throat, gulping half its contents in one swig.

Weston extends his hand and I hand him the bottle. He guzzles it until it's empty, hands the bottle back, and wipes his mouth with the back of his red and white jersey.

"So? How does it feel?" He stares at me, his intense blue eyes boring into me inquisitively. God, he's as nosey as my sister—worse, even.

I roll my eyes. "Cold. Refreshing."

"Ha ha, real funny smartass. You know I'm not talking about the water. Come on, come on, spill it before everyone shows up for the team meeting," he says, referring to the Badger Hockey team's imminent arrival for a postgame recap meeting. We arrived early and suited up solely to put together a few plays for the Lightning.

I rest my elbow on the wooden wall and sigh. "Do you have a vagina somewhere under your pads that we don't know about? Christ, you're worse than my mom." This does nothing to deter him. In fact, I think it only encourages him more.

He presses on. "Just repeat the part where Cecelia tells you to shut up."

Glaring at him, I shove off the boards and skate toward the door to the locker room, my skates cutting into the ice in fluid motions, leaving shavings in my wake. I hold my arm in the air, raising my middle finger in a salute.

He trails after me, his laughter echoing off the high rafters in the ceiling. "Oh come on baby, don't be like that," he croons.

My skates stop on a dime, and he almost slams into the back of me as I spin around to face him. "Jesus Christ. What is wrong with you?"

He shrugs, and I fight the urge to punch his well-defined jaw.

Defeated, I sigh again as I prop my stick out, jut my hip for balance, and lean on it. "I don't know where to go from here. I laid it all out there and now I guess it's her decision."

Weston scrunches up his face in thought then slowly asks, "But did you bring it up to her before, or just that night at Starbucks?"

"What do you mean?"

He rolls his eyes. "Did you just spring it on her out of the blue, or have you had an actual conversation about it, one where you laid out all the facts?"

I wipe away the sweat that's dripping down my forehead under my helmet, give my hairline a scratch, and let out a confused "Er..."

"*Er*? Is that your answer? Man, no wonder she got pissed."

"What the fuck was I supposed to do?" I yell, flapping the free arm at my side in frustration.

"You were *supposed* to sell her on the idea, dipshit. Give her the reasons she should go with you. Fuck, dude, are you that clueless?" He watches me for a few seconds, assessing me, then blows out a stream of breath. "Look man, I'm hardly the one to be giving you advice, and this one might be way over my head. My advice: you either wing it and try your luck again with Cece, *or* call your sister."

"Why do neither of those options sound appealing?"

Weston shakes his head and nods toward the locker room. "It's your call but you need to decide quick." He gives his pits a hard whiff and makes a face. "The shower is calling my name and the meeting starts in twenty. Let's not be standing here like a couple of girls at a slumber party when everyone gets here. We look like goddamn Sallys."

***

I hate admitting when I'm wrong, but in this case…Weston may have a point. I need to get this shit figured out, and quick.

Hopping out of the shower in my condo, I stand on the terry cloth floor mat, running a white towel up and down my arms to dry off, debating my options.

I look at myself in the mirror, gazing back at my reflection, taking in the hard edges of my mouth, the deep scar above my left eyebrow, and the crooked bridge of my nose.

Last night at practice with the Lightning, little Kyle Adams—who has terrible aim—took a slap shot at the goal but nailed me instead, narrowly missing my eye and giving me a nice, purple and blue shiner.

It hurt like hell and looks even worse.

Obviously I wasn't pleased, but Kyle cried and apologized repeatedly for a solid thirty minutes, snot dripping out of his nose and onto his practice jersey, so I cut him some slack.

I touch the bruise and find it still tender, then give pause to study my other contusions: fractured collarbone, gashed lip, chipped tooth.

Wincing, I continue to dry off, wrapping the towel around my lean hips before walking into my closet. I grab a ratty t-shirt, jeans, and a Michael Kors henley sweater, and then I throw them on quickly before adding shoes. I head to the foyer and grab my cell phone and keys off the dresser, stuffing them in my back pocket and heading out the door.

Cecelia

Back in the good old days—you know, when I was in high school—one of my favorite things to do was shack up in my bedroom and hunker down to study. I'd throw myself across my bed, lying flat on my stomach with textbooks scattered out in front of me, and do my homework that way.

So, in homage to those days, I'm spread out on my comforter, textbook and papers fanned out, laptop glowing, and yes, even a bag of pretzels is on standby not too far away on the desk.

I'm comfortable—black yoga leggings and a heather gray, off-the-shoulder cashmere sweater. On my feet are the most comfy (see: worn) chenille socks I own. Basically, it's like I'm giving myself a big warm hug, and I snuggle down with my butt in the air, Pandora playing Taylor Swift's new *1989* playlist softly through my pink ear buds.

I tap the keys on my laptop, humming to her new single "Style", and I briefly space out before stopping to stare blankly at the plain white wall of my bedroom. I'm so *so* ridiculously close to being done with this last paper, but right now I'm finding it impossible to concentrate. Rather, my mind continues to drift, wandering everywhere—my master's program, where I'm going to live in a few weeks, and then, yes…it eventually wanders to Matthew.

I wonder what he's doing right now—is he home, or out? Alone, or with his friends? *Is he pissed at me?* I haven't heard from him since Starbucks, which was two days ago, and for someone who claims he wants to *live* with me, it seems pretty telling that he hasn't had the decency to even text.

Rude.

I'm so lost in thought that I don't hear the bedroom door crack open, and I gasp when a large pair of strong, solid hands slowly run up the back of my calves, up my inner thighs, and squeeze my ass cheeks.

I pull out the ear buds and look over my shoulder at a grinning Matthew.

"How'd you get in here?" I ask, not the least bit put out by his presence. "You scared the crap out of me."

"I came down the chimney," he smarts, stepping in between my legs, which are sticking halfway off the bed. His hands lazily run up my spine and he leans forward, planting a kiss on my naked shoulder. "I missed you." Matthew's breath is on my neck and I swallow a shudder, determined to remain nonchalant.

"Did you now." I gulp, voice sounding *way* too throaty to be calm, cool, and collected. If I don't watch myself, I'm going to be a puddle of mush within minutes. "*Never* would have guessed it. You never called."

He leans forward and presses another kiss on my shoulder, his chest pressed against my back as he trails his breath along my neck. I close my eyes and bite my lip— I'm sorry, but it feels so good. "I wanted to, but I also wanted to give you some time."

I lie there on my stomach as Matthew hovers over me, bracing one strong arm on the bed and running his other hand up my rib cage and under my sweater, all the while breathing warm kisses on my bare neck and shoulder. I tip my head to the side and let out a soft moan.

"Did you miss me, too, Cecelia? It sounds like you

did." His tongue slips in my ear and my traitorous body tingles all over.

"Of course I did, you big idiot," I groan, amazed at my ability to speak under the circumstances.

Even as he chuckles deep in his chest, Matthew's pelvis pushes into my backside, and I can feel how hard he is through the thin fabric of my leggings as he begins grinding himself slowly into my ass crack.

Seriously, it feels so *good* I want to pass out from the pleasure of it all, and we're both fully clothed—*that* takes talent.

"We need to talk," he whispers, the low timbre of his voice sending ripples of lust coursing through my body, through my cerebellum, down my chest, and to the apex of my thighs.

"Whatever it is, yes," I moan, arching my back and pushing my rear into his denim-clad erection.

"You little hussy," he says as his free hand finds its way up my shirt and unclasps my bra. "Flip over and give me a peek at the goods."

Giggling, I squirm under him until I'm on my back, staring into his heated gaze. We lock eyes for only a moment before our lips crash into each other, teeth and tongues clashing in a frenzy. Gasping for breath, I unlatch my mouth only to ask, "Did you lock the door?"

Matthew grunts, burying his face in my neck while his hands roam up my chest, under my bra. Fingers idly trace my skin then skim the underside of my breasts, back and forth, back and forth goes the tip of his index finger, grazing the delicate skin with every teasing stroke. "What do I look like, a fucking amateur?"

"Shut your foul mouth or I'll shut it for you," I hiss, pulling his head down to mine, my lips like a heat-seeking missile as his calloused palm covers my aching breast. "Mmmm…" I moan into his mouth for what seems like the tenth time tonight and arch into his hand.

"I love your tits," Matthew groans out into my mouth, squeezing one softly then lavishing attention on the other. "They're the perfect handful."

Hearing him refer to my breasts as…as…well, *t-i-t-s*, makes my cheeks blazing hot—sso hot, I'm surprised he hasn't noticed my flaming red face. While it is embarrassing me, I'm also extremely turned on by his crude description. It makes me feel a bit saucy, sexy, and incredibly desirable.

Before I can stop myself, I blurt out, "Baby, that feels so good," than clamp my mouth shut before I can utter anything else that sounds so cliché.

"Talk dirty to me," Matthew demands, his hand now in the waistband of my leggings.

"I am *not* talking dirty to you." I laugh and wiggle my hips, encouraging his hand to go lower. "Nice try though."

"It was worth a shot." He grins down at me and studies my face, his messy auburn hair falling in his eyes. "Wanna get naked?"

I nod, and immediately we're both fumbling with our clothes, pants flying this way and that, shirts, panties, and boxer briefs landing on chairs and the carpet, and just like that, he's back on top of me.

Somewhere in the recesses of my mind, I hear a door within the apartment open and close, dismissing it in favor of running my hands along Matthew's insanely muscular torso, the tips of my fingers alive with a thousand nerves. He shudders when my fingers circle his nipples, giving them a little tug before I take one in my mouth and give it a good suck.

After that, it's nothing but the sound of skin on skin. Mouths and tongues. Moaning, gasps, and groans. At one point, he leaps off the bed to retrieve his jeans, leaving me writhing around the bed like a limp, turned-on, two-dollar hooker as I wait impatiently for him to slide into me.

When he does, my head goes back, and although we try to be quiet, we aren't the least bit successful. "*Uh… uh…*oh god," I gasp.

"Oh fuck…oh fuck, baby…you feel so good," he counters, thrusting so hard the headboard knocks against the wall…once, twice, *oh god*, three times (I'm not surprised; a hockey player's success is all in the swivel of the hips). It feels too good to give a shit that the bed is pounding into the wall behind us.

My hand snakes down between our bodies and, in a move I once read about in Cosmo (and one you might want to look into yourself), my finger finds its way up under his boys and presses down on a sweet spot there.

"Oh my god, this is why I love you." His low gravely moan is like a prayer whispered into my hair.

His words are an aphrodisiac to my soul, and I can't stop the threat of tears at the corner of my eye. My breath hitches as he grinds his pelvis. "You…do?"

His reply is to grunt, and within moments, we're both throwing our heads back, shuddering and going limp.

Being with him tonight is like a dream, a glorious, romantic, dream—only this dream is real.

And he's here.

And he's *mine*.

Matthew

For a while, we just lie there, Cecelia's head buried in the apex of my armpit, hauled up close next to my body by arms of steel. She's biting her lip and wants to say something, but she either can't find the right words, or she's completely chickenshit.

I put her out of her misery, crossing my free arm over my chest to rake my fingers through her hair as we lie there. "Yes. I love you. I mean, did you *really* think I'd ask you to move across the country with me if I didn't?"

She avoids my gaze, the ceiling becoming real interesting all of a sudden, and shrugs her bare shoulders. "How do you know?"

"How do I know *what*?"

"How do you know you *love* me? It's only been like… a few weeks."

I snort. "Please. Besides the fact that you're fucking *amazing*, you're the only woman on the planet that I didn't sleep with immediately. That's saying something."

"Um…and what is that saying, *exactly*?"

I look down at her, tilting my chin down to get a better look. "That I respect you. Better yet, that I liked you from the very beginning. You led me on a merry chase, but it was worth it."

She smacks me in the chest. "I did *not* lead you on

a merry chase! Well, not on purpose anyway. I simply loathed you."

"Tuh-may-toe, tuh-mah-toe. You call it loathing, I call it playing hard to get. In the end, I win." Her elbow digs into my ribs, and I gasp. "Hey! Watch the merchandise!"

"Who wins?"

I roll my eyes. "*We* win."

Cecelia
Later that night

"So, next time you decide to screw in the apartment, could you at least give me a little advance warning?" Molly just walked in the door and is setting her bag and keys down on the kitchen table. Hands on her hips, she turns to glare at me from my spot on the couch. "Well?"

My face turns bright red. "I am so so sorry…"

"Yeah, well, you didn't sound sorry. It sounded like you were *both* being murdered. Oh Matthew, *UH, UH, UH. Oh. My. Gawd.*"

"But I…I thought you'd left?" *Hoped* she'd left is more like it.

"I did, but not before the Banging Headboard Show began. You're lucky he didn't *bang* you through the freaking wall. Jee-zuz." She makes a loud gagging sound and walks to the fridge, opening it and peering inside. Her voice carries over the refrigerator door, and I can hear food being moved around. "As God is my witness, if I ever—*ever*— have to hear my own brother having loud porn sex again, I will *literally* stab myself."

Molly walks back into the living room holding a Coke in one hand and an apple in the other. "So, besides you kids screwing each other's brains out, did the two of you actually seal a deal?"

I cringe inwardly, still embarrassed and ashamed to have acted like such a dirty, filthy roommate. In all actuality, Weston has his own apartment, so I rarely have to listen to them *doing the deed*. It fills me with shame to know she heard so much of my intimate night with her brother.

Molly props her Coke can on her hip, giving me the eye and impatiently tapping her foot. "Well?"

Biting my lip and summoning up all my courage, I finally begin telling her all the details.

Cecelia

December 23rd

"This is slowly becoming my worst nightmare," Matthew mutters under his breath as his mom bustles out of the room to fetch yet another dish from the dining room. His entire hand gropes my butt and gives it a firm squeeze. "Your ass is the only saving grace," he jokes.

"Please don't be so dramatic." I laugh, turning to fill up a water glass at the sink. "Come on, everyone is getting ready to open presents in the living room."

"Ugh, I hate this part. It's white elephant and it takes everyone forever. Plus, I never get anything good," he says with a frown.

"That's because I rule the white elephant," Molly says as she enters the room with a tray. She sets it on the counter and grabs a fresh glass from the cabinet. "Besides, everything you bring is always sucky. Even for a gag gift, your gifts suck."

"What? They do not!" Matthew shouts indignantly. "We didn't fly all the way here from California to be harassed."

Molly scoffs. "Please. Did you *really* think anyone wanted that used bike helmet you brought last year? I mean, what the hell. And the year before that, you brought a yoga mat. "

"At least he's sticking to a theme," I add. They both look at me like I'm crazy. "Um, sports? Bike helmet, yoga mat…"

I don't have the heart to mention the gift he's brought this year: a nasty old bowling trophy he found at a resale shop, and I swear if I end up with it, I'm going to be *so* pissed. But hey, on the bright side, at least he picked it out on his own (which is more than I can say for most guys in my experience).

We're ushered into the room by his dad, and soon we're all sitting around their large, cozy living room. It's Matthew, Molly, their parents, a few aunts, uncles, and cousins, and the fireplace is blazing. Mrs. Wakefield has a vintage holiday record playing and a plate with different varieties of Christmas cookies sits on the coffee table.

Matthew stands near the tree, seemingly scanning the room for an open spot, but instead of taking a seat, he clasps his hands together and clears his throat. "Hey everyone? Before we get started, I have a little announcement to make," he begins.

"You knocked up your girlfriend?" his cousin Jack shouts.

"*Jackson* Michael Wakefield!" his mother admonishes

from her spot on the couch, clearly embarrassed.

Mrs. Wakefield laughs nervously.

Matthew shakes his head, and with a grin, winks at me. "Not quite, but I am glad you're all here, because I've got some really exciting news to share. In fact, I haven't even told Cecelia."

All eyes turn to me, and I feel a blush creep up my neck. Molly nudges me in the ribs from her spot next to me, humming the opening bars from "Wedding March". I shoot her a *hey, knock it off* glare as I rub my side.

Again, Matthew clears his throat and directs his attention toward me. "Cecelia, *sweet*heart." I hold my breath. "I've been traded to the Blackhawks."

Suddenly, everyone jumps up and begins shouting, and Mr. and Mrs. Wakefield embrace in a congratulatory hug. I stand and take a few steps toward Matthew, but he meets me halfway, cupping my face in the large hands I've come to cherish. "I'm so happy for you!" I whisper when our noses meet, my hands covering his.

"Don't be happy for me, baby. Be happy for *us*. We're coming *home*. You'll only be a half hour from your parents, closer than you were before."

Closer to my parents? *Oh joy*, I think, noting that even my thoughts are bordering on sarcastic.

"When did you find out?"

"Honestly? This morning. Bill's been working on it for a while. They couldn't agree on a salary, but they faxed over a number this morning and we'll sign the contracts tomorrow. Are you happy?"

I'll have to remember and send Bill (Matthew's agent) a thank you card.

I look up at Matthew, brushing my mouth against his lips. "Yes, I'm happy."

"I love you, Cecelia. *So* much."

I kiss him again. "I love you, too."

Someone pulls at the pant leg of my jeans, and I look down to find Molly staring up at me with a grimace on her pretty face. "Ugh, could you two *not*? Stop pawing at each other and sit your asses down so we can start opening presents." She rolls her eyes and glares at her brother.

Taking my hand, Matthew pulls me to the carpet, and we sit, hands entwined.

Life is good.

And I have a feeling it's only going to get better.

Preview the next book in the Kiss and Make Up Series:

A KISS *like* THIS

SARA NEY

Abby

*I*t all started innocently enough on a Friday just like any other, with classes and a coffee run, then straight to strategic planning for the evening ahead.

Now, normally, I'm not the first person to volunteer for a night out, even on the weekends. The simple truth is, I would much rather stay home, rent movies, read a book, and eat snacks on my couch—one hundred percent of the time, hands down, no debate.

However, tonight is different. Tonight, my cousin, Tyler Darlington the Third—when I was younger, I used to call him Tyler Darlington *the Turd*—became an officer of his fraternity, and in his mind, *that* is something to celebrate.

I also want to point out that Tyler becoming an officer of *anything* is kind of a big deal—to both his parents and mine. Believe me when I say, the whole entire Darlington clan is in a *tizzy* over the fact that Tyler has been admitted to a Big 10 school. Not only that, but he's managed not to flunk out of that same Big 10 school or cause any property damage to or burn down his fraternity house.

Naturally, these things alone are cause for celebration (that was sarcasm) and my parental units are practically *forcing* me to attend his celebratory frat party.

Okay, maybe forcing is a strong word, but they did have to promise me a fifty-dollar pre-paid Visa gift card if I went.

To put it bluntly: Tyler is kind of a moron.

And by moron, I mean pothead.

So, despite my usual penchant for staying in on the weekends like a hermit, there is definitely something to be said for the simple act of getting ready to go out with friends that is *more* fun than the actual act of going out.

For example:

1. Cramming multiple young women into *one* bathroom, then crowding around the only mirror in the apartment—unless of course you count the cheap mirror hanging behind your bedroom door, which you do *not*.

2. Borrowing clothes that never seem to look as cute on you as they do on your friend or roommate. Damn her.

3. Getting sprayed/blinded by the hairspray because you were standing too closely behind your friend wielding the can, which we all know is inevitable. Someone always get sprayed in the eyes.

4. Smudging your eyeliner because you get el-

bowed by your friend every time you lean over the counter to draw a more precise line. We call this irony.

Sounds like funsies, right?

That's because it is...for the most part.

There's always tons of wild laughter, annoyed grumbling, and in the end, everyone looks stunning and ready to take on the town—or in this case, a house party.

Tonight is no exception.

It's a short walk to the fraternity house from our crappy rental house, and even though the air is a tad too chilly for my liking, we chose to walk the short distance rather than drive, despite the heels most of us are wearing.

Having already decided it's going to be an early night, we spend the remainder of the evening huddled together in the corner of my cousin's fraternity house, not because we're wallflowers, or party poopers, or stuck up. No. We're huddled together because the house is dirty and falling apart, and the crowd it draws isn't exactly my "scene".

My scene is the library. A quaint coffee shop with an acoustic guitar player, smelling of rich coffee grounds. The campus study center with its overstuffed couches. My small but tidy bedroom in my off-campus rental.

This crowd...this crowd is collegians on academic probation. Drunks. Potheads. Girls with loose morals and even looser panties.

I brave the party with my friends in the corner I've forced us to occupy, where we laugh, my friends drink, and we lose track of time.

Before I know it, my friends have disappeared and my

cousin is at my side, half-baked (as usual) but in protection mode. Tyler actually convinces me to be responsible and *not* to walk home alone in the dark, even though the last place I want to be is here, in this fraternity house, alone without my friends.

Before the party thins and the crowd downstairs disperses, I'm upstairs in Ty's room, door locked, throwing clothes and books off his queen-sized bed, grateful that it's not a twin or a simple mattress on the floor, and flinging myself on top of it in a tired heap.

The one beer my friends Tabitha and Maria persuaded me to drink is the sleep aid I need to close my eyes and shut out the racket below me.

Find Sara Online

Facebook: https://www.facebook.com/saraneyauthor/
Reader Group: https://www.facebook.com/
groups/1065756456778840/
Twitter: @SaraNey
IG: saraneyauthor
Email: saraneyauthor@yahoo.com

Other Books by Sara Ney

Kiss and Make Up:
Kissing in Cars
He Kissed me first
A kiss like this
One Last Kiss (Early 2018)

Three Little Lies
Things Liars Say
Things Liars Hide
Things Liars Fake

How to Date a Douchebag:
The Studying Hours
The Failing Hours
The Learning Hours (Fall 2017)

With Author M.E.Carter:
FriendTrip
WeddedBliss
Kissmas Eve